# BETTER OFF RED

## Vampire Sorority Sisters Book 1

Visit us at www.boldstrokesbooks.com

# BETTER OFF RED

## Vampire Sorority Sisters
## Book 1

*by*

Rebekah Weatherspoon

2011

# BETTER OFF RED: VAMPIRE SORORITY SISTERS BOOK 1

ISBN 10: 1-60282-574-2
ISBN 13: 978-1-60282-574-1

This Trade Paperback Original Is Published By
Bold Strokes Books, Inc.
P.O. Box 249
Valley Falls, NY 12185

First Edition: November 2011

---

**CREDITS**
EDITOR: CINDY CRESAP
PRODUCTION DESIGN: SUSAN RAMUNDO
COVER DESIGN BY SHERI (GRAPHICARTIST2020@HOTMAIL.COM)

# Acknowledgments

I must thank the following people:

My parents and my brothers and sister for letting me be myself.

The boys of Cilley Hall and the girls of Amen, Dunbar, and Bancroft; the other Five Heartbeats and the ladies of the Upsilon Xi Chapter of Zeta Phi Beta Sorority, Inc., for helping me lay the foundation.

Ellee, Jenny, and Ariana for sharing their experiences with me, and Jordan for showing me around the house.

Ari, Kim, and Carole for the dance parties and the makeup lessons, even though they didn't stick.

Erica and Rosana for finding me and encouraging me to keep going, and the readers who embraced my online stories. Your support has been phenomenal.

Summer and Tecora for holding my hand through every chapter of this book and beyond. To Aiden and Zac for existing, Steph for the chubbles, I.T. for introducing me to so many things, and Weebs for keeping me awake. Vanessa for being you.

The entire Bold Strokes family for their warm welcome , Cindy Cresap for her amazing eye, and Sheri for the fantastic cover art.

And lastly, many, many thanks to Radclyffe for giving this story a chance.

## Dedication

To my mother, Jackie, who taught me how to swim
and my father, Russell, who never let me drown.
And to T. I love you, baby. Wanna go have lunch?

## CHAPTER ONE

I have an idea." Amy threw her bag on the floor and perched on the edge of her mattress. I put down my pen and turned around.

"What?"

"Let's rush."

"Where?"

"No, no. Rush, stupid. Like join a sorority."

"Hell no." I had just gotten used to sharing a broom closet worth of space with another human being. Our entire hall had a single shower. I was even getting over the fact I had to plan my masturbation me time around my roommate's class schedule, but this was asking too much.

"Ginge, come on."

"Amy, my darling, you are more than welcome to auction off your brain in exchange for endless amounts of upbeat to the highest bidder. I won't stop you," I said. "But there is no way in hell, no way, I am joining a sorority. I already have a ton of studying to do."

"You're majoring in gym," she said with a condescending glare. "Just hear me out."

"Ugh, fine. And I'm not majoring in gym."

"Right. Anyway. Here's what I'm thinking. We're too young to get into any of the good bars downtown, and all the eighteen and up places will just be packed with people from our gen ed classes. There are parties on the Row all the time. Parties I want to go to."

"The Row? You're already into this. You're in deep, using the lingo and everything."

"Just let me finish. My sister said the parties on the Row are the best and they're 'invite only.' If we rush, we get to meet all of the people who throw these parties. So even if we don't actually pledge, we'll meet tons of guys. Guys who will invite us back when it's all over."

I chewed the inside of my lip, thinking over the nonsense she was talking. I didn't give a crap about meeting guys. There were thousands of them on campus. I even sat next to a few in my classes. I had worked hard to get into Maryland University. Their exercise science program was one of the best in the country, and my workload this semester was more than enough to keep me busy. Getting involved in Greek life was not another slice of pie I wanted to add to my plate.

Even if I had all the free time in the world, there was still no draw. I didn't have anything against sorority girls, but I never considered myself to be that kind of a joiner. If Amy asked me to go out for the Frisbee golf team, then sure, that was the sort of group activity I could handle. The thought of slapping on a smile for the next however many days, pretending to be perfect just so some girls I didn't know and had no real interest in getting to know, could tell me I was cool enough to walk around with them wearing matching shirts, well, it made me want to roll my eyes at Amy and dive right back into my chem notes. From the eager look on her face, I knew that type of blow off was not gonna fly.

"Please. There's this mega cute guy from Chi Nu in my econ class. I would love to see him in his natural habitat."

I had only known Amy for a few weeks. She was cute. A perky blonde. Perky in every way. We got along great, except for moments like this. It was obvious she wasn't used to taking no for an answer. I, however, had no problem saying it. I just wasn't sure if telling Amy to shove it was a good way to keep the air peaceful between us.

I took a deep breath and squeezed my eyes shut. Maybe it was the right moment to tell Amy I was seventy-seven percent sure I was a lesbian, but that might create a whole other problem. The last thing I wanted was a roommate who was scared I was going to feel her up in her sleep or check her out while she was getting dressed in the morning.

When I opened my eyes, Amy started clapping. I watched the dopey grin on her face stretch to full capacity and then stared at her as this weird squeal came through her clenched teeth. Apparently taking a moment to get my head together was the same thing as saying yes in her book.

"Fine."

"Fine?" Her voice pitched higher than I'd ever heard it before.

"Yes. I will go through rush with you, but that's it. I'm not pledging."

"Stop sulking," Amy said. "I'll do everything. You just come with me and pretend you're having a good time."

"I said fine." I snatched my pen off my notebook and turned my back on her. She finally dug out her books and settled down to study.

"It'll be great," she squealed again.

"Yeah. I bet."

❖

Amy managed to let me get my chem notes done without mentioning rush again. The next morning was a different story. While we got dressed, she told me about each sorority's dedication to particular charities and causes. Apparently there was more to the ladies' side of the Greek system than bake sales and bikini car washes.

I listened as patiently as possible. I wanted to change the subject, but I figured I'd just let her get it all out, then move on to music or current events once she'd tuckered herself out. By the time we made it over to the cafeteria for breakfast, she was already talking my ear off about rush week etiquette.

"Why do I have to wear white?" I asked.

"Either white or black. Every sorority has colors," Amy told me, the poor clueless fool that I was.

"I know that."

"Well, if you show up parading around in teal and yellow or purple and pink, you're sending a message."

"What, that I like to mix my pastels?"

"No. That you have Xi O or Mu Phi on the top of your list."

"Okay, what else?" I asked. This was all so stupid.

"They'll each have tables set up on the quad today, so we can cruise by and meet a few of the girls from each house."

I took a bite of my eggs and spit them right back out into my napkin. "Ick. Those are off." Amy reached across the table and took a forkful.

"They taste fine to me. Here." She handed me her untouched bagel and snatched my plate of eggs and fruit.

"You have any faves yet?" I asked.

"Xi O actually." She didn't seem bothered by the eggs. "My mom's a Xi O."

"Oh. Isn't being a legacy an automatic in?"

"Yeah, I guess, but I don't know. I kinda want to do my own thing."

"Nothing spells independence like joining a sorority." I ducked just in time to dodge a grape.

"I just want to see what else is out there. We have to check out the Tri Pis and ABO."

"Why ABO?" I knew that Pi Pi Pi was one of those old school sororities everyone had heard about, but I knew nothing about Alpha Beta Omega.

"I heard their house is gorgeous and huge. The guys in their brother fraternity are smoking hot and they have a reputation for only picking pretty girls. I know it sounds shallow." She tried to save herself before I called her out.

"Um, yeah."

"I don't know. It would be cool if they asked me to join. Knowing they think I'm foxy." The tip of her tongue stuck out as she wiggled her head a bit. I had to laugh. Admitting girls to your sorority based solely on their looks was the definition of shallow, but I figured that's how sororities worked. They were sanctioned cliques set up on prime real estate, hiding behind the guise of good deeds and sisterhood. It would only make sense to have the hottest girls on campus at your side when you walk into the local soup kitchen. Accepting my fate, I bit into my newly acquired bagel. This week was going to suck.

❖

I met up with Amy again before lunch, and just like she said, every fraternity and sorority on campus had tables and booths set up around the huge lawn between the library and the Liberal Arts building. I followed Amy from table to table, feigning interest in what each of the recruitment chairs had to say, growing more and more annoyed that terms like "recruitment chair" were becoming a part of my vocabulary. I was a little disappointed to have most of my assumptions confirmed.

Every sorority had its type. Three blue-eyed, platinum blondes bubbled around the Theta booth. Four African-American girls with identical deep toffee skin tones chatted up prospective members at the Sigma table. Every nationality, hair color, and body type was represented from group to group, never mixing together. It was boring and predictable, and Amy was loving every single minute of it.

Each girl we met was perfectly nice, but there was something fake and overzealous about all of them. Except for the girls of Alpha Beta Omega.

By the time we reached their table, I was dying for a sandwich and a power nap. I also hadn't masturbated in three days and had every intention of doing just that while Amy was in her two o'clock class.

"This is the last one. I swear." She held out a stack of pamphlets for me to hold while she opened her backpack. I shoved the bundle of papers inside then followed Amy toward the final table.

The sisters of Alpha Beta Omega had their booth set up at the far end of the quad. Their brother fraternity, Omega Beta Alpha, was set up across the grass, in clear view. I glanced over as we walked closer to a group of four girls dressed in white, black, and red. Their frat brothers were pretty cute. The girls behind the table, though, were much cuter.

Right away, it was obvious that this group of girls was different from the other sisters we'd spent our lunch break talking to. A gorgeous brunette stood, her arm linked with her curvaceous, golden haired soror (another word I learned that day). An African-American girl with a beautiful, full afro laughed along with whatever conversation they were having. A bright red ribbon added the perfect blast of color to her ebony curls. A fourth girl, a petite Asian beauty with boobs a little too big for her frame, refilled a bowl of red candies. All four girls wore small teardrop rubies hanging on delicate platinum chains around their necks. It was shocking to see such a diverse bunch and a pleasant surprise that, for once, Amy hadn't been wrong. They were all hot.

The laughter and chatting died away naturally as we walked up to the table. The golden haired girl greeted us first. Some would have considered her heavy or even fat, but I thought she filled out her ABO T-shirt perfectly.

"Hi," she said, extending her free hand. "I'm Danni. This is Cleo." The girl with the chocolate brown skin checked us out with an upward nod of her head. "And Barb." The Asian girl replied with a bright hello, her warm almond eyes sparkling in our direction. "And this is Paige."

The girl on Danni's arm didn't smile, but gazed over Amy and me before offering her own quiet, "Hey."

"I'm Amy and this is Ginger."

"Ginger?" Cleo asked, taking in my long red hair. "I thought my parents were cruel. Tsk, tsk, naming a ginger kid 'Ginger.'"

"Yeah, it could be worse," I said with a shrug. "At least it doesn't rhyme with anything."

"True. It could be worse. My last name is Jones." I couldn't say what sucked more, a name tag mocking your hair and your God-given beauty marks or being named after a blaxploitation character. Biting back my chuckle, I glanced at Amy who didn't get either joke. Luckily, Barb spoke up before Amy had a chance to ask any questions.

"So are you ladies interested in joining Alpha Beta Omega?"

"She's not." Amy thumbed in my direction. I was instantly annoyed. Yeah, cheery meet-and-greets weren't my scene, but this was the first group of girls who actually had my attention. I wasn't about to tell them I thought their sorority was a complete joke. I should have explained that to Amy. "I had to beg her to come out with me…"

While Amy continued to assassinate my amazing character, a small movement off to the left snatched my attention. I fought to keep my mouth from popping open as Paige casually brushed her finger over Danni's nipple. Again, I quickly glanced in Amy's direction. She'd completely missed it, but Danni had caught my gawk and scramble. She cocked an eyebrow at me before grazing her teeth over her full bottom lip. I could feel the heat blush my face red as I looked back toward Amy. She hadn't noticed a thing.

"You too cool for all this Greek mess?" Cleo poked at me playfully.

"What? No. I, uh, I just didn't think about going through rush until she brought it up," I replied lamely.

"We'll be having our first open house tonight. How about you leave us your info and we'll give you all the details." Danni tapped a sign-up sheet sitting on the table.

"Okay," Amy said instantly. I shrugged and took the pen Cleo handed to me.

All the slots of the first page were filled so I flipped to the next, looking for a blank line. And then the third and fourth. On the twelfth page, there was one open slot. Something felt off about their popularity. There hadn't been a single girl at their table when we walked over, but it looked like every single freshman and sophomore girl on campus had signed up to rush ABO. Not sure what to make of it, I gripped the pen, ready to sign my week away. Before I could, my phone rang. I pulled out my cell and looked at the display.

"Excuse me. I gotta take this." I handed the pen to Amy and tucked myself out of the way, under the shade of a nearby tree. "Hi, Mom."

"Hi, sweetie. I just wanted to check on you. How's my baby?"

"I'm fine. Amy's trying to drag me through rush week with her," I said loud enough for Amy to hear, forgetting that the girls of ABO could hear me too. Thank God they waved my comment off as a joke before dragging Amy into more pointless conversations about mascots and themed parties.

"Are you going to join a sorority?" Mom asked.

Keeping my voice low, I replied, "Probably not, but I'll keep Amy company until rush is over."

"Aw, honey. You're such a good friend. Oh! Toddy's here. He wants to talk to you." I heard my mom tell my brother I was joining a sorority as she handed him the phone. Not my exact words. Linda Carmichael had a special sort of short-term Mom memory I had grown accustomed to.

"What up, Gingey?"

"Hey, Todd." I didn't fight the smile that spread across my face. My brother was twenty-three and still never turned my mom down when she offered to cook for him in exchange for manual labor around the house. I loved him. He made it so easy. He knew me so well, knew that I hated my mom's salmon cakes, her favorite thing to make for us. He knew I secretly loved my freckles, and although our parents were great people, it meant a lot to me that the both of us were adopted. Todd knew exactly what it felt like to know that your birth mother was dead, and he knew the way your heart ached once you realized you'd finally found a real family. My brother was my best friend.

Our dad was out of the country, lending his surgeon's hands to the Red Cross in a coastal region of Brazil that had just been hit by an earthquake. He would be gone for several weeks, and I was glad Todd was still around looking after our mom.

"What'd she break?" I said flatly.

"Nothing. Dad got her a new DVD player, but he didn't install it before he left. I'm hooking it up for her."

"You're such a good boy."

"That's what she keeps telling me. So you're joining stuff now?"

"No. My roommate wants me to, but—"

"You should." I didn't bother holding in a burst of laughter. "Easy now. Just listen. You move into the house. All those girls are walking around in their jammies, taking showers together, making breakfast naked. It'll take about five point five seconds for you to figure out which ones are muff divers and which ones aren't."

I would have been eight shades of red having this conversation with anyone else, but Todd also knew I liked girls. He'd caught me kissing our neighbor, Kristen Lander, over the summer. I wasn't exactly sure whether I was bisexual or what, but he knew I was trying to figure it out. After Paige's little nipple maneuver, Todd may have had a point. A sorority might be a good place to start.

"That simple, huh?" I kicked a rock at my feet. I could feel Amy's eyes on me, but I wasn't ready to rush off the phone just yet.

"It is."

"I don't know yet. I could still totally like guys."

"Well, sister, college is a great place to find out. It's where I discovered my love for Sam Adams in the ongoing battle of liquor versus beer."

"Yeah, thanks, Todd. I gotta go. Kiss Mom for me."

"Will do." Then Todd shouted, "Come here, Linda! I got a kiss for you!" I hit end, shaking my head. I hadn't been away from home for very long at all, but I missed my family like crazy. Amy, on the other hand, seemed perfectly at home with the girls of Alpha Beta Omega.

"Sorry about that," I said bashfully as I walked back toward the table.

"Don't worry about it," Danni said sweetly. "We were just telling Amy more about the mixer we're going to have tonight. You two should stop by our house around nine?" She quirked her head in Cleo's direction.

"Yeah, nine."

I picked up the pen, turned to the thirteenth page, and wrote down my information. We said our good-byes and Amy finally agreed it was time for lunch.

"See, that wasn't so bad, was it?" Amy handed me a black pamphlet. On the cover of the tri-fold was the red silhouette of a panther below the script of ABO.

"No. They seemed pretty cool." I tucked the info page in my bag and headed off toward the cafeteria. As we walked, I looked back toward the Alpha Beta Omega table. The info sessions on the quad were supposed to go until four that afternoon, but the girls of ABO were already packing up to leave.

❖

I wanted to kill Amy. All in, she'd planned to visit six information sessions, which meant I had to stop by six sorority houses.

The night went a little something like this: Amy and I would walk up to the front door of any particular house. We both wore white shirts with our fitted jeans. Amy wouldn't let me wear green. Giggly Girl A and her sidekick, Giggly Girl B, would greet us at the door and quickly invite us in. Over-anxious Girl would ask us to repeat our names and ask us our majors. Amy was undeclared, so she'd just bite her lip and shrug. I'd explain to everyone within earshot that there was actually a lot you could do with a degree in exercise science. Then I would repeat exactly what kinesiology was to the girls who had stumbled into the middle of the conversation.

After these in-depth analyses of our true personalities, we would be given a brief tour of the whitewashed living room and the granite topped kitchen. We'd accept a drink and a snack, then stand around with three dozen other prospective new members and talk more about classes and, of course, boys. I'd met thirty-four girls named Jessica, twenty-two named Kaitlin, sixteen Jennifers, and a very interesting girl with one arm named Parnin, who I suspected was admitted to a particular sorority for karma points.

I was on upbeat overload, and if I was being honest with myself, seriously considering giving up my quest for a female who could be more than a friend. I'd had enough estrogen to last me a few lifetimes. If the Alpha Beta Omega house hadn't been our last stop on this slow tour through hell, I would have ditched Amy the moment I heard how much it cost to join a sorority. Screw Todd's advice. There were other ways to meet girls.

At the Xi O house, I had to give myself a break. Amy was talking another Jessica's head off about how skinny jeans didn't flatter anyone, and all I could think about was what time I should meet my lab partner on Saturday. I excused myself to the restroom, then wandered out the front door. I texted Amy, telling her where to find me when she was ready. She showed up a few seconds later.

"Is it that bad?" she asked, closing the door behind her.

"Yes, it is. Do you want to hang out with these girls? I mean, really?" If the answer was yes, I might have had to rethink the terms of our friendship.

"So far, no, but we haven't gotten to know them yet and they haven't gotten to know us."

"Right, but why do we have to go through all this and pay to get to know them better? I'm perfectly happy just meeting people the normal way. You know, study groups, hanging out at the gym, at the cafeteria, crap like that."

"No. I know, you're right. But, Ginge, we only get to do this sort of thing once in our lives. Let's just get through this week. If you get any bids, just turn them down. I promise, if I do end up pledging, I won't let it affect you at all."

"We live together. It'll affect me."

"Look, it's only eight thirty, but let's just head over to the ABO house now and we can get the night over with."

"Deal. And then we need to find food. Cheese and crackers do not a meal make."

"Deal," Amy said with a firm nod. "Let's go." She grabbed my hand and I let her drag me down the street.

You could spot the Alpha Beta Omega house from a mile away because the ABO house wasn't a house at all. It was an enormous colonial mansion. You could have seen it from the moon. The other houses on the Row were nice, big enough to accommodate all their members, plenty of room for entertaining, but this place was amazing. A wide brick path rose up the front lawn to the front door, framed with several white columns. The brick facade stretched for yards and yards in either direction, and it would have taken me a few minutes to count all of the black shuttered windows that covered the three visible floors. In the center of it all, the seven-foot high Greek letters for Alpha Beta Omega sat molded to the face of the vaulted porch roof.

"Wow," Amy gasped.

"Yeah," I said breathlessly.

"You planning on going inside?" We turned around to see Cleo coming up the path, her arms loaded down with several boxes of pizza.

"Yeah. Of course," Amy replied.

I held out my hands for the boxes. "You need help?"

"Nah. Can you just grab the door for me?"

We scampered ahead up the steps and opened the heavy white door. The house was filled with girls, but the mood was strangely subdued. Pop music was playing from one room, and from another we heard an episode of the hot new *90210* coming from the TV.

"Look what I found lurking on the front lawn," Cleo yelled. Danni came walking into the foyer. She looked great in a simple pair of jeans and her ABO colors.

"Hey. You're early."

"Yeah, we just—" I started.

"Ginger was getting bored at the Xi O house so we just came over here," Amy finished.

"Shut up. I wasn't bored. I just—"

"You missed us, didn't you?" Danni said, winking at me.

"Something like that." I swallowed when she took a step closer. Danni gently pinched my arm. "Well, come eat."

We followed her into the kitchen where a bunch of girls were already diving into the pizza Cleo had spread out on the counter. There were a handful of prospective new members mingling in with the sisters, but not as many as I'd expected. At all the other houses I felt like a cow being packed shoulder to shoulder into the slaughterhouse. Not at the ABO house. I could breathe, move around, find a seat. Everything was just so casual. I wondered for a moment if we'd missed a big crowd earlier.

After we grabbed our slices, we followed Danni into the living room. A few would-be pledges were playing cards with a few of the sisters at a round cherry wood table behind the huge sectional couch. Other girls were parked around the TV. Some were talking, answering questions, and giving out actual information about the sorority while others were just vegging out. It felt…normal.

Paige, the beautiful stern-faced brunette we'd met that afternoon, was there on the couch. It turned out she was the chapter's vice president, a role that didn't quite seem to fit with her penchant for stroking other people's nipples in public. She made room for us on the couch before liberating a slice of pepperoni from Danni's plate.

"You ladies pick your house yet?" Paige asked.

"That's it, Paige. Get right to it," Cleo said. Amy blushed uncontrollably, glaring at me for support.

"Oh no, don't give me that bug-eyed look. This is your party," I said.

"It's okay, Amy," Danni said as she reached out and touched Amy's hand. "It would be kinda hard to keep a sorority going if no one new wanted to be a member. Tell us where else you guys have been looking."

Amy swallowed nervously. "Well, we went to a few places, but my mom was a Xi O, so—"

"Bitches," Cleo coughed.

"They flat out told Layna over there"—Paige pointed to a caramel skinned black girl with blond streaks in her hair who was playing cards—"that they didn't take her kind."

"Wow." Amy gasped. I bit my tongue. There was no way we were going back there.

"You look pretty pissed about that, Ginge." Cleo's eyebrow went up as she looked at me.

"My brother's black," I said. "We're both adopted. I don't know what I would do if someone talked to him like that."

"I knew I liked you." Cleo chuckled, swatting my thigh. I let her encouragement calm my rage as Amy filled them in on the other houses we'd visited that night. In return, they gave us their honest opinion of each sorority, pointing out legit pros and cons and throwing in bits of gossip that would interest anyone whether she gave a crap about rush or not.

The big-chested Asian girl, Barb, joined in halfway through our conversation. She was the chapter president, but in a refreshing twist, Barb didn't walk around with that same "I can't wait to make you wear adult diapers to class" attitude the other chapter presidents wore proudly.

"I'm supposed to ask," she said, "Have you picked a major yet?" This time the question didn't annoy me. Barb's tone made me feel like she actually cared.

"I'm going for a BS in exercise science. I'm trying to get prereqs out of the way."

"What are you going to do with that?" Paige asked, looking at me with the same bored expression she'd worn all night.

"Teach gym," Amy said.

"No," I shot back.

"It's okay. Heather is majoring in gym too." I looked in the direction Cleo nodded. A pretty girl with chestnut brown hair greeted us as she plopped on the floor between Cleo's legs. Cleo leaned over and kissed her gently on the forehead. Thoughts of how close they really were had me shifting in my seat.

"I want to be an athletic trainer in the NFL. MU has a good relationship with the Baltimore Ravens." I was from Massachusetts and admittedly a bandwagon Patriots fan.

"Oh, wow. That's cool," Barb said.

"I know," I said, playfully glaring at Amy.

A while later, I excused myself on a legitimate search for the bathroom. When I came back into the room, I noticed immediately that the number of people had grown by one.

A stunning girl, dressed all in black, had pulled Barb into the corner and was talking quietly in her ear. I'd never considered whether I had a type before, but looking at this girl with her spiky midnight black hair made me think I had one now. The black tank top she wore showed off her perfectly toned arms and the low-cut front showed off a generous amount of cleavage. The bright red lipstick that would have screamed five-dollar whore on anyone else looked amazing against her golden skin. The shade matched perfectly with the ruby studs in her ears. The shape of her eyes, her nose, and her high cheekbones said she had some sort of Hispanic blood flowing through her veins. Her bright hazel eyes that were focused directly on me said something else.

She continued to whisper to Barb, but her eyes stayed on me. For a moment, I noticed her nostrils flaring as if she were trying to catch a scent in the air. My face grew hot. My stomach tingled, and I didn't miss the fact that my underwear had suddenly become wet. I swallowed nervously, all the while trying to catch my breath. I'd never had that sort of reaction to anyone.

It was the perfect moment for Barb to catch me staring. Feeling the heat of embarrassment crawl up my neck, I scampered back over to the couch and took my seat next to Amy.

The conversation continued to flow, but I couldn't resist glancing back at this new mystery girl. I waited a few seconds then pretended to fix my ponytail. When I peeked back over my shoulder, she was gone.

"We should get going," Amy suddenly announced. I was a little shocked. We were having such a good time. I had to agree though. I looked at the clock and saw that it was almost midnight. Danni and Cleo walked us to the door and hugged us good-bye.

"Do you guys need a ride? We can get the boys to take you." Cleo pointed across the street to the Omega Beta Alpha house. I hadn't noticed, but the house where their brother fraternity lived was just as big and breathtaking.

"No. We're right over in Cramer. We'll be fine," Amy said. I wasn't sure I'd heard her right. I didn't need "the boys" to drive us anywhere, but Amy seemed like she'd been waiting her whole teenage life to get into a car with a fraternity boy.

"Okay. Well, come back tomorrow around nine," Danni said. We happily agreed.

❖

On the way back to the dorm, Amy explained to me how the rest of rush would go. Every night we would narrow down our options and skip the places we decided to drop off our list. Come Friday, Bid Day, we would get invitations to join whichever sorority wanted us for the next round of initiation, a round that Amy would go through solo. I agreed to keep her company through the rest of the week on the grounds she would actually back off after Bid Day and we would never set foot near the Xi O house ever again. She was more than okay with those terms.

So every night, we went to one less house, mingling with Jessicas and Kaitlins. I went through my colorful collection of low-cut, v-neck tees. Amy was smart and kept her mouth shut about my wardrobe choices.

We crossed the Betas off the list when one of the girls referred to my favorite talk show host as "a nasty fucking dyke." The Kappas counted us out when I actually yawned out loud during their philanthropy presentation. The rest of the time, I nodded and smiled, just counting down the minutes until we could hang out with the girls of Alpha Beta Omega. Somehow, they actually made the idea of joining a sorority, well, at least their sorority, sound appealing. I actually listened during their more informal info sessions and bothered to retain a few bits of history.

The sorority had been formed in 1863 as a literary club for ladies in Washington, DC. It was one of the oldest sororities around, but only counted twelve chapters at various universities across the country. Maryland University was home to the Alpha chapters of both ABO and OBA. Alpha Beta Omega had the biggest house on the Row, but the least amount of members. Danni told me they capped membership at thirty-six. This year they had room for only twelve new girls. Xi O boasted a roster of one hundred and seventy-four sisters. How did you get to know one hundred and seventy-four girls well enough to call them sisters?

Aside from the added bonus of small numbers, Alpha Beta Omega didn't charge for membership. That included the semester dues the other sororities and fraternities required. ABO had a collection of financially successful alumnae, and the families of the founding members had invested millions in every chapter to ensure the sorority attracted girls who truly wanted to belong and not just girls who could afford to.

Their charitable hours were spent supporting Types of Hope, a foundation that catered specifically to women and children with HIV/AIDS. The teardrop ruby necklaces represented not only their bonds of sisterhood, but their support for those they pledged to help. It was hard to hate girls like that. You couldn't make fun of people who actually cared and actually managed to be themselves.

I started noticing the girls of ABO around campus more and more. By Wednesday, Amy and I were joining Cleo and Danni for lunch and hanging around the quad with them between classes. I knew people thought we were trying to kiss up to the chapter's recruitment chairs, but I sure wasn't. I genuinely liked them. And I still didn't want to be in a sorority.

Even though joining Alpha Beta Omega would cost me nothing but time, time wasn't something I had a lot to give. I was determined to get a 4.0 my first semester, and joining any sort of organization that would demand so much of my nights and weekends was something I couldn't swing. Still, I found myself wanting to be around Danni, Cleo, and the rest of the girls. They made us feel welcome, and they made me feel more open to being myself.

During the hours we spent with the girls, they seemed to become more and more comfortable being physically affectionate with one another in front of me and Amy. In some cases, like with Heather and Cleo, it seemed like they were just close friends. Things were different with Danni. By the time Thursday night rolled around, I was convinced she was sleeping with Paige, if not Layna and Barb too.

They were always touching and kissing. Nothing so intense that it made me feel like a sick voyeur, but just enough to make me a little wet in the pants. Amy was as straight as could be. She was back on the prowl as soon as she learned the Chi Nu in her econ class had a girlfriend. I thought watching Paige feel Danni up would have made her uncomfortable, but she barely seemed to notice.

I found all the girls of ABO very attractive, but that type of intimacy always made me think of the girl with the spiky black hair.

I found myself thinking about her constantly. Constantly would have been a lot if she and I were dating. What I was into was a tad obsessive considering we had never said a word to each other. I ended every night we spent at the ABO house disappointed because she never made an appearance, as if she owed me the chance to just look at her again. I never saw her around campus either, but her lips and caramel-green eyes were always featured in my fantasies. And every time I pictured those eyes and considered the possibilities of those full red lips, my body reacted as if she were right there with me, watching me the same intense way she had that first night of rush. I did my best to spare Amy from the feelings this nameless girl sparked in me. Okay, I masturbated like crazy whenever I had the room to myself, and still every night after I was sure Amy was asleep, snoring somewhat softly across our tiny room, I couldn't stop myself from conjuring up images of that gorgeous face, that amazing body, and all things I wanted her to do to me. I tried to fight it, but eventually my fingers would slip past whatever pajama bottoms I'd worn to bed, into my underwear, through my short curls. The shock at just how wet she made me faded the second my fingers passed over my clit, all sensitive and hard.

I had to swallow heavily to choke down my gasps and my sighs as my body rocked eagerly against my hand, aching for so much more than a warm-up, but dreading the cool, foolish thoughts that snuck up on me as soon as I came.

Every time it started the same way, in the same place. I would find her back in the ABO living room, but in my imagination, we would have the place to ourselves. No other girls, no interruptions or pointless conversations about majors and stupid boys. Mostly, she was silent as she beckoned me across the room with her crooked index finger. The one night I'd driven myself crazy, wanting more than a fantasy, my imagination forced her to speak. She asked me my name, and even though her voice sounded exactly like mine, it was that one thing, her just wanting to know me, that keyed me up even more.

I would walk to her, and every time, she would kiss me, deep and slow, letting her warm hands gently trail along my sides, up my back, and if I was feeling secure in my squeaky dorm mattress, around to my breasts. She'd flick at my nipples, pinch them through thin layers of cotton until an almost shrill moan from me made her stop. I would tease my clit as I liked to do before my fingers moved to my opening. One of her hands would follow the same path, spreading my wetness around. Her other hand rested at the small of my back, holding me in place as she pulled her lips away from mine and kissed a hot, wet path down my neck.

That was always the best moment, when I could squeeze my eyes shut and forget about all the sights and sounds and the stupidity of how and where we'd first laid eyes on each other and just feel what I was doing to myself, what she was doing to me.

I'd draw it out as long as I could. I had to be reasonable for Amy's sake, but I always made the best of the imaginary minutes Hazel Eyes and I spent together. Something simple would push me over the edge. A single intense stroke of her fingers against the inner walls of my pussy or one forceful downward thrust of her palm against my clit. Or like during the last time, the best time, the way she whispered my name tripped me up in my covert pleasure operation and had me coming in heavy, saturated pulses all around my fingers.

I have no clue how I didn't wake Amy up. I did moan out loud. My bed did creak and groan under the grinding of my hips into the shitty springs, but even if I'd come out of my hazel-eyed stupor and seen Amy sitting straight up in her bed, staring at me like the sicko I was, I still couldn't get this girl out of my mind, and the fantasies I had about her wouldn't let me keep my hand away from my crotch. And that was just back at the dorm. Out on campus, I started to become a little desperate.

I wanted to see her. I wanted to know her, but short of stalking the ABO house twenty-four hours a day, I didn't know how to find her. MU had a pretty big student body, so running into someone who lived off campus and didn't share your major or anything resembling your schedule would have been a little much to expect. Asking Danni or Cleo about her was an option, but I felt foolish bringing her up, like a freshman asking a senior to prom.

I decided once they were through with their weeks of initiation, my pruned fingers and I would find her. If she shot me down, I could suffer the embarrassment of rejection without Danni or Cleo being involved. I just had to get through this silly week of rush.

❖

On Friday morning, Danni told us to be in our room between four and seven p.m. to receive our invitations to initiation. I wanted to get ahead in my English reading, so I stayed in with Amy while she waited. By six o'clock, she'd already received three floral-covered envelopes, life-changing offers, sealed and delivered, but for some reason she didn't seem all that excited.

"What's the problem?" I asked. "Three is pretty good."

"Yeah. I know. I was kinda hoping ABO would ask me and not 'cause I'm so cute. I really like them," she said.

"You know, so do I." I looked at the clock. "You want to go get some dinner?" It was almost seven, and these chicks all seemed so anxious when they came to the door, I doubted any of them would wait this long.

"Yeah. Let me put my shoes on."

"Don't worry. Something tells me the ABO girls would hang out with us even if we didn't join."

I pulled the door open and walked smack into Cleo.

"Oh! Hey."

"Ladies," she said with a calm smile.

I was going to invite Cleo in, when I glanced at her hands. She was holding two bright red envelopes. One for Amy. And one for me.

## Chapter Two

A my and I dropped onto her bed and stared at our envelopes. I turned mine over and gazed at the circle of thick black wax pressed with the Greek symbols for Alpha Beta Omega. It was the most beautiful presentation of stationary I'd ever seen.

"Are you going to open it?" Amy peered up at me. She was so excited I thought she would bounce off the bed.

"Are you?"

"Of course. Here, let's open them together." We tore into the wax, and inside the envelope was a small square of black paper. Below the crest, the day's date, and my first, middle, and last names, it read:

We invite you to join us in our eternal sisterhood.

Interesting word choice, but I wasn't surprised. Amy told me her mother still met with her Xi O sisters twice a month, and she was almost fifty. Joining a sorority meant you were in it for the long haul. I read the words over again, running my finger across the indentations the print made in the thick paper. The red script looked gorgeous against the ebony background. Something else was off, though.

"Do you remember filling out anything with your middle name?" I asked.

"No, but they could get them from the housing department or the chancellor's office," Amy said. "This is weird though."

"What? Let me see." I grabbed the small piece of paper from Amy's hand. The words were exactly the same, only this invitation had Amy's name instead of mine. "What's the problem?"

"It's a bid card. There's supposed to be a check box or a blank line or something, like a yes or no option so if we decide we don't want to go through initiation, we can check no and send it back."

"You think what, they aren't giving us a choice?"

"Or they are assuming we're going to say yes?"

"Are we?" I asked.

"I don't know, Ginger. Are we?" I didn't like it, but she had every right to give me crap about accepting the bid. Going through initiation with the sisters of Alpha Beta Omega was not something I wanted at all. I was glad that Amy and I had made some new friends, but my priorities hadn't changed. School came first.

I should have told Amy that, right then and there, and I would have, if it weren't for one small problem. I thought of the dark-haired girl with the hazel eyes and her perfect red lips almost every time I closed my eyes. I didn't know what role she played in ABO, but I had a feeling it was something important. If I went through initiation, maybe I could see her again.

I also had to consider Amy. She had a big mouth. Having a big mouth didn't mean she knew when, or even how to stick up for herself. Cleo, Danni, and the rest of the girls seemed perfectly normal, but any girl who had survived high school knew a thing or two about mob mentality. Greek culture carried with it the unshakable stigma of hazing. There was no way I would put up with that kind of crap. Amy would, if she knew it meant she could belong. Stalking Hazel Eyes and keeping tabs on my roommate were perfectly valid reasons to at least go through initiation. I reminded myself again, I could always quit.

"Okay," I said confidently.

"Are you sure? You're really going to do it?" Amy gasped. I could hear that horrible squeal of hers aching to get escape.

"I'm going with you, but only for two reasons. One, I don't want you going into this alone. We barely know these girls and I don't want you getting hazed."

"Aw, Ginge."

"And I can always quit. Which I will if this takes up too much time. I'm serious, Amy. I need to keep my grades up this semester. I'm not going to let any parties or canine diabetes fun runs mess up my GPA."

"Oh, Ginger. Thank you. Thank you. I swear this will be fun. Thank you," she squealed.

"Yeah, great. So what do we do now?" I flipped the card over as if instructions had magically appeared on the back.

"Um, we could call Danni or we could wait—" Amy was cut off by a knock on the door. We glanced at each other then I jumped up to answer it. Danni was standing in the hallway.

"Hey, we were just about to call you," I said.

Her face dropped, her eyes bugging wide. "You're not backing out are you?"

"No, but how did you know we'd—"

"One hundred and forty-seven years and no one has ever said no."

"Fair enough."

"So now what?" Amy asked over my shoulder.

Danni handed us each a garment bag. "You'll be ready at nine p.m. sharp. Someone will come for you." She cocked her head to the side and looked us over before she went on. "Camila prefers it if you wear your hair down. Bye." She grabbed the knob and pulled the door closed before we could ask any questions.

I unzipped the garment bag and laid the white eyelet dress on the bed. Well, it wasn't exactly a dress.

"Is that a nightgown?" Amy asked.

"Yup." There was a small red bag pinned to the hanger. Inside was a long white ribbon. I ditched it on my bed along with the hanger, then I held the baby-doll-style nightie up to my body. It came about an inch or two below my crotch.

"See! This is exactly what I was talking about. They're going to parade us around in lingerie and then make us screw the Omega Beta Alpha boys and tape it."

"Shut up. They would never make us do that," Amy said, holding her own scrap of lace up in front of her chest. "It is kinda kinky."

"Yeah, kinky. Amy, I swear if pictures of me in this thing end up on the Internet, I'm going to kill you."

"They won't. Hey, who's Camila?" We'd met all twenty-four active members of Alpha Beta Omega, but there hadn't been anyone named Camila.

"Oh. I don't know." I didn't, but I had an idea of who it might be.

❖

Three girls on our floor had accepted their bids to different sororities. All three of them beat Amy and me to the shower. I let Amy go first while I got our curling irons out. In an effort to up her overall sex appeal, Amy had brought a warehouse worth of black lace bras and panties with her to school. Lucky for her, we were nearly the same size and I swore by simple white cotton. I threw her one of my bras. I drew the line at lending her a pair of underwear. She had to settle for a light yellow pair she usually wore on laundry day.

After I pulled on the nightie, I almost reconsidered the bra. The tight lace of the top pushed my boobs together plenty without the use of underwire, if only it hadn't been see-through.

We took turns doing each other's hair. My red mane was so bright that sometimes I could swear it glowed in the dark. Thank God it was fairly straight. We both added some volume to our locks with big, soft curls. We had no idea what to do with the white ribbon, so I wrapped Amy's around her head like a headband, tying a small bow off to the side. She did the same with mine. They didn't say anything about shoes, so we both grabbed a pair of flip-flops from our closets. Then we sat on our beds to wait. For some reason, I couldn't stop playing with my hands.

"You don't think they'll hit us, do you?" Amy asked. I looked at her. I'd never seen her frightened before. I don't think Amy had given the idea of us getting hazed any real thought until we actually started getting dressed. She'd been so focused on getting a bid, on getting into parties and meeting a cute guy, that she never considered the reality of what might happen to her if she agreed to go through with initiation. I knew I'd made the right choice to go with her.

"They won't. But…"

"But what?" Amy's eyes sprang wide.

"Nothing. They won't hit us, and if they do we leave, okay?"

"Okay."

I patted Amy on the knee and then I sent texts to Todd and my mom, telling them where we were going, just in case.

❖

At nine on the dot, there was a knock on our door. I gave Amy a weak smile and went to open it. She hadn't said a thing while we waited. It freaked me out a little.

This time Paige and Cleo stood in the hallway. The playful glint in Cleo's eye made me feel a little bit better. I didn't think they would actually do anything cruel or painful to us, but I was still a little rattled. I swallowed, trying not to sound nervous.

"Hey. We're ready."

"No, you're not." Cleo's tone was dry.

"But what—"

"Lose the underwear. All of it." I cursed under my breath as Cleo and Paige stepped into the room. Amy and I quickly pulled off our undies and our bras. I glanced up at her. Considering I was in the same nightie, it was clear you could totally see my nipples, and even though I did some pretty decent landscaping in the shower, I should have shaved my pubes all off. Amy looked back at me and I could tell she wished she had too.

"I need your keys, your dorm cards, and your cell phones," Paige said. The look on her face was typically blank. Now she looked annoyed, and I knew we needed to hurry. We grabbed our stuff and dropped it in a black sack Paige seemed to pull out of thin air.

"Now you're ready. No more talking from here on out," Cleo said, all humor gone from her voice. She handed Paige a white blindfold before she stepped behind me and told me to close my eyes. The cloth wasn't uncomfortable, just tight enough that it would have irritated the crap out of me if I tried to open my eyes.

"Open your hand." Cleo's voice was right by my ear. I lifted my hand and felt my open palm cupped with Amy's. She was shaking. I was able to sneak in a quick reassuring squeeze before we were led out the door.

❖

If the sisters of Alpha Beta Omega had set out to leave us disoriented and confused and, in Amy's case, scared shitless, well then, they deserved some sort of award for their efforts.

After getting over the initial embarrassment of everyone in the lobby seeing my nipples at full attention and knowing that my hair color did match, floor to ceiling, I had the pleasure of tripping down the front stairs. I almost took Amy with me. Cleo managed to catch me before we both face planted into the concrete. I was pretty uncomfortable from the start, but the blind misstep had my heart thumping in my chest.

They loaded us into some sort of bus. I only knew because we had to walk up a few steps before we were seated. Then they took our flip-flops. A few moments later, we were moving. Danni had told us there would be twelve new members total. I didn't know how many girls were with us when we got on. From the amount of unsteady breathing and the way the air moved, I knew it had to be at least eight or nine.

We'd been driving for a long time and it became obvious they were driving us in circles to keep us in suspense before they brought us back to the ABO house. At least I figured that's where we were going.

After an hour or so, the bus stopped and the door hissed as it opened.

"Take the hand of the one beside you." The tone was formal, but I could tell it was Barb.

Amy hadn't let go of my hand since we'd left the dorm, so I reached to my left in a clumsy attempt to grab at the nearest person. A soft, warm hand with thick fingers intertwined with mine just as Barb told us to stand. We were led off the bus slowly. Barb had probably been warned about my spill.

I tried to take in everything about my surroundings as we walked, but I couldn't. Amy was still shaking, and once we were inside, we were led through several halls, each with sharp turns.

When we finally came to a stop, our hands were separated and then we were gently turned so we were standing shoulder to shoulder. I could feel Amy take a few deep breaths, and slowly, she stopped trembling. The girl to my left was taller than me. Her arm felt like her hand, warm and soft and a little bit doughy. When my blindfold was removed, I wanted to look to see who it was, but what I saw in front of me told me I should wait.

It didn't take long for my eyes to adjust to the dim candlelight. The dark marble room around us was definitely set up for a ceremony, but I ignored the details. I couldn't focus on anything but the woman standing on the other side of the wide marble floor. The one I wanted the most, the one with the gorgeous red lips and the beautiful hazel eyes.

There were other women standing beside her. To her left was a tall female with white-blond hair cut sharply along her chin and bangs trimmed bluntly across her forehead. Beyond her stood a muscular woman with wavy brown hair down to her waist. Her skin was pale and her eyes were big and the same deep brown color as her hair. A short woman who looked Native American stood beside Hazel Eyes on her right, and on her other side there was another woman of African descent, whose hair was in perfectly shaped locks that hung past her shoulders. The last woman was Asian, and she had the most seductive look about her. Something about the curve of her mouth and the way her hair was swept up in an elegant loose bun. All six of them carried an erotic air, lustful and lethal.

I wouldn't have noticed any of the others at all if it weren't for the fact that they were nearly naked. A delicate weaving of black chain mail laced with small rubies barely covered the spot between their legs. Each woman was beautiful in her own way, but I couldn't keep from staring at my Hazel Eyes.

From across the room, I could tell she was just a little taller than me. Her red lips were just as plump and full as I'd remembered them. Her proportions were flawless. I gazed over her golden skin, tracing the curves of her perfectly shaped thighs up to her full breasts tipped with dark brown nipples that were meant to be worshiped. My heart was racing again and my palms started to tingle. If I hadn't been under the watchful eye of about three dozen other people, I would have made a move to touch her, or at least ask her her name.

A movement to her left snapped me out of my trance. The woman with the white-blond hair stepped down from the elevated marble rise where the six of them stood. Her eyes were bright blue and she wore the same red lipstick as Hazel Eyes. When she spoke, a thick Eastern European accent dripped from every disinterested word.

"We are going to do things a little differently tonight. You will have three chances to leave. If you decide that you must, no one will stop you. There will be no repercussions, but you will not speak unless you are asked. Unless you are asked individually, you will answer as one. Is this understood?"

To my surprise, we all replied with a confident "Yes."

"We are not like the other organizations on campus," she continued, her tone unaffected. "If you choose to remain with us through this night, you will remain with us always. Is this understood?"

Another "Yes" filled the air. I don't remember mustering any effort to agree, but my voice was there joining in the reply.

"Now is your first chance. If there are any of you who wish to leave, please step forward." Nobody moved. "Are we to understand that you all wish to remain?"

Again, "Yes" echoed off the marble.

"Wonderful," she continued. "My darling Danielle, you may begin." The woman turned and walked back to the platform. When she was back with the other women, my gaze shifted to Hazel Eyes.

I nearly gasped as her eyes settled back on me. Even as Danni began to speak, her eyes held mine.

Danni's voice came from just behind me. I could feel that she was standing just between Amy and me.

"My Queen. If you will allow, it is my honor to present to you thirteen potential donors. None are without fault, but all are pure of heart and of clean body. They will all serve you as we and our sisters before us have served you. And when they have completed their term, they will go forth willingly and serve our master."

It took me a moment to register the exact words Danni had said. I was too busy staring at the woman in front of me, but finally they clicked, and I wasn't sure I was comfortable with what they meant. Danni hadn't mentioned anything about serving anyone, master or otherwise. It was time to grab Amy and go.

As if she could read my mind, Hazel Eyes's gaze narrowed and her nostrils flared. Fear pierced through me, fear and arousal, which scared me even more. My hand twitched toward Amy's, but for some reason I jerked it back before I touched her. Hazel Eyes's expression returned to normal and I realized I wasn't in control of my own body. She was. When she seemed confident I wouldn't run, she took a step forward. She must have been the queen.

"Do they understand the true nature of their purpose?" the queen asked. Her voice was like silk, deep and smooth, so much better than I'd imagined it. I felt myself sway a little as I blinked, before refocusing on her face.

"No, they do not," a group of voices called out from behind us.

"And do you believe once they discover the true nature of their purpose, they all will remain?"

"We do," the sisterhood behind us said.

It seemed to take some effort, but the queen looked away from me and focused on a girl far to my left. If I glanced in that direction, I could only see the thick neck and shoulder of the girl beside me. I had no idea who the queen was looking at.

"Anna-Jade, tell me why are you here?"

A shy voice replied, "I've wanted to join a sorority. Layna and Heather were really nice to me so I accepted the invitation."

The queen nodded then looked to the other end of the line and addressed a girl far to my right. Her name was Laura and she gave pretty much the same answer. Two of the sisters of Alpha Beta Omega had reached out to her and shown her the upside to making friends through Greek life.

The queen carried on like this, back and forth down the line, asking each of us why we had accepted our bid. Even though we hadn't been given the option in writing, we could have turned Danni down when she showed up with our dresses, but we didn't. Danni and Cleo had completely won us over. Now I was terrified about what they had gotten us into.

Finally, the queen spoke to a girl named Samantha, a few people to my left.

"Samantha, tell me why you are here."

"I just got a position on the university paper. There was a rumor going around that ABO was involved with some underground secret society involving vampires and demons." The queen burst out laughing, a rich, intoxicating sound. The others beside her laughed as well, but they let Samantha continue.

"We all knew it was bullshit, but my editor wanted me to get in and see what rumors I could confirm."

"We welcome you, Samantha. Although, I doubt any of this will end up in print," the queen replied with a slight shake of her head. I couldn't believe the girl had admitted to spying. She could have been born without a filter, or maybe she felt the same pull toward the truth that I did.

The queen went on with her questioning, a slight grin on her lips. "Benita, please."

The girl next to me tried to speak up, but her voice was still low and shy. "My mother is married to your master. He felt this was the right place for me."

"Ah, so you are the one. Do you feel this is the right place for you?"

"Yes, my Queen. I do. Danni and Cleo have made me feel less anxious about being away from home," Benita replied with a little more confidence. She was the only one of us to address the queen so directly. The queen seemed to enjoy it.

"I have to agree with your father. This is the perfect place for you. And you prefer to be called 'Benny'?"

"Yes, my Queen."

"Benny it will be. Amy…" she went on with a teasing tone. "Why are you here?"

Amy's breathing had calmed completely. There was still nervous energy coming off her body. She inhaled deeply before she answered. "I wanted to get into all the good parties," she replied.

"But that's not why you accepted our invitation?" the queen asked.

"No, ma'am."

"Have you ever been with a woman before?" the queen asked bluntly.

"No, but I do have a crush on Danni." It took everything I had not to turn to Amy. She'd never mentioned anything about liking Danni like that. I didn't think it was something she would freely admit, ever. Forget confessing it to a room full of people she'd just met. I knew then I was totally screwed. I wasn't a liar and I didn't have anything to hide, but this confessing of the truth was beyond embarrassing. The queen gave me about two seconds to figure out what I was going to say. My name coming from her lips wiped the response from my mind immediately.

"Ginger."

"Yes."

"Why are you here?"

"I wanted to look out for my roommate, and lately, I've been questioning my sexuality. My brother suggested joining a sorority might help me find some other girls who feel the way I do about other women."

She relaxed slightly. "Is that right? I've heard there are a few girl bars downtown. You didn't start there?"

"No, I didn't, but I did like hanging out with Cleo and Danni."

"They are very special. Are you attracted to my favorite pets?" She winked at Danni behind me.

"Yes, but…"

"But what?"

"I'm more attracted to you." I couldn't believe what I'd just said, but I couldn't take the words back. They were out there for everyone to hear and analyze, everyone including the queen. Quiet laughter filled the room. I swallowed again, keeping my eyes focused on her. Her nostrils flared slightly as she licked her bottom lip. I felt a small rush of moisture between my legs.

"I see," she said. She swallowed then and tipped up her chin to address us all. I exhaled, glad I hadn't pissed her off.

"We will proceed." The queen's eyes closed as if in a brief moment of prayer before she looked at me again and spoke. "I thank you all for your honesty, and now it is my duty to reveal the truth in your presence. Samantha's editor may have had some valid suspicions." She paused, then started pacing in front of us. "Our kind wandered and scavenged for centuries, taking of the innocent and the evil, the undeserving and the unaware, to feed our bodies and maintain our survival."

I didn't want to believe what she was saying. This wasn't a cheerful "welcome to the party" type speech. The queen was talking about something ancient and deadly. She could have been trying to scare us for the sake of the ceremony, but the intense green and golden glow of her eyes told me she was being completely serious.

And there was something else. I watched the queen as she talked. I hadn't noticed at first, but as she went on, her canines grew larger and longer. The tips were sharpening, and the length was making it harder for her to close her mouth all the way when she paused. Those teeth were real and they kept growing.

"Our kind grew tired of the death and the pain, the destruction of lives and families. We humbled ourselves at your ancestors' feet and we were given all that we would ever need in return for our undying loyalty." I turned these words over in my head as quickly as possible. I looked at the mouths of the five other women flanking the queen and saw their lips were parted now to make room for their elongated teeth. My eyes shot to back to the queen. I didn't know what she truly was—vampire, demon, overzealous comic book fan.

Either way, I knew she and the other women were not human and we'd been brought there to feed them.

I did a quick scan for the exit but couldn't find one. I focused ahead again as the queen and the others stepped from the platform. I hadn't noticed before, but there were large cushions on the floor. The six women sank to their knees on the cushions in front of us.

They bowed their heads and turned their palms up as if they planned to worship us.

The queen went on. This time her tone was low and somber as if she were begging for forgiveness and asking for permission at the same time.

"We need your trust and we want nothing more than to offer our own. Your sacrifice is a gift, and in return, we pledge to honor and protect you." Her voice dropped even lower. "I will ask for a second time. Those of you who have been brought before me and my sisters, do any of you wish to leave?" The queen lifted her head and scanned the line of girls beside me as she spoke. Again, her gaze settled back on me. Nobody moved. I knew we all had our reasons. I was too scared.

"Layna, Heather, please. Make your presentation to your sister-queen."

For the first time, I got a good look at one of the other new girls. This must have been Anna-Jade, the first girl who was questioned. She was much shorter than me with jet-black straight hair to her waist. She had on the same see-through slip. I'd forgotten how exposed we all were. She was shaking. Layna and Heather were wearing long black hooded robes that dragged behind them on the floor. The hoods were down, covering their shoulders. Their hands peeked out from under the draping fabric as they led Anna-Jade forward with a gentle touch to her elbows. Layna carried a knife.

They knelt on the cushion in front of the first woman, the one with the blunt blond haircut. I watched her face for a moment as she looked over Anna-Jade.

"Most gracious Natasha, our sister-queen, I present to you Anna-Jade Wilson. She is kind and giving and in need of love and respect," Layna said softly.

Heather continued with the same soft murmur. "We know you will bring her the same joy you have brought to us, and we know you will offer her your protection."

Natasha gently lifted her finger and tipped Anna-Jade's chin up so she could look her in the eye. "Do you understand what I ask of you?"

"You want my blood?" Anna-Jade replied. I shuddered, hearing my fears confirmed.

"That is correct. If you will give yourself to me, never will you fear again. I will love and protect you and your little sister." Anna-Jade made a small hiccupping sound and her body shook more. Natasha gave her a moment before she went on. "I ask you one last time, my sweet, will you allow me to bind you to myself, my sister-queens, and your sisters?"

The decision was up to her now, not the group. This was her final out, her last chance to escape, but Anna-Jade nodded and said, "Yes."

I was captivated by the vows between them. I didn't know Anna-Jade at all, but despite the size of Natasha's teeth, her words were enough to take the fear away, for Anna-Jade at least. I hadn't lost sight of what was going on here. They were asking us to feed them, but even I couldn't fight the comfort Natasha offered...until she took the knife Layna held out to her and pulled the blade across Anna-Jade's palm.

The air hissed between her teeth, but she didn't move. Natasha dipped her head slowly and licked the blood away from the opening in the gash. She ran her mouth back and forth across Anna-Jade's skin. I wanted to be horrified. I wanted to puke, then grab Amy and run. I'd promised I wouldn't let them hurt her, and hand slicing fell under the umbrella of pain. I was still paralyzed by what I was seeing.

When Natasha lifted her head, Anna-Jade's palm was clean and the cut was completely healed. Natasha brushed her cheek gently before leaning forward to kiss Anna-Jade on the lips. She pulled away and stroked her cheek one more time.

Then Heather handed Natasha a slim black box. I couldn't see what was inside until Anna-Jade bowed her head a little. Natasha fastened a delicate platinum chain around her neck. I knew there was a small teardrop ruby hanging just above her breasts.

"You are safe here and we all will love you," Natasha said before she looked to Heather and Layna. They took that as their cue to usher Anna-Jade up from her spot. The three of them shuffled behind Natasha and settled comfortably on the cushion. Anna-Jade was still crying. Heather wrapped her arms around her and let her sob quietly. I got the feeling they were tears of relief.

The queen had our attention again as she looked off to my right. "Kate, Jordan, please make your presentation to your sister-queen." Kate and Jordan led Laura forward toward the chocolate-skinned woman. Her name was Omi. The vows were nearly the same. She promised to protect and care for Laura, whose palm was swiftly cut then resealed with a few swipes of Omi's tongue. A ruby necklace was placed around her neck and Laura was kissed. Then she took her seat with Kate and Jordan behind Omi.

The queen went over the line again. On either side of me, one by one, a new girl was brought forward and presented to a different sister-queen. Natasha. Omi. Kina. Faeth. Tokyo. All exotically beautiful, all terrifying.

Then, Danni and Paige brought Amy forward to the queen. The most important sister-queen, the hazel-eyed leader of this insane ceremony. The queen made her pledge to Amy, then closed her wound. I watched Amy for a moment while she twirled the teardrop ruby between her fingers. When Benny went forward with Cleo and Barb, I realized I was the only one left. I was the thirteenth girl.

As Benny crossed the marble floor, I finally got a good look at her. She was heavy like Danni, but she didn't carry her weight as well. Her long dark brown hair was frizzy and she had acne all over her back and shoulders. I hated myself for thinking it. I didn't want to believe the queen found Benny more attractive than me.

And even more, I was filled with this irrational stab of jealously. Danni and Cleo had brought Benny and Amy for the queen, and I was left out. The other girls were involved in their own sister-queens, exchanging small kisses and petting strokes. They didn't notice just how uncomfortable I was standing in the middle of the room alone. I felt like crying. And then I felt crazy. I actually wanted this—vampire to pick me. At least over Benny.

"It looks like you and Cleo have brought me one extra," the queen said to Danni as she looked me over. I watched her hands as she gently stroked Amy's leg. That pissed me off even more.

"She didn't want any part of this, but we thought maybe you'd like to meet her. Ginger Elizabeth Carmichael, meet Camila, our kind and loving and most gracious Queen," Danni replied. I couldn't tell whether she was messing with me or Camila.

"You are too sweet, Danni. I want you to take Amy and Benny." I took a step back as all the women stood at once. Danni handed Camila another slim black box. "I would like to have a word with Ginger alone."

Everyone ignored me as they filed out of the room. Amy didn't even glance back to see if I was okay. She was so wrapped up in Danni. She and I were going to have a long talk.

When it was just the two of us, Camila held out her hand for me.

"Come."

I stepped forward and took Camila's hand. Her skin was warm and soft. Up close, she smelled like fresh cinnamon with a bit of sugar. My mouth started to water, and other parts of my body became more and more wet. I swallowed and followed her silently as she led me from the room.

## CHAPTER THREE

The other girls disappeared down a long hallway. Camila tugged me in the opposite direction. I glanced back after Amy. The dimly lit corridor made it impossible for me to find her in the sea of black robes, white nighties, and bare skin. I wanted to trust Danni and Cleo to keep her safe because I'd never forgive myself if she were to get hurt. Or worse. If I found Amy the next morning with her perky demeanor intact, I'd let her know I was a little annoyed she had bailed on me so easily. At the moment, though, Amy was the least of my worries.

Considering how much time I'd spent thinking about Camila, I should have been anxious to actually be with her alone, but that was the Camila I'd dreamed up in my head. The harmless, yet outrageously sexy college student, maybe a senior with a thing for girls my height with green eyes and freckles. The reality of what I had just witnessed, the blood oaths and the fangs, left me a little conflicted. While we walked, I pictured the short blade cutting open Amy's skin and the satisfied look on Camila's face as she licked the blood away. If she was fulfilled by the taste of blood, there was no way I was safe with her alone. I might not live to see the morning. Were amazingly good looks reason enough to trust your blood lusting captor?

I suppose I didn't have to hold her hand. My body didn't see that there was another choice. Camila, the queen, my Hazel Eyes, was a vampire. Vampires were supposed to be cold, undead creatures of the night or something just as cute and cuddly. Camila's skin was incredibly soft, and even though her grip was confident and firm, she was surprisingly gentle as her fingers interlaced with mine. I inhaled another hint of her warm, mouthwatering scent as she pulled me closer. I had to get away from her.

I tried to focus on where we were going instead of on Camila's bare ass. It was difficult. Her backside was so round and perky. The black chain around her body shimmered as she moved, following the curve of her hips, up around her back. I looked at her smooth shoulders and the graceful line of her neck. Her haircut was so… cute. The dark spikes were in perfect disarray, short in the back and slightly longer over her ears and bangs. It wasn't a style many people could pull off, but like the bright red lipstick, it looked amazing on her.

My clit wanted to see just how close I could get to her. The throbbing pulse between my legs wanted to touch her. It was telling me to run my fingers over her whole body. The logical side of my brain wanted to make a run for it. If I only knew which way would take me to an actual exit and not back into the arms of the other sister-queens.

Our long walk brought us to a red door. Camila opened it and patiently ushered me inside. I don't know what I was expecting. I found a pretty regular lounge area. A dark carpet covered the floor. There was a black couch, a few chairs, and a coffee table centered around an enormous flat screen TV. In the corner there was an elegant bar. Along the far wall were three more red doors. Camila led me to the door in the center.

She flicked a switch and a soft, golden glow lit the room. I glanced up and saw small yellow bulbs hidden in the molding around the ceiling. There was an enormous bed covered with black satin sheets and thick black blankets. Another flat screen TV was mounted on the wall across from the bed, over a large dresser. On the far side of the room, a set of black curtains were pulled open on either side of a sitting area with two oversized armchairs and a chaise lounge. All the furniture was black and there were no windows.

I stood by the door and watched Camila. I was fascinated by the way she moved. Her hips and shoulders rotated in lithe, synchronized movements, like a jungle cat. I almost felt rude staring. I had to take advantage, though. I didn't know if I'd ever see her again. I needed someone to slap me. If I lived, I had to get out of there.

She walked over to her dresser and stashed the thin black box. I think it held a necklace for me. A necklace that I'd have to shed blood for. Camila unhooked the weaving of metal and rubies from around her waist and placed it gently in a wooden box lined with black silk.

"You may sit if you like." Without looking at me, she nodded toward the bed. My stomach clenched at the sound of her voice. The bed seemed like a bad place to sit and I'd have to walk past her to get to the chairs.

"I'm fine."

She opened a drawer and pulled out a pair of black lace underwear and a black tank top. It was a shame to cover any of that perfect golden skin. As she pulled on the underwear, she turned toward me a little bit. She was completely bare between her legs. The skin of her slit glistened. For a split second, I wanted to know what exactly had made her wet.

"Kinda overdoing it with the black, huh?" I blurted nervously.

She pulled the tank top over her head. Her hard nipples puckered through the fabric.

"I have to offset Natasha. Her room is all neons. It's hideous. Besides, don't you think it's fitting?" She turned around and leaned against her dresser, folding her arms across her chest. "For a vampire."

"Is that what you are?"

"It's what you think, isn't it?"

"Something like that." I took a deep breath and stood up straight. It was time to leave. "You guys seem pretty stocked up on food now. What do you want with me?"

"Tonight, I was hoping you would feed me. And then I was planning on fucking you to sleep." Heat surged across my chest and face. No one had ever said anything like that to me—ever. I had no idea what to say back. That didn't stop my body from reacting to her even more. My nipples started to tingle and my feet shuffled, my thighs pressing together.

"But we have some things to discuss before that." Her fangs had retracted for the most part, but the light still caught their sharp tips when she talked. She caught me looking at them before she licked her plump bottom lip and glanced at the floor. The red lipstick didn't budge at all. I shifted my weight more to my left foot.

"Wha—" My voice cracked so I coughed and tried again. "What things?" Camila pushed off the dresser and turned to rummage through another jewelry box. I wanted to back away as she came back toward me. Instead, I watched helplessly, my eyes glued to the long needle she carried. She picked up my hand and pricked my index finger, then pinched it so the blood came rushing to the surface. I gasped as she took my fingertip in her mouth. Her warm tongue swirled over my skin. She looked up at me, still sucking on my finger, and my pussy gushed.

"I figured," Camila said. She straightened and let go of my hand. "You saw me that night, didn't you?"

"When?" I glanced at my finger. Every trace of the pinprick was gone. "The night of the open house?" She nodded. "Yeah. You were talking to Barb."

"Did you see any of the other sister-queens?" I scanned my memory. There had been so many people in the past week. Something clicked, though.

"Yeah, Faeth? The tall one with the brown hair." Camila nodded again, pursing her lips. "Yeah, I saw her last night when we came over. She was standing by the window for a little while."

"Cleo tells me you were adopted."

"I was. What does that have to do with you or Faeth?"

"What happened to your birth mother?"

"She died." I shook my head with a humorless chuckle, wanting to move away from the painful truths of my past. "She died twice actually. She used to joke that women had nine lives, like cats."

"What do you mean twice?"

"She was found clinically dead when she was about five months pregnant with me. A mugger or something. The doctors saved her."

"Ah, okay."

"What?" My relationship with my real mother had been short and painful, but I didn't appreciate anyone being so casual about her death. "Why are you asking about her?"

"Because I am not sure a doctor saved your mother or even you, for that matter. You have vampire blood in your system. Unless someone tried to turn you—and you'd remember that—I'm fairly sure your mother fed from one of my kind while she was pregnant with you."

I stared at her, completely confused. "How can you know that?"

"You shouldn't have seen me or Faeth. It's not much, but the blood of my kind is in you. I can taste it and it's the only way you could have seen through the cloak. We only used it to mask ourselves against humans."

My mother had been a stripper who sold the rest of her body on the side. The idea that she'd known a vampire, considering they were now very real in my universe, didn't seem all that impossible. That didn't make the idea that I had vampire blood in my veins any easier to process.

It took me years to feel comfortable enough to call the Carmichaels Mom and Dad. There were still days where I was shocked my new family hadn't picked up and left me in the middle of the night. They had helped me become the person I was now, a person I was happy and comfortable with. I didn't need a know-it-all vampire I'd just met telling me that I didn't know myself at all.

I sat on the bed. Camila sat next to me. The bed barely shifted under her weight. I got the feeling she wanted to touch me, but she kept her hands to herself.

"You think I'm not human?"

"You are. You blood simply isn't pure. What happened the second time, to your mother?" she asked.

"She…um. She killed herself. Slit her wrists while I was at school." I couldn't say anymore—about how I'd found her. I didn't want to think about the envelope of cash or the note she'd left for the neighbors, asking them to keep me. And I didn't think Camila wanted to hear anything about the year I spent in the system.

"Do you know anything about your father?"

"No. She never mentioned him." I looked into her eyes. "Do you think he was like you—a vampire, I mean?"

"No. We can't breed. Drinking from one of us is the only way to get our blood into your system."

"Well, he must have been a redhead. My mom was a brunette." I looked back at my hands. I usually traced patterns in my freckles while I thought, but they had suddenly blurred together.

"We haven't had a redhead in a while. That's part of the reason why I wanted to keep you." I could hear a hint of pleasure in her voice. Then I knew I'd let my guard down. She was trying to gain my trust and it made me sick.

"What's the other reason?" I stood and backed away from her. "Don't you have enough food?"

"Ginger, this isn't about food."

"Then let me go."

"You can leave right now. I'll even lend you some sweats so you can walk back to the dorm. But I'd like to explain first." I looked down at the see-through dress. There was no way I was walking across campus in that thing.

"Fine. But I'm not feeding you."

"Fine," Camila said. "Will you come sit down, please?"

"Why?"

Her eyes started to glow a bit as she gazed over my body. I took another step back.

"Because I like the way you smell. And I feel rude making a guest stand."

"No. I'm fine, really."

"Okay." She shrugged dismissively.

"So, what? You guys use the sorority to lure unsuspecting girls to your lair?"

"It's not that simple," she said. I closed my eyes and leaned my head against the wall.

"The others are hearing the truth for themselves right now. Please. Just let me tell you."

"I already know too much, don't I?" I could just see Camila and her sister-friends letting me get five hundred yards before hunting me down and ripping out my throat. I wasn't in the mood for that kind of silencing.

"Well, yes, but we can always strip your memory. It's your choice." Camila was trying not to chuckle.

"You're enjoying this aren't you?"

"A little bit. Yes. How about you ask the questions?" She nodded toward the spot next to her on the bed.

I walked past her and sank in one of the big chairs. I was actually surprised by how comfortable it was. I tucked my legs under me and tried to relax. If she was telling the truth about my mixed vampire blood, I at least had to hear her out before making my escape.

I thought for a moment. There was a lot I wanted to know, but I couldn't decide what was the most important bit of information. Apparently, I was taking too long.

"Why don't I just start from the beginning and then you can ask me to fill in the blanks?" Camila said.

I nodded, wrapping my arms around myself.

"The first of my kind were the children of demons." Camila laughed again as my eyes darted to the door. "Just listen."

"What? I'm listening."

"Let me ask you this? You are familiar with the idea of fallen angels?"

"Yeah." I kept the duh to myself.

"Well, the first of our kind were essentially…enlightened demons."

"You're saying some demons grew a conscience and wanted out of Hell."

"It's not exactly your idea of Hell, but something like that. Several of them escaped, but they could only make it as far as this plane."

"And these were blood drinking demons?" I said. Warm-blooded, soft-skinned, beautiful demons.

"Yes. We are here as guests, you could say. Our master has an arrangement with whom you would call God."

"What do you call him?"

"The Divine has no name."

"Okay. So God and your master struck what kind of an arrangement?"

"My master's children, my sisters, and I are permitted to feed as long as we do not interfere with God's plans."

I still didn't see the upshot of this conversation. It had been a while since I'd been to Mass, but I was raised Catholic. If memory served me right demons weren't something you were supposed to mess with or bind yourself to even for the sake the time honored traditions of a sorority. Still I listened, trying to wrap my mind around what I knew she believed to be the truth.

"So why all this?" I motioned around the room. "I thought vampires were supposed to be all powerful. Why go through all this to play nice with your food? There's like eight billion people in the world. Why not pick some randoms off the street?" I flinched as she stood. She grabbed a blanket off the bed and brought it over to me. I was freezing. I hadn't even noticed. She tucked the thick fleece around my shoulders then reclined in the other chair across from me.

"Have you ever been hunting?" she asked.

"No. I don't like guns."

"Neither do I. Well, you eat meat, right? Imagine if you had to chase the cows. You don't have a gun, so you have to use your fists and you can only chase those cows at night." I coughed to cover my laughter. The idea of trying to fistfight a cow to death at night was pretty ridiculous. "Wouldn't it be easier if the cow showed up at your door and let you take all you needed?"

"So you do view us as food?" I frowned.

"We used to. We need a lot of blood to live. We eat regular food just like you, but we'd die without what humans give us."

"You mean what you take?"

"Part of me wants to tell you to shut the fuck up, but you're kind of cute like this." I wanted to tell her to fuck off, but I couldn't deny how being around her made me feel. The flirting was not helping me formulate an escape plan.

"I meant what I said. We live off what humans give us. Humans were beginning to suspect our existence. When we are starving, our kind can drain a human in a matter of minutes. That sort of feeding leaves bodies, and they began to hunt us. A few vampires realized if they could just find humans to volunteer to feed them on a regular basis, no humans would have to die and there would be no trace of a monster to hunt. Our master finally settled on this sorority as a guise and many of us have become accustomed to finding our feeders this way. It's about convenience, comfort, and routine."

"Oh, I see. So you rounded up thirty-six, well, thirty-seven girls, to feed you and your friends. In exchange, we get a kiss and a ruby necklace and the bragging rights that come with being an ABO?"

"You insist on making this sound much worse than it truly is."

"Please tell me the good part. Tell me why I shouldn't grab Amy and leave right now. Why use Cleo and Danni to trick us? Why the mind and body control back there—if it's all our choice?" I was getting pretty riled up, but I didn't care.

"So you did feel my influence?"

"Of course I did. I was scared out of my mind, but I couldn't move."

"You prove my point. The other girls weren't aware they were losing control. You were able to feel it—"

"Because of the blood. Right, right. So tell me what makes this any better? They weren't scared. So what? You didn't give them much of a choice. What's in it for us?"

Camila's fang bit into her bottom lip as she tried to hide another snicker at my expense, and that just made me even more upset. For all I knew, my roommate was taking her last breath and I had the queen of the vampires thinking about how cute I am when I get mad. If I didn't love the way the light was catching her eyes or the way her lips looked when she smiled, I would have stormed out of the room and found my way back to the dorm barefoot and nearly naked.

"They were given a choice, Ginger. The control was to stave off the fear and release honesty. They will be pleased with their decision to stay. The humans who feed us are very well taken care of. We sent Cleo and the others out to find other girls they believe deserve to be treated like queens." I wasn't following and she could tell. "There are vampires all over the world. Some live on their own, hiding in the dark and hunting their prey at their own risk. Hell-banishment is the cost of exposure, so most demons who live this way are careful, but our lives are safer if we serve my master."

"Benny's dad?"

"Her step-father. He is the most powerful vampire in this part of the world. Now he works with your government to ensure our survival. In return for their cooperation, he takes care of the humans who feed us."

"Why?" I asked. Camila wasn't making any sense. Who'd ever heard of a vampire trying to be a diplomat and a humanitarian?

"Because we need you to live. Why is this so hard for you to believe?"

"So you're saying if I feed you, you'll take care of me financially for the rest of my life?"

"I'm saying that if you feed me, I will take care of you in any way you'll let me until you graduate."

"And then what?"

"You'll go out in the world and my master will find another vampire for you to feed and they will take care of you for the rest of your life. Or if my master grants you permission, you may become a vampire yourself, but—" She stood. "That doesn't apply to you."

"Why?"

"Because you wanted to leave." Camila walked over to a large closet. She pulled out a black tracksuit and laid it on the bed. "Amy is probably having the best orgasm of her life right now. I'd hate to interrupt that, but I promise to send her back in the morning. Unharmed."

"Wait. They're having…sex?" I wanted to smack myself as soon as I said it. I sounded like a twelve-year-old.

"If my sister-queens are feeding, then yes, it typically leads to sex." She threw me the bottoms of the tracksuit. I caught the waistband just fine. Too bad one of the legs wrapped around my head. Camila did her best not to laugh. Again.

"They might be a little long. Get changed and I'll drive you back to the dorm."

"Why did Cleo and Danni bring me here in the first place? You never told me. I'm...extra." Why was I still talking? She was letting me leave.

"Your blood isn't pure in either direction. In that respect, you're not as useful to me as your roommate, but you are rather beautiful. I just wanted a taste."

I flinched, looking at the floor.

"What bothers you more? That I want to fuck you or that I want you to feed me?"

"Jesus. Stop saying that..." My voice drifted. Apparently, Todd was dead-on about where I could find a girl to experiment with. I still wanted to explore my sexuality, but I wanted to be used as Camila's sexual scratching post just as much as I wanted her to use my neck as her chew toy. I thought maybe I'd find a nice girl who had a little bit more experience than I did. We'd take things slow, work out a casual arrangement, hopefully something more. I had no intention of getting with someone like Camila who would just use me until she was full. Or bored. It didn't matter how beautiful she was. If I ever saw Todd again, I would tell him to keep his advice to himself.

Camila came around the bed slowly. "Ginger, tell me what's the matter?"

"I've...never..." I stumbled over the words. Camila had probably slept with hundreds of people. How was I supposed to tell her I was a virgin? "I've only kissed one person before. I've—I've never done anything else."

"But you know how to pleasure yourself, right?"

"How'd you—"

"I could taste it on your finger."

"Of course you could," I muttered back. I closed my eyes and let in and out a deep breath, too embarrassed to look at her.

"Ginger, look at me." I opened my eyes. Camila was standing right in front of me. I didn't fight it when she took my hand. "I am telling you the truth. About myself. About you. I understand if you don't trust us. You were lied to, but I want to make it right. Stay a little longer. I promise I will not hurt you."

I wanted to believe her. Even though the things she had told me were hard to take in, they made sense. I'd seen the other girls' skin heal right before my eyes. I'd heard the sincere pledges the sister-queens had made to them. It was a whole lot of trouble to go to if they just wanted to kill us. If what Camila had said about my mother—about my blood—was true, she had no real reason to keep me around. I was useless to her. If she couldn't live off my blood, maybe it wasn't crazy to think that on some level, Camila did want me.

I looked between our bodies. Camila turned my hand over and started tracing little squares over my freckles. Her fingers were so warm. She was putting me under her spell. This time I didn't mind.

"If I stay, what will we do?"

"We can do whatever you like," she said softly. "But for right now, why don't you change." She nodded toward the tracksuit on the bed. "Then we'll go check on your roommate."

Ditching the transparent lace helped mellow me out, but just a little. I didn't think it was possible to be completely at ease around Camila. She didn't bother to cover up any more than she already had, and this time as we walked down the hall, she walked beside me, our fingers intertwined. More than once, I caught myself trying to sneak a sideways peek at the outline of her nipples in the thin black cotton. She caught me looking every time.

We entered a different corridor and the energy in the air seemed to change.

And then I heard the moaning.

Camila led me to a large open archway, to the source of the erotic sounds. Black and red cushions covered the carpeted floor of another dimly lit room. The space was filled with naked female bodies. The girls had broken off into groups of six or seven. Every girl was touching someone else and being touched, lips on lips, in every way. Bare thighs and bare asses being pinched and stroked.

Everywhere I looked there was naked skin on naked skin, the mounds of flesh pulsing in different rhythms that in some way all seemed to match. No doubt the scene was an instant turn-on, but there was no real sense of any emotional connection when there are forty some-odd people trying to get off.

I scanned the room looking for Amy. She was in the middle of a heap of breasts and thighs. Danni was on her knees with her face buried in Amy's crotch. Surprisingly, Amy was kissing Paige passionately on the mouth. Barb was lying on her back with her arms wrapped around Paige's thighs. She sucked Paige's pussy, making her moan in Amy's mouth.

Cleo sat a few feet away from the group. Benny was sitting between her legs, her own knees drawn up to her chin. Cleo had her ceremonial robe wrapped around them both. When she saw us, Cleo waved us over.

We crossed the room, stepping around bare feet and steadying hands. When we reached Cleo and Benny, Camila pulled me in front of her and sank to the floor. I sat between her legs and tried to act natural when she wrapped her arms around my waist.

I stared at my toes, listening closely while Camila leaned over to whisper to Cleo.

"Is everything okay?" She must have been talking about Benny. It made sense that she didn't feel comfortable enough to join in the activities. I didn't have Benny's weight or acne problems, and there was no way I was ready to dive headfirst into a girl orgy.

"We're going to take it slow until Benny's ready," Cleo replied. I glanced over in Benny's direction. Cleo was gently stroking her hair as if patting it would tame the wild frizz. Benny caught my eye and the corner of her mouth turned up in a weak attempt at a smile. I did my best to smile back in understanding.

Then Benny looked over at Camila. "I am ready to feed you, whenever you need me." Her voice was low, but there was no hesitance in her tone. She knew what she was here to do and she was completely ready to offer her blood up to the sister-queens. I wished for a moment that I could boast that kind of confidence in any kind of purpose.

Camila pulled her arm from around my waist so she could touch Benny's cheek. I didn't miss the devotion in her voice.

"Thank you."

Benny seemed to relax then turned her eyes back toward the scene in front of us.

Camila's arms came back around my middle and she pulled me closer to her body. I felt her warm breath on my ear and I swallowed, fighting to keep my eyes open. I failed. Camila's nipples were hard, so hard I could feel their perfectly puckered tips on my back through the layers of our clothes. Lower, I felt the heat from her pussy against a small bit of my exposed skin. I'd never been held like that before. It was comforting and arousing all at once. A little overwhelming. Suddenly, I realized I didn't care what Camila was; I didn't want her to let go.

"Just watch," she said through the whimpers and pants that filled the air. "No one is hurting. No one will experience any pain. Only pleasure."

I took a real look at the erotic scene in front of me. I knew why Camila had brought me here. I could have watched a group of girls go at it on the Internet. She wanted me to witness a feeding firsthand.

I searched around, looking specifically for one of the sister-queens. A swish of white-blond hair caught my attention. Across the room Natasha's new "pets" were crawling all over her and each other. Layna's tongue was buried deep inside Natasha's mouth. Heather's fingers were buried deep inside Natasha's bare pussy. Samantha was latched on to one nipple and Anna-Jade was suckling the other. Another older member of ABO, Georgiana, rubbed the clit of a girl named Julia. Julia was handling Samantha with her mouth.

It seemed so…complicated, but so perfect at the same time.

"Watch," Camila said again. "Natasha likes to feed before she comes. She's so close. Look at her, the way her stomach moves. So close." My eyes followed the path over Natasha's body. Her hips thrust up, swirling down on Heather's fingers. Her belly moved in gentle waves, her muscles tensing over and over beneath her smooth, pale skin.

Natasha gripped the back of Layna's head and broke away from their kiss. With her other hand she gently encouraged Anna-Jade up her body, so her neck was level with Natasha's mouth. Her lips peeled away from her teeth and her fangs quickly elongated, shooting down from her gums. She paused, gazing at Anna-Jade's throat, and at that exact moment Camila's hand slid under the top I was wearing. Her fingers and her open palm slid over my stomach. Higher and higher, cupping me gently.

I swallowed again and found myself leaning into her body even more. She took that as a sign and slid her hand over my breast. The sensation of her warm palm grazing over my tight, tingling skin shot right from my nipple to my clit. I ruined the bottoms of that tracksuit for sure. I was soaking wet.

Natasha waited a half second more then bit into Anna-Jade's neck. Anna-Jade cried out and I whimpered in sympathy, imagining the pain.

"Shh," Camila said. "There's no hurting. No pain."

As Camila's words sank in, Anna-Jade's body went rigid for a moment and then she started coming even harder, her legs flopping and straining on the red cushion. Layna whispered something to Heather who took that as her cue to drive her fingers even harder into Natasha's slit. Natasha released Anna-Jade from her grasp and started to ride Heather's fingers shamelessly. I stared in awe at the red-stained tips of her large fangs. A drop of blood trailed down her lip, dangerously close to rolling down her chin as Natasha rode out her own orgasm. She blinked heavily when the tip of her tongue caught the drop. And as she savored it, Natasha fixed her sights on her next meal. Samantha. There were a few seconds that passed where Camila continued to touch me, one hand stroking over my stomach and the soft, but confident fingers of the other hand playing with my nipple. We watched Samantha anxiously climb up Natasha's lean body. She steadied herself on her hands and knees and boldly offered her neck. Natasha bit into Samantha's skin hard and fast, keeping her in place with a firm hand on the back of her head as Samantha's body arched away. She came with a loud and hard groan.

That's when Camila's right hand slid into my track pants. But she waited.

I knew exactly what I wanted, and at the same time I had no clue. I'd thought about having her hands on my body so many times before. Silently, I'd begged her to touch me, but now that her fingers were so close to where I'd wanted…I was scared.

Her vampire senses or magical powers must have caught my hesitation because her fingers slowly began moving back up and to the side, drawing light circles between the width of my hips.

"I can stop," she said. "You can leave."

"No. I…" I wanted to stay right where I was, there on the floor. I wanted to watch the girls touching each other in front of us. I wanted this queen of demons to touch me. I was tired of my fantasies and the low-grade stalking. I wanted the real thing with her. But I couldn't force myself to say the words. This wasn't just some random hookup, even if I did get up and walk away as soon as it was over. This was the girl literally of my dreams asking for my body. Asking for permission to bite me.

I didn't know if I could say yes.

A shiver tore through my shoulders as she placed a single kiss to my neck.

"Do you want me to stop?"

I shook my head. My desperation must have been obvious because Cleo coughed back a laugh beside me. I whipped my head in her direction, but before I could ask her anything, Camila slid her hand between my legs. She wasted no time spreading my short curls and finding my clit. I moaned, forgetting all about Cleo's mocking.

Camila's fangs grazed the side of my throat, and even though I should have been, I couldn't bring myself to be scared anymore. Pathetic, yeah, but her fingers felt that good. My head dropped back against her shoulder. I closed my eyes and pushed the fact that Benny and Cleo were right beside us, watching me now, out of my head. I basked in the feminine sounds of ecstasy flowing through the room and I let myself feel Camila's fingers as they caressed my body.

She pinched my nipple, drawing the already throbbing peak out even more. I shuddered, wanting more, getting more as two of her fingers slid inside my pussy. My hips pitched up off the floor. My body pressed against her palm and I groaned helplessly.

"Please, Ginger," she said. A purr, a deep tremble of noise that made me even wetter accented her voice. "Please. I just want a taste."

And there it was, the voice I'd been wanting to hear all along. I turned slightly, just enough to face her, but not enough for her to pull her hand away. Those beautiful eyes glinted back at me. She didn't try to deny the truth of what her bite would mean. She'd be claiming me as one of her own, even if my blood wouldn't truly feed her. I was giving her a part of myself. Before I could chicken out, I faced forward again and arched my neck to the side. I didn't feel the initial puncture of my throat. Instead, a cool, tingling sensation spread out under my skin, and as she drank, I felt the sweet sucking all the way down to my toes. She held me in an iron grip until she'd had her fill, but long before that, I came as she stroked me and erupted all over her hand.

❖

Sometime later, I woke up in Camila's bed. She didn't have a clock in her room, but I got the sense that it wasn't morning yet. I stretched and rolled over. Looking around, I realized I was in bed alone and completely naked.

"Hi," I heard her murmur.

I sat up and blinked until my eyes settled on Camila. She was sitting in one of the armchairs, reading a book. She'd ditched her tank top. I couldn't help but think about how badly I wanted to suck on her full brown nipples.

I cleared my throat then looked down. I started smoothing the blanket over my thigh while I tried to think of what to say. Camila got up from her chair and crawled on the bed next to me. I couldn't ignore the way her breasts swayed under their lush weight as she crawled on all fours through the sheets. When she was settled next to me I thought, screw it, and gently stroked her nipple. She hissed and I could see the tips of her fangs peeking out from between her lips.

"What happens if I agree to this?" I asked, my voice thick with sleep.

"During the day, things don't change. You go to class. You study. You spend time with the girls."

"And at night?" I rotated my finger, pushing the very tip up before swirling it back downward. Her nostrils flared again, but she didn't try to move my finger.

"At night, we find out more about what having our blood inside you means. You feed me, if you like, and I continue to worship your beautiful body."

"But my blood does nothing for you."

"I wouldn't say that. You have a wonderful taste." She touched my cheek. "I want you to stay."

I dropped my hand to my lap, turning her words over in my head. The girls of Alpha Beta Omega and the sister-queens they served had plenty of opportunities to hurt us, but my initial bout of outrage and brattiness aside, they had been nothing except kind and gentle, showing each one of us undeniable pleasure.

I wanted to keep the friends I had made. I wanted to know more about myself and, all said and done, I wanted Camila. Yeah, she terrified me in some ways, but I didn't want to consider going the rest of my life without seeing her again. I doubted they would let me just hang out if I turned this chance down.

I held out my hand, palm up. Camila was out of bed and back with a short silver blade and thin black box in less than a moment.

She took my outstretched hand and waited for me to look into her eyes.

"Ginger Elizabeth Carmichael..." She smirked as she said my middle name.

"Okay. Don't get cocky with it." I scowled.

"Will you allow me to bind you to myself, my sister-queens, and to your sisters?"

"Yes." I barely said the word with any volume, but I knew she'd heard me. My palm burned as the blade came down across my skin. I was proud of myself for not flinching. Camila dropped the knife and quickly sealed the cut. As her tongue trailed over the wound, the cool, soothing sensation spread through my hand. She lifted her head and the cut was completely healed. I watched her patiently as she reached for the thin black box and took out the last of the thirteen necklaces.

She held the ruby up, letting the dim light catch it before she fastened the platinum links around my neck.

"You're mine now, Red," she said with an evil grin. I had a snappy comeback, but I didn't get a chance to use it.

Camila pushed me back on the bed and then she kissed me.

# CHAPTER FOUR

The kiss didn't last long enough. The soft sweep of her tongue over my lips was perfect, intoxicating, and the moment she pushed her way gently into my mouth I realized that she tasted just as delicious as she smelled. I lifted my head, wanting more, but she pulled away and sat back on her knees.

She looked over my body, at my breasts, and down to my hips that were still covered with her blankets and sheets. I followed her gaze and suddenly struck shy, pulled the blanket over my chest.

Camila chuckled to herself, flashing the sharp tips of her fangs.

What?" I asked, all my nipple-stroking confidence gone.

"Nothing," she said with a slight shake of her head. "I was just wondering what would be the best way to repay you."

"Repay me?" I didn't like the way that sounded.

"Repay may be the wrong word." Her tongue crept out and traced her bottom lip. I gasped a little. "I understand how my bite can make you feel, but I want to give you more than that."

"Why?" I pulled the blanket up even further.

She leaned forward and kissed me lightly on the lips, but she left the blanket where it was. "I've already told you." She kissed me again. "You've bound yourself to me, and you've given me your blood, but remember that last thing I wanted?"

"The part with the fucking," I managed to squeak out.

"Right, Red. The part with the fucking. I'm just wondering where you'd like me to start."

"Uh…" I had my ideas, but I had no experience to go on. Not to mention her "Do Me Now" voice and those eyes were making it impossible for me to form a complete sentence. And the kissing, it wasn't helping either.

"That is if you're okay with, you know, going all the way," she said.

Did I want my first time to be with the sexiest being I had ever seen, even if she was an undead demon-queen? Yes. Yes, I did. I may have even wanted her to bite me again.

I nodded wide-eyed.

"Why don't you lie back down?"

Right, I could do that. I slid back against her pillows and made myself comfortable—well, as comfortable as I could be while nearly hyperventilating.

She pulled back the sheets and climbed over me before wrapping the sheet back over us both. It was still dim in the room, but light enough that the dark sheets didn't hide the curves of her breasts as they swept past mine. I swallowed thickly as she held herself up with one hand and pulled off her underwear with the other. A tingling set off in my throat as our legs brushed together.

Once her underwear was tossed aside, probably lost to the abyss at the foot of the bed along with the tracksuit, she settled herself casually between my legs. My pussy throbbed as her stomach pressed against me. My clit pulsed through my soaked hairs, the only thing keeping the over sensitive tip from rubbing directly against her skin. My heart thudded up somewhere near my throat. I almost choked when she reached up and pulled my new ruby pendant from my hair and centered it back on its chain between my breasts.

"So." Camila's finger began tracing the edge of my nipple. It felt pretty close to awesome. "I have good news and I have bad news, which might also be good news depending on how you look at it. Which would you like first?"

"Um, the bad news." I looked at her lips, hoping she would kiss me again soon.

"I haven't gotten off in the way I like to in a few days. That's a long time for me, so we might be here a while."

Watching her mouth move while she was pressed against my crotch was a little too much. I looked up to her eyes. Possibly a dumber idea. "What's the bad news?"

"You're so cute." She huffed a short laugh. This time the flirtatious comment was just that. If my cuteness kept her between my legs, then cute it was.

"What's the good news?"

"It would be better if I showed you."

"Okay." My voice came out just above a whisper. This part should be easier. She'd already fingered me, kissed me, gnawed on my neck a little. Having sex with Camila was just a matter of taking things a step further. I could do it. Piece of cake.

My eyes stung for a moment as I swallowed. Again.

"Don't be nervous, Red," Camila said. She lightly brushed my hair away from my forehead. That worked. I closed my eyes and let out a deep breath. When I opened my eyes she was smiling down at me. I bit my lip and almost managed not to grin back.

"Come here," she said. I lifted my head and met her halfway as she kissed me once more, slowly brushing her lips back and forth across my mouth.

"Just move with me."

And that's what I did.

Camila braced her hands on either side of my shoulders then shifted herself up and over until our legs were intertwined, her wet, bare slit pressed against mine. She was so wet. Slippery and hot. It felt so good I almost didn't want her to move. The pressure on my clit was perfect. Or so I thought until she started rocking her hips.

My hands flew to her waist and I held on. I had no idea what I'd been missing, just how good it would feel to have someone between my legs, someone like Camila.

Her mouth was on mine a second later, swallowing my moans and cries while we thrust against each other. She wasn't gentle, but I liked it. She dipped her tongue into my mouth over and over. I caught it when I could, sucked on its soft sweetness, and when that wasn't enough, she used her teeth, matched the push and retreat of her hips with light nips of her fangs along my bottom lip.

Heat flashed through my whole body as we continued to move together. This was so much better than rubbing myself in the privacy of my dorm, so much better than I thought it would be with anyone else. I moved my hips faster against her body, but kept my hands where they were on her sides. I wanted to touch her all over. I wanted grab and pinch her breasts and her perfectly round ass, but I was so close to coming and suddenly doubting any acute motor skills I'd acquired in the last eighteen years, doing what she'd said, moving along with the thrusting motion of her body seemed like the best thing to do. We could come and then later, much later, when I had some clue what I was doing, I would get fancy with my hands.

Without warning, Camila broke from our kiss and threw her head back. Her fangs were all the way out, long and shining in the dim light as she purred my name.

"Ah. Ah," I panted desperately in response. My clit twitched sharply against her, overcome by the sensations my own pussy lips and her warm body had to offer. My eyes squeezed shut as I was blinded for a moment and then I came all over her leg.

Camila was right behind me. She ground down even harder against my thigh, and then I felt the wet rush of her orgasm.

"Fuck! Me!" Her scream echoed off the high, black ceiling. The sound sent my body off, shuddering with one last aftershock as her rocking motions slowed then stopped completely. I stared up at her, trying to catch my breath.

With a loud exhale, she rolled off me, licking her lips and fangs.

We lay there together for a few moments, both of us panting, me a little more so because she hadn't stopped touching me. Her fingers swept the now damp hair off the nape of my neck then she brushed across my collarbone. I looked back at her, gazing at her smooth, golden skin and her beautifully hard nipples. I couldn't stop staring.

"What is it, Red?" she asked.

"I was just wondering…" She sounded genuinely interested in what was on my mind, but I couldn't finish the thought. It was too ridiculous.

"Don't make me bite you again." Some threat, but I knew she was serious.

"I was just thinking…you're not human, right?"

"Not anymore, that's correct."

"Well, it's just interesting. I think I was expecting you to do something differently when you came." I mean, the way she purred my name was a little different, and I didn't sprout razor-sharp teeth at the heights of ecstasy, but I mean…

"You have to remember, Red, I'm still a woman. Same parts."

"I know." I scowled back at her.

She jumped up to her knees and grabbed me by my legs.

I squealed as she threw my calves over her shoulders. "What are you doing?" She paused before our pussies made contact. I knew exactly what she was doing, I just didn't know why.

"Are you tired?"

"No." I wasn't tired at all. That first orgasm had barely taken the edge off. I could definitely stand to come a few more times, especially with her.

"Well." She nicked my ankle with her teeth then slowly licked my calf before she went on. I whimpered pathetically and let my eyes roll back in my head. They stayed there as she rolled her hips and drew her pussy down the length of my spread slit. I made a strangled noise, something between a moan, a scream, and a gargle.

"We can do more of this." She kept up the motions, back and forth, rocking against me. Her clit brushed against mine. "Or I can tuck you in and you can go to sleep."

"No." My head flopped from side to side on the pillow. "More of this," I said. "Definitely more of this."

When I woke up again, it was actually morning and Camila was in bed with me. I couldn't keep the smile off my face as I stretched between the sheets. My body was sore in all the best places. My inner thighs had been held open to make room for Camila's strong hips and her soft, wet pussy. My shoulders ached from having my hands pinned above my head when she decided to take me again.

But my neck felt amazing, even though she had bitten me again and then one more time before we were completely spent.

I felt the warmth of her chest against my back. Her soft fingertips gently caressed my hair and my cheek. I rolled into her embrace, looking into her eyes.

"Hey."

"Hello." Camila leaned forward and kissed me. Her soft tongue gently moved past my lips. She slowly pulled her tongue out, then pushed it back in, and my pussy soaked for her all over again. I was still half asleep, my eyes and my head still clouded with memories of the night, but that only seemed to make the kiss better.

I'd slept like the dead, that deep, dreamless sleep where you're surprised you didn't drool all over yourself when you finally lifted your head off the pillow. I might as well have been in a coma. Those few hours of unconsciousness hadn't been enough to make me forget just how talented Camila was with her hands and her mouth.

I had no idea if I was a good kisser or not. Todd had burst in on my one and only kiss. My neighbor, Kristen had left for soccer training at UVA before I got a chance to ask her for an honest assessment. Camila could have been faking it, letting me feel like she enjoyed kissing me as much as I enjoyed kissing her, but I didn't get that feeling at all. Camila made me feel like I was a freaking expert. As the night went on, I loved the way she moaned when our tongues slowly touched. It took a few tries, but eventually I figured out that licking her fangs was a surefire way to make her growl. And she really growled, this deep, rumbling noise like a tiger, a sound that made me shiver.

So at least I had the kissing thing down. I wasn't sure about everything else. I'd lost count of how many times I'd come the night before, but I did know that Camila had done all the work and I had a lot to learn. Hopefully, she would teach me.

She pulled away slowly, but continued to lay soft kisses across my cheeks. Then on the tip of my nose.

"Are you still angry with me for bringing you here?" Her voice was low but clear. Vampires probably never woke up groggy. She kissed me right below my ear.

"I'll let you know when I see the inside of my dorm room again," I replied. Finding my voice wasn't much of a distraction from her hand slipping between my legs.

"That sounds fair. I'm glad you're awake."

"Really? Why?" I moaned.

"Cleo is going to barge in here any moment to wake you for breakfast." Her middle finger parted my slit.

"You're the queen. Can't you tell her to go away?" I gasped as she moved up and down. This was no way to carry on a conversation.

"I'd love to keep you in my bed all day long, but maybe I should let you see the outdoors. It's better to keep a willing captive."

I'd planned on spending my whole day in the library. I had an English paper to start, a stats test to study for, notes to organize for my dance and culture class—my favorite and the most pointless prereq for my major—and I had to meet with my lab partner, Greg. I knew she was safe, but I needed to talk to Amy. When Camila slid her fingers back inside me, I figured all that could wait.

"Was it so bad?" She was talking about more than just my initiation.

"No," I whimpered.

"I'm glad I could change your mind." She pulled her fingers from between the sheets, and my eyes snapped wide as she licked them clean. "If you'll excuse me for a moment."

Camila slid out of bed. If her back hadn't been to me, she would have seen my tortured looks as she pulled her clothes back on. She walked over to the door and opened it for Cleo and Paige. They hadn't knocked.

"Hi," Cleo said, smiling bashfully at Camila.

"Hi," she replied.

"We came for Ginger." I'd only known her a few days, but I'd never seen Cleo acting this sweet.

Camila turned toward me and licked her lips before she said my name. My cheeks and my neck were instantly hot. "Ginger, you have some visitors."

"Outta bed, maggot." And like that, the Cleo I knew and loved was back. "We got a full day ahead of us. Breakfast is at oh-nine hundred sharp. You will be on time or you will not eat and you will get left."

"Are you done?" Camila asked.

"Yeah, thanks. I've been wanting to yell at the new girls all summer," Cleo said.

"I bet you have."

"Breakfast is in thirty. Here are your clothes." Paige held up a black canvas bag with the white letters "ABO" stitched on with bright red threading. I looked at the sheet covering my boobs. I would have hopped out of bed to take the bag, but I was still naked. Camila took it from Paige and put in on the dresser.

"Thanks," I muttered.

"She'll be up in thirty minutes," Camila told them.

"Okay," Cleo replied. And then she and Paige waited.

"Good-bye," Camila said as she started closing the door. Paige huffed and rolled her eyes, and Cleo actually pouted. I got a weird tight feeling in my throat. "I'll see you both tonight."

"Fine," they both whined. Camila laughed to herself as she shut the door all the way. She came back over to the bed and sat beside me.

"What was that all about?" I asked, trying not to sound jealous, which I instantly realized I was. She must have sensed it because she tried to distract me by drawing her fingertips across my shoulder.

"Nothing," she said. "They just missed me last night."

"Did I keep you away from them?"

"No. I'm fed. They're just needy. Ignore them." Before I could ask who'd fed her properly, she kissed me, another painfully slow, warm, wet kiss. I couldn't remember what day it was when she pulled away. She smoothed my hair away from my face, gazing between my lips and my eyes. I wanted her again, but I didn't have time.

"So what does a vampire do during the day?" I asked.

"I sleep for a few hours. I get some work done—"

"Work?"

"Someone's gotta pay for all those necklaces. I own a few businesses downtown. I call down there and make sure everything's okay while I'm trapped here. I check in with Types of Hope."

"So the foundation is legit?"

"Doing good works is one of the best ways to blend in. Except with Types of Hope, there is no catch. We like our humans healthy and we want to help the humans who aren't."

I don't know why the thought of her being trapped inside all day made me upset, but it did, almost selfishly. I'd walked around clueless to what made up my DNA for eighteen years. What else kept Camila from normal human behavior? I wasn't much for silver jewelry, but I loved garlic. What if I was experiencing some sort of delayed reaction? What if there was some sort of puberty I hadn't reached yet? I had more than thirty minutes' worth of questions.

"You really can't go out in the daytime?"

"I can. Just not in this form."

"What do you mean?"

Camila thought for a moment before she answered. "Our… nature allows us to shift form. We can take the shape of other living creatures, but we can only go out in the daytime in an animal form."

"Wow." Of course I'd never tried, but maybe if I did, I could—

I looked up as she combed her fingers through my hair. "Don't worry, Red. Clearly, the sun doesn't affect you. And though the shifting is something you can control it's not as amazing as it sounds. If you get trapped somewhere as a cat or a blue jay, you're stuck that way until nightfall. And then of course, when you shift back, you're naked."

"Yeah, I can see where that would have its drawbacks." Even if I did prefer her in the buff.

"We'll figure you out, okay? Have fun with the girls, and later you can ask me anything you want to know."

"Okay."

"Come. Let me show you the bathroom."

I followed Camila back out to her living room. Apparently, the door all the way to the left opened to an enormous black-tiled bathroom. Double glass doors opened to a shower that ran the length of an entire wall. Every single member of ABO could fit inside that thing.

Camila walked silently across the midnight floor and pressed a small button hidden along the wall. A hot spray came from thousands of tiny showerheads in the ceiling.

"Shampoo and soap in the shower. Towels in the closet, and there's toothpaste right there." She pointed around the room before turning back to me. She took a step closer. I bit my lip to keep my lungs in my chest.

"I'd join you, but what I have in mind would take more than thirty minutes."

I swallowed. "Can't be late for breakfast."

"No, Red. You can't." She took a step closer, letting her delicious cinnamon scent rush cross my lips.

"You're going to keep calling me 'Red,' aren't you?"

"Unless you ask me to stop." I didn't want to. "That shower is heaven. Don't take too long." She slid past me and out the door without kissing me. I don't think I've ever showered that fast. I had to get back to her.

❖

In the bag Paige brought me was a new toothbrush, travel size bottles of my favorite lotion and deodorant, and some clothes. Another tracksuit. It would have been cute if it wasn't white. What was with all the tracksuits and all the white? I was starting to think I'd joined a cult, which I supposed I had. The ruby hanging around my neck was proof enough that I had given in, traded my brain and my blood for sex and then some.

The terrycloth jacket had my name stitched in elegant cursive on the breast. I looked at the red lettering for a while before putting it on. I wanted to know what I had gotten myself into. I had to find out what was going on with my body. I had to know how deep this vampire/human relationship ran. I wouldn't find that out standing in my vampire's bathroom. I found some white underwear in the bottom of the bag, then finished getting dressed. I was still trying to figure out Paige and her less than cheery attitude, but I would thank her for the new brush and the hair ties.

When I got back to the bedroom, Amy was sitting on the foot of the bed, wearing the same white tracksuit, watching Camila get dressed. Seeing her was a bigger relief than I'd expected. My night with Camila had been nothing short of perfect, but Amy was my one connection to the real world. Knowing she was in one piece made me realize just how afraid I had been for both of our safety.

Amy smiled brightly. "Hey."

"Hey. Are you all right?"

"Yeah. I'm fine. I crashed in Danni's room last night." She looked between Camila and me. "Cleo said you slept down here."

"Yeah. I did," I muttered. Come on, Amy. Go ahead. Embarrass me in front of Camila.

She turned right back to Camila. "See, what did I tell you? Not even a full day and she's already teacher's pet." I took a deep breath and reminded myself that starting a catfight in the middle of the floor wouldn't be a good idea.

Camila finished zipping a pair of dark skinny jeans. Her thick thighs looked perfect in them. "Your roommate was telling me how serious you are about your studies," Camila said.

"I just want to do well. That's all."

"There's nothing wrong with that. There is a minimum GPA to be in ABO, but I'm sure Amy knows that as well." She winked at me before pulling on a red tank top. "I'll show you out."

Camila led us down a different hallway to an elevator. She told us it led to a concealed walk-in space hidden inside the kitchen pantry. We'd find Danni easily once we got there. The door opened smoothly, and as soon as Amy and I were inside, Camila punched in a series of numbers into a keypad on the wall. She backed out of the doorway and waggled her fingers at us, flirting some more with a flash of her fangs.

As soon as the doors closed, Amy was on me.

"Oh my God. Okay. Tell me now. What happened?"

"I'll tell you when we get back to the dorm."

"What? No. Tell me now."

"No." She followed my finger as I pointed to a small camera mounted in the corner of the ceiling.

"Ugh. Fine, but when we get back to the dorm, you better spill." The door opened into the pantry in the kitchen. Danni was there waiting for us, a perfect reason to keep quiet.

❖

"We have to lay out some ground rules." Cleo paced around the kitchen. The thirteen of us were lined up in front of an enormous breakfast buffet. My stomach was trying to eat itself, but we weren't getting anywhere near the mountains of croissants and cubed melon until Cleo was finished. Danni, Barb, and Paige sat on the counter by the fridge, stern looks plastered on their faces.

"There are two ways to get kicked out of Alpha Beta Omega. The first way is to talk about what goes on on the bottom floor of Alpha Beta Omega. You do not mention our sister-queens to anyone. Not your friends, not your mom, not your editor. Outside of this house, they don't exist. You talk and you're out. You talk to the wrong person and Camila will have you killed. Benny, am I lying?"

"No, Cleo," Benny replied quietly.

"Are we clear?" Cleo asked.

"Yes," we responded together.

"Good. Now here are a few other things you should remember. Curfew is nine o'clock. Every night. During the week, if you're not at work or on campus studying, you're here at the house or you're in your dorm room, studying. On the weekends, it doesn't matter where you are, you check in at nine o'clock. Is that clear?"

"Yes."

"At nine p.m., you text someone, you call someone and tell us exactly where you are. What time should we hear from you?"

"Nine p.m."

"Excellent. Not nine-oh-one, not nine-oh-two. Nine. If you are out after nine and you are walking back to your dorm, you will call one of us first and someone will escort you." I think that bit applied to all of us. We were all freshman, and Maryland University didn't let freshman keep cars on campus. "A few of us might come meet you or one of the OBA boys will. I know you are all strong, independent women, but this is a big campus in the middle of a big city. Even I don't walk around at night alone. That brings me to the next item on the list. Boys."

I could feel Amy beside me trying not to giggle.

"You can date whoever you want. Yeah, things get a little freaky when the sister-queens feed, but not all of us like to bump clit twenty-four seven. I know I do, but that's not the point. Date whoever you like. Come back here with VD and you're out. As of last night, we know you're all clean. It should stay that way. The sister-queens cannot contract our diseases, but we play together too much to be giving each other the clap. Plus, that's just fucking gross."

That time, I laughed. Cleo ignored my weak attempt to make it sound like a cough.

"Until you move into this house, which you are all allowed to do next semester, you are not allowed down into the sister-queens' quarters unescorted. This is our playhouse, that space is their permanent home, and you will respect it. Is that understood?"

"Yes."

"The rubies around your neck do not come off. Consider it your Med-Alert bracelet. If you get hurt, hit by a car, fall down some stairs, drink yourself half to death at Chi Nu house, you'll be taken to a hospital that is bound to our sister-queens. Seriously, don't take it off. If you know your turn to feed is coming up, do not drink or take any illegal substances. Our sister-queens can taste it in our system and I've been told it makes our blood taste like piss."

Just then a short, wide Hispanic woman waddled into the kitchen. Her hair was cut close to her head and dyed an unnatural yellow. She sidled right up to Cleo who draped her arm around the woman's chubby shoulders.

"This is Florencia. She's our housemother. She's not here to cook for you. She's not here to clean up after you. She speaks English when she feels like it. If she likes you, she might ask you to join her in a game of Hearts. If she doesn't, just stay out of her way."

Florencia jabbed Cleo in the stomach and muttered something in Spanish I couldn't understand. My Spanish was decent, but she was speaking too softly.

"Okay, okay. The university says we have to have a housemother, but we don't exactly need one. Flor used to feed Omi's maker and we love her to bits. And it's funny to watch the other housemothers try to be PC around her. But seriously, don't get on her nerves. She's good people."

"Buenos días," Florencia muttered to us before she shuffled away.

Danni hopped off the counter and grabbed a black bag. I remembered it from the day before. She and Paige walked down the line and started handing us our cell phones as Cleo rattled off the last of her instructions.

"Eat your breakfast, make whatever calls you need to make. Ginger, text your brother and tell him you're not dead." Amy did giggle then. "We're hitting the spa in an hour."

No one said anything; they just lined up at the buffet and started scrolling through their phones. I wasn't going to be the only one to tell Cleo I already had plans.

"Crap," I muttered. I had to call my lab partner Greg and cancel.

I had two texts—one from Mom telling me she was glad I'd decided to join a sorority, and one from Todd saying he hoped I got lucky. Considering the rules Cleo had just laid out, I'd have to tell him no. He'd start asking questions and then I'd have to make some stuff up and then he'd ask more questions.

I checked my voice mail. There was only one and it was from Greg. He sounded like crap.

"Hey, Ginger. It's Greg. I had some shit come up today. Let me know if you can meet up tomorrow. Later."

I shot him a text letting him know I was busy too and we could reschedule for tomorrow.

I loaded my plate and headed into the dining room. The table had been set just for the thirteen of us. I took a seat next to Amy and Benny sat on my other side. Then we all took a few minutes to reintroduce ourselves. As we went around the table, it was clear most of us had nothing much in common. We repeated our names, threw out information about our majors and where we were from, but there was still a nervous vibe among the group. We were all the new kid and Cleo had left us without a teacher. We were silent for a few moments before Samantha, our spy from the school paper, decided she'd held her tongue long enough.

"Anyone want to tell me what the fuck we just signed up for?" Her tone was light enough that we burst out laughing. Part of it was nerves and part of it was from the fact that, just like Samantha, we all couldn't believe how the past twenty-four hours had turned out. We'd accepted invitations to join a sorority. None of us had dreamed we'd be greeted by a coven of female vampires. We were bound to them for the next four years, and I think, to the race as a whole, for the rest of lives. Not the Friday night any of us planned for.

When the laughter died out, I was surprised at who spoke up first.

"They don't want to hunt us." Benny took a bite of bacon. She chewed a few bites before she continued. "It varies from country to country. Culture to culture. Here, it's easiest to get to us this way. A sorority is an easy cover."

"So what happens now?" Ruth asked. She was bound to the sister-queen, Faeth.

"Same thing they told us last night," Mel, a Puerto Rican girl who belonged to Tokyo, said, looking to Benny. "We're in a sorority now. Everything's normal but the feedings, right?"

"Right. We feed them and we get our degrees," Benny said before she bit into a muffin the size of a softball.

Anna-Jade's tiny voice squeaked from the end of the table, "They meant what they said last night...they won't hurt us?"

"No. They won't. These vampires have taken an oath stronger then the pledge we made. If they take advantage of us in any way, they are terminated immediately. There are homicidal demons out there, but they won't bother us. The sister-queens' scents are all over us now. Plus, our necklaces. They know better than to cross Camila."

"How'd you get so smart?" Samantha asked. I wasn't so amused with the tone she was taking with Benny.

"Your dad's one of them, right?" Laura asked.

"My step-father. He oversees the vampires north of the equator, between Greenland and Alaska. The seat of power is in Asia though," Benny said.

"What happened to your real dad?" Anna-Jade asked. I'd been thinking the same thing.

"He was my step-father's main contact in the White House. He'd planned to blackmail a group of vampires in China. After he was disposed of, my step-father took my mother and me in."

"You don't sound too sad about that," Samantha said.

"I'm not. He wasn't a good man." Benny left it at that.

"What happens after graduation?" Amy finally spoke up.

"You go on with your life, feeding another vampire wherever you decide to live. I don't know if you noticed, but they picked a diverse group for a reason. None of us would hang out normally. No more than two of us share a major. When we graduate, we'll go off to different places and work with vampires in different fields. Each of the sister-queens only needs to feed from three of us, but they take on six at a time to bring more feeders into their world. This is all just to prepare us to share our lives with them. To show us how to live with the secret."

It got quiet again, all of us letting what Benny had just said sink in.

"It's easier this way. They will feed no matter what. It's better if they trust us and we trust them. No one gets hurt that way and we both can exist," Benny added as a final note.

It had been hard to believe Camila, but I knew Benny was telling the truth.

"So why'd you sit out last night?" Samantha looked pointedly at Benny. "Not into the lady loving like the rest of us?"

"Hey. Back off," I snapped. Benny was giving us a lot of useful information. What did it matter if she wasn't into the group sex scene? Samantha had no reason to be a bitch.

Benny replied calmly, ignoring my attempt to defend her. "Because as kind as they are to us, I don't believe in having sex with people I barely know." She kept her voice low and even, but she didn't back down. "It has nothing to do with my sexual preference. I can serve Camila and the other sister-queens without fucking them or any of you. We all can. They love us for our sacrifice, and if we get to know them better, they will like us as friends."

She looked directly at Samantha. "Natasha has had close to one hundred and eighty lovers since this house was built. Her husband is the King of Omega Beta Alpha. His name is Rodrick, if you were wondering. The feeding is a necessity. The orgasm is a bonus. The sex is for you to brag about. We all feel affection for our sister-queens, but it's part of the blood bond we all agreed to last night. Nothing more. Thinking it can be something more is a waste of everyone's time."

That shut all of us up. Benny was completely right. The agreement we'd struck made sense. We work with the vampires; they don't kill us for sport. But the sex was a whole other issue. I'd enjoyed my night with Camila, but I didn't know her at all. I didn't know how many lovers she'd had. I didn't know if she was married. Natasha was just as involved in the sexual escapades as the rest of us, and we didn't know a thing about her personal life.

I'd been seduced thoroughly, but like Benny, I wanted something more than to be Camila's one hundred and eighty-first plaything, and when the time came, I'd never intended on sharing my first girlfriend with thirty-six other people. I'd thought I wanted to experiment, get some clarity, but that wasn't true. I wanted something special with one special girl. And I wouldn't get that from Camila or anyone else in Alpha Beta Omega. No matter how much I wanted her.

Benny broke the silence once more. "Sex complicates things for humans. Not for them. Why do you think we're free to date? They don't want us to get attached to them that way. I'd hate to fall in love with one of the sister-queens seeing as how they've already prepared to let us go in four years. I'll stick to the sidelines, thanks."

And with that kick in the gut, Cleo entered the room.

"Benny. Come here a sec," she called from the doorway. Benny stood and walked out of the dining room on Cleo's heels. The rest of us finished our breakfast in silence.

## CHAPTER FIVE

Between Benny's information bomb and where and how I'd woken up this morning, I had to rethink my approach to my role in the sorority and my relationship with Camila. I knew my vampire blood had been the main reason Camila had pulled me aside, but the other girls had no clue why I'd been the only one to get the queen to myself. I wasn't going to bring it up. Amy had already razzed me for spending the night alone with Camila. Would the rest of the girls think I was trying to weasel my way into her favor, her bed, and her heart?

Aside from Samantha, I liked my sisters in Greekness. We were obviously in this together, for good. I knew a thing or two about cattiness and jealousy. Cozying up with Camila seemed like the perfect way to set myself up as an ass-kissing target for both. As I finished my meal, I decided that last night was the last time I would put myself in that sort of situation with Camila. From now on, I would focus on getting to know the other girls better, on making new friends. And on putting up with Samantha.

Thirty minutes or so later, we were loaded into a black limo bus, probably the same bus that had brought us to the house. It had been a relief to see the top floors of the ABO house again. It was fantastic to be outside in the mid-September sun, breathing some fresh Baltimore air.

I took my seat next to Amy, and we chatted about how much longer we'd be forced to wear all white. I looked up when the bus grew strangely quiet.

Benny walked down the aisle and took her seat next to me. When she'd left the dining room, her hair looked liked the aftermath of a bomb going off in a very long brunette rat's nest. Now her coffee brown locks were amazingly straight. The acne that had riddled her face was magically gone. I imagined it was the same below the neck. We all stared at her for a minute. She ignored us and started playing a game on her cell phone.

Cleo and Danni hopped on the bus and the driver pulled away from the house. Amy and I picked up our conversation, moving on to what Amy was going to tell her mom now that she officially wasn't going to be a Xi O. I listened for a few moments, but then I had to take a crack at Benny.

I glanced across the aisle. Laura and Anna-Jade were in their own world. Mel was staring out the window, and Ruth and Ebony were talking animatedly about the one professor they shared, a college algebra teacher who wore his pants up around his nipples. Samantha was staring right at Benny, but I had a feeling Sam's hostile attitude wasn't going to change anytime soon.

"You're looking a little different," I said. I felt Amy inch a bit closer to me, straining to hear Benny's response.

"Their blood has healing properties. Camila offered to let me take from her, so I said okay."

"Your step-dad wouldn't feed you before?" Amy asked.

"Would you ask your step-dad if you could take from his wrist?"

"Good point," Amy and I both muttered. We were quiet for a moment before I patted Benny on the knee. "Well. You look good."

"Thanks, Ginger."

❖

As we got closer to the spa, Cleo and Danni made us all memorize the address and the phone number of the Alpha Beta Omega house for emergencies. Then they explained how the rest of our weekend would go. Our mandatory morning of pampering would be followed by a few hours we'd have to ourselves. We could head back to the ABO house, go to our dorms, whatever. We had to be back by seven to get ready for a formal mixer with the boys from Omega Beta Alpha. I'd expected some of the other girls to be excited about meeting them, but they took the news with casual amusement.

For the rest of the sororities and fraternities on campus, initiation lasted eight to twelve weeks. Our initiation ended sometime around dawn that morning, a blood bond making all the other Greek traditions seem a little lame. We still had activities and chapter meetings to attend. Sunday would be ours, but our Friday nights and Saturdays belonged to Alpha Beta Omega. We had to make it look like we were going through the process just like the other Greek organizations.

When we arrived at the spa, we were put back in our line and shuffled off two by two to see the estheticians. Even if they weren't all that invested in us emotionally, the sister-queens preferred our lady parts bare. We all snickered at the shrieks of pain coming from inside the room and offered our condolences for the pubes that had fought the good fight.

A chubby woman with light brown hair and too much eye makeup helped me onto the table then showed me my options for designs. I seriously wanted to kick myself. When she asked me which I liked the best, Camila immediately popped into my mind. I wondered, just for a second, which was a second way too long, what she would like to see the next time we were together. But there wasn't going to be a next time. That was the perfect reason for me to push any thought of what Camila might like out of my head.

I liked the idea of maintaining a little proof I was a natural redhead, so I decided against the full Brazilian. I went back and forth between the straight landing strip and a plain triangle. They actually offered a heart-shaped design that could be dyed pink on request.

I held up my necklace. "Can you do a landing strip shaped like this?"

"Like a teardrop?" she asked. I nodded. "Of course."

She stirred the hot wax, and I did a pretty good job of not making any weird animal-like noises when she poured it all over my crotch—and along my ass. It hurt like hell, every single tear-jerking yank, but it suddenly felt surprisingly light and breezy between my legs. The woman gave me a mirror so I could examine her handiwork upright. The leftover patch of hair looked so ridiculous I knew I'd have to shave it off at some point. My pussy looked kinda nice. It was a little swollen and blushed a bright red, but it was nice to see what I was working with from that angle. It didn't look half bad. Blinding pain aside, I knew I'd be waxing from then on.

After a facial, a massage, and watching Danni and Amy make out in the sauna for a good fifteen minutes, Amy and I decided to head back to the dorm for a little while. She managed to keep it together on her way up to our room. She'd been waiting all day for me to spill about my night with Camila. We were finally alone and I didn't have the excuse of security cameras or eavesdropping sorority girls to keep her questions at bay.

When we hit our hallway, Amy's nosy questions took a backseat. Our door was covered in red, black, and white decorations. Our names were cut out in big red block letters around an even bigger ABO cut out in black construction paper. The letters were surrounded by white stars and hearts, glitter, confetti, and streamers all over the slab of faux wood. It looked like a piñata threw up.

Amy laughed at my bug-eyed look. "This part is actually normal. They decorate our room."

"Oh. How long do we have to keep this up?"

"All semester," she said as she unlocked the door. We stepped inside and then we both stopped in our tracksuits.

Our beds were piled high with gift boxes and shopping bags.

"What the? Okay. I knew about the decorations, but I don't know what all this stuff is," Amy said.

We glanced at each other for a moment before we tore into the packages. Inside each bag and box, we found item after item of Alpha Beta Omega swag. Under the tissue paper, I dug out four different ABO T-shirts, in different arrangements of the sorority's colors. There was a vintage letterman's sweater in black with an enormous red "A" stitched to the rib with white thread. Custom ABO sweats from Victoria's Secret. Custom underwear and camisoles from Victoria's Secret. Three different hooded sweatshirts, a fleece jacket, socks, a scarf, knit and baseball caps, key chains, a watch, headbands and hair clips, plastic bracelets, and flip-flops, all in red, black, and white. The only thing missing was a pair of Alpha Beta Omega low-rise jeans.

There was a giant plush panther on my pillows wearing an ABO collar. Between its paws was a paddle that Amy assured me was just for decoration. The sizable piece of carved wood was decorated with my name, the year, and of course, the letters ABO. Apparently, we were supposed to hang it somewhere.

I couldn't decide what my favorite piece of apparel was. It was a toss-up between the letterman's sweater and a T-shirt that read, "Once you go red, white, and black, you never go back." I had the sneaky suspicion Cleo had something to do with that one. We allowed ourselves a good half hour of girlie frenzy and then tried to make some order out of our room.

"Are you going to sleep at the house tonight?" Amy asked.

"I guess." I hadn't planned on meeting up with Greg until after lunch on Sunday. I could spend the night acting the fool with the girls.

"I'm sure there'll be plenty of room in Camila's bed." Amy poked her tongue out at me between her teeth.

"Probably. I won't be sleeping there."

"Why not?"

"Why would I?"

"Um, because Camila's gorgeous and she wants you. Why else would she have picked you out?" I didn't think now was a good time to tell Amy about my curious blood. I wanted to know more before I talked to anyone about it.

"She sensed I wasn't into the idea of joining a sorority even if it's all some elaborate ruse, so we just talked about that."

"And then after you talked, you and Camila…"

"We watched you get it on with Danni and Paige and Barb." I turned around and grinned at her.

"Wait. You were there?"

"Uh, yeah."

"I didn't see you."

"Well, you were a little busy getting it on with Danni and Paige and Barb."

"Yeah." Amy got quiet, nibbling on the inside of her lip. "I like Danni a lot." That explained the making out in the sauna.

"Did you tell her that?"

"No. I mean, I found out she's not dating Paige. They just hook up a lot, so at least she's single. Officially, but..."

"What?"

"Ginger, I've only known her for five days and I'm over guys."

"Whoa. It's that serious?" I know it sounded like I was giving Amy a hard time, but I wasn't. She was pretty damn boy crazy. For her to consider sleeping with a girl—I mean outside of the vampire-induced group sex—was a big deal. Wanting to be in a relationship with another girl was huge.

"I just—I know what Benny said was mostly about the sister-queens, about them not wanting to get serious with us, but I'm afraid to say something to Danni. What if she looks at us new girls the same way? I'll feel like a total idiot if she shoots me down."

"I hate to say it, but you'll never know until you try."

"You're right." She took a deep breath then sat up straight. "You're right. I'll talk to her tonight."

"Good." I turned to the closet and started hanging up my new shirts.

"So what happened after you watched Danni and me getting it on?" Damn it. Changing the subject hadn't made her forget.

"We went back to her room and then we fucked like crazy until I passed out. Is that what you wanted to hear?"

"Yes. Thank you." I turned back to the closet to avoid the smug look on Amy's face.

❖

Power naps were in order before we got in the Saturday night line for the shower. Amy listened when I told her it would be dumb to assume Camila wanted to spend the night with me again. She might not even be around for the mixer. We'd had a blast together the night before, but it was a one-time thing. I told Amy I'd let some other girl in the sorority be Camila's bed buddy. Amy laughed and I cringed a little inside, hoping foolishly that Camila would decide to spend the night alone if she couldn't spend it with me.

Amy called Danni who told us Anna-Jade, Mel, Laura, and Benny were planning on spending the night at the ABO house, sex free. Then I texted Cleo and she texted me right back, telling me her bed was big enough to sleep her, Benny, and me. A genuine slumber party sounded like the perfect thing to keep my mind off Camila. Even if she would be sleeping or working a few floors below.

Our outfits for the party were at the house waiting for us. The limo bus was waiting for us downstairs at seven. When we climbed on, Kyle, Ruth, and Laura were already joking about what we would be forced to wear in front of the brothers of OBA.

"Ten to one, it's white," Kyle said.

"Twenty to one, Cleo doesn't let us wear underwear," Laura added.

Once we were off the bus, we raced up the enormous staircase and found our way to our big sisters' bedrooms. Cleo and Danni were waiting for Amy, Benny, and me with our red chiffon dresses. The fabric was gorgeous and ran no risk of showing off our nipples and newly manicured crotches.

The dresses were strapless, and mine fell just above my knees. I didn't need a bra thanks to the tight bodice, but Cleo had been nice enough to lay out a few options of boy shorts and thongs. I risked the thong and was very happy with the way it felt along my bare slit.

I did my own makeup while the girls descended on Benny. After her hair had been tamed, it was easy to see how beautiful her face was. She didn't need much makeup, if any, but she didn't argue when Danni and Amy wanted to put a few curls in her hair. She looked fantastic in her dress, and it was even more obvious why she'd wanted to handle the acne situation on her back and shoulders. Now her creamy pale skin was even and smooth. I was tempted to touch her just to see if it was as soft as it looked. I kept my hands to myself as I passed by.

I stood in the bathroom putting the finishing touches on my mascara, when Camila appeared in the mirror behind me. She looked beautiful. Her strapless chiffon gown was black and went all the way to the floor. An elaborate web of diamonds and rubies hung around her neck. Her lips were bright red again, and her eyes sparkled their heart-stopping shade. I whipped around to face her.

"What are you doing here?" I asked like a total idiot.

"Well, technically, this is my house. It's nice to see you too." Her fangs gleamed in the vanity lights as she smiled at me. I felt my face go hot and then blinked a couple times to clear my head of a few fantasies that had just popped up.

"No. Sorry, I just—I wasn't expecting to see you before the party. I didn't know if you were coming to the party at all."

"I am. I brought a little something for my girls." She held up a small black box I hadn't realized she was holding. She opened the lid and showed me a pair of teardrop ruby earrings resting on the black velvet.

"Oh, wow. Those are beautiful. You didn't have to."

"I wanted to." She glanced at the bottle of mascara dangling from my fingers. "I'll let you finish up." She put the earrings on the counter then paused by the door. Her gaze trailed over my body as her fang caught her bottom lip. I'd seen that look in her eye the night before. She wanted to bite me. "I'll see you in a few minutes."

"Okay," I breathed. Camila slipped out of the bathroom. When I stopped trembling, I finished putting on my makeup.

❖

In the place of nametags that read "Hi. I'm new," my fellow initiates and I were given white roses to wear in our hair. The seven of us who fed Camila were the last to head down the grand staircase.

Cleo said to me, "Camila will introduce you three around, and then you're free to mingle." I nodded, trying my best not to trip on my stilettos as we followed our queen into the buzzing crowd.

The guys from Omega Beta Alpha wore black suits with black shirts and ties. The newcomers were set apart by their red ties and the same anxious look we new girls couldn't seem to shake. Gelled spikes were in perfect place. Trimmed heads had sharply traced edges. Every bit of facial hair, where there was some, was perfectly manicured. We'd spent the morning at the spa. The boys had all been to see a very professional barber. Apparently, onyx-plated dog tags hung below their shirts, markers of exactly whom they belonged to.

Benny's claim that we'd been chosen for our diversity was reflected in the brothers of OBA. I didn't bother to remember all their names on the first go-round, but almost every ethnicity was represented. Where the sister-queens seemed to embrace a wider range of body types, the boys were all tall and in excellent shape.

The six brother-kings were easy to spot. They carried themselves in the same smooth, graceful manner that was anything but natural to a human. Camila led us toward a man who was nearly seven feet tall. His eyes were eerily blue, and his spiked hair was a bottomless shade of black. He introduced himself as Rodrick, a thick Russian accent coating his words. He didn't bother explaining his significance, but I'd remembered what Benny had said about him at breakfast. This was the king of Omega Beta Alpha. And Natasha's husband.

Camila introduced Benny, Amy, and me. I didn't look away from his intense blue eyes until he began introducing the two boys by his side. A baby-faced blond with soft brown eyes stood to Rodrick's right. His name was Micah. If Amy hadn't been so wrapped up in Danni, I'd have thought Micah would be right up her alley.

To Rodrick's left was my lab partner, Greg. He cleaned up well. I'd never noticed that his eyes were almost as green as mine. I had never noticed him period. He was smart and hardworking, and we both wanted to get an A in our lab. I knew better what the back of his hand looked like holding a pen than what shade of pink his lips were.

He usually wore a ratty Cubs hat over his chin length curly brown hair. He hadn't cut the curls, but they'd been brushed behind his ears. Greg was pretty hot. That wasn't the reason I was staring at him. He looked like he was about to throw up or cry.

"Ginger?" I glanced at Camila.

"Oh, sorry. I…ah…"

"I believe these two already know each other." Rodrick smiled, flashing an enormous set of fangs.

"Um, sorry. Yeah, Greg's my chem lab partner," I finally spit out.

"That's wonderful," Rodrick said. "Gregory's very focused on his studies. Maybe Ginger can convince him to get a little socializing in."

"Good luck with that," Amy muttered.

"Ginger takes her schoolwork seriously as well. Perhaps their new brothers and sisters will be able to coax them both out," Camila said, slowly drawing her finger down my back. I held back a shiver of pleasure and fought the urge to step closer to her.

We chatted with Rodrick and Micah for a few more minutes. Greg stood by, only answering when asked a direct question. He was always polite when he responded, but the whole time his body was tense and he never smiled.

After an appropriate amount of small talk, Rodrick excused himself to go find Natasha, and after a gracious "It was lovely to meet you" to Micah and Greg, Camila let us off our leash. Benny took off to find Cleo. Amy was eating her dust on a mission to find Danni. I made a move to follow Greg to the bar, but Camila's warm fingers on my arm stopped me. I almost asked her what she needed, what quick bit of advice she had for me before I ventured into the crowd. Instead, I froze the moment I was locked in her trance.

Camila took a smooth step toward me, then she kissed me softly on the lips. I knew instantly that she was labeling me as her property in the midst of the crowded room. I should have stopped her from marking me with her perfectly juicy lips. I should have been pissed. I was already bound to her and the sisterhood. She had no right to make a show of me being her pet. But the second I was surrounded by her warm scent, I couldn't find the will to fight her. My body caught fire, starting at my mouth as she gently teased me with the tip of her tongue. And then further down, my pussy throbbed, soaking the thin strip of fabric between my legs.

When she pulled away, my eyes blinked open just in time to see her nostrils flare as she raked the tips of her fangs and her tongue across her bottom lip. Again, her lipstick didn't smudge.

"Play nice with the other kids," she said quietly. She looked me over one more time before blending seamlessly into the crowd.

When I came back to myself, I'd lost track of Greg. I made my way over to Anna-Jade who was standing by herself in the corner. She'd set herself up in the perfect nook to people watch and gave me a small wave as I walked over.

"You having a good time?" I asked.

"Yeah, it's just a lot of people to meet in two days."

"Yeah, no shit." I was surprised when Anna-Jade actually laughed.

Just then Greg and Micah strode over to us.

"Hey, I was wondering where you went," I told Greg. Micah answered for him.

"We were scoping out the kitchen. Yours is nicer than the one at the OBA house. I'm Micah, by the way." He held out his had to Anna-Jade.

"Oh, my bad." I didn't know when I'd forgotten my manners. "Micah, Greg, this is Anna—"

"A.J. My friends call me A.J.," she said.

"It's nice to meet you, A.J.," Micah replied. Micah seemed like an outgoing kind of guy. I wasn't shocked by his end of their back-and-forth. My jaw was on the floor because I was almost positive our sheepish little A.J. was flirting.

"A.J., I think my friend here was hoping to have a word with your friend. Would you like to join me on my quest for chips and dip?" Micah asked. Anna-Jade blushed then nodded and tucked her hand into Micah's elbow. I chuckled to myself as they walked off, but my mood dropped the moment I turned back to Greg.

"Can we go outside for a minute?" he asked. If he was trying to keep something from Rodrick, I had a feeling we'd have to go to the next county to keep from being overheard. Still, I led him toward the front door. It was the illusion of privacy he wanted.

Surrounded by the warm night air, I leaned against the porch railing. Greg tilted his head back against the ornate brick and let out a huge sigh.

"Are you okay?" I asked.

"No. I'm not." He took another deep breath and looked at me. "How'd you get wrapped up in this shit? I didn't peg you for the sorority type."

"My roommate tricked me. You could have said no, Greg. What's going on?" I refused to believe the guys of OBA hadn't been given the same chances to back out. The mood in the house was pleasant all around, if not sexually charged. None of the new guys seemed upset about how their initiation had turned out. They all seemed downright happy. All of them but Greg. And then it clicked.

"They fed from you guys last night, didn't they?"

Greg looked at his shiny new shoes, shifting uncomfortably. I'd had my own issues with how instantly sexual our relationship with the sister-queens had become. I could only imagine how a guy like Greg, who was very straight, had felt when he thought back to the previous night. He must have freaked out when he realized he'd let a male vampire sink his fangs into his neck. He must have been disgusted when he thought about how hard the feeding had made him come. And that's assuming Greg didn't participate in the orgy that had probably gone down.

Ignoring the other complications of our nonexistent relationship, I loved the feeling of Camila's hands on my body. I craved the grip of her fangs on my throat. That was only after a few hours with her. I was pretty sure I was gay. Greg was not.

"Greg, just tell Rodrick you want out. Or…" I thought for a moment. "I know. Ask him if you can switch with one of us. A few of the girls don't care who they feed. I'm sure one of them would love to feed Rodrick. Then when we graduate you can serve a female vampire." At least I thought he could.

"It's not that simple, Ginger. I'm legacy. My dad was in the Beta chapter at Carolina." He gritted his teeth before looking back up. He refused to make eye contact with me though. He looked over my shoulder at the OBA house across the street.

"He just—he could have fucking told me. I mean, I get it. This shit's important. I'd rather help Rodrick out than have him offing little kids every time he's hungry. He's a good dude. I just—"

"Wouldn't have gone through with it if you knew?" His silence gave me his answer. "I wouldn't have either. Trust me."

"So what the fuck do I do now? I mean Micah wasn't into it. Some of the guys were into it, but he didn't fight it either. Fuck. I don't know if I can do this for four years."

"Do you want me to talk to Camila? Maybe she can work something out with Rodrick?"

"No. Ha!" Greg's reaction was grim and a little crazed. "I don't want to be the one pussy who can't hang."

"Well, one of our girls refuses to participate in the sex part. I know some things are unavoidable, but the sex isn't a must."

"Shit. I don't know. I'll think of something. Don't say anything. Rodrick's probably using his X-ray vision to watch us through the wall, but don't go telling your friends or whatever."

"I won't. I promise." I had my own secrets now, secrets my birth mother could have shared with me before she died. I understood why Greg was upset. "Listen, Cleo said we can still date and stuff. Let's go inside and find you a nice girl."

"Yeah. Sounds great," he muttered.

❖

For the most part, no one seemed to notice as we slipped back into the house. Of course Camila locked eyes with me the moment I closed the door. When she seemed satisfied I was where she could see me, she focused back on her conversation with one of the other brother-kings. He was tall, with a slighter build than Rodrick, with long, light brown hair pulled back in a low ponytail. I think his name was Pax.

Greg and I found Micah and Anna-Jade hanging out by the bar. It was only serving soda, juice, and water. Samantha and Kyle had their high beams focused on Greg. There was nothing I could do for him right then and there, so when he was distracted enough with their attention, I took off to find Amy.

As the party went on, I periodically scanned the room for Greg. He and Samantha had made themselves comfortable on the couch. I wouldn't have handpicked her for him, but toward the end of the night, she actually had him talking and laughing. I'd take that over the helpless desperation I'd faced on the porch.

The whole night, I felt Camila's eyes on me. It drove me nuts. I made up my mind to ignore her. She may have been the reason for the slow, aching burn between my thighs, but I wasn't going to let her know that. The power of her kiss didn't negate Benny's warning. I refused to be another one of her meaningless, semi-nutritious hookups. I enjoyed the rest of the night with the satisfaction of knowing she wouldn't get another crack at me, in bed at least.

A little before one a.m., Rodrick started sending the boys back toward their house. Soon, Micah was the only one left.

"Micah, the young ladies need their rest. Miss A.J. will still attend the university in the morning," Rodrick said with a gentle grin.

"All right. I'm coming." Micah leaned closer to Anna-Jade. "I'll hit you up later," I heard him whisper. Her cheeks turned bright red, and at least two other girls had to hold in their "aws" as she waved a bashful good-bye.

Camila employed a maid service who would be there first thing in the morning. Still, a bunch of us pitched in for a preliminary clean up. The other sister-queens and a handful of the girls had returned to the bottom floor. I had no idea where Camila had gone, but she must have completed her Ginger surveillance for the night because I didn't see her anywhere.

I was the last one up the stairs, openly mocking Cleo for her use of the word credenza, when I heard Camila call my name.

"Ah, teacher's pet," Cleo coughed. The other girls bit their cheeks to hold in their comments. Gritting my teeth, I slowly turned around. I felt like I had been caught sneaking back into my parents' house after a late night of drinking in the woods.

Camila was waiting at the bottom of the stairs. The telling look on her face didn't make things any better. I carefully inserted my foot in my mouth and decided to accept Camila's offer before she made it.

"Let me just grab my stuff," I told her. We both ignored Cleo's snicker.

"I'll be waiting in the pantry." Camila gracefully strode away. I cursed then walked to get my bag. I was sure to flip off Cleo and Amy as I went.

❖

We made the trip to her place in silence. She watched me the whole time, that sly grin glued to her lips. I excused myself to change and take off my makeup. I nearly threw a hissy fit when she made a move to stop me. I just wanted a second to get my mind together. Good thing I'd bit my tongue because she'd only meant to unzip my dress for me.

"Just leave it on the counter. I'll have it dry-cleaned."

I murmured my thank-you before slinking away.

I closed the bathroom door and considered banging my head against the sink. How in the hell did I end up back in her room? I was so spineless. I hadn't even attempted to say no. Not a maybe later or a not tonight. I stuck the apple in my own my mouth, right beside my foot, then started basting myself for Camila's amusement.

And after I changed, I'd wished I brought different pajamas. I'd been anxious to try out my new ABO boy shorts and cami. I turned to the side, looking at myself in the mirror. She hadn't even touched me and my nipples were straining under the stretch cotton. The simple kiss she'd given me during the party had left me so wet I could almost wring out the thong I'd been wearing.

I turned to the other side and ran my fingers over my stomach.

"I'd kill for a snowsuit or a chastity belt," I muttered to myself.

"Now why would you do that?"

My heart jumped up into my throat. Camila stepped behind me in the dimly lit bathroom. She had changed into another black tank top/lace panties combo. She looked so good.

"You have to stop doing that," I said when I started breathing again.

"What? Coming into the bathroom?"

"Sneaking up on me."

"I like that little noise you make when you're surprised."

"What noise?" I scowled at her.

"Don't worry about it, Red. I want you to tell me something."

I watched her hips as she walked over to me. Her smooth gait reminded me of the shocking power hidden in those feminine curves. When she reached me, she gently gripped my waist and placed me on the counter in one effortless motion. Her strength took me by surprise again, and it left me breathless.

"See. You made that noise."

"I'll take your word for it."

The lump in my throat went down hard as I looked at her full lips. She had gotten rid of the lipstick, but her lips were still tinted pink and they shined with some sort of unscented gloss. I wanted to kiss her.

Slowly, her hands slid up my ribs. She gently guided my arms up and around her shoulders. Her skin was so soft and warm it was hard to believe she was the spawn of some demon race. She was too gentle and so accessible. She tasted too sweet.

Camila slid in a little closer and my legs automatically wrapped around her hips. I knew right then I was screwed. My body was holding hers captive, but she had all the control. She had me. I wasn't going anywhere.

Her lips parted slightly as she looked me over. I caught a glimpse of her sharp teeth.

"So tell me, why do you seem so embarrassed to be spending the night with me?"

"I'm not embarrassed."

Her head dipped and she gently nipped me on the shoulder. My hips shifted all on their own, chasing some friction from Camila's body. Her arm wrapped around my back and she pulled me closer, rubbing her stomach against my slit. I whimpered, arching my body.

"I just want to fuck you again. I loved watching you come. I don't believe that's something to be embarrassed about."

"No," I moaned. "It's not."

"You'll stay with me tonight?"

"Yes."

"Good. I've been thinking about your taste all day," she said. "Come to bed with me."

She didn't wait for my reply before she helped me slip off the counter. We walked back to her bedroom, and I didn't pull away from her when she tried to hold my hand. There was no will to resist her. I wasn't thinking clearly at all. There was no use in denying what I wanted. Camila got me so worked up, there was no flicker of logic sparking in my brain. I wanted to touch her and I wanted her to touch me.

When she laid me down on her bed, I pushed everything I'd wanted in terms of a relationship, and everything Benny had told us, out of my head. I'd focus on tonight and Camila and worry about everything—school, Greg, my affected DNA—tomorrow. Now I wanted the beautiful vampire queen to take the pleasure between our bodies where we both wanted it to go.

Her deep gaze held mine as she prowled over my body. When we were eye to eye, she kissed me. Her perfect tongue slid in and out of my mouth with slow, penetrating strokes. Her cinnamon scent surrounded me. If I could have lived off the flavor of her lips and the juices from her tongue, I would have. The words I wanted to tell her, the confessions of how she was making me feel, were lost in the swirl of my senses. I couldn't have ended the kiss to share them with her, so I moaned deep in my throat. She smiled against my lips then kissed me even deeper.

My body started to grind against her stomach. Camila took that as her cue to pull away. I watched her, licking all trace of her off my lips. She rose to her knees and hooked her fingers into the fabric at my hips.

"Did you have fun today?" she asked softly.

I nodded in reply.

She pulled my underwear down my thighs and off my feet.

"Well, I'll say." She ran her fingers over my newly styled pubic hair. "Very pretty."

She gazed between my legs. Her lips parted again, and this time her growing fangs kept her from closing them. A low purring sound rumbled in her chest and my pussy clenched, soaking, aching for her. Her nostrils flared and the purring grew slightly louder.

"God, Red." Her palm came down on the juncture of my hip and thigh, and she slowly ran her finger down the length of my slit. My mouth fell open and I did my best to keep from arching off the bed. My pussy tingled like crazy, dripping even wetter with each gentle stroke.

Camila took her time driving me insane. I could hear myself panting. I wanted her to hurry up and bite me. The sweet crushing orgasm that came with the cool sting of her fangs was better than any orgasm I'd ever given myself, undoubtedly better than any orgasm anyone else could give me. But then there was the other part of me that wanted Camila to go slowly. When I had the time and the privacy, I liked working myself to the point where my clit ached and throbbed. Finally giving in and letting myself come again and again had always been the best reward for my patience. Camila made the torture so much sweeter.

She dipped her thumb into my dripping pussy then drew my juices up, spreading them around my clit. She was purposefully avoiding the tip.

"And Cleo and the girls took good care of you?" she asked.

"Yes." I bit my lip and moaned to keep from finishing my sentence. The words *but I still missed you* almost tumbled out. I was completely freaked out that the thought had even popped into my head. It was true that I hadn't experienced anything better than Camila's seductive touch, but the time we spent together was very limited, and as I'd been reminding myself all day, meaningless.

Plus, I'd only known her for a little over twenty-four hours. Saying I missed her just made me sound like a total nut bag. I wouldn't even bother considering whether it was true.

Camila had no problem fucking me, so I could fuck her and go about my business. I wasn't attached to anyone else, human or vampire, and no one but Camila had caught my eye, so why couldn't I enjoy the time we spent together?

Her thumb swirled over my clit once more and my hips jerked off the sheets. Enjoying wouldn't be a problem.

"Red," she whispered. I peeled my eyes open and stared at her beautiful face as she slid onto her belly between my legs. "I'm going to go slow." All I could do was nod, swallowing a gasp as her thumb pushed back inside me.

She worked my body at a brutal pace, taking her time as she moved through different motions with her fingers and her palm. I fought to keep my hips still. The moment I pushed back or tried to ride her hand, I knew I would come. I wasn't ready yet.

Finally, she lowered her head, her shoulders bunching. This time she didn't have to bite me. The moment her lips locked on to my pussy, I came.

## CHAPTER SIX

Instead of a sexy naked vampire, I woke up next to a tented piece of white stationary. I grabbed the note Camila had left me and I rolled onto my back. The sheets on her side of the bed were cold. I shivered and rolled back into my pocket of warmth before I opened the note.

Red, I'm right next door.

Her handwriting was swirly and feminine. For some reason, I expected something more angular or maybe even typed. She didn't sign the note. A small heart was etched on the paper in the place of her name. I stared at the little symbol for love, and my chest fluttered a bit. I was in trouble.

Our second night together had been perfect. Better than the first. I didn't know it was possible to let yourself go that way, leave yourself completely at the will of someone else. Every ounce of resistance fell to the side. Camila took over, took every inch of me, twice before we fell asleep and once more in the middle of the night.

There were sensations I never thought existed, positions I'd never considered. And then there were the emotions, ones I wasn't ready to feel for anyone, ones I should never feel for her, that grew stronger and stronger with every kiss and every touch. I was so fucking screwed.

I was in love with Camila.

There was no falling about it. I'd packed my bags sometime during the week, and last night I'd changed my address and moved into the You're Insane Manor.

I looked at the note again and imagined receiving hundreds more like it, hopefully with heavier meaning and more thoughtful or x-rated content. As if she would slip little pieces of paper in my locker after study hall. I needed to get a grip. Before long, I'd be imagining myself with her last name, if she had one.

I rubbed my neck where she'd bitten me. She had kept her word. There was never any pain, and even now as I brushed my fingers over the healed skin, my clit tingled. I wanted to equate that feeling to the amazing sex Camila and I had, but it was more than that. It was the way Camila made me feel when she kissed me, the smile that touched her lips every time she called me Red. So many things about her that I loved.

"You are mental," I muttered. Then I got out of bed. I pulled one of my new ABO shirts and a pair of sweats out of my bag. My sanity kept her opinion to herself when I slipped Camila's note in the side pocket.

After I pulled my hair up, I went looking for Camila. I heard her voice off to the left, from the one room of her underground apartment I hadn't seen. The door was open. I peeked around the jamb and saw Camila pacing around, talking on her cell. She was back in her uniform: the black tank top and undies. Bedhead never seemed to affect her perfect black spikes that I had yet to run my fingers through. Her lips looked soft and perfect.

She held out her hand, beckoning me across the room. My feet carried me over to her immediately. I wanted to throw my arms around her and nuzzle my cheek against her shoulder, the kind of stuff you do first thing in the morning when you see someone you love.

Instead, our fingers intertwined and I felt her warmth spread through me. My stomach flipped and I could feel the heat rising up my face. Unless we were actually having sex, holding hands was pretty much all we did. But I loved when she touched me, so I didn't see any reason to complain.

"No. I told him that was not okay…No. He cleans himself up or he's done," she said. She held the phone away from her cheek and kissed me softly on the lips. While we touched, I could faintly hear some guy muttering on the other end. She took a small step back, looking at our feet. I could tell she was pretty pissed at whoever she was talking about, but there was still a gentleness to her tone.

"He's useless to me in more ways than one, and there's no way I'm sending him to someone else…No, I took him off Faeth's hands as a favor on the terms that he wouldn't feed again. I'm not running a rehab."

There was more muttering on the line. She shook her head with a quick laugh then kissed me again.

"I'm not yelling at you. Don't worry about it. This is not your problem. Thank you for telling me, and I'll handle it. How was last night?"

I finally peeled my eyes off her gorgeous face and gave myself a chance to look around the office. She let go of my hand, and I strolled across the cool hardwood floor. There were shelves and shelves lined with books, everything from old leather-bound volumes to brightly colored paperbacks. There were trinkets on every available surface.

Figures of round-bellied fertility goddesses in different stones and sizes lined the top of her bookshelves. Between her volumes of poetry and seven versions of the Bible was what looked like the first soccer ball ever stitched together. On a low sideboard near the door sat three long black feathers tied together with a yellow ribbon, the fragile leaves of a dried palm frond, a raw ruby the size of my head, an antique tea set, and an ashtray from Colonial Williamsburg.

There was no real theme to the decorations, just evidence she was the type of person who kept things that interested her or had meaning. And maybe that she'd been alive for a very long time.

There was only one piece of art. A graffiti mural covered the wall opposite her bookshelves. Bright swirls and blocks transformed the space from floor to ceiling. In the center, the mash of colors came together around a smooth black and gray portrait of Camila. Her eyes were cast down, and there was a bright red rose in her hair. It captured every detail of her beauty and more emotion than I'd seen from her in the little amount of time we'd spent together.

I couldn't hold in the "Wow" that whispered through my lips.

I turned around and found Camila grinning at me.

"Kina did it," she said, nodding at the painting. I turned back and stared at the details in the image. It was amazing.

I spun slowly and did a final sweep of the room. On the far wall three computer monitors were set up on her long desk. I took a few steps forward, being a little nosy. I held in a laugh when I looked at the first screen. Camila was shopping for more books online. It was adorable to think of her doing something so normal like partaking in online retail therapy. The others showed a few dozen split screen videos captured from various security cameras.

I looked at the gray images of an empty storefront, a busy hotel lobby, and a short man covered in tattoos sitting in a small office. The phone up to his ear made me think he had Camila on the line. I glanced at the other monitor and saw images from around the ABO house. Cleo's Honda and Danni's beat-up Jeep were parked in the back among the other cars. The elevator was empty. Florencia sat in front of the TV with Kate, Jordan, and Ruth, drinking coffee.

Upstairs was relatively quiet. Most of the girls were still asleep. Julia and Georgiana were passed out in Julia's bed. There was an early morning gab session going on in Cleo's room. Benny was there, cuddled up with Cleo under her comforter. Amy and Danni were both squeezing into Cleo's papasan chair. Anna-Jade was passed out at the foot of the bed wrapped in an ABO fleece blanket. They all had that rumpled from sleep look, but they were laughing at something Cleo was saying.

I wanted to feel left out, but I didn't. Not when Camila's arms wrapped around me. She'd gotten off the phone without me noticing.

"Did you sleep well?" she murmured against my cheek.

I nodded and then asked, "Are there cameras in every room?"

"Yes. Just making sure my girls are safe. Last spring, the boys from Iota planned to 'kidnap' a member of every sorority. They were supposed to give Florencia a warning, but they didn't. The footage of their botched break-in was the only thing that kept me from pressing charges."

"Who'd they get?"

"Nobody. Jordan caught wind of it and told everyone. It took them ten minutes to get in, and the house was empty."

My eyes drifted back to the shot of the girls in Cleo's room. Kyle and Mel wandered into the room just as Anna-Jade had rolled over.

"Do you want to join them?" Camila's lips softly brushed my neck.

"Not right now."

Camila reached across the desk and pressed the speaker button on a regular looking office phone. Considering the computer setup, I was a little shocked she didn't have something a little more high tech. She pressed "four," and it started to ring. A few seconds later, I saw Cleo pick up a phone next to her bed.

"Helloooo," she drawled.

"Do you ladies have plans for this morning?" Camila asked.

"I think we're going to hit up the cafeteria in a little while and then go to the library."

"How long is a little while?"

"Maybe an hour or so." Cleo gently poked Anna-Jade through the sheets with her toe. "A.J. was on the phone with Micah until five this morning. We're going to let her sleep for a while before we go. Why? Does Ginger feel like rejoining us day dwellers?" I watched Amy on the monitor as she leaned toward the phone.

"Hi, Ginger!"

"You want to roll with us, Ginge?" Cleo asked.

"Yeah. I have to meet Greg." We agreed I would meet them in an hour and a half before we said our good-byes. When Camila hung up, I watched as Cleo said something to the girls. They all burst out laughing. I knew they were making fun of me for being teacher's pet and all, but whatever. I couldn't bring myself to care. I'd just bought myself more time with Camila. If things kept up this way between us, there would be plenty of chances for Cleo to give me crap for hanging out with Camila.

I looked back to the image of the empty elevator.

"Are there cameras in every room down here?"

Camila slid in closer, pressing the curve of her hips against my body. I swallowed, pressing back. Her breath came out raggedly as she replied.

"Of course. For my sister-queens' protection. They still have their privacy, but what's stored here is more important for reassurance." Camila reached over and grabbed the mouse. It took a few clicks to find the right file and cue it up to the right time. The camera above Camila's bedroom door was hidden, but the angle of the lens captured the whole room. The whole bed.

It was strange to see myself asleep, but not strange enough to quash the heat that rushed over my skin as I watched Camila's body between the sheets, close to mine. The covers were pulled up to our shoulders. I still remembered drifting off, the feeling of Camila's fingers pressed against my stomach.

And the next second she was gone. I gasped as the sheets on the screen fluttered flat, covering the spot where Camila had been. I had woken up alone not even ten minutes ago, and I was in her arms now, but something about seeing her vanish, how quick and easy it was for her to disappear, left me hollow. I watched myself roll onto my back. Even in my sleep, I grimaced, sensing my loneliness.

"Where'd you go?" I asked.

"Not far, Red. See." And at that moment Camila walked back into the frame. She had her cell phone pressed to her ear. "Rodrick was simply checking in."

The proof that she hadn't abandoned me calmed my shaky nerves. Her lips brushing against my cheek started my breathing again.

On the screen I watched her take a seat on the end of the bed. She gently lifted the sheets and began caressing my legs. My sleeping self took a deep breath and relaxed against the pillow. A few seconds later, Camila ended her call and tossed her phone onto the dresser. Then she crawled between my legs, under the covers. My eyes traced the path she took underneath the silky black fabric until the outline of her head and shoulders reached the tops of my thighs.

My body tensed the moment her head dipped lower, on the screen, and there in her office, standing in Camila's arms. I didn't remember the first strokes of her tongue, but I could feel it now along with the tips of her fangs, dragging down my neck.

My shirt was pulled up and over my head just in time for me to see myself wake up on the computer screen. The night before, I had gently grasped Camila's shoulders, rolling my hips. Now I gripped the edge of the desk as she moved me to step out of my sweats.

On the monitor, my head pitched back into the pillow. There in the office, she rose behind me and found my hard nipples with her warm fingers. There was no sound on the video so I knew the moan I heard in my ears was echoing off the walls and the wood floor and not coming from the speakers of her computer.

She played with me forever, only touching my breasts with her hands, refusing to go any lower. That didn't stop my clit from throbbing as I watched myself coming on the screen.

I remembered how the orgasm had brought me fully awake, how I'd whimpered her name. But that hadn't been enough to stop her from licking and sucking. My thigh went up over her shoulder, and I remembered the feeling of her tongue thrusting into my pussy. A shiver ran through me now as my core clenched and dripped.

"Ginger, do you want me to make you come?"

"Yes," I whispered. "Please."

"Why don't I take you in the shower and you can come all over me. Would you like that?" she replied with a deep, lusty growl.

"Yes."

Camila turned me in her arms. I saw that same fierce burning I was oddly starting to crave light up her eyes. A sudden bashfulness tackled me out of nowhere and I gave in to the urge to cover my boobs with my arms. She was just so sexy and so beautiful and powerful. Of course I wanted her again, but I was nervous about what would happen next.

We'd hopped the fence from the area of playful experimenting I'd been hoping for and skipped right into porn territory. Not somewhere I ever thought I'd go. And then there were those pesky love feelings that only seemed to intensify as she looked at me. I knew she could eat me alive, and this weird part of me almost wanted her to. I wanted to give her everything, and that scared me even more.

Cautiously, like prey easing its way to safety, I passed her and took a few steps closer to the door.

"Go," she said with a soft pat to my ass.

I walked faster into the lounge but stopped when I felt her lagging behind. When I turned, she had just crossed through the doorway of her office and was shedding her tank top and her underwear.

Camila bent to pull the black panties off her foot. That delicious smile flashed across her mouth as she licked her bottom lip. "Don't worry. I'm still coming." She straightened and looked me slowly up and down.

"Do you want me to chase you?"

"No," I blurted out. "I'm not a tease." But I might be a little afraid you might disappear again, I wanted to say, but I bit my tongue. I wanted her close, no space in between us, for as long as possible. The sun and school would separate us soon enough.

Camila came toward me and cupped my face. I sighed into her mouth as she kissed me. God, the way she kissed should be illegal. It wasn't right or fair to unleash that kind of perfect, brain melting technique and that taste into someone's mouth. When she pulled away, I realized my pussy wasn't just wet; the insides of my thighs were soaked.

Her nostrils flared.

"No, Red. You surely are not a tease."

She turned me again so I was facing the bathroom then wrapped her arms around my waist.

"Is this better?" she asked, nuzzling her chin against my shoulder, pressing her breasts against my back.

"Yes, it is," I managed to say.

Her feet staggered on either side of mine, Camila shuffled us into the bathroom, keeping her arms tightly around me. She flicked on the lights and then maneuvered us over to the shower. Under the hot spray, I turned my face to her, struck silent by just how hot she looked covered in water with her dark spikes slicked back. I wanted to lick her all over.

She pulled me close and kissed me again, letting her hands wander all over my back and further down to my ass. I let her go wild, wanting her to touch me everywhere, aching even more as she pressed herself against me. Feeling her hot slickness and the firm ridge of her clit almost sent me over the edge.

The full curve of her thigh slid between my legs while she guided my arms up and around her shoulders.

"Hold on to me," she said into my ear. I slid my palms further down her back and let my fingers grip her soft skin. She leaned back slightly, taking both our weight as if balancing another person on her thigh was no big deal. I gasped and tried to pull away. I know she'd picked me up before, but she hadn't held me up. That didn't sound like it would be much fun for her. Plus, breaking her ankle or my face against the black tile was not the kind of shower sex I had in mind.

"No," she breathed. "Come on me."

I blinked, licking away some of the water rushing over my lips. I'd already given her my heart, whether she knew it or not, and she had settled me on the counter the night before like I weighed nothing at all. Maybe I could trust her lower body strength. I leaned back into her and my clit thanked me with several sharp twitches once I settled my weight back on her thigh. With our bodies melded together, head to toe, a rush of air left my lungs.

"Yes, Like that." She purred deeply, her chest puffing in and out against mine. "Don't worry. I can hold you, Red."

My body starting swaying on its own, rocking against her as she held her legs perfectly still. Her lips and her hands, though, were very busy. She threaded her fingers through the base of my ponytail and lightly gripped the back of my head then set about torturing me with light passes of her tongue and her fangs along my neck. I lost it when she nipped my skin.

I came. Not as much as my body wanted to, but enough to make me jerk and shudder against her body, enough to make me want so much more.

Camila chuckled and licked my jaw. "Are you okay?"

"Yeah. I—I want—"

"More?"

"Yeah." I nodded before going after her lips. She kissed me back, sucking my tongue into her mouth.

That's when things got interesting. That's when she spread me open.

Camila's fingers slid down behind me. Slowly, she began slipping her finger in and out of my pussy. The feeling of her gentle thrusts drove me forward, and I continued to press myself against her leg, grinding my already throbbing clit harder against her body. That should have been enough to make me explode all over again. I wanted to, so badly, but Camila seemed to be keeping me just far enough away from that point, pushing me just enough that I wouldn't let go.

Her finger pulled back, dragging a trail of my juices up to my asshole. She'd barely touched the puckered surface, but I tensed, pulling away slightly.

"Camila," I protested weakly. I didn't want things to stop altogether, I just—

"Shhh," she whispered, trailing soft kisses across my lips and my cheeks. "Remember what I told you? No pain. Only pleasure."

"Okay, but I've never—"

"I know, Red," she murmured, sliding her finger into my pussy again. She added another and another, working me up all over again. This time when her hand slipped a little higher, my body didn't resist. I wanted to come too much. I was way too high to even ease back down.

She pushed in gently, easing just the tip of her finger inside me. She was right. It didn't hurt at all. Just the opposite. The pressure nailed me right at the height of my slit. A violent shudder spread over my belly and down through my kneecaps. I surged forward and back, harder and faster, as fast as I could while our bodies were still connected. Her finger slid in deeper and deeper.

Suddenly, there was a small prick of pain. I gasped and winced a little, but she held me tightly, distracting me more with her kisses and purrs, and the pain started to fade.

I could tell she was close. Camila's nips and licks were becoming needy. I had no idea if she'd fed before I woke up, but she definitely wanted to bite me now. I could feel the tips of her fangs just before our tongues would meet. My blood probably wouldn't help with any legit craving. Still, maybe it would give her something she needed.

I craned my neck to the side and offered her my throat, letting the hot shower spray rain down on my face. She hesitated a moment. Her finger stilled inside me. Her fangs extended all the way, ready to strike.

"Red," she groaned.

"Do it," I murmured, grinding down as hard as my body could stand on her thigh. She snapped, her finger plunging as far as it could go as her fangs broke my skin.

Her name came out of me as a high-pitched scream, and I soaked her already slick thigh, my thick wetness coating her skin. She trembled against me, sucking harder for a few more moments before she licked the puncture wounds closed.

Her finger eased out and she slowly righted us both, cradling my head against her neck. I kissed her beating pulse point, trying to catch my breath.

"Better?" she asked then kissed my shoulder.

I swallowed, soaking in the gentle strokes of her other hand through my hair. My ponytail had fallen loose somewhere along the way.

"No. My legs are broken and I can't see. I think you 'repaid me' plenty."

Camila kissed the corner of my mouth. "Not even close, Red. Not even close."

We walked to the elevator hand-in-hand. Camila was trapped inside for another eight hours, at least. I had a ton of studying to get done, but the last thing I wanted to do was leave her.

"I have to be downtown a few nights this week, but any time you spend the night here, you're welcome to spend the night with me," she said.

"Is that a formal invitation?"

"It is, Red. You might not be much for my health, but you're in me now. You set foot in that front door and I'll know. You stay past bedtime, and I'm coming to get you." The gold in her eyes glowed as a deep purr came from her throat.

"Okay, that was creepy."

"Sorry." Camila laughed. It was a warm, apologetic sound, but she couldn't joke like that, being what she was. "But I can sense you."

"Maybe next time we can actually talk. I want to know more about your creepy powers," I said.

"And yours."

"Mine? No. I've been thinking about it, and beside my hypersensitive taste buds and my preference for chicken over fish, there have been no perks to having demon blood in my system."

"I'd like to find out for sure." She touched my cheek just for a moment, then pressed the button for the elevator door. With a slight swishing sound, it opened. I stepped inside. She'd already invited me back. The last thing I needed to do was hang around like a pathetic little puppy.

Camila punched the same series of numbers into the elevator's keypad and then kissed me with a soft good-bye before the door slid closed. I knew it would take everything I had not to daydream about the taste of her lips—or how good she looked naked—as the day went on.

The decision to be a grown-up about our interesting relationship had been made, so I was going to be a big girl and stick to that plan. I still had to focus on school and whatever new responsibilities now came with being a member Alpha Beta Omega. Adding occasional sex with the head sister-queen to the equation was simply a matter of changing where I slept at night. It could work.

And I felt good about my decision, or at least I knew I should have. My life had changed over the weekend. New friends, new secrets, new jewelry, and stylish new pubes. But one thing irked me as I took the short ride up to the pantry. It was lame, but I couldn't keep from thinking of it. I had no way of getting in touch with Camila. So far, she had been the one to seek me out. Sure, I could have asked Cleo the best way to reach Camila. I also could have asked her myself before I hopped on the elevator. That logical detail was pushed out of my mind.

We weren't a couple, but I figured after as much time as she spent with her tongue between my legs, swapping digits wasn't all that unreasonable. She could sense me, so it wasn't like she needed to speed dial me to lock in on my location, but I couldn't even text her if I wanted to. She'd been pretty consistent with asking me what I wanted. Not that I ever would, but I truly felt like I could turn her down if I felt like I should. I had plenty of choices in terms of if and how. She had all the control over the when and where.

By the time I reached Cleo's room, I realized that bothered me a lot more than it should.

The day before, the sunlight on my face had been a gift, nature's way of showing me that even though we were now bound to the sister-queens, our lives were still our own. We were safe and we were free to come and go. Now, as we stepped out onto the porch of Alpha Beta Omega house and I didn't burst into flames, I silently cursed the sun as a harsh reminder of several things I had no interest in thinking about. I still had a stats test to study for, an English paper to start, and Greg and I had to complete our lab write-up for the week.

As we walked to campus, the UV blast on my cheeks was also another bit of unavoidable truth standing between Camila and me. Forget any obvious age or possible generational gaps or the fact she had several businesses to run or that I had freshman year to get through. The sun itself would keep us apart no matter what we had to do. Even if she felt the same way I did, which would be nuts because what kind of a freak show falls for their fuck buddy after two days, we could never really be together.

Having sex and watching the highlights on her computer over the weekends was one thing, but her world existed at night. Unless I decided to switch to all night classes, things would remain this way. And then I just hated myself for even considering rearranging my schedule, my life, for Camila. We'd just met. She more than had a life of her own, and I was just some kid she liked to play with. Distracting myself with homework seemed like a better idea every minute.

Amy and I took a quick detour to the dorm to grab our books. I wanted to ask her if she'd gotten a chance to tell Danni how she felt, but I couldn't because Danni tagged along with us. Still, it only took a few minutes to figure out that something had changed between them.

When we were getting ready to leave the house, Danni was particularly touchy-feely with Amy. The fact that they held hands as we walked to the dorms wasn't a big deal. I'd held hands with Camila plenty of times in the past few days. But when we got to our room they started exhibiting more couplesque behavior.

Amy couldn't find her laptop cord. Danni helped her look for it while I was busy texting Todd. I was lost in a back-and-forth about who he favored in the Monday night game, when something Danni said caught my attention.

"Baby, where was the last place you saw it?" she asked Amy. I peeked up and watched them both.

"I think…Oh! I know." Amy dug into the crack between her mattress and the wall and pulled out the missing cord. The crisis was handled, but I was still caught up in their interaction. At some point in the night, they'd moved on to pet names.

They'd probably swapped numbers too.

"Ginger? You ready?" Amy asked me. I blinked and looked away after I realized I was staring at Danni's hands on Amy's hips.

"Yeah. Let's go." I waited for them to walk out and locked the door behind us. The whole way to the cafeteria, they blissfully ignored me, completely wrapped up in each other and more pet names. Danni even chased Amy across the quad, threatening to tickle her. I was glad Amy was happy, but I just wasn't in the mood to be their third wheel. Amy noticed. Once we grabbed our food she cornered me by the juice dispenser.

"Hey, what's going on with you?"

"Nothing." I looked around to make sure we were alone. Danni was across the cafeteria, digging into her own lunch.

"You're all quiet. Is everything okay with…C?" I snickered as her eyes darted around. I wasn't planning on mentioning Camila's name in public either. I cleared my throat and glanced around.

"I mean there's nothing to be 'okay' about. We had a good time last night. I'll see her again when I see her."

"Is that what you want?"

"Amy, what are you talking about?"

"I just mean, maybe you...It's obvious you like her," she blurted out the last part.

"Is it? Because you've seen us together when?"

"Ginger, you're so serious about everything. Well, just school. I'm not saying you're uptight, but it seems like she's the only thing that distracts you."

"I'm glad I'm not too uptight." I scoffed. "Listen. I do like spending time with C, but it's nothing beyond spending time. Let's just consider what and who she is, all that stuff Benny told us, and then maybe you'll see that even if I did like her, it wouldn't matter. Right?"

"No. You're right," Amy reluctantly agreed. Then that perky grin spread across her face. "But Danni did say you're the only girl who has spent time alone with her, you know, since initiation."

Yeah, because of my blood. "We were just talking. It's nothing."

"Whatever. I still think you like her."

"Great. You keep thinking that. I'm going to eat." Amy drove me insane, but she did care about me and my feelings. It was hard to stay annoyed with her.

We grabbed our trays and Amy followed me to a secluded table where the girls had saved us seats.

"Danni asked me to be her girlfriend," she said as we walked.

"I figured as much. What did you tell her?"

"Nothing. After we got ready for bed, she just asked me."

"That's good. I'm very happy for you."

"Liar."

I winked at her and plopped next to Laura. She'd put on about eight pounds of Goth makeup and a tutu, but traded in her fishnet sleeves I'd seen her wear around campus for an ABO shirt. It worked for her.

"I thought we weren't allowed to talk about this stuff," she said to Cleo. Apparently, we'd missed the beginning of a juicy conversation.

"Not with people outside of Alpha Beta Omega or OBA," Cleo said.

"So we can talk to the boys about stuff?" Anna-Jade muttered.

"Yes, A.J. We can." Anna-Jade blushed at Cleo's teasing reply.

"So what exactly happens when they change you?" Mel urged Cleo to go on. Cleo looked over at Benny, our source on the inside thanks to her step-dad. Benny coughed like she was about to lower her voice. It was almost comical the way we all leaned in closer to hear.

"I've only seen it done once, but basically they drain you and then you drink from at least four others. The most powerful is your primary. They're the demon you have to answer to. Or if you break the law, they will be the one who has to answer for you."

"Does it hurt?" Amy asked.

"Of course it hurts. You die." I'd been trying to ignore the fact that Samantha had joined us for lunch, but her bitchiness made it impossible. So what if she did have a point.

"I've heard it's different for everyone. If you fight the change, it is painful," Benny went on.

"The pain doesn't bother me. It's the shit afterward you have to deal with," Cleo said.

"What shit?" I asked.

"It's a complicated process. Most demons live in small groups with a specific feeder, but the house has to be sealed from sunlight," Benny said.

"I think you're forgetting something." I didn't feel good about the scowl on Cleo's face. Benny didn't either, but she let Cleo go on.

"They have to wipe you off the human grid. Fake your death, all this shit. No way I'm letting my mama think I'm dead. Immortality is not worth giving Cynthia Jones a heart attack." There were a lot of nervous laughs around the table, but Cleo brought up a very serious issue. Becoming a vampire meant giving up your entire human life, and that just wasn't something I was willing to do. There was no way I could let my family believe I was dead.

"Hey, Benny, how about you don't bring your bad news to breakfast anymore?" Laura said playfully.

"I'm sorry," Benny said back. "I'm just being honest. I'll sugarcoat from now on."

"No, B. You keep it real. It's the only way they'll learn," Cleo said with a firm nod.

"Is your mom still…like us?" Mel asked Benny.

"Yes. She's waiting until I graduate."

"Why then?" Amy asked exactly what I'd been thinking.

"My step-dad can't go out in the daytime. She didn't like the idea of me facing the day alone. So if I decide to, with my step-dad's permission, we'll both go through with the switch after graduation."

"Nope." Cleo laughed. "Even with your step-dad's permission. Not doing it."

I looked up as Amy whispered to Danni. "Do you want to?"

Danni kissed her on the cheek with a dismissive smile. "I don't know, babe. I haven't decided yet."

"So what are the perks?" Sam asked.

Benny paused, probably contemplating what someone like Samantha would see as a plus. "You've seen what their blood can do. There's the issue of immortality, and when it comes to money or possessions, you want for nothing."

There was more that Benny wasn't saying, like how vampires could change form, but I didn't want to be the know-it-all to bring that piece of information up. All that would do was bring more attention to me and the time I was spending with Camila so I kept my mouth shut.

The conversation slowly shifted then. We went on talking about the sister-queens and gathering other useful bits of info. Camila and the others needed to feed three times a week. When school wasn't in session, they had various feeders scattered around the city, and from the way Benny explained it, around the country. They didn't mind if they had to travel to feed. I decided it would be better if I didn't think about who would be lucky enough to experience Camila's many oral talents at any given time. The sex wasn't necessary, and Camila wasn't mine. Other than Benny, I knew none of the other girls would turn her down if a simple drawing of blood turned into something more. She had to feed to live and I just had to deal with it.

After we took a few minutes to give Anna-Jade a hard time about Micah, Cleo and Danni gave us the rundown for the coming week. We had our first chapter meeting on Tuesday night. Friday night was movie night at the ABO house. Saturday morning, all the fraternities were hosting a pancake breakfast for the sororities. The brothers of OBA would issue our formal invites sometime during the week. Saturday night, the Chi Nus were throwing an honest-to-God toga party, but it wasn't mandatory. Sunday night would be spent in the ABO kitchen getting ready for our first bake sale to benefit Types of Hope.

Of course, Camila was on my mind. I couldn't wait to see her again, but the weekend ahead sounded pretty good without the prospect of spending the night in her arms. You couldn't go wrong with all-you-can-eat pancakes and hanging out with the girls.

❖

The moment we left the cafeteria on Sunday, things in my life went from pretty darn interesting to utter crap. Micah and an agitated Greg were waiting for Anna-Jade and me at the library. I had an idea of what was pissing him off. If we'd been alone, I would have asked Greg if he wanted to talk, but he was being such a moody jerk that staying with the group seemed like the better move.

Halfway through the afternoon, Samantha showed up. She'd finished her work over at the paper early and decided to come study with Greg. And by study, I mean rub his leg under the table as we finished our lab report. She appeared to lighten his mood, but I still didn't like her.

I left them right before dinner, grabbed a sandwich from the cafeteria, and ate in my room. Amy sent me a text at eight thirty telling me she was spending the night with Danni. She texted me again to remind me to check in with Cleo at nine. I thanked her because I had completely forgotten. I worked on my paper until midnight when I finally climbed into bed. At one, I stopped waiting to hear from Camila. If she could sense me, she could at least get my phone number from Cleo.

Monday morning, things got worse. The late hours I'd spent with Camila finally caught up with me. I hit the snooze button four times and was almost late for class. That night Amy invited me to join her over at the house, but I passed. I was determined to get some sleep. Instead, I tossed and turned until two a.m., hoping to hear from Camila. She didn't call.

Tuesday was more of the same, except Greg was even more pissy in lab. I was starting to think I should carry Samantha around in my backpack just to get him to chill out. He did apologize after class, explaining in hushed, coded tones, that Rodrick liked to feed more than three times a week and even after receiving a thorough apology from his father, Greg hadn't come up with a plan about getting out of OBA. I was too tired to care.

That night we had a real chapter meeting that was outrageously dull. Omi was the only sister-queen to show up, and she didn't say anything. The entire time, all I could think about was Camila. She didn't poke her head in after the meeting or call me later that night, but Rodrick did. He wanted a sample of blood.

Wednesday after class I met him and Natasha at the ABO house, down in Natasha's quarters. Camila wasn't joking. Her whole apartment was decorated in neons. It looked like she was set up for the ultimate 80s themed party, but I was distracted from the décor by the two vampires who greeted me. I realized how comfortable I'd become with Camila. Vampires are pretty intimidating when they weren't the object of your own obsessive lust. Rodrick towered over me as he led me to the couch.

"We are lucky to have found you," Natasha said. She sat on the arm of a nearby chair, watching with casual interest while Rodrick had me roll up my sleeve.

"What makes you say that?" I winced as Rodrick slid the needle into my arm.

"We prefer to take care of our own," Rodrick answered with a wink. I looked at the blood filling the vial and wondered how much of that notion was true. From latchkey kid to orphan to Carmichael to vampire foster undergrad? I wondered what exactly had happened with my mother and if the events leading up to my birth could have saved her from herself. The blood of these demons had somehow kept me alive, not to mention the bang up job its magic had worked on Benny's acne. Having no clue when I'd hear from Camila again, I took a chance.

"Can I ask you something?"

"Of course." Rodrick handed my sample off to Natasha then swabbed my arm. She stuck the sample in a satchel on the chair. Then they both moved to the couch beside me. I don't know what I expected from them, but it was sweet to see Natasha settle comfortably in Rodrick's arms, almost like they were a normal couple and not part of some vampire underworld.

"Do you really live forever?" I asked, looking up as Natasha rubbed Rodrick's forearm.

She looked back at Rodrick, but he kept his eyes on me. "We can be killed, but I think you're asking if we die of old age," he said. Now that he brought up the distinction I realized I wanted to know the answer to both questions.

"We don't know. In our master's time there have been recalls of his children, twice."

"What do you mean by a recall?"

"There are rules we must follow to stay in our God's good graces. Our identities must be kept a secret from humans from whom we do not feed, and we are not to act in any way that will alter the lives of humans on a large scale. Twice those rules were broken and twice the earth was swept clear of all demons like us," Natasha said.

"But not your master?" I asked.

"Losing all of their vampire children was punishment for not keeping them in order," Natasha said. "It was many years ago and we were both born into this life centuries later."

"What did they do? The violators?" I wanted to know if we were talking about jaywalking with your fangs out or staging a major coup.

"There was a major uprising in Egypt one thousand years ago, but it was not recorded in your history. Many humans were sacrificed to a vampire who had become a slave to his own power."

"And the other time?"

"I think your school books would call it the Black Death," Rodrick said.

I gasped, unable to hide my shock. Natasha touched my elbow gently. "We didn't cause the sickness, but vampires flocked to the region and fed freely without permission then tossed their kill among the plague victims. They didn't bother to hide what they were."

My stomach started to churn. "Could something like that happen again?"

"You must know, Ginger. We were born human, but our master and his lot were born in hell and what we have become is rooted in genuine evil. Only a pure heart can overcome that part of our reborn nature. Now, our master is very careful to select humans who can handle the burden to join our flock," Rodrick said.

"It could happen," Natasha went on. "Anything is possible. But we do our best now to prevent those types of incidents, and the sorority helps. You girls help." I tried to let her hopeful grin comfort me. "With our bonds with our feeders in place, our master was able to secure our eternal judgment on an individual basis. If there is another global sweep of our kind, only those who are truly at fault will be damned. Still, we take violations very seriously. Those who cross our master are terminated immediately and banished right back to hell."

"How do you terminate a vampire?" I asked. I braced myself for a gruesome answer when Natasha pulled Rodrick's hand closer to her stomach.

"You have to remove the head or the heart and expose it to the sun. The rest of the body will follow once the vitals are destroyed."

"Oh." Not a pleasant way to go. "Do the other girls know about this?" Did Benny know?

Rodrick's lip turned up in a slight grin. I could see the tip of his fang. "We try not to tell humans how to kill us. It's difficult for us to be overpowered, but people like to find ways."

I finally saw the need for the sorority then. Their master was here to stay and if he'd come up with an arrangement that kept his vampires happy and fed and the girls and the OBA boys safe, then why rock the boat.

"So why are you telling me? I'm still technically a human, aren't I?"

"We intend to find out," Rodrick replied, nodding toward the satchel. Somehow his answer didn't help.

"I'd like to stay that way." I didn't want my feelings on changing species to offend them, but I had to be clear.

"Then you will have it that way," Natasha said sweetly.

We talked for a little longer, and the more time I spent with them, I saw that vampires like Rodrick and Natasha were not the kind I should fear. Rodrick's size was still a bit intimidating, but they were cute together. They answered more of my questions, the whole time holding hands or exchanging gentle touches. They let me know I was clear to go back to church with Mom and Dad come Christmas time. I wouldn't catch on fire if I set foot on hallowed ground. Even if I was suddenly craving the taste of human blood, garlic was still safe to eat, and if someone came at me with a wooden stake, Natasha reminded me I had bigger problems than what made up my blood. The decision to let the other girls know about my mother and the mysteries of her pregnancy was completely up to me. Rodrick advised that it would be best for me to wait until they knew exactly how much vampire blood was in my system and how it affected me. I thought it was a good idea.

I spent the rest of the day with the girls, still a little worried about what my DNA would say, but it was nice to know I had Natasha and Rodrick to talk to. I just wished I would have talked to Camila instead of spending nearly every waking moment I had with her naked.

By Friday I was a complete mess. I'd slept like crap all week. The little sleep I got was riddled with frustrating dreams about a certain vampire—horrible, mocking dreams where she always seemed to be just out of reach. When I wasn't dreaming of her slipping through my fingers, there were nightmares about my birth mother, the kind I hadn't had in years. Chest-crushing images of her smile melting, blood dripping from her hair. One night there had even been a man, tall with no hair and no face, holding her close to his chest as a gash across her neck oozed onto the floor.

The heel of his hand was pressed to her bulbous stomach. As a kid I'd always tried to scream during nightmares of my mother, but the sound never came. It was no different this time. I'd wake in my bed, sweating and sobbing breathlessly, hurting even more that Camila was nowhere around.

At least the anger and frustration, both physical and emotional, drove me to ace my stats test.

After class all I wanted was a self-indulgent cry and a nap, but that wasn't going to happen. The head of the department had arranged for the chair of the Professional Football Athletic Trainers Organization to come speak to all the exercise science majors. There had been a lot of grumbling about why the hell they'd have him give a talk on a Friday night, but his Q and A was scheduled to end at eight. Just enough time for me to go back to the room and grab my stuff for movie night.

I trudged back to the dorm, contemplating paying Laura or Mel for a massage. Or Anna-Jade. She had little hands. I was beat, and my mind was a muddled mess. So muddled that I didn't register the moans coming from my room before I opened the door. For the first time all week, I actually wished I had the pleasure of walking in on Amy and Danni. And I wished I'd known that Friday was Amy's night to feed Camila.

## Chapter Seven

Even with Amy draped all over her, it was impossible to miss how gorgeous Camila looked. She wore a red hooded sweater under her motorcycle jacket and skintight jeans under her knee-high riding boots. I would have complimented her, but I was too busy fighting the intense wave of rage and arousal that swept through my body. Amy was fully dressed, which didn't matter. She was grinding her crotch against Camila's stomach. The layers of clothes between them probably added to the friction quite nicely.

Camila and I stared at each other. She didn't release Amy's neck. Her fingers were tangled in her blond waves to keep Amy in place. I could tell from the way Camila's brow contorted that she was frowning at me. I realized then that I was standing in the hallway with the door wide open while a vampire was making love to my roommate's jugular. I quickly stepped inside and closed the door.

Camila didn't look like she had any intention of letting my presence interrupt her feeding, so I didn't let their erotic exchange stop me from getting ready for movie night. Amy's chorus of moans and grunts grew more urgent as I grabbed my pajamas. I'd crash with Cleo and Benny. The pair of boxers I liberated from Todd and my Reading Memorial High T-shirt were as sexy as it was going to get. A couple pairs of fresh undies, some clean jeans, my favorite green V-neck, and a black ABO hoodie to wear to pancakes the next morning would be enough to cover me until I came back to the dorm.

As I was shoving everything in my bag, Amy came with a loud "Oh God!" and then after a few moments of nothing but harsh breathing, I heard her shuffle off Camila's lap. Amy cleared her throat and excused herself to the bathroom. A clean up in aisle two was definitely in order after busting that loud of a nut.

I froze at the edge of my bed, my knees pressed into the crappy mattress, my throat and chest clenching in frustration. I squeezed my eyes shut and tried to clear my head. It didn't work, but my hands and feet decided to cooperate. I snatched the last few things I needed—my phone charger and my brush—then I sat on my bed to text Mom.

"Amy let me know about your seminar. I dropped by to give you two a ride to the house," Camila said hesitantly. The sound of her voice tore at my stomach. So sweet and warm, nothing like the person it belonged to. It annoyed me that she had the balls to actually say anything to me, but I refused to be a brat about it. I wouldn't give her the satisfaction of knowing all the hateful things that were running through my head. "Yeah. Whatever. Fuck you, bitch," was not the reply to go with.

I looked up from my phone and ignored the pained way she was looking at me.

"Thank you. I'm pretty tired. A ride would be great."

I glanced over when Amy came back in the door, looking flushed and refreshed.

"I'm ready," she said as she glanced nervously between Camila and me.

I locked up after Camila and Amy stepped into the hallway, then followed them down to the car. When we reached the curb it was obvious how out of it I had been when I'd come back from the Q and A. I hadn't noticed the matte black Range Rover parked in the fire lane.

I was tempted to join Amy in the backseat, but I could tell by the way she closed the car door behind her that she was giving me a chance to ride up front with Camila. I hopped in and forced myself not to show just how impressed I was with her car. The cream-colored leather smelled just like her and the fancy dashboard settings were lit up like a very expensive Christmas tree. It was easily the nicest car I'd ever seen or sat in.

Camila started the SUV, and a low R&B tune came through the speakers. I knew the song, instantly remembered singing along to it with Todd and Mom, but those happy memories only made the trip to the ABO house worse. I wanted to be at home with my family instead of riding in the dark with a vampire I had been stupid enough to fall for. There was no way to be slick about wiping the few tears from my eyes, so I did it quickly with the sleeve of my fleece.

We rode in silence for a few minutes, time I took to calculate just how many days of the silent treatment Camila deserved. A month sounded fair. Starting tonight. Totally appropriate for the week of silence she'd given me.

And then Amy's cell rang. From the way she giggled like a fool, it had to be Danni.

"Hi…Yeah, we're on our way right now. Okay. I'll see you soon…I love you, too." It took everything I had not to jump from the moving vehicle.

We pulled up in front of the house and Camila put the car in park. I reached to grab my bag, and I almost escaped before Camila gently put her hand on my thigh. I froze. The feeling of her palm burned through my jeans. She moved her hand before I had a chance to slap it away.

"Ginger will be up in a minute," she told Amy.

The song changed to one I loved even more.

"Okay," Amy said slowly. I looked over my shoulder. Amy strolled out with her hand on the door. Instantly, my anger with her drifted away. She had this desperate look on her face that told me no matter what Camila said, Amy wouldn't leave me until she knew I was okay.

I gave her a slight nod of reassurance, which she took as her cue to hop out of the car. None of this was her fault, and I had every intention of apologizing to her for being so cold. As soon as I got this horrible conversation over with.

Avoiding Camila's gaze, I watched Amy run up the front steps. She stopped halfway to the door, and three other freshman, Ebony, Gwen, and Maddie, ran to meet her. They were safe inside before Camila said anything. Her silken voice floated over the soft music. I missed the way it used to soothe and excite me, even if it had only been for a few days.

"I'd prefer it if I didn't have to read your thoughts, so would you care to tell me what's the matter?"

"Do you really want to know?"

"Yes. I do."

I thought about how happy Amy and Danni were. I pictured just how cute Micah and Anna-Jade looked walking hand-in-hand across the quad. I'd wanted that, and I would never have it with Camila. I thought of how things had been just a week ago, the night Camila and I met and how shitastic things had been since. Now seemed like a perfect time to draw a new line with her. There was no way I could spend another minute wishing she wanted a relationship we couldn't have.

I looked back toward the house and took a deep breath, pushing my sadness aside and replacing it with some bitterness and a little rage that had been fighting to get to the surface. Then I worked up the nerve to let Camila know just how crazy I was before she formed any more opinions about me. Or before I spent another day infatuated with her. It was better to just spill the beans now and have her kick me out of the car so we could both just get on with our lives.

She could fondly remember me as the little lunatic who fell for her after two nights of hooking up, and I'd think back on the forty-eight hours I'd actually thought I was adult enough to handle no-strings-attached sex with the most beautiful creature I'd ever seen.

"Fine." I turned in the seat to face Camila. "I'll tell you what's bothering me."

She cut the engine off and settled back against the leather. Her expression was calm, but that didn't ease the air between us.

"I'm in love with you. Well, obsessed might be a better word considering I don't actually know enough about you for it to be considered love. But yeah, I'm obsessed with you. I've been thinking about you non-stop, all week. Actually, that's not true. I masturbated thinking about you last week, so really I've been obsessed for about ten days now. I didn't sleep at all because I was praying you would call me."

She hadn't even blinked so I just kept going.

"And then I spent hours and hours just thinking about how stupid it was for me to feel anything for you. You're, well, you and I was actually sad because I want to be with you and we can't be together. Then, just when I'm sort of coming to grips with the fact that I'm crazy and pathetic, I come back to my room to find Amy feeding you. I forgot what she sounds like when she's coming, so thanks for that." I started losing some steam. I took another deep breath and drove my point home.

"That's what's wrong with me. I'm obsessed with you and there's nothing I can do about it. Oh, and I have to spend the next four years knowing that you're making my roommate come at least once a week, but that's none of my business, so we can ignore that part," I said as I slapped my thighs.

Finally, she blinked. "Is there anything else?"

"Nope. That's it. I'm gonna head inside. I hope you enjoy your weekend."

"Ginger."

"What?"

"At any point were you planning to tell me how you feel?"

"No." Why would I do that?

"You've assumed I have no feelings for you, that I've been avoiding you, and that I intentionally fed from Amy to rub all of that in your face?"

I thought for a quick second. "Well, yes and no. I don't think you were rubbing Amy in my face, but the avoiding and the no feelings, that sounds about right."

"I apologize for the situation with Amy. I need to feed, but I understand that doing it in the space you share with her was a mistake. I won't do it again."

"I don't care. Seriously. I know now, so it's not a big deal."

"I do care. It will not happen again." She looked down for a moment and then turned toward me. I think she was actually nervous. I didn't think vampires could get nervous.

"I had to fire one of my guys down at my tattoo shop because he's been self-medicating with meth. I think you heard part of that conversation on Sunday morning."

"Yeah. I remember," I muttered.

"He came back on Monday and got himself shot three times trying to rob the shop. That kept me busy through Wednesday night. That's why I wasn't there when you met with Rodrick and Natasha. I wanted to be there. They enjoyed spending time with you by the way."

"I like them too. And I'm sorry about the shop."

"Jamie is fine now, but thank you. I didn't call you or come see you last night because Cleo told me you had a statistics test today. I didn't want to distract you from your studying."

"Oh." Okay, now I was feeling bad.

"I thought about you all week. I almost switched forms today and followed you to class, but I thought that would have been a little insane."

"I wouldn't have minded," I said quietly.

She sat up quickly, a scowl touching her face. "And where are you getting these ideas that we can't be together?"

"Cleo and Benny—"

"What? They told you I wasn't allowed to date? Listen, the two of them may know a lot about my kind and how our world operates, but they don't know a thing about my personal life or the personal lives of any of the other sister-queens. A while back, Faeth dated one of the girls for eight years. Kina has been seeing some kindergarten teacher for the last six months.

"I can do whatever the fuck I want. I didn't say anything to you because you've been through plenty of changes lately, including joining a sorority against your will." I looked away from her wry grin as she went on.

"I didn't want you to feel pressured into a relationship with me because it would be complicated, but if you wanted me, it would be something. Please don't listen to the girls when it comes to things between the two of us."

"Because it'll lead to a conversation like this?"

"Exactly. So, Red, what do you want?"

"I…I…" I wasn't expecting her to ask me that.

"Because I'll take you out tomorrow night on a real date. If you'll let me. We'll eat at one of the restaurants I own, and if you'll allow it, I'll make love to you in the best penthouse suite of my best hotel—till about four a.m. I have to be back before sunrise."

"You want to go out with me?" I said. At this point, the bitterness and the rage were replaced by something like sunflowers and daisies.

"Yes." She reached across the center console and tucked my hair behind my ear. My skin tingled where her palm brushed against my cheek. "We can go out tonight if you want to, blow off the girls."

"I'd like to watch movies with you tonight. And I need a little time to find something to wear on our date."

"I'll take you however I get you, Red, but I won't complain if you want to get all prettied up. Are you sure there's nothing else?"

"I want your number. Right now."

"Your phone, please."

I dug my cell out of my pocket and handed it to her.

"And what's your last name?"

Before she answered, she got out of the car and walked around to my side, entering her number into my cell as she went. When she opened my door for me, I hopped down and let her slide my phone back in my hand as she took my bag from me. Her hips guided me off to the side so she could close my door. The grooves in the rear handle pressed into my back. I barely noticed as Camila leaned into me. Our faces were only inches apart. Our breasts were touching. My nipples were instantly hard, and I realized how hard her nipples were, even through all our layers of clothes. And with a dull ache, my pussy started to drip.

She looked at my lips, licking her own. "My driver's license says Sanchez. I change it every ten years."

She leaned in closer and my head automatically fell to the side. Her warm breath on my neck made me drip even more.

"Why would you think I wouldn't want to be with you?" she asked.

"Um, I don't know. I'm a college freshman and you're…"

"An undead lady creature of the night?"

"That and I…"

She pulled back, hearing the hesitation in my voice. "What?" The genuine concern on her face melted my heart. I had to be honest with her.

I took a deep breath and blurted the rest out. I told Camila everything that Benny and Cleo had told us, about how the sister-queens viewed us and how they only wanted us for our blood and for the sex, which had been my suspicion from the very beginning. I even spilled to her how jealous I was of Anna-Jade, Amy, and their new relationships. Even Rodrick and Natasha. And then I told her that I understood we had no real future together. I'd be gone in four years. I wrapped things up with the reasons I didn't want to be a vampire myself. I was cool with being in on the secret, but I loved my family and I had no need to serve the master in any new ways.

"I do want to go out with you," I said. "But I understand there's an expiration date to us. Even if your master was okay with me changing all the way, I can't leave my parents. It would kill them if they thought I was dead."

"Red, you're so smart, but you think too damn much. You understand you started our relationship and planned our breakup before I even knew you liked me? Sorry, before I knew you were obsessed with me."

"When you put it that way…"

"Let's try a date first and then we'll discuss your plans for after graduation. Maybe somewhere in there we can get to know each other a little better. No changing necessary. Okay?"

"Okay."

"Okay. And so you know…" She dropped her voice to a whisper and leaned in close again. This time her lips brushed against mine. "I'm pretty obsessed with you too."

The next thing I knew, we were kissing, her soft lips slowly caressing mine. God, I'd missed her so much. Her arm came around my waist and I wrapped my arms around her shoulders. Our breasts rubbed together. It was a perfect kiss until her tongue slid past my lips.

The most mouthwatering taste hit my tongue, something beyond her own delicious spice. It sent a tingle over the crown of my head and straight down to my clit, followed immediately by a thousand-volt shock to my heart.

I jerked back, covering my mouth.

"Ginger, what's wrong? Did I hurt you?"

I shook my head. My tongue was still tingling, my skin vibrating. I squeezed my eyes shut and tried to locate the source of the pain, but there wasn't any. There never was, only tiny aftershocks in my fingers and toes, a jolt I confused with pain. After a moment, I opened my eyes and slowly pulled my hand away. Camila gently placed her hands on either side of my face.

"What happened?" she asked.

I swallowed, scanning her face before I answered. I didn't want to freak her out even more.

"When you drink our blood—human blood—what does it taste like?"

Her eyes shot wide as she processed the question. Her hands dropped to my shoulders.

"I, uh, I guess it has its own unique flavor. I wouldn't know what to compare it to."

"I think I just tasted Amy." My face had to be glowing in the dark. I couldn't believe what I was saying.

"Oh." She grimaced. "I'm sorry. Did it make you sick?"

"No. I-I like the way it tastes." It sounded so wrong, but it was the truth. I shuddered as the thought ran through me again. I knew the flavor of Amy's blood now and I enjoyed it. The taste was delicious, sweet with a zipping tang, like berries electrified.

I gazed at Camila's face in the golden glow of the streetlight. She'd been living off the stuff. It would have been a little hypocritical of her to judge me for wanting to taste more, but that's when the weight of what I was hit me. The daylight didn't affect me, and I couldn't vanish into thin air, but I had a thirst for human blood. The demon was in me.

I took a deep breath. The pocket of hysteria inside was balancing on the edge between laughter and tears. Camila picked up on my anxiety before I crashed either way. She stroked my hair affectionately, kissed me softly on the cheek. The heat from her touch helped calm my heart.

"Just think of it as another thing to add to the list. You can see through my cloak. You can feel my influence, but you can't fight it, and now we know you do like the taste of human blood. And there's nothing wrong with that. The same part of you that craves was the same thing that saved your mother's life. And the life of her baby."

"You're right." I let out a deep breath and welcomed Camila's arms around my waist. I'd spent the whole week sulking over my lack of love life that I didn't stop to consider what having vampire blood pumping through my veins meant. And I was angry at myself for assuming all sorts of things about Camila's actions and motivations. A reality check was in order, on all fronts.

I don't know how long we stood there together. The tingling faded. My body stopped reacting to the blood and started reacting to the body tucked tightly against mine. The firm but slow sweep of her hands up and down my back, the baby soft leather of her jacket under my own fingers, her amazing scent. The night weather had begun to get cooler, but I would have spent hours in front of the ABO house as long as she didn't let me go.

A deep sigh escaped when I realized that wasn't going to happen. There was a movie to be watched, and I had sorority bonding to do. Damn sisterhood. My mind was exhausted. All I wanted was the heat from Camila's body. Add her bed. Minus the clothes.

She took a small step back. "I'll be more careful next time. Are you sure you're okay?"

I looked down at myself, patted my stomach and my chest like an idiot.

"Yeah. I'm fine. That was pretty weird, though."

"Come. Why don't you go join the girls? I'll let Rodrick know about your reaction." She took my hand and led me to the front door.

"When will he know about my blood makeup?"

"By Monday. We'll hold off on any other 'experiments' until then, and I'll be sure to brush after I feed from now on," she said.

I glanced at her just in time to catch her smiling at me. Then I giggled like a total dork. In a weird way, her fangs made the grin even sweeter. Screw an apology. I owed Amy a solid for dragging me through Rush. Ignorance about my blood would have been one thing, but I never would have met Camila without Amy's perky insistence. And maybe Todd's nudging helped. Missing out on any part of Camila would have been an absolute shame. Even if I'd become a little obsessed.

As I reached for the door handle, there was one more thing I wanted to clear up.

"So we're dating now?"

"Sure." Camila's upper lip twitched into a little grin. "What's on your mind?"

"I'm just wondering what or even if I should tell the girls. Cleo and Amy love to give me shit about you."

"Yes, I caught that. You tell them whatever you want, Red. If you want to tell them I'm your girlfriend, you can. Or you can tell them to mind their own business. It's completely up to you."

"I like the way the girlfriend thing sounds," I muttered in reply, biting my lip.

"Then I'll tell Cleo to shut the fuck up." I laughed at her toothy grin. The porch light made her canines shine. "You're sure you're okay?"

"Yes. Good as new."

"Okay. I'll see you in a few minutes," she said, touching my cheek with the back of her hand.

This time, I kissed her, but just a quick peck on the lips. Then I slipped inside before we ended up making out on the porch.

❖

I met the bright light of the foyer like a new woman. Again, my life had changed in a matter of minutes. Camila knew the truth, and

I hadn't died of embarrassment. Not only was I still upright, but she actually liked me back. I damn near skipped past Kyle and Julia on my way up to Cleo's room, greeting them with perky hellos. They looked at me like I was nuts, but I didn't care. I had a girlfriend now. I also had a bizarre interest in biting Amy, but that wasn't the point.

There was music coming from Cleo's room. When I opened the door, I felt like I'd stepped in on an impromptu Soul Sisters of ABO meeting. All the African-American girls in our sorority were there. Cleo was singing along with Carlos Santana while flipping through a magazine. Ebony was watching Layna's handiwork as she put the finishing touches on a fresh set of micro braids in Irene's hair.

In high school, I'd spent a weekend in Atlanta with my friend Morgan and her family. Her cousin Shanice ran a salon out of her house. She'd walked me through some simple braiding techniques, but nothing as fancy as what Layna was doing.

I stood in the doorway and looked over at Cleo. "Should I come back, or is the meeting almost over?" Ebony and Layna laughed. Irene smiled and then winced. Her new do was a little too tight for her to show any drastic emotions. Just then, Benny came out of the bathroom. She'd already changed into her pajamas.

Cleo flipped the pages of her *People*. "Amy and Danni will be back in a sec. Either way, you're black by association. And B here's got booty for days." She reached forward and slapped Benny on the ass. Benny didn't even blink. She just plopped on the bed and curled up with her cheek on Cleo's thigh. I knew they were just friends, but they would have made a cute couple.

"How'd your stats test go?" Benny asked me.

"Oh, good. I think I got an A."

"Is that what you're smiling about?" Ebony asked.

As a reflex, I frowned. "I'm not smiling."

"Well, not now."

Before I could rebut, Cleo's bedside phone rang.

"Aloha." Her eyes shot to me. Crap. It was Camila.

"Oh really?…Okay," she said. "Sounds good." She tucked the phone against her shoulder. "I promise…Okay. Later." She hung up and turned to me. "Anything you want to tell us?"

"I have no idea what you're talking about," I said casually. I walked into the bathroom and closed the door behind me. I quickly changed but took my time brushing my teeth and putting up my hair. I'll admit, I was giddy. I'd become a pro at publicly denying my feelings for Camila. Now I had to think of what to say since it was okay for us to be "out" to the rest of the girls.

Danni and Amy were perched on Cleo's bed when I came out of the bathroom. They were both pink cheeked and giggly. Clearly, a quickie had been in order the moment Amy came upstairs. I felt bad for being angry and jealous and even worse when it dawned on me that Amy had probably been thinking of Danni during Camila's feeding. Amy had been embarrassingly honest about her feelings for Danni. It was so stupid of me to think that interactions between Amy and Camila were anything beyond their arrangement as blood donor and vampire. I had some serious apologizing and explaining to do.

After Cleo was done harassing me.

"Out with it, bitch." Cleo snickered.

"Okay. Fine. I have a date tomorrow."

"With Camila?" Amy squealed.

"Yes. Tomorrow night."

Amy squealed again.

"But I have no idea what to wear. My closet is full of going to class stuff and maybe looking decent for brunch stuff. Not date stuff."

"Where are you going?" Layna asked. She sprayed some glossy mist on Irene's hair and gently spread it over the tight braids with her palms.

"I don't know for sure. Dinner I guess and then we might spend the night at a hotel."

"Ooh, girl," Cleo sang.

"We are getting you some lingerie."

"Amy—" That's as far as I got before she cut me off.

"No. Have you seen the underwear she has?" she asked Cleo.

"Yeah. We broke into your room to get your sizes," she said with an odd grin.

I did a double take in Cleo's direction before turning my attention back to Amy. I'd talk to her about my feelings on their necessary breaking and entering later.

"She hasn't complained about my underwear so far," I told them.

"Probably because she took them off the first chance she got," Danni joked. Sort of.

My mouth popped open as if I had some sort of response, but she was right. I hadn't spent much time fully dressed around her. And now I was seriously regretting the revenge pj's I'd grabbed for tonight.

Just then Barb stuck her head in the door.

"Come on, ladies. Movie time."

"After pancakes, I'll take you to the mall," Cleo said to me, leaving no room for argument.

The girls headed for the door, but I hung back. I needed to talk to Amy now.

"I'll be right there. Amy, hold on one sec." She kissed Danni on the cheek and plopped in Cleo's papasan chair. I closed the door behind Benny and sat on the bed.

"I'm sorry, about being all pissy back there," I said.

"No, I'm sorry. I know how it looked. I didn't mean to…hump her like that." She frowned. "But either way, we both thought you would be gone longer, and she told me she'd nearly missed her feeding with Benny on Wednesday. We were just trying to get it out of the way."

"Yeah, she had a crazy week. Things are just, well, they're complicated." Rodrick's suggestion that I keep the truth about my blood a secret for a while came to mind, but now I wanted to tell Amy. She had become a true friend, and I was starting to see that keeping things from her wasn't helping either of us.

"Promise you won't say anything?" I threw out the unnecessary precaution.

"Of course. I won't even tell Danni, I swear."

"Okay. It's kind of a long story, but somehow I have vampire blood in my system. Camila thinks my birth mom drank from one of them when she was pregnant with me."

"Wow," she gasped. "So what does that mean?"

"I don't know yet, but Camila can't live off my blood. And I think it's just another reason I've been acting so weird about all of this. I already feel like the odd one out, and then I went and fell for the most important vampire in the house."

"Yeah, that makes sense," Amy said. "I promise I won't say anything. And you can talk to me, Ginger. Seriously. I know I get all girlie and annoying sometimes."

"Only sometimes?"

"Okay, a lot of the time. But seriously. I love Danni, but you're my friend. I might not be able to understand the vampire stuff, but you can tell me about it."

"I will. From now on. Trust me, I will."

Amy walked over to the door. "Okay, so what happened in the car?"

"Walk with me," I said as I wrapped my arm around her shoulder. "I'll tell you on the way."

## CHAPTER EIGHT

I didn't know how good a red cami, black flannel pants, and heart-shaped, fuzzy slippers could look until I saw them on my new girlfriend. I did my best not to push the other girls out of the way to get to her, to tell her just how adorably cute and human she looked. Instead, I waited until she greeted them each with a kiss on the cheek as we stepped off the elevator. The hello she had for me was a minty, open-mouth kiss. She'd actually brushed her teeth.

Just for me.

Movie night as a sorority event had started off with a bizarre, yet erotic twist. We met the rest of the girls and the sister-queens in the carpeted room that had been the setting for last week's feedings and sexual festivities. There were still big cushions on the floor, but this time a few comfortable couches had been set up around a large projection screen that dropped from the high ceiling. Tokyo had decided we'd watch *Mean Girls* and *Teen Witch*, but before the movie started, there was the matter of a formal punishment to be handed out, literally.

Samantha had missed curfew twice. The dumbass had gone off with Greg and couldn't be bothered to check in.

Camila gave Sam a piece of her mind, reminding her the nine o'clock check-in time was a rule of Alpha Beta Omega and not a suggestion. When that tongue-lashing was over, Natasha had Samantha wait on all of us, bringing us drinks and candy from a small kitchen in the back. And once everyone was served and settled, Samantha was told to strip.

Her physical appeal was totally overshadowed by her bitchy mouth, but as she pulled off her clothes, it was hard to ignore just how gorgeous Samantha was. Her whole body had a natural olive tone to it. It went perfectly with her brown hair with its sun-kissed highlights. My opinion of her hadn't changed. Still, she was beautiful.

Conversations hushed as everyone's attention settled on Samantha, naked and on her knees between her sister-queen's legs. Natasha had her gently by the chin with one hand and was pinching one of Samantha's light brown nipples with the other. Sam whimpered as she tried to sit still through Natasha's lecture. It had definitely been a sound of frustration and pleasure and not pain.

Natasha took Samantha over her lap. She gave her one hell of a spanking, twelve licks, two for each of the other girls who served Natasha, including Samantha herself. I had no idea how anyone could be turned on by that kind of pain, but it seemed like she was enjoying the punishment. It was hard to look away as each blow hit its mark, and it was hard not to react to every pathetic sound Samantha made.

I enjoyed the spectacle of it all; I couldn't help it. Watching Samantha's whole body blush to pink, the cheeks of her ass flashing to red every time Natasha's hand came down, the sharp jiggle of her breasts as her nipples pointed toward the floor. Or maybe I was caught up sharing the experience with Camila. We were cuddled together on a nearby couch; Danni, Amy, and the girls around us, Camila's arms around me. My pussy had started to ache the moment I stepped off the elevator and into her embrace, but it soaked and throbbed when I felt her lips and her fangs drawing slowly across my neck as we watched Natasha go to work.

The final smack left the whole room silent except for Samantha's breathless sobs. Natasha pulled her upright and immediately sank her teeth into Samantha's neck. She fed deeply, pinching Samantha's bright red ass cheeks the whole time. Samantha came instantly. It didn't seem fair that she would get to come so hard after breaking curfew, but as soon as Natasha was full, Samantha was forced to spend the rest of the night on her knees at Natasha's side, watching the rest of us play.

When the lights were dimmed and the movie started, all around the room, articles of clothing started to hit the floor. I was anxious and prickly, hot and wet from watching Natasha's passionate enforcement of the rules. I eagerly welcomed Camila's strong fingers as they slipped gently between my legs. She'd stroked my clit through my boxers and my underwear, her rhythm bringing her fingers lower, soaking the layers of cotton even more. And then she bit me. My shuddering moan echoed across the room, and I remember thinking in the back of my mind that another of the sister-queens must have decided to feed at that exact moment.

Camila didn't drink from me for long. I don't know if she'd read my mind or if she'd felt the same way, but the second after I came, she turned me in her lap and kissed me, hard and slow. The movie played in the background, coupled with a chorus of cries and lustful sobs that had filled the room. We barely made it halfway through *Mean Girls* before I was begging her to take me back to her bed.

As our bodies rolled together under her satin sheets, I noticed there was a different sense of desire. There were still the fluttering in my stomach and the heat that would rush over my skin. All the physical reactions were the same, but somehow heightened and transformed by an overwhelming sense of happiness. I honestly didn't know emotions like that existed.

I knew what it was like to love someone and to see others in love, but now I finally understood why Danni and Amy were so darn cute together, why Anna-Jade would light up if you even mentioned Micah's name—the unconditional way my mom cared for my dad. Now when Camila reached for me I truly felt weightless. She hadn't said the words, but I felt loved and I felt wanted.

❖

The morning came way too soon. Our shower together was way too short. Camila excused herself to let Cleo, Benny, Danni, and Amy in while I was getting dressed. I heard Amy blab that they were taking me shopping for our date after the pancake breakfast.

I cautiously took the keys when Camila offered to let us drive her Range Rover to the mall. I argued with her for a few minutes when she offered to pay for my outfit. I hadn't spent a cent of the money I'd made bagging groceries over the summer. I was happy to have this new title to our relationship. Okay, I was happy there was an actual relationship at all, but I wasn't looking for a sugar mama. She claimed the girls had shopped on her dime every chance they got. I wasn't buying it. Cleo settled the debate by snatching the wad of cash from Camila and dragging me toward the door. I got Cleo back, though, the second she asked to drive the Range Rover.

"This is some kind of bullshit, and you know it," Cleo grumbled. She channeled her frustration into the satellite radio, changing the station again.

I pulled the Range Rover into the entrance of the mall and bit my cheek. Cackling in Cleo's face would have been a bad move.

"Stop cursing at me and maybe I'll ask her if you can drive back to the house." I glanced over and then snickered at Cleo's poisonous glare. There was no way I was letting her drive Camila's super expensive, custom SUV without her permission.

"I don't like you anymore, Ginger."

"Why?" I coughed, choking on my laugh.

"You used to be so nice."

"No. You thought I was nice. Ask Amy. I'm a total bitch."

"She's right," Amy said playfully from the backseat. "Total bitch."

"Cleo, I'll ask her if you can drive back. I want to get ready at the dorm anyway."

"Make it a real date?" I caught Danni's smile in the rearview mirror.

"Exactly."

We hopped out of the car, and just as the alarm beeped, I heard my cell phone go off. It was a text from Camila.

*How's my baby?*

The fluttering lit off in my stomach just from seeing the words on the display, thinking of who they were from. I knew I must have looked like an idiot, nibbling the inside of my lips as I texted her back, but I didn't care. I typed away and let Amy's voice guide me through the parking lot.

*She's good. I parked her away from the other cars.*

She texted me back right away. *Smartass. I miss you.*

And that was good to know. Pretty freaking sweet actually. I kept myself from singing and dancing, skipping and high-fiving strangers, but I couldn't keep myself from the upper levels of cloud nine. I was cheesing so hard I thought my cheeks would burst.

I texted her right back, telling her I missed her too and asking her if Cleo could drop me off.

*She can drive. Tell her not to crash or she's buying me another whip.*

I stopped walking. *Okay. Can't wait to see you.*

"Damn, Ginger." Cleo grabbed my shoulder and shoved me through the door. "You'll see her in a few hours. Let's go."

I flicked her off and then hit send. "She said you can drive, jerk."

"Did I mention how much I like you and your new girlfriend?"

"Yeah, I bet." I put my phone away, even though it beeped again, and I gave my undivided attention to Amy, our self-assigned shopping coordinator. She walked and talked, leading us to the first designer store. I loved a good skirt and a cute, high-heeled shoe, but I was more of an Old Navy girl, not couture.

"Okay, dress first and then we get you some new pan-tays," Amy drawled.

"Please, just tell me where we're going," I begged. Camila had told Amy and Cleo where she was taking me on our date. Of course they told Danni and Benny. That couldn't be helped, chatty bitches. But Amy was setting a record, keeping a secret from me for a whole three hours. I had zero leverage to make her crack.

"No. Jesus, Ginger. Just let the woman surprise you," Amy whined.

"Fine."

We started searching the racks. I wasn't seeing anything that yelled "My girl will love this," so I pulled out my phone and continued to text Camila, handing the quest for the perfect date dress over to the girls.

"What's your best color?" Danni asked.

"Green," Amy and I said at once.

"We need to get something to match your eyes," Amy said.

We all took a quick glance around. Everything in the store was in different shades of cream and tan and black.

"Let's go somewhere else," Amy said. We all nodded in agreement and followed her across the mall into a co-ed store that catered more to our age bracket and the desires of Amy's color scheme.

"I hate this place. They've never heard of my size," Benny grumbled as we browsed through the racks.

"I know. Let's get Ginger squared away and then you and I can hit the big girl stores," Danni said.

"Here, take this." Cleo handed me the first green dress she found. Then she looked up at us. "So who hates Samantha?"

"I was waiting for you to say something!" Danni said.

"If you guys hate her so much, then why'd you pick her?" I asked.

"Two reasons. Well, three," Danni said. "Natasha thinks she's gorgeous. And as you now know, Natasha loves fucking her. Two, she is serious about journalism, and Camila thinks she'll go far with it. It's always nice to have someone in the media aligned with them."

"That is true," Benny said.

"Three, and she won't tell you this, but her dad was in OBA," Danni said.

"What?" Amy and I yelled. Benny didn't seem surprised by this news.

"Did you know that?" I asked her. She just nodded and held up a shirt, pretending to read the tag.

"Why was she asking all those bitchy questions then? Her dad should have told her everything," I said.

"You'll love this. When she was like ten or something, her dad just up and split. Six months later, he sent her and her mom a shitload of cash and a note explaining that he'd gone nocturnal. And that he was gay."

"Ooo burn, Sam's mom," Amy snorted.

I couldn't help laughing. "That does suck for her mom. And maybe that's why Sam's such a bitch."

"It is sad, but the bitchiness is no excuse," Benny said.

"You're right." My life before the Carmichaels had been terrible, but I knew how to treat people. Samantha was missing that part of her brain.

"How did you find this out?" I asked, taking a green skirt Amy passed to me. I looked at it and passed it back. "I don't like that."

Danni didn't skip a beat. "One of those nights she was too busy to check in, she was up late, over with the boys. Greg fell asleep and she stayed up talking to Micah. Micah told A.J.—"

"And she told us," Cleo said.

"Weird," Amy said, frowning.

"And God, she loved getting spanked last night. That whole teary-eyed lip quiver thing was bullshit. She'd probably miss curfew again if everyone wouldn't really hate her," Danni said.

"So it's okay if we don't all get along?" I asked. Ninety percent of the time, I wanted to punch Samantha in the face. I was relieved to find out those feelings were okay to share with the group.

"Oh, yeah. Our president last year, Kelly—" Cleo started to say.

"Oh, God," Danni added.

"She was the biggest bitch ever, but Kina loved her. And she was so freakin' organized."

"Which is key." I nodded sternly.

"What's she doing now?" Amy asked.

"Works for Congressman Whitmore," Benny said.

I turned to her. "Remind me to keep you close, Benita. What you know scares me a little."

"It should." And then I was rewarded with one of Benny's rare smiles.

"Okay. I like these. Into the dressing room you go," Amy said, shoving four more dresses in my face.

"Before I do that, just tell me where we're going."

"No!" was the unanimous answer I got.

I marched into the dressing room and got a good look at the dresses Amy had picked out for me: a short cocktail number that I knew would make me look like a slut, a green and blue puffy thing that I knew would make me look like a bird, a solid green tank dress with a tutu skirt, which looked ridiculous for the fall weather, and a knit shirt-dress that was too casual. I was in and out of the dressing rooms in record time. All four dresses were cute in theory but looked terrible on me. We tossed those options and moved on to a dozen more stores.

By the time we had a dress, shoes, a clutch, a jacket, a bra and pantie set, and jewelry, I was ready to tap out. Danni and Amy were just warming up, running into Sunglass Hut. I took a seat on the bench outside. Cleo and Benny parked it with me, and the three of us watched Danni and Amy kiss in front of the Prada frames. They both came up for air, giggling like mad when the sales guy got up the nerve to approach them.

"I can't believe Danni found an even bigger spaz to go out with. They're perfect for each other," Cleo said.

"I was just thinking the same thing. Hey," I said as the thought popped into my head. "Do any of the older girls want to change?" Cleo knew what I was getting at.

"Paige is thinking about it. She has no real family to speak of. Her mom's a bitch. Barb's a no. Why? You thinking about your future with our fearless leader?"

"Actually, no. I already told her I wasn't going to do it. I'm kinda in your boat. I can't cut myself off from my family."

"I'll be back." Benny stood and I watched Cleo's expression as she watched Benny walk away. At that moment, I wished I knew what was on Cleo's mind. She was never hushed about anything, except Benny. Now that I wasn't distracted with the doubts of my own sanity, I started to wonder if there wasn't something more between them.

Benny disappeared around the corner, headed toward the restrooms. Cleo took a deep, almost sad breath then turned to me.

"There are ways to keep the ties with your family, but it's just as fucked up."

"How so?"

"Everyone who knows has to become a feeder."

"Oh. Yeah, that's not…"

"Exactly. Mama Jones is a preacher. I still haven't told her I'm gay. No way could I convince her to become demon food. She'd out me and the sister-queens and then have the whole congregation praying for my soul."

"What about your dad?"

Cleo shrugged. "Her word is gospel in the house too. He knows better than to rock that boat, but for me the whole thing's a risk. B's step-dad is an actual demon. Like a real demon. You change and you piss him off, you actually go to hell. It's one thing to think there's a hell and something completely different to know there's a hell. If staying human increases my chance of not going there, that's where I'll place my bets. Mortal I shall remain, Miss Ginge."

She was quiet for a moment. I was quiet too. I figured it was better not say anything about the things Natasha and Rodrick had told me. I glanced toward the restrooms.

"Does Benny want you to change?"

Cleo replied with a deep nod. "She wants to feed me. I just—I can't."

So that was it.

"Is that all she wants?"

Just then Benny came back around the corner. There was no way she had gone to the bathroom. She was back too quickly.

"She won't say. Come here, juicy booty," Cleo said as she pulled Benny into her lap.

"I'm going to crush you," Benny muttered. Cleo's arms went around her waist. She closed her eyes and nuzzled her cheek against the back of Benny's ABO sweatshirt.

"No. You won't."

❖

I gave credit where it was due and admitted Cleo was a better driver than I was. I'd gotten us to the mall safely, but she handled the Range Rover like she was born behind the wheel, weaving smoothly between cars, getting us back across the city in record time. She pulled in front of the dorm, and I couldn't help shaking my head laughing at her. Cleo was so proud driving that thing like she owned it.

"You guys run up and I'll park this bad boy," she said almost seriously.

"Actually, I'm going to get ready by myself," I said, looking back at Amy.

"Are you sure? I can help you with your hair."

"I'm sure." The afternoon had been filled with the kind of pure girlie fun I hadn't experienced in months, but I was exhausted and needed to clear my head. I also hadn't had a single second to myself in the past twenty-four hours. Luckily, they understood. They wished me luck, and before I hopped out, I made them promise they would take pictures at the Chi Nu toga party.

Upstairs in my room, the peace and quiet only gave my mind more room to wander. There was this interesting back-and-forth between the part of me that knew this date was going to lead somewhere good, that this was the beginning of something that had a chance to last, and the part of me that refused to overlook a few truths.

Camila was a vampire. I was not and never would be. My life was going to go on, evolve, and at some point, I was going to die, hopefully of natural causes in my sleep, at age eighty, after the best sex ever. Camila would outlive me and almost everyone we knew. There were other things, like wanting her to meet my family, wanting to know everything about her, that might prove to be difficult. My family couldn't know about her, and something told me that an immortal might have secrets she might never want to share. Past lovers, past lies. We would never really know each other.

But I had to remind myself all of that came with the territory. I wanted her. Bad. And I had to deal with everything that came along with Ms. Sanchez and her never-ending life. I had to trust her and leave our future to the future. Things with her, with Alpha Beta Omega, had turned out surprisingly well so far, and if I could just bring myself to stop stressing so much, things would be okay.

Then Cleo's words about her mother popped into my head. Not her concerns about her mortality, but her fears about her mother finding out she was gay. I knew now I was definitely attracted to women, and I knew that wasn't going to change. There were things I couldn't tell my family about recent developments in my life, but I could tell Todd I was no longer confused. I could tell my mom not to expect to hear about boys from my classes anytime soon. I could tell them both that I had met someone. I'd just skim on the details about who or what that special someone was.

I should have told them in person. This was a huge deal, confessing that Dad would never get a son-in-law to call—well, he had Todd for all that son stuff, but maybe he wanted a son-in-law. My parents were never going to get truly biological grandkids out of me anyway, so I figured Mom wouldn't mind that part, but still I imagined at some point she'd imagined she'd help me pick out cake toppers, a man and woman, or that she'd be telling her friends in her quilting club about the amazing man her daughter had met during her academic adventures near the Chesapeake Bay. None of that was going to happen, so I had to tell them.

I felt like a coward using the 3G network to make this announcement, but it would be a while before I got to see my family, and Camila was better than waiting a while. The phone would have to do. Knowing Mom, she'd find a way to tell Dad before I even got the words out of my mouth.

I knew Todd didn't care who I fell for, and I think my parents felt the same way, but still I found my stomach tying in knots as I stared at my phone.

I chickened out on calling Mom and decided to send Todd a quick text. Then I'd call Mom.

I sat on my bed and typed as fast as my fingers could fly.

*Not confused anymore. Have a date tonight.*

I hit send and then I waited. Paced around my room and waited some more. When I hadn't heard back from him fifteen minutes later, I admitted to myself I was stalling. I had to call my mom.

But I'd get undressed for my shower first. So I did that, then I dug out my towel and my shower shoes. And then I checked my e-mail.

Then I called my mom.

Okay, I started to, but my finger didn't seem to want to make contact with the words Linda/Mobile on my screen.

"Just do it, you puss. You're already eighteen. It's not like she's going to unadopt you. Just call her," I scolded myself. "Okay. Okay. Okay. I'm calling her."

I walked over to my desk then skittered back over to my bed. I pressed my mom's number, sat on my comforter, and closed my eyes.

"It's Saturday night. You should be out," she said instead of hello.

"Hi, Mom. I'm going out soon." I swallowed and started picking nervously at the stuffed panther on my bed. Amy had named him Thackery Binx. I dug my fingernail into the rim of his plastic eye. "There's something I wanted to talk to you about."

I should I have phrased that differently. I set her off in her typical, Linda-style rampage.

"What's wrong? You're not pregnant, are you? Ginger, we've talked about birth control. You promised me—"

"Mom, no. I—" I took a deep breath. How the hell do you tell your mom something like this? "I think—I think I'm a lesbian. Well, I know I am. I'm going out with a girl."

I fell over and buried my face in Thackery's plush fur, waiting for Mom to disown me.

"Oh." She actually sounded relieved.

"What do you mean 'oh'?" I said, sitting bolt upright.

"Sweetie, you've never mentioned liking a boy a day in your life. I figured we'd be having this conversation sometime around your freshman year in high school."

"Oh." That threw me big time, but she had a point. I'd talked to my mom about everything. School, sports, my friends, Todd's ex-girlfriends. I'd never come to her about any boys or even hinted I had my eye on anyone at school. No heartbreaks, not even a crush. I wondered for a moment if that part of it bothered her, that we didn't have that kind of a relationship to share.

"You're not mad?" I asked quietly.

"Why would I be mad?"

"I don't know." I adjusted my towel and dragged Thackery across my lap. "I just thought…"

"Honey, I'm an ex-pothead who married a mobster's son then adopted a black kid. You think I'm going to judge my only daughter for being gay?"

"I guess not."

"It's your crotch, Gingey. I'm just glad you're not pregnant or on any powder drugs or pills. Just be safe and get tested regularly like I told you. I kissed my roommate in college. She was nice; it just wasn't for me."

"Oh." I laughed a tad hysterically. "Well, good."

"Just be a good girl and your dad and I will be happy."

"And just don't get pregnant?"

"I'm too young to be a grandma. Are you going out with this young lady tonight?" It was weird to hear someone talk about Camila like she was any regular girl.

"Yeah. Nothing big, but I have to get ready."

"What's her name?"

"Uh, I'd rather not jinx it." Mom made a little scoffing noise. I could just see her rolling her eyes at me. "Let me see how this date goes before I start talking her up. It could be nothing, but yes, it's girls for good." It felt good to say. It felt great to say it to my mom and to know she still loved me either way.

"Okay. Well, thank you for telling me. And I'll be sure to tell your dad."

"Thanks, Mom." I shook my head in disbelief as we said our good-byes. I didn't realize till the moment she picked up the phone how terrified I had been of upsetting my parents for any reason. I felt much better as I headed down the hall, a huge weight I'd been oblivious to, lifted off my shoulders.

❖

The bathroom was empty so I took a long shower. Afterward, I didn't feel bad taking my sweet time blow-drying my hair since my roommate was gone. I turned up my music louder, singing along with Katy Perry at the top of my lungs while I lotioned up and put on my makeup.

The music and the solitude revived me, but when I was done getting ready, the end result in the mirror gave me a much needed boost of confidence. Amy had found the perfect dress. The emerald green silk showed off "just enough leg and not enough booby," as Amy liked to put it. The perfect mix to drive Camila crazy. I liked it because it made me look older. So many of the dresses we found made me look my age or younger with crazy cuts and patterns.

This one accentuated all the right parts. The neckline scooped just low enough to show off my ruby necklace, which I had grown completely accustomed to wearing twenty-four seven. The fabric had a slight shimmer to it. It hugged my stomach and my chest, and the skirt came just to my knees. I decided to wear my long red waves pulled back in an artful bun. The whole package said classy but willing. The ruby red platform pumps Amy had picked out for me said willing and ready. Amy had grabbed some silver hoops and bangles to match my necklace and a gray cropped motorcycle jacket to complete the look and match Camila's overall style. Amy insisted I needed a little pattern to make the look complete. I didn't argue and shoved my phone and my wallet into my new leopard print clutch.

Camila was right on time, knocking on my door at exactly eight o'clock. If I hadn't been so determined to go on an actual date with her, I would have yanked her inside, mounted her, and called it a night. She looked too good. I blinked, my mouth actually flopping open. The difference in our height had only been an inch or so. It was a safe guess Amy had told her what she'd picked out for me because Camila's peep toe heels were just a little bit higher than mine.

A part of my brain noted that her toenails were red, but my clit forced my eyes to skip up to her skintight vinyl leggings. The loose black shirt she had on covered her perfect ass, but hung off her shoulder, giving me a peek of the black satin bra she had on underneath. My favorite red lipstick was back and there were black spiked studs in her ears. I forgot all about any sort of readiness or willingness; her outfit demanded that I fuck her right then and there.

I got as far as, "Uh, hey."

"You look good, Red," she said a little too sweetly, knowing just how amazing she looked.

I swallowed anxiously. "Thank you. Where did you get those pants?" I said.

She just smiled wide, flashing her fangs.

I'd been to downtown Baltimore once, and even then, my dad and I had only driven down a few streets on our way to the university. I hadn't gotten a good look at the skyscrapers and local vendors or the harbor, and the city lights were the last thing on my mind now. I was focused on the woman next to me and our hands intertwined on her vinyl covered thigh. The side of my hand was on fire resting against her leg.

"So where are you taking me?" I asked.

"A Japanese place on Pratt."

"Do you own this place?" I asked, absolutely loving the love sexy grin I got back.

"Yes, I do. I own mostly restaurants and hotels here and there. And the spa you ladies visited. I'd take you by the tattoo shop, but I'd like to get on with the dinner portion of the evening if that's okay with you."

"Yes. It's more than okay," I said. "I'm just waiting for Cleo and Amy to pop up in the backseat." Which wouldn't have been a surprise. It was no one's fault, except maybe Camila's meth-addicted ex-employee, but we hadn't had much vertical, fully clothed time alone. I wanted tonight to be about Camila and me. And only us.

"There will be none of that. I just want to be with you."

"That's exactly what I was thinking," I replied.

She lifted our hands and brushed the back of my palm against her cheek, a sweet, adoring gesture that had me cursing the console between us. I sighed and settled back into the seat, finally watching the storefronts that passed by.

We arrived at Hama, Camila's Japanese restaurant and sushi bar, a few minutes later and left the car at the valet stand. The restaurant was packed. The deep wood accents on the walls and ceiling soaked in the golden light, giving the open space the best sense of intimacy. I followed Camila past the hostess who greeted us with a simple nod. I wondered if she knew exactly who or what Camila was. It felt silly to ask, but I still got the impression she knew Camila was free to navigate the space on her own.

She led us right to the sushi chef. After talking to him for a few moments—in Japanese—she turned to me with a wink and led me to a huge private booth toward the back. I let her take my coat, shrugging out of the gray faux leather, and settled comfortably next to her on the padded bench.

"And you speak Japanese?"

She leaned forward and kissed me. "I'm not sure there's a language I don't speak, Red. I ordered a few things for you to try. I hope that's okay." My mom had always told me that someone who orders for you without your permission is an arrogant prick and not saying so is an invitation for them to control your life. When it came to Camila, I was willing to let it slide.

"It's fine. My Japanese is a little rusty."

"I'll help you brush up," she said, scrunching her nose. Just then a female server brought us two glasses of water. Camila thanked her sweetly—in Japanese—before leaning back and gazing over my face. "So tell me more about you, Red."

"Oh? The way Benny talks, you guys already know everything about us."

"We know what's on the books, so to speak, and I know the adorable things I love about you, but I want to know more. Tell me about your family."

Now that was easy. I pulled out my phone and started scrolling through my pictures. I pulled up a recent favorite, my mom and me posing on either side of my dad and Todd, both in pizza comas on the couch.

"Oh, your brother is cute."

"Hey!"

"I'm just saying." She chuckled. "When was this taken?"

"Right before I came to school. My dad left for Brazil a few days after he dropped me here, but I'm guessing you knew that."

"I did, but tell me about him. And your mom."

"I don't know. They're just...amazing." My focus instantly dropped to my lap. I started choking up. It happened every time I thought about my family, every time I considered what they meant to me. Camila's arm went around my shoulders and she pulled me closer. I took the comfort, leaning into her warm body. My arm brushed her nipple through the layers of her clothes, and my clit throbbed. But that only made me feel more secure, knowing I wanted her in every way and that now she was there for me in all the ways I needed her to be.

"I'm sorry." I took a deep breath and gave it another try. "I was in this group home in South Boston. It wasn't bad it was just..."

"A group home?"

I swallowed, trying to pull it together. "Exactly. After my birth mom, I didn't talk for over three months. I played with the toys they gave us and paid attention in school and stuff, but I just wouldn't talk. I remember them trying every day to get me to say something.

"My mom—Todd calls her Linda, still," I said through my sniffling. "She came in to volunteer and she brought Todd with her. He's just so—he brings people out. It's impossible not to like him. He walked right up to me and goes 'Linda, let's keep this one.'"

"You're joking?"

"No. I'm dead serious. She looked at me for a minute and then turned back to Mrs. Farnham, the lady who ran the place. I was coloring and Todd just sat and picked up a crayon and started coloring with me." It took Todd a few moments to realize I wasn't going to talk to him, but he didn't care. He just talked and talked, going on about nothing important. None of the kids were mean to me; it's not that much fun to pick on someone who doesn't bother to fight back, but Todd was the first person who made me feel liked.

"Two weeks later, Linda came back with her husband Fredo and Todd. Mrs. Farnham told me the Carmichaels wanted to adopt me, no trial foster home, but full, immediate adoption, as immediate as those sort of things are. I wish you could have seen Mrs. Farnham's face when I said I was okay with it. Lawyers conferred, paper work was finalized, and a few months later, I was a Carmichael. I found out later Dad had called in some serious favors to get me out of there as quickly as possible."

"I have to thank Todd though. He's my best friend." I shrugged. "I was safe in the group home, but Todd saved my life, I think." I took another deep breath, relief and joy rising to a smile on my face at the thought of the wonderful family I still had.

"And he's taking a year off?" Camila asked. I scowled at her, knowing her vampire spies had given her that information.

"Yeah. He volunteers at a youth center near his first foster home. He's going to start med school next fall. Following in Dad's footsteps. Unlike me, who just wants to cozy up to football players."

"Well, something tells me your parents are proud of you either way."

"You'd love my parents. My mom is so silly. She's so much fun, and my dad, he's just a good person."

"I think it takes a genuinely good person to do the work he does."

"It does."

"I'd love to meet them," Camila said.

"You would? But I thought—"

"If your next statement has anything to do with anything Benny or Cleo said, I'm going to kill them," she said.

"Well, Natasha and Rodrick too. I just figured…"

"If you want me to, I can meet them. It'll have to be at night, of course, and they can't exactly know what I am, but I can still meet them."

"What about your fancy teeth?"

Camila opened her mouth. I blinked three or four times. The sharp tips of her fangs were there one second and gone the next.

"How'd you do that?"

Camila shrugged. When she opened her mouth to speak, the sharp tips were back. "It takes a little effort, but it's not impossible."

"I'd love for you to meet them." To express my gratitude, I kissed her softly on the lips, giving myself a hint of her delicious taste.

I hadn't realized how hungry I was until the sushi hit the table. Camila watched me demolish almost an entire spider roll before I realized she wasn't eating. I grinned at her, my mouth full of crab, avocado, and rice.

"You are so adorable, Red." She picked up the last piece and put it between her perfect lips.

I swallowed and took a sip of my water. "Sorry. Those pancakes wore off some time around two."

"Don't apologize. Eat all you want and then tell me more."

The years between my adoption and the moment I met Amy, had been pretty boring. Camila still wanted to know everything about me. I bragged shamelessly about my straight A's in math, which she seemed to appreciate. I told her about my four year run on an undefeated field hockey team, the many things I'd learned about the perks of paper over plastic, how much I loved Starbursts.

We got on the subject of friends and relationships. I explained to her that school took priority over boys and how I started to realize boys might not have been on my mind at all. My prom date had been a last minute thing with a friend who'd just gotten dumped. I'd planned on going stag. Then I accidentally told her about how my summer ended with my first kiss.

"About that," she said playfully. "You hinted you were a virgin when we met."

"Stop. I know what you're getting at." I knew this would come up. I was virgin, technically, in the sense that I'd never been with anyone else, but I knew she would question how easily she'd been able to slip sometimes three fingers inside me without a single protest.

"My mom tried to supplement the crap sex ed I was getting at school with extra info sessions at home. I got a little curious when she got to the section on masturbation." I squeezed my eyes closed, thinking about how stupid I'd been. "I accidentally de-virginized myself with a cucumber."

"Oh, Red!" Camila's shock was appropriate for how painful it had been. I went on, telling her how Mom had discreetly left a smaller, more hygienic vibrator on my dresser after she'd found the abused cucumber in the bathroom trash.

"It wasn't one of my finer moments," I said. "But still, before you, I'd only kissed one other person, even though I'd spent many hours with myself."

"And was she any good? At the kissing I mean," Camila asked. I pushed aside images of the day I maimed myself and thought about that muggy August afternoon, standing between our houses. Kristen and I had been talking, swapping bits and pieces of info about our soon-to-be roommates, when suddenly she just kissed me. At the time, it was amazing, hot and wet, with a lot of tongue. I'd wanted her to take the kiss further, which she would have if Todd's nosy ass hadn't come around the corner. It had been the peak of my sexual experience and prepared me in no way for the beautiful demon queen I was with now.

"She was okay," I muttered.

"Well, baby, as long as she treated you right." Camila's fingers brushed across my knee. My thighs automatically opened for her. I looked down as if I could see through the table, imagining her hand going a little higher. She slid closer, closing the natural distance that had come between us as we ate, and kissed me gently on the neck. Her warm tongue poked out between her parted lips and caressed my vein. Then her soft fingers started their trip north. I had about ten seconds before a wet patch stained my dress. When she brushed the thin fabric covering my clit, my thighs squeezed together.

"Is that lace?" She smiled against my tingling skin.

"Yes."

"I think we need to get you out of this dress." Coming with other people around was something I was starting to get used to, but I had a feeling the middle-aged couple beside us might not appreciate my high-pitched moans. I turned my head just a little, brushing my cheek against hers.

"Can we go?" I whispered.

"Of course, Red. Just one moment." Something was suddenly off about her voice, so I pulled away. And then I almost jumped back when I saw the tall, gray-haired woman standing next to our table.

# CHAPTER NINE

Camila withdrew her hand and gently pushed my legs together. My heart sank at the thought she was actually ashamed of me, until she turned slowly and pulled me tightly against her side. The way her body suddenly gripped with tension told me she wasn't ashamed or embarrassed. She was protecting me.

At first glance, there was nothing overtly threatening about the woman, or the two young men she had beside her. They didn't look much older than me, but the woman was older than Camila, possibly in her late thirties, although her gray hair made her look even older. Her outfit was a little distracting. The Lycra tube dress was skintight over her firm breasts and just long enough to barely cover her crotch. It matched her brightly colored stilettos perfectly.

Only highway road crews wore that shade of orange at night, but even the most dedicated of crews didn't wear that much neon chest-to-toe. With the black and white streaks of her hip-length hair, she looked a little overanxious for Halloween. The fact that both boys wore thick leather collars around their necks only added to the hilarity of the situation, but as she looked me over, there was no urge to laugh. Her eyes were a little too bright and silver. And when she opened her mouth to speak, her fangs were obvious in the dim light.

"I am so sorry to interrupt, but if I'm not mistaken, it's been months since I've seen you last. I had to come over and say hello." The woman's Southern accent was so thick you could almost taste the sweet tea on her lips. But despite the velvet twang of her pronunciation, her husky voice was anything but charming.

"It's nice to see you again, Moreland," Camila said.

"I've decided to treat my pets to supper out. They've been so well behaved these past few weeks." She reached up and gently stroked the moppish, brown hair of the young man to her left. He gazed at her as he leaned into her affections, the way a dog would to his owner. I cringed. Moreland turned back in our direction just in time to see the look of disgust on my face. If my reaction bothered her, she didn't show it. She kept right on talking.

"I see you're treating one of your beautiful pets as well."

Camila slipped her arm from around my shoulders and threw a hundred dollar bill on the table. I could feel the tension coming off her as she frowned. "She is not my pet."

"Oh. My. I do apologize. She is wearing your ruby." I automatically patted the small jewel as if she meant to snatch it from my neck, but Moreland just smiled wider, prattling on. "I assume you are borrowing from Kina's stock, then?"

I glanced at Camila just in time to see her jaw tighten; her plump red lips twitched. This would have been a perfect time for this woman to shut the hell up, but she didn't.

"I do so envy you and your sisters. Our master has provided me with such beautiful playthings, but you ladies always get the freshest…" The bitch drew in a deep breath through her nose before she made a dramatic show of licking her lips. "…the sweetest little girls. Do tell me your name, sweet pea."

Fuck my name; I wanted to let my gag reflex fly. I grabbed Camila's hand under the table and slid closer to her.

"Uh, it's Ginger."

"Well, my darling Ginger, you must come see me after you graduate. I would hate for your flavor to go to waste."

And that's when Camila snapped.

I'd seen a pretty decent chick fight on my way to English class last spring. Lots of screaming and hair pulling. One girl had even landed a solid kick to the gut. That was kind of hilarious to watch, the drama of it all. This was much more frightening. No punches were thrown. There was no yelling, but the silent, deadly grace that came over Camila would have scared the shit out of me if I had been on the receiving end of her glare.

Camila slowly rose from the table, guiding me up along with her. She spoke calmly, her voice so low and focused, you'd have been a fool to let down your guard.

"I thought you knew how much I don't like to repeat myself. Ginger is not one of our pets. She is my mate."

Moreland's silver eyes flashed for a brief moment as Camila's words registered. The look of satisfaction immediately dropped from her face. Camila ignored her shock and looked at each of the boys as she went on.

"Andrew, Luke, you contact me immediately if she mistreats you. Promise me?"

"Yes, ma'am," they both replied with quiet respect.

I followed Camila out from behind the table. Her steps were measured and confident, but where she usually channeled sex with her every move, now I was waiting for her to lash out and punch Moreland in the neck. Instead, she helped me into my jacket and handed me my clutch. She was still strung tight, but I felt calmer and safer the second she reclaimed my hand. She walked slowly toward Moreland until their shoulders were almost touching. Moreland immediately dropped her gaze to the floor, finally too afraid to look Camila in the eye.

"You seem to have forgotten who I am to you. Don't ever approach one of my girls," Camila said with a treacherous purr. "And if you ever speak to me like that again, I will strip you of your adoring pets." She looked down Moreland's body, past her hardened nipples. "Or I can just rip your throat out."

"I do apologize. Please forgive me," Moreland whispered.

"Enjoy your meal," Camila replied. As we walked away, there was no doubt in my mind Moreland would have nightmares about the parting smile Camila gave her.

A little nervous and very turned on, I followed Camila outside. The valet stand was empty, but that didn't seem to faze her. She pulled me to the side, wrapping her arms around my waist. I rubbed her shoulders feeling the tension drain out of her body.

"I'm sorry," she said.

"For what?"

"I didn't mean to scare you."

"You didn't," I said. "She did."

"Well, you and the girls don't need to worry about Moreland. We've never passed anyone on to her."

"What's her deal?"

"Nothing. She does view you girls, well, all humans, as food and sex toys. But her feeders always love her and she's never had any violations, so there was nothing I can do."

"Was?"

"You don't disrespect me in front of my girl," she said.

"You have my full permission to rip her to shreds anytime. Ugh, she's wicked gross!"

I smiled when Camila laughed. "Thank you, baby. If she pulls some shit like that again, I will."

"So what's the difference between being your girlfriend and being your mate?" I asked.

"Girlfriend is very temporary in her eyes. It means that I'd let her play with you on the weekends if she asked nicely. Mate means if she runs into you on the street thirty years from now, she'll still have to deal with me and I'd still kick her ass."

"Oh. What do the other sister-queens see me as?"

"My mate, Red. Don't worry."

"Good."

We kissed, just for a moment. I never thought I would be so attracted to power or such an intense display of aggression, but I was, even more so because I knew Camila would never use it against me. That sense of security in her, and myself, made me want to kiss her even harder, letting myself go in her arms.

She pulled back, putting a small step between us. When I opened my eyes, the SUV was there at the curb, the valet standing with my door open for me. Camila tipped him generously, then held my hand as she helped me up into the high cab. That kind of chivalrous attention had never been paid to me before. It was something I could definitely get used to. After a few seconds, she was beside me again, pulling the Range Rover out into traffic.

She took my hand and pulled it back into her lap just before she needed both her hands to take a slow left. I took advantage and spread my fingers over her vinyl-covered thigh. Her lips parted, just barely, and a soft sound of pleasure came from her chest.

"So," I said cautiously. "Where are you exactly in the whole vampire power pyramid?" Camila had the type of presence that demanded attention and respect. Anyone could see that. Even though she deserved more than the reprimand, it was interesting how quickly someone as rude and clueless as Moreland would cower to Camila.

"Power pyramid, huh. In this part of the world, I'm second in command."

"Really?" That shocked me.

"Our hierarchy is based on the origin of your maker. My maker was never human."

"You only had one maker? Because Benny said that when you turn, you feed from at least four others."

"Yes. That is true. That's the safest way…for the vampires." A dark look closed over her brow. And there is it was. The secrets. But she'd pushed me to tell her the truth about myself and my family, and now I would push her, just a little.

"You killed your maker, didn't you?" I said.

She rubbed the back of my hand with her thumb, squeezing me gently.

"I'm sorry, Red. I haven't had to explain myself in a long time."

"And you don't have to now." I lifted our hands and kissed her knuckles. "I was just wondering. So it's based on the rank of your makers?"

"Essentially, yes. Abrah was a pure demon. I took on all his powers and his rank."

"So what are you doing with the likes of us lowly sorority girls?"

"I'm on vacation," she said, licking her lips.

"Oh?"

"Yes. When I get bored with you pets, I'll go to DC, hook back up with Dalhem. That's Benny's father. And I'll let you in on a little secret, baby. He's pure demon as well." Which wasn't actually a secret to me thanks to Cleo. "I'm watching over this chapter as a favor to him. I'll go back to work keeping the rest of my demon friends like Moreland in line when I'm done."

"Oh. And when will that be?" I asked, dreading the answer. Of course she would move on. Who the hell would want to live under a sorority house forever?

Camila turned to me, the gold in her eyes sparking a glow in the swirling green.

"Whenever you're done with me, Red." She met me halfway as I leaned across the seat, both of us trusting her senses to keep us on the road as our lips pressed together.

"Not yet." My whisper caught in my throat.

"No. Now is working just fine for me."

Camila was cheating. I wanted to wait until we got inside the hotel room before I came all over myself. All I had was the tiny bit of security in the fact that she wouldn't actually fuck me in the elevator of the hotel to keep me from coming apart in her hands. But she had those lips, those soft, full lips and, God, those fangs.

There was a camera mounted somewhere in the over-sized mirrored box. Only she knew where. Fear of having her sharp teeth revealed to the security guards downstairs was not something on her mind. Her fangs grew to their full length, lightly pricking the pulsing vein running down my neck to my heart.

"Baby," the word slipped out of my mouth, but it felt right. "Just wait."

"Why should I? I've been waiting all day. I want to taste you now."

My back arched off the wall. I pressed my body between her hips.

"Exactly." I pressed against her even harder, forcing her gaze up. Her breath was coming hard, a sawing purr sweeping her scented breath across my lips. "I want to come in your mouth."

She stepped to the other side of the elevator and casually tucked her hands behind her back.

"Oh, is that all it takes? Does my pussy taste that good?" I asked softly. It quickly turned into a gasp as she was on me again in a flash, her knee pressing between my legs.

"Yes, Red. That's all it takes. You taste good. Like sweet fruit. Here…" Her knee pressed even harder. And then she licked my neck. "And here." The elevator door dinged open as a shiver rippled through my body.

I tried to gather myself before we stepped off and right into the penthouse foyer.

The hotel room had a foyer.

My gaze followed Camila's hand as she pointed to the right.

"Hot tub, television, bar, and view of the west side of the city that way."

"And that way?" I nodded to left.

"A bathroom with a pool sized tub, two more TVs, and the bedroom with a view of the south and east side of the city. A beautiful view of the water. Your pick."

My neck and my tingling clit had made the decision back at the restaurant.

"Bedroom." I nodded confidently.

"After you."

The bedroom was easy enough to find down a short, marbled hall, through an enormous sitting room. We paused for me to ditch my jacket and my clutch. I slid my hand back into hers, letting her guide me deeper into the penthouse. We stepped into the bedroom and she gave me a moment to look around. Right away, I noticed a pattern in Camila's taste in decor. I followed the strips of electric blue illumination coming from lights hidden along the seam of the ceiling. But the soothing hue against the marble didn't keep my attention for long.

Floor to ceiling windows lined the walls, allowing the lights of the distant houses and surrounding skyscrapers to bounce off the smooth white floor. My nerves had calmed some during the short walk from the elevator, but as I approached one of the huge panes, my breath caught at the buzzing world thirty-five stories down. All on its own, my hand pressed against the cool glass. I checked quickly to make sure I didn't leave a mark then gazed back across the miles and miles of white, yellow, and red dots and out over the shimmering water of the bay.

"I can see my house from here," I said, turning to Camila. She was standing patiently in the center of the room, watching me, a slight, but adoring smile touching her lips. The steps I took led me back to her and she guided me toward the bed, a quadruple California king-sized beast. I'd been too distracted by the view to notice it.

I'm not sure how far out of her way Camila had to go to plan our date, especially since she took me exclusively to places she owned, but that didn't make the surprise waiting for me on top of the fresh linens any less special. From all the movies I'd seen, rose petals and chocolates or even strawberries and champagne, seemed like the customary bedroom seduction tools. Camila had skipped right over any sort of floral displays and sweets and gotten right to the point.

Three dildos—one green, one pink, and one black—a pink vibrator, and a harness sat on a neatly folded cream blanket surrounded by a variety of lotions, oils, and lubricants. I looked at the plastic cocks in their different shapes and sizes and the shiny new leather then turned to Camila.

"Oh, I see what's going on here," I said sternly.

"Do you?"

"You've been wanting me to take you over to the bed and fuck you crazy, but you didn't know how to ask. So you just laid this stuff out and hoped I took the hint."

She wrapped her arms around my waist, looking over my lips then up to my eyes. I swallowed at her deep stare and my pussy quivered, adding another bit of moisture to the already damp fabric between my legs. It was more than about time I took my underwear off.

"There's that. Ultimately, it's your choice, baby. We can do it the old-fashioned way," she said. "You know I love feeling your clit against mine. Or I can fuck you this way." She nodded toward the toys on the bed. "Or you could fuck me."

"The green one," I decided before I took a step back out of her arms. Without another word, I walked toward the bathroom. The confidence in my strides was utter crap, but Camila didn't seem to notice or mind. Glancing over my shoulder one last time, I caught her wink before shutting the door behind me.

I turned and faced a cavernous marble room, completely devoid of any sort of light.

"Smooth," I mumbled in the darkness. Note to self. Know where the light switches are before walking off alone.

There were no windows in the large bathroom and no light coming in from under the door. I couldn't see a damn thing. A short moment before I started feeling along the counter for the wall, the door cracked open and the lights flicked on. My eyes adjusted to the bright glow just as Camila's hand slid back out the door.

"Thanks," I yelled.

"No problem, Red," she yelled back.

Days could be wasted thinking over the difference between my level of overall coolness and subtlety compared to Camila's. The fact that she was more mature, more experienced, and of another more magical and powerful species, would never change. So after one glance in the mirror I figured it was best to just focus on shucking my outfit and getting back in her arms, instead of how lame I was.

I kicked off my shoes and then ditched my dress and jewelry on the counter before I gave myself a quick once-over. The underwear Amy had picked was perfect. A slowly turned circle in front of the mirror gave me a chance to check the hem of the lace tanga shorts that barley covered my ass. They were soaked, but I wanted Camila to see them on me before I ditched them in a wet ball on the floor. The matching black bra pushed my already plump breasts up and together. I could see the blushing pink of my nipples easily though the black lace pattern. They were so hard and sensitive already, aching to be sucked. I hoped Danni was giving it to Amy good at that very moment. She deserved it.

I opened the door, flicked the switch off, and got somewhere around three feet back into the bedroom before I froze. There was music playing, soft techno rhythms that reminded me of something I'd heard in the dressing rooms earlier that day. The low lights that had cast the room in a pretty neon glow had switched from electric blue to an emerald green. Little changes that set a perfect mood and couldn't have mattered less when compared to the woman in front of me.

She knew I was there, even though she didn't look up as she fastened the harness around her bare thighs. I got the feeling she wanted to give me a moment, a moment I needed, just to look at her. I'd seen Camila in various stages of undress during the times we'd spent together, but nothing had hung so perfectly off her gorgeous hips the way the straps of leather did now. Not the patch of jewels and chain mail she had worn the first night we met, or the vinyl pants she'd had on just moments ago. It was a shame I hadn't gotten to pull the tight fabric off her. I had a feeling there would be plenty of chances to lend her an unnecessary hand out of her clothes. For now, I couldn't help but drool over the goddess in front of me.

My gaze traveled up her body, over her waist to her lush breasts with their tight brown nipples. I swallowed as soon as my mouth began to water, my tongue aching to trace every inch of her skin. Even her bare feet looked nice planted solidly beneath her curvaceous frame, the caramel of her skin in soft contrast with the pale marble floor.

She pulled the right strap tight, making the green cock bob between her hips. A moan actually slipped through my lips. I tried to catch it, my throat clenching. It only bubbled up harder as the air leaving my lungs forced it from my mouth.

Camila glanced up finally, smiling at me. But then she froze, just for a moment. The amusement dropped from her lips and she straightened, placing her hands on her hips. "Come here, Red," she said softly.

I was halfway to her before I'd realized my feet had started working, and I was in her arms, the green cock pressing against my belly, before I took my next breath. I didn't know it was possible to want someone this bad.

"Faeth and Tokyo fought over you," she said suddenly and quite seriously.

I frowned. That was not where I saw this conversation going. I was shocked there was any conversation at all. "What? When and what for?"

"Faeth saw you first and she wanted you. Tokyo saw you a little later and she wanted you, too."

"So they fought over me?"

"Not physically. Tokyo would win, but they argued. And I settled it."

"I see. What did you say?"

"That I wanted you more."

"And you don't argue with the queen?"

"No, baby. You don't."

"Hey, is Tokyo her real name?"

"No," Camila said. "Her name is Miyoko. She had a feeder who called her Tokyo and it just stuck."

"Oh. Well, as nice as Tokyo and Faeth are…" Which was a complete assumption because I'd never talked to them. "I think I got the better end of the deal."

I wanted to tell her I loved her right then, but I couldn't. I'd already embarrassed the hell out of myself the day before, spilling my feelings all over the interior of her car. As the emotions rolled through my head, her expression softened, but in a way that made me a little uncomfortable.

"You can read my mind?" I asked.

"I can."

"But you're not right now."

"No, I'm not and I haven't. Ever."

Why not, I wanted to say, but I didn't. The strange look on her face, the speculation and something close to pity, told me I wouldn't like what she would say. And I wanted her inside me way too much to start that kind of conversation right now. She'd asked me out, told me I could call her my girlfriend, even elevated me to a seemingly important status to the sister-queens, but she'd never said anything about loving me back. She wanted me and she made me feel special, so I would give her the same back. No more doubts, no more hesitation.

"If you ever do, just give me a heads up. I'd hate for you to catch me thinking about something boring like my stats homework."

"You'd never bore me, baby," she said. "Ever."

She swallowed, the deep rolling of her throat catching my eye. Her hesitation slipped away and the calm, seductive Camila was back. Whatever doubts had been on her mind she'd clearly decided to save for another day. Her hand slipped between our bellies and lower until her fingers brushed the wet lace between my legs.

"When I fuck you, we're gonna leave these on."

I nodded deeply before I said okay.

"Lie down."

I turned and walked to the bed, feeling her gaze heating the skin on my back. She didn't move from the spot until I was settled on the sheets, and that's when she walked toward the bed, prowled on her hands and knees until her head was between my legs. I met her feral gaze, the glowing stare that set my nipples aching even harder and made my clit twitch.

Her lips parted, her fangs growing back to their full length. I knew what artery she would go for. She had yet to feed from the inside of my thigh. But she only cocked her head slightly. I felt a pinpoint of pressure just above my clit, then a small brush of air and the warm brush of her cheek as it moved along the split she'd just made in the fabric. I shivered, swallowing nervously, unable to keep from biting my lips as my chest rose and fell.

She gently lifted my hips and moved down even further. She raised her head when she finished and I could tell that my underwear had been split from my clit to my asshole, giving her every inch of access. When she dipped her head back and licked me, a warm, wet, dragging stroke, front to back, top to bottom, I knew for sure. It was too much for me to moan. Too many sensations for me to whimper. I just went on shivering and gasping for air.

"God, Red. Don't make me wait," she begged me. It was strange; I knew she wanted me, but she was usually more in control. I wanted her bite and I wanted to give her my blood, but there were other things I wanted more, like more of her tongue on my body and every inch of the cock between her legs. She let her head fall to the side and nuzzled my thigh with rough affection, the way a loving cat would do to its beloved owner. I ran my fingers through her jet-black spikes for the first time. They were so soft. Her purr grew louder and she rubbed her cheek and then her chin along the inside of my hips. My body arched up to her face. I spoke boldly before the courage to ask went away.

"Please," I said. "Lick me first."

"Okay, baby," she groaned in reply.

My legs were spread wide by her strong hands, forcing my knees almost to my chest. I shifted on the bed just as her lips covered my slit. With a slight upward motion, her tongue spread me wider. The moaning couldn't be helped. My body needed her, wanted her more than I could handle to keep in.

Despite the desperate sounds she was making, Camila managed to work me slowly, gently sucking my clit into her mouth. Paying affectionate attention to my opening with her tongue. I gripped her hair tighter and let my body go with the motions of her lips.

With her, there had never been any time for me to consider what I liked, what subtle skills or advanced tricks someone would have to use on me to make me come. With her, everything worked. Everything she did with her mouth, the soft scraping of her teeth over my clit or the insistent thrusts of her tongue inside, all of it brought me closer and closer to coming.

She alternated, her hands never leaving my thighs, just her lips and her tongue, teasing me, torturing me. Our eyes met. She was all animal in that moment, all demon, and I could see how hard she was fighting to keep her control in check. That heat in her eyes, the want, that pushed me over. I cried out, whimpering nonsense into the cool air above us, clutching on to her head. She met my downward thrust, grinding her face harder between my legs, taking every bit of my trembling into her body.

With one more slow, sweeping pass of her tongue, Camila silently rose up to her knees. There was no warning and no hesitating. The cock between her hips pushed inside me with one sharp thrust, my dripping juices easing the way. My eyes slammed shut. I gripped the sheets. The cock fit perfectly inside me, the same firm way Camila felt perfect on top of me.

She pulled back a little then pushed forward again, pausing just for a moment when my body decided to roll its hips. My pussy spasmed along the firm plastic and spasmed again when I thought of who it was attached to. My eyes fluttered open and I stared at her beautiful face.

I love you, I wanted to say, but I didn't. "Kiss me," I said instead. She answered by pressing her lips against mine. My mouth parted and she entered me again, kissing me the way I needed her to, letting me taste the traces of myself on her lips. She was like honey and sweet fruit with that hint of spice I'd been craving all along. My arms wrapped around her shoulders and her arms came around my back. I arched off the mattress giving her plenty of room to unhook my bra. I let go just long enough to slip it from my arms, and then she was lifting me.

"Ride me," she said as she fell back on her heels.

I nodded, wrapping my body around hers and the cock. I followed her motions, rising and falling, grinding in her lap. She took advantage of the shift between us and suckled my nipple between her red lips. And then I lost it. She let go of my nipple the second I started coming and gently cupped the side of my neck. She thrust up into my pussy harder and harder and I came again. This time I moaned her name.

"Baby," she growled deeply as I shuddered against her. My head tilted to the side. I gave her my neck. Her bite was hard. Hard and perfect, the cool sting sending thundering shocks through my veins to every inch of my body. I came again, crying out desperately, soaking the leather in her lap and the insides of my thighs.

Her head dropped to my breast as her own orgasm rippled over her. She cried out, groaning my name, licking my damp skin around my ruby and my chain, kissing and biting at my nipples, refusing to slow the pumping of her hips. And I kept riding her, harder, neither of us willing to stop even as she added a finger to the equation.

She may not have been in love with me, but I was in love with her, and the same way my blood was in her, she was now inside me, inside my heart in every way, making me come over and over. There were no thoughts of where the morning would take us, but as she gently used her middle finger, soaked in my juices, to tease the tight ring of my ass, I couldn't help but wonder where the security cameras were in the penthouse and just how well they were capturing the show on the bed.

When there was time, I'd love to see the playback.

# CHAPTER TEN

There's a heart here." Her fingers brushed across my shoulder blade. "And if I squint, there's a frog right here." And then in a small circle at the top of my spine.

"But only if you squint?"

"Precisely."

I giggled, unable to control the tremble that rippled through my body. Her fingers moved up and down my back, across my shoulder and my neck, and back again.

There were only a few hours left before sunrise, hours I refused to waste sleeping. Camila had fucked me perfectly one more time before giving me a break to stretch and hydrate. At some point, we decided an ice cream sundae was in order. She called downstairs and what felt like a whole minute later, Camila returned from the elevator carrying a huge bowl on a silver tray. I complained for a moment that it was too big for me to eat alone, but quit arguing when she made a very seductive move to feed me the sugary dessert. It's hard to turn someone down when they lick your lips.

Our little dessert break left me cranked up all over again. My pussy pulsed and clenched with every sloppy spoonful she brought to my mouth. She intentionally made a mess, letting me lick the chocolate syrup and whipped cream from her fingers. The sugar rush led to a laughing fit that somehow gave me the bright idea to actually try to screw Camila with the strap-on. That plan came up short the moment she pulled the straps around my hips.

Something about seeing me in the new leather set off the beast in Camila's brain. One moment I was standing at the foot of the bed looking down as her confident hands secured the harness on my body, and the next I was on my back on the floor, Camila's head buried between my legs. Annoyed that she hadn't even let me try the pink dildo out, I actually put up a fight. Which was pretty stupid. She gripped my hips tighter and drew the length of her fang down the side of my clit. My back shot up off the marble floor and my orgasm shuddered through my body. Momentary blindness didn't keep me from feeling my juices gushing over her tongue and chin.

She pulled away, not bothering to ease me down from the high peak she put me on. As soon as I could see straight, I pounced on her. She let me take her to the floor. I wasn't surprised how easily her legs fell open. She let me in, letting me taste her for the first time. I almost came again the second my tongue lapped across her hardened clit. She tasted so sweet, just like her strong scent mixed with honey.

She had been so commanding and so dominating when we'd been together, even though I wanted to badly, I never thought to go down on her without explicit instructions to do just that. But she hadn't even flinched to stop me. She opened herself to me, letting my clumsy lips and fingers explore the tight warmth of her gorgeous slit. I admired every bit of skin, the stiff length of her clit, every crevasse. So soft and wet. I knew it wasn't all my doing, but I was pleased when she came, psyched when she began rolling her hips harder against my face until she fell apart, gripping and soaking my fingers. She'd taken no time to come back down. She hopped to her feet, still panting and purring, and led me back to the bed. And for an hour, we lay there talking and touching.

I thought falling for Camila that first night we'd spent together had been a mistake. Even having a crush on an immortal creature like her had seemed like a bad idea. Finally feeling her react to me, tasting her as she came apart because of something I had done, threw my priorities completely out of whack. Now the part of my world that mattered the most existed at night. School was still important. I wanted my degree and I wanted to make my parents proud. Lying in the curve of her hips, my cheek resting on her warm breast made the real world, the one I belonged to, seem so unimportant and so far away. No part of me wanted to go back to the ABO house, back to school or my life. I just wanted to spend forever lying with her.

I got the distinct feeling Camila felt the same way. She was stalling, breaking in her story as often as possible, using the freckles along my back and arms as an excuse.

"This one looks like a bunny," she whispered against my hair.

I yawned then nuzzled her pert nipple with the corner of my mouth. "You'll have to show me tomorrow. Tell me more about your maker."

Finally she gave in. She picked up her tale where she'd left off, but kept up the soothing strokes along my back. I never wanted to move again.

For as long as anyone in her family could remember, Abrah had lived in a system of caves just north of the Sierra Norte de Oaxaca mountain range in Southern Mexico. I listened as Camila described the beauty of the region. It was impossible to ignore the adoration in her voice when she talked about the mountains and lush valleys she'd explored as a child.

An hour before, all I knew about Mexico involved escalating drug violence, tales of dangerous border crossings, and of course the ongoing debate over Cabo versus Jamaica for spring break. I pictured Camila, in a different time and place, a completely different person from the one who lay underneath me in the sheets.

Her village had been small, but a true community that lived peacefully between the mountains and the river. The nearest town was a considerable walking distance, but news had always reached them. There had been devastating changes to the country and there was always the fear that outsiders would stumble across their small haven in the wilderness and interrupt their pleasant lives. The head of the village had taken care to reassure his people that the outside world would never be a threat. Their village was too remote. And then there was their protector. Abrah, a true demon or a demon-bourne as Camila explained it, one of only seven to escape from the bonds of hell.

The tale of Angel de las Cuevas had spread all over the land north and south of the mountains, but only the members of Camila's village knew just how real their Angel of the Caves was.

His relationship with her people was very different from the relationship the girls and I shared with the sister-queens. There was still a sense of ceremony. When every member of the village reached adulthood, they were first presented to Abrah, then to the village for marriage. But everything else was different. Abrah never took human form, living his life in the mountains as a full demon. When he emerged to feed, he never hid the crowned horns of his head or his majestic black wings. And he never slept with any of his humans. Anatomically, it wouldn't have worked, but his fangs still gave the cold shock of ecstasy.

"He could sense our physical pleasure and our pain," she said, explaining why she'd never asked me to touch her. I practically came from looking at her. The orgasms-by-contact she must have received just from feeding would keep anyone sexually gratified. Forever.

Camila was a late bloomer, the youngest of six children, the only girl among five boys. Her grandfather had been a green-eyed Scottish missionary who had been separated from his group. He stumbled upon the village one rainy morning, and after he realized they had absolutely no interest in killing him, decided to stay. He took a wife, a young widow. A generation later, Camila had arrived, hazel-eyed, and as I imagined, just as perfect as I saw her now.

Her first encounter with Abrah had been typical, but as time passed, it became clear to everyone in the village that Camila was his favorite. He always socialized on his visits down from the mountains, but his main purpose was to feed. On the night of her wedding to Lino, the young man who had won her hand, Abrah was there with gifts and well wishes. It was the first time he'd appeared for such an event.

"He came back the night I found out I was pregnant."

My head snapped up. "You had kids?"

She nodded with a soft, sad smile.

Camila had given birth early in the spring. The very same day the developers first approached the head of the village, demanding he take his people elsewhere. Their homes sat directly in the path they wanted to take to the river and further on to the ocean.

"The place was no bigger than a city block," Camila said.

"But they wanted you out."

"They wanted the land, the trees, and uninterrupted access to the river." Something they would go to extreme lengths to get.

The head of the village had sent the men away, telling Camila's family and the families of her friends and neighbors not to worry about the intruders. They celebrated the arrival of Camila's children, twin boys viewed as a blessing for the whole village, two males who would grow into strong and proud men. Camila and Lino lived their lives blissfully for three more years, raising their sons in peace and willingly serving Abrah.

Camila paused for a moment. I fought the urge to ask, "Then what happened," like some foolish little kid. She sighed and went on without any prodding from me.

In the three years she'd had with her family, the developer's company had made the decision to clear out the village and take the land. They had heeded the warning from a neighboring town. They may not have believed in the myth of Angel de las Cuevas, but they were smart enough to plan their ambush for high noon, a time when the men were away from the village, the women and children at their most vulnerable as their demon protector, if he actually existed, slept. She found out later that two groups had been sent out: one to surround and burn the village, the other to round up and slaughter all the men out in the forest.

Camila had been by the river, gathering water, when she first heard the screams and smelled the smoke. She made it to the edge of their clearing as the shots that killed her boys rang out. She had never thought twice about leaving them with their grandmother, but suddenly she wished they'd never left her side. She ran to them anyway, ignoring the shouts of the men brandishing torches and rifles. She described the scene to me, the fire and the blood and bodies everywhere, but I could hardly picture it.

She'd been shot in the back at the entrance to her parents' home. The blow had knocked her to the ground. A thick-heeled boot to the head had knocked her out. The fire burning through her clothes ripped her back to reality sometime around dusk. I shuddered uncontrollably against her as she said the words.

"If you can avoid it, Red, I don't recommend being set on fire." She looked at me, trying just as I would have, to make light of the situation.

"I'll do my best."

She took a deep breath and went on.

She'd been placed at the edge of a pile of bodies and lit on fire along with them. She forced herself to ignore the choking smell of burning flesh, her own flesh and that of her loved ones, and managed to roll away from the heap. She put out the flames that had begun to engulf her by rolling in the blood soaked dirt. With her senses better under control, she could finally hear voices in the distance, voices she ignored. She knew her husband was dead, knew her sons were somewhere in the flaming heap. Heartbroken and in searing pain, her body made decisions she didn't think to override as she crawled to the edge of the forest, toward the caves.

"I didn't make it that far before I passed out again, and when I came to, Abrah had me in his arms." He spoke soothing words to her, promising to save her. She was the only one left, his only child, and he refused to let her die. She barely held on to consciousness as he carried her swiftly through the forest all the way back to the concealed ledges of his cave. She remembered cool ferns against her charred skin and the golden glow of his eyes in the darkness, but nothing else.

"When I woke up, I was completely healed and Abrah was dead. There was a huge gash in his neck. For a long time I wondered how I'd overpowered him, but Dalhem told me it was impossible for a healthy human to take down a demon, especially at night." She was silent for a moment staring at the ceiling. There was no need for her to go on. I didn't want to know the rest. I saw the pain on her face.

My birth father had never existed to me and my mother had been a piss-poor definition of the word. It couldn't have been easier for the Carmichaels to replace them. It was amazing to think how great they'd turned out to be, how they'd healed me.

Abrah had saved Camila's life, a life that she had no one left to share with.

In the remaining darkness, her instincts had told her to drag her maker's body to the exposed cliffs just outside the cave. She hid in the shadows the following day, ignoring the scent of scorched demon flesh as Abrah's body was ignited by the rising sun. And that night she set out to find the men who had killed her family. She'd drained three of them completely before Dalhem found her.

"He found you the next day?" I asked.

"The seven bourne-demons are linked, but Dalhem and Abrah were spawned twins. Dalhem knew the moment I'd taken his brother's life and his powers." Camila had fought him when he tried to pull her away from the developer's encampment. She was strong enough to show some genuine resistance, but there was still human in her. Dalhem's demon quickly overpowered her and pulled her back to the cover of the forest. Somehow, he'd been able to talk some sense into her, convince her that the mass-murder of her family's killers wouldn't bring her sons or her husband back. That age-old lecture of the downside to revenge. He promised he would prevent them from destroying the land, but there was nothing he could do about the events that had already unfolded. The approaching sunrise had been the only reason she'd given in and followed Dalhem back to the States.

"He'd had a home set up in DC for years by the time I met him, so he brought me there. Taught me how to use my powers, figure out my weaknesses."

"You have weaknesses?"

"I do, baby. Redheads being one of them," she said, letting out another deep breath. I looked up at her just as she looked at me and that's when I saw the blue tears, a few stray, translucent blue streaks of moisture trailing down the side of her face. There hadn't been a hint of a tremble in her voice, but of course she would cry thinking of her family. Or course she would miss them.

I jumped up on the bed beside her and didn't hesitate to brush the tears gently away from her face. More followed. And more even though her voice continued with its solid rhythm.

"Lino and I would be dead by now, but Acui and Lan could still be alive."

"Really?" I pulled back and gazed at her young face. "How old would they be? How old are you?"

She burst out laughing through her tears. "I'm eighty-three, Red."

"Oh." The disappointment in my voice made absolutely no sense. "I thought you were older. How old were you when you died?"

"Eighteen."

"What?" I actually yelled that time.

She huffed a short laugh, then wiped her face and sat up. "I'm not human, baby, and you'd be surprised what a difference a little confidence makes."

"I guess. So we're the same age, sorta?"

"Sorta." She smiled.

"When's your birthday?" I had to stop sounding like a complete tool.

"July twenty-fifth. I think. Your birthday is December fourth, if my information from Benny is correct."

"Ha ha. Yeah, it is."

"Well, that gives me plenty of time to pick out a present for you." I felt myself blush, embarrassed by just how good the idea of us being together three months from now sounded. I wiped away the last traces of her tears with my thumb.

"You still want me? Even though I'm younger than you hoped?" she asked, faking a pout. I shoved her shoulder gently.

"I'm the obsessed one, remember. I'm sorry about your family. I can't even imagine what that must have been like."

"I don't want you to. I miss them. I always will, but I have my sisters. I have Cleo's smartass mouth and I have you."

"Poor substitutes," I said, knowing I only meant it in terms of me.

She cupped the side of my neck, stroking me with her thumb and I found it was impossible not to look up into her shimmering eyes.

"Not a substitute, just something different and special." Instantly, I was done with the subject. I didn't want her to have to remember anymore, at least for the rest of the night.

I squared my shoulders and frowned very seriously. "There is a cluster of freckles on my butt that I am positive looks like a jack-o-lantern."

"Oh, this I gotta see," she said. I met her laughter with a shriek, giggling uncontrollably as she flipped me over.

There was nothing that could have been done to fix our screwed up, tattered pasts, and I had no clue what our future would be like, but I had her with me now. I held on to that thought and let the feeling of it warm my heart as she used her body to warm mine all over again.

I dreamed about cats. Cats crying. I could hear the meowing coming from the dark corner of an unfamiliar room. Every time I thought I found the source of the sound, the corner would be empty. It sounded like kittens, crying out for their mother. I couldn't stop looking, but I did once I felt something brush across my face. Something rough and sandpapery.

I shot up in bed, gasping in the bright sunlight.

The early morning sunlight.

It was morning.

"Shit!" A small heart attack ripped through my chest when a sleek black cat jumped into my lap. "What the—" My hand automatically went to its soft fur, my body realizing before my brain that the animal in the sheets with me was indeed Camila and not some stray who had magically learned how to work an elevator. It was the brightest morning Baltimore had probably seen in years, and we were sitting atop the city's tallest hotel, in a penthouse with wall-sized windows. With open curtains. Of course Camila would take a safer form.

I looked around the room, checking stupidly to make sure the cat and I were alone. Then I stared back at Camila.

"Oh, this is really happening." I sighed deeply. Her hazel eyes were exactly the same, gazing back at me. She meowed again before jumping off the bed and running toward the bathroom. I followed, thankful I didn't get tangled in the covers.

I closed us inside and double-checked to see if any light was coming in from under the door. I flicked the light switch, praying the room was truly UV free.

"Jesus." I jumped. Camila, the hu—vampire version of her, was standing behind me in the mirror. I spun around facing her.

"I'm sorry," she said frantically.

"What the hell happened?"

"I overslept."

"Second most powerful demon in all of North America and you overslept. Please tell me how."

"I haven't slept in four months."

"Why not?" I gasped. "We slept together last weekend, and I mean before that—"

"We spend the summer setting the older girls up with their new feeders and just all the shit with the shop—" She cut herself off, hanging her head, frustrated.

An unusual calm came over me. I could freak out later. I had to get her back to the house.

"It's fine. What do we do now?"

She rubbed her palm over her eyes before looking back at me. "There's a shopping bag in the closet in the bedroom. Throw all our stuff in there. When we get downstairs, tell the valet you're picking up Ms. Sanchez's Range Rover. He doesn't know me, but he knows my name and he knows which car is mine. He'll bring it up. You remember the address to the house?"

"Yeah." Right, because I'd been too busy trying to make out with her and feeling up her vinyl pants to pay attention to the way we'd come. I had no fucking idea where the hotel was in relationship to the house. This was just getting better.

"The GPS is unnecessarily fancy, but it'll get you back to the house."

"Good. And you're okay?" It was my turn to ask.

"Yes, I'm fine. I shifted in my sleep. Red, I'm—"

"I know. It's cool. Let's just get out of here." Camila let her apology drop, and then a fraction of a second later was down on all furry black fours looking up at me.

"This is really fucking happening," I muttered before opening the door for the black cat at my ankles. I wasted no time digging up the shopping bag. I threw in Camila's clothes and shoes, all the toys she bought me. No way was I leaving them behind. Even though I was freaking out, I'd want them later. I chucked my jewelry and my shredded underwear in the bag and cursed out loud when I realized the only shoes I had to walk and drive in were four-inch platform pumps. I wanted to kill Amy.

I felt like a complete whore as I slithered back into my bra and my dress. After a final sweep of the penthouse and reclaiming my jacket and my clutch, I turned to the cat.

"So do I just carry you…"

She meowed, pawing the air under the shopping bag.

"Of course." I put the bag on the floor. Camila hopped in, meowing at me again when she was settled on top of the toys and her vinyl pants.

I clicked my heel on the marble floor as I waited for the elevator. I nearly bit through my lip; my teeth wouldn't stop gnawing at it. I could not believe this was happening.

The ride down was a fucking nightmare. Three old ladies got on on the eighteenth floor. The situation would have only been worse if it had been Nanny and Pop-Pop Carmichael in the elevator with me instead, may they rest in peace. One of the old ladies was just rude enough to peer into the huge bag slung over my shoulder. I didn't realize she was even looking in my direction until she screeched, "Oh, what a gorgeous cat." The other two women had been purposely ignoring me. My dress, my red do-me pumps, and my messy ponytail did not make for presentable Sunday brunch attire.

I wanted to die. The woman actually reaching into the bag and stroking Camila's head made it the best walk of shame ever. They hopped off at the dining room on the second floor, and that gave me about fifteen seconds to prepare myself for my power walk past the front desk.

The valet, Frank, had apparently seen worse morning-afters and spared me his disapproving stares. Once I was behind the wheel, Camila hopped out of the bag and into my lap. My thigh twitched under her weight, a mix of annoyance and arousal. It twitched again when I looked at the clock on the dash. It was seven fifty-five a.m.

There were only three menus to get through before I could enter the address to the house. I gripped the steering wheel the whole seven point three miles back to campus, doing my best to ignore my mewling girlfriend in my lap.

I knew I had to do something to keep my mind off the anger boiling in my stomach. Reciting the code to the garage over in my head was the only thing that seemed to work. At mile three, I realized repeating the numbers was only putting me more and more on edge. If Camila could sense my pleasure and my pain, there was way no way she couldn't sense my emotions now. By the time we pulled into the safety of the underground garage, my knuckles were white and I was nearly shaking.

I opened the door and Camila hopped off my lap. She trotted slowly down the hall and I followed, wondering why she hadn't changed back. Then I remembered I had her clothes in the bag at my side. She wasn't shy on nudity, but this wasn't the time. I felt bad for a moment, thinking of how crappy waking up four-legged and furry would actually be.

The tension in me started to ease, until we turned the corner to the sister-queens' quarters. Tokyo, dressed in nothing but a kimono robe, had Mel, naked, up against the wall. I could only assume the hallway was the perfect place to feed this time of the morning. The two of them had probably never been to bed. At least they had the good sense to remain underground.

My annoyed grunt brought Tokyo up short.

"What's wrong?" she asked a moment before she looked at Camila. "Oh shit. I'm sorry, Ginger. It sucks when that happens."

"I bet it does," I grumbled as I stormed by, feeling Tokyo's receding laughter like a punch in the back.

We hung a right to Camila's door. She sprinted in front of me, blinking into her two-legged, two-armed, very naked form. My stare lingered on her ass just for a second. I forced myself to look at her feet once she opened the door. I stepped inside and waited.

"Red—"

"May I use your shower?"

"You know you can. You don't have to ask. You're welcome to my space and my things. Just let me—"

"Thank you." I dropped my stuff on the couch, and without another word, marched into the bathroom.

The shower was perfectly hot, but I didn't wash. I just stood there under the raining spray. My body was still for a long time as I let the hot water trickle in and out of my mouth. There was no shampooing my hair. I couldn't be bothered to lather up my body. All I could do was stare at the black tile because every time I closed my eyes all I could see was Camila's ashes piled next to me in the white sheets.

For months after my mother died, I'd pictured what it must have been like to drag the razor across my own wrists. I wondered if it would hurt or, if you were someone like my mother, would you enjoy that sort of pain. Would you only be sad because you realized ending your life meant you would never be able to feel that sort of agony again. I thought of my mother, thought of my dreams, new and old, of her dead and bleeding, pregnant and bleeding. And I thought of Camila.

"Baby." I didn't jump this time when she appeared behind me. I didn't even flinch when her arms came around my waist. My gaze traced a line across the black floor as she gently turned me toward her. Still too afraid to close my eyes, I looked as high as her navel. She couldn't ask me for more than that.

"Don't be angry with me," she pleaded softly. "*Querida*, please." For the first time, her heritage thickly coated her voice with emotion. It made me shiver.

"I'm not angry with you," I croaked.

"Then please tell me—"

"No. I can't."

"Why? You can tell me anything."

At that moment, something in me broke. A string that ran from my brain to my heart, that had been tangled up in my courage and my soul, just gave way, making room for nothing but vulnerability and fear. And somehow that crack in my will gave me the power to invite Camila into my head.

Her eyes snapped wide the moment she was inside and even wider, shocked with the pain I was feeling and the horrible things I'd been imagining. She saw my dead mother lying against the white tile, saw how I pictured her own death, the way she had burned and bled.

"Red." She choked out a sob, the sympathy spreading across her face. For some reason, her reaction pissed me off. I took a step back out of her arms.

"Don't do that," I shouted. "You can't do that, okay? I know I'm just some stupid kid with mommy issues, but what I feel for you is real. And it doesn't deserve your pity. I know you've been through a lot of girls, but you mean more than that to me. Thank you for taking me out and claiming me as your mate, but we both know you don't love me."

"I love you. Let's get that straight right now," Camila said back. The feral tone of her voice and the anger that snapped into place on her face shut me up. "Damn it, this is going to sound bad, but you're the reason I slept so hard this morning. For the first time in over sixty years, I got a real night's sleep. Losing my children and Lino—it ripped my fucking heart out, Ginger. Don't think for one second that you didn't give it back to me because you did.

"I love you so much and I've only known you a week. I almost killed Moreland in a crowded restaurant just for looking at you, and that has nothing to do with sex or possessing you. I can't stand the thought of anyone else making you laugh. It makes me sick to my stomach. The thought of someone else counting your freckles makes me want to punch a hole in the wall. I love you, no matter how old you are, whether you're immortal or not. I'm sorry about what happened this morning. I swear to you it will never happen again."

"You swear? Because I can't protect you. You have to protect yourself. I don't care how tired or stressed out you are. I don't want to lose you." My eyes started to mist up. The admission of her love right on the heels of the very real idea of being without her, pushed the tears over the edge. It all happened so fast, but I truly did love her.

"Yes. Jesus Christ, Red." Her arms came around me again. I let her pull me against her body. The water slicked our skin making our nipples bud against each other. "I keep fucking this up. It's been years since anyone cared what I did with my time, if I took care of myself. I'm going to stop hurting you."

I leaned back, staying close enough for her to keep a hold on me. My fingers traced across her collarbone. Touching her made the goose bumps rise on my own skin.

"You haven't hurt me. We just, we keep missing each other. I'm assuming one thing and you're assuming another. I know you know how to take care of yourself. You wouldn't let yourself go out in the sun carelessly. I was just scared. I don't want anything to happen to you. This is new for me, but it's worse because you're not just some girl in my class I have a crush on. I don't know. Does that even make sense?"

"Yes. It does." She gently lifted the ruby pendant off my chest. "I have given this necklace to so many girls. Cleo is one of the few I would consider a true friend, but there have been others like her. There's never been anyone like you, Ginger. Four years, grad school, fuck, even if you stay here for your PhD. I don't want to let you go."

"You curse a lot when you get worked up."

"I know. I'll work on that too."

"How often do you need to sleep? Honestly."

"I can get by on six hours a week, but twelve is better. The closer you are to a bourne-demon the less you need, but my human side does need some."

"I know you had a crazy week, but what in the hell were you doing the times I slept in your bed?"

She shrugged. "I got some work done. Thought about what the hell I was going to do with you."

"Okay, well, will you please get some sleep for me, squeeze some nine or so hours in, here and there? And please let me know when you're going to feed again. I know it wasn't anything emotional with Amy, but it's unreasonable to ask a girl not to get a little excited when you're sucking on her neck. I'd rather not walk in on that again"

Her laugh forced me to smile. There was no helping it. "I promise. Will you let me in again?" she asked cautiously. I took a deep breath and nodded. This time I didn't try to do anything, but I did feel her inside my head, a light pressure just behind my forehead. I twitched and winced a little. The pressure didn't hurt, but something about another person occupying your brain while you're fully conscious of it just didn't feel right.

"It's okay, baby. Just relax."

I exhaled deeply and did my best to hold still. The feeling of the intrusion didn't ease, but suddenly the painful images were gone, not for good, she silently told me, but for the moment. She slipped out just as quickly as she had slipped in. My mind was my own again even though her influence lingered. When I closed my eyes there were no memories of death, hers or my mother's. Just calm, weightless darkness.

My eyes stayed closed when she kissed me, and I didn't open them again while she washed my hair and rubbed down my body. Afterward, she dried me off and carried me to bed. I kept my eyes closed the whole time, relieved that the next time I opened them, some four hours later, Camila was still wrapped around me under her black blankets, sound asleep.

## CHAPTER ELEVEN

Todd would not stop texting me. It was my fault. He'd gotten my text the night before and responded sometime between our run-in with Moreland and our ride up in the elevator. He'd texted me back and told me that Mom had mentioned that I was officially "out," but now he wanted specifics about my date. And specifics about my girl.

I could have told him the truth, that my first date with Camila, my first date ever, had been amazing. I could tell him that right now I wasn't in the library studying with my sorority sisters, because that wasn't the truth. The truth involved me sitting on the floor in Camila's lounge, nestled between her legs. My attention was split between the Colts/Pats game, a used copy of *Tess of the D'Urbervilles*, and my demon-angel's soft kisses across my shoulder.

My first mission for the afternoon had been to avoid Amy and the girls and their barrage of post date questions, which I pulled off, thanks to Camila. God, I loved her even more. She gave me the keys to the Range Rover. In a borrowed pair of sweats and one of her signature black tank tops, I took a quick, covert trip back to the dorm to grab more clothes and my books. Her SUV could be recognized by any of the ABO girls, but it was way more likely that I would bump into Amy or Cleo on foot. I wanted to dish about my night and just how amazing Camila had turned out to be, but I had hours and hours of daylight to spend gossiping with the girls. Camila was rested and had some free time before she had to get back to her role as demon enforcer and successful business owner. If she wanted to spend the afternoon watching me read my English homework and studying my stats notes, there was no way I was going to turn her down.

After our talk in the shower, the reality of just how different my relationship with Camila would be hit me. And it left me exhausted, even after our nap. She had shown me a special side of her world and her personal life outside of Alpha Beta Omega. Parts I loved, like the toys and the hotel room. And parts of it made me nervous, psychos like Moreland and the danger of UV exposure. Now I welcomed any moments of normalcy we were allowed. Any moments where her demon blood, my waking nightmares, and nosy sorority sisters wouldn't come between us. Spending the day lying low in her underground apartment seemed to take care of those intrusive factors, but they didn't keep my brother from texting me.

The display on my cell phone lit up as it vibrated. I wanted to ignore it, but I couldn't look away from the alert box in the center of the screen. I picked it up off the coffee table. He was satisfied I'd spent Friday watching movies. Now he wanted to know about my Saturday night. I loved Todd so much, but for once I wanted him to give a little less of a shit. I groaned, running my thumb over the screen. Camila hugged me tighter and kissed my neck. I pressed back against her even more. I loved feeling her warmth around me.

"What should I tell him?"

"What do you want to tell him, baby?"

I wanted to tell him the truth. I wanted to tell him everything, but that wasn't going to work. It wasn't my truth to tell. Not all of it anyway.

"I should tell him something about last night. He'll keep asking about that."

"Okay," she said, trailing hands down my sides. My eyes slipped closed. It was so hard to focus on anything when she touched me. I swallowed and tried to unscramble my hormone-riddled brain. Task one, get Todd off my back and off my phone. Task two, finish my damn homework, with my clothes on.

"And I want to tell him about you. Stop that." Her fingers found their way up my borrowed tank top.

"Why?" Her fingers slid higher up to my bra.

"Because. I'm trying not to have sex with you. Until after I finish my homework."

"Okay. Excuse me," she said. Then she moved to stand up. I grabbed her hand before she got very far.

"Where are you going?"

"I'm going over there." She pointed across the room to the armchair.

I shoved her hand back up my shirt. "You stay. Just keep it above the belt, Ms. Sanchez."

"This would be a lot easier if you didn't smell so fucking good."

"Well, you're stuck with me and my fuckable scent. What should I tell my brother?"

"Tell him you have an amazing girlfriend. And be sure to include a detailed description of how cute I am."

"Fine. I will," I said defiantly. I started texting. "Your name's Mila. You're a Mexican-American freshman from Washington, DC, studying business. You don't have a Facebook account so I'm telling him not to bother looking." I hit send then swapped my phone for my book, dropping my cell on the coffee table.

Her breath tickled my ear as she chuckled softly. I breathed in her delicious scent and gave myself over to her advances, only for a moment. I turned my head enough for her to kiss me. Our lips met and when her tongue slid into my mouth, I forgot all about Todd and my homework.

Until my phone vibrated again. I turned away from Camila with a frustrated grunt.

*Brady sucks ass this season. Is she hot?* Todd's text read.

"He wants to know what you look like. Are pictures banned by the master?"

"Sort of. Here." She snatched my phone out of my hand and turned it around. "Say cheese." I flashed my teeth just as she pressed the bottom. "Send him that."

Of course I looked like crap. Camila looked like she had just walked off a centerfold's page, all sweet cheeked and pouty lipped. She'd even managed to smile in the most adorable way that hid her canines. So unfair. If it had been anyone else but my brother, I would have demanded a re-shoot. Something else bothered me, though.

I twisted around so I could see her face.

"Are you sure you want me to send this? There isn't some demon law about not showing yourself to non-feeder humans or something?" I did want Todd to know her, and I trusted him more than anyone. I knew he would never intentionally do anything to hurt me or Camila. But after our scare in the hotel, the last thing I wanted to do was put her at any sort of risk, even if she did want to meet my family.

She looked at me for a moment and gently tucked loose strands of my hair behind my ear.

"This is why I love you," she said. "You call me Mila and that's who I'll be, whenever that's what you need. And Todd will be safe. And so will Linda. And your dad. And so will I. Yes, I have to be careful about some things, but I don't have to hide from the people you love."

"And what if they want to meet your parents at some point?"

"Well, Rodrick is well-versed in shifting form, and Natasha's Spanish is pretty damn good."

"Very funny." I kissed the tip of her nose. "I love you, Mila."

"Good. Now send the picture. Then finish your reading. And then, I'm sorry, but I'm going to have to fuck you again. Or eat that sweet pussy."

My teeth grabbed at my bottom lip as I tried to hold in a shiver. It didn't work. My crotch was hardwired to her every word, and now my underwear was drenched.

I sent the picture and then made a real effort to try to read. Three pages in, the TV snatched my attention. The Pats scored on an interception. And just as Peyton Manning threw a subtle sidelines hissy fit, Todd texted back.

*DAMN! And she's in Alpha Beta O O O?*

"You're not meeting my brother," I said.

"Why?" she asked taking my phone from me. I ignored her burst of laughter and turned back to my book. "I'm sorry. Would it be better if I were homely? I can shift form to an ugly girl."

"No! I mean I'm not that shallow. I just—"

"Yeah. That's what I thought. Don't worry. Your brother's not exactly my type."

"Is it the fully human part or the penis you don't agree with?"

I jumped as she suddenly kicked the coffee table out of the way. It skidded across the carpet, stopping right in front of the TV. Somehow my book and my phone stayed put, right on the dark wood surface, but I had no time to marvel over that work of physics. Camila picked me up and spun me around in the same swing of her arms. Before I could blink, I was facing her, straddling her lap. I wanted to argue, but it was useless. She pulled my tank over my head. My bra wasn't far behind.

"He's not you, baby," she said lightly. She took my nipple in her mouth, stroking the very tip with her tongue and her fang. I was done. My body was hers.

"I'm never going to get this reading done," I said, fighting back a moan.

"Yes, you are." She nipped at my other breast, torturing me some more. "Just not right now."

A shred of determination lingered, but that didn't stop me from settling myself against her stomach and twisting my fingers through the soft, short hair at the back of her head. I looked down, watching her tongue slide back and forth over my tight nipple.

"No," I pretended to protest. "Stop. Stop. Please. No. No. My homework. No…" She bit down gently and my head rolled back on my shoulders. I let out a shameless groan. "Don't stop at all. Oh God. That feels so good."

Her scent washed up between us as she breathed against my skin. Such an ass. She knew she had all the control. She knew the moment my resolve turned to crap. I had to do something about that.

"Actually. Wait."

Camila gazed up at me wide-eyed. My nipple was still in her mouth.

"I want to make you come," I said quickly.

She released my nipple and her grip on my waist and leaned back against the couch. I glanced at the smooth skin of her shoulder as she stretched her arms out along the cushions, all cool and calm.

"Do you?"

"Yes." Sure, I had made her come at the hotel, but for some reason, that felt different. She was already keyed up and we'd already had sex twice at that point. It was my turn to initiate something. Even if it was five minutes after she initiated something first.

"Well, Red." She started to move so I climbed off her lap and watched her stand. She pulled off her tank top and the small red track shorts she had on. She hadn't bothered with a bra, but she ditched her underwear just as quickly before stretching out on the floor. She crossed her hands behind her head and peered up at me like she wasn't butt naked with the figure of a sixties pinup girl. Her small waist and enormous breasts with large tips taunting my intentions.

"Have at me," she said playfully.

I stood next to the couch, fiddling with my hands. Camila just lay there patiently waiting for me to back up my bravado. She shifted a little and crossed her ankles. The simple motion made her thighs look even fuller. I had to get in there.

"Do you want a pillow or something?" I asked, mentally slapping myself for sounding lame.

Her mouth twitched, fighting a smile. "No, I'm fine. Thank you for asking."

I waited a moment, thinking of the best way to approach the situation until my crotch reminded my brain that there was a naked woman lying on the floor waiting for me to get on with it.

"Okay." I sounded ridiculously determined. I got on my knees beside her and crawled over her body. Now I knew I was being ridiculous. I bit my lip, trying not to crack up. "Don't move."

"I'll try not to." Camila snorted, grimacing to keep her reaction under control.

"Don't laugh." My own snort crippled my demand.

"You're laughing."

"Because you're laughing. Okay, seriously." I sat up with a deep breath, letting my butt settle on her hips, and fixed a stern expression on my face. Then I collapsed to the floor with my hands beside her shoulders and glared at her. She glared back, but the gold in her eyes still twinkled. "This is serious. I'm sexy and you're turned on. And I'm about to give you the best orgasm of your life. Don't you dare laugh."

She licked her fangs, eyeing my mouth while she spoke. "Come here, Red." Giving up control, again, I leaned forward until our lips met.

"Give me your hand," she whispered softly. She took my fingers and guided them between our bellies, then between her legs. I gasped the moment my hand brushed against her spread slit. She was so wet and hot.

Camila held my fingers as we teased her clit together for a few moments, gently toying with the length and the tip. She sighed a little and closed her eyes, but her interest in the external play didn't seem to last very long.

Camila moved my index finger to the opening of her pussy. She arched her back slightly and let her thighs open wider.

"Now. Fuck me."

She let go and let me gently trace the most delicate bit of her skin, coating my fingers in her wetness. She watched me, breathing steadily, patiently. I appreciated that. I was talking a big game, but I did want to know her more, without the dim lights and the music or the ice cream hangover. We might have been at her place, but I needed to know this part of her on my level of the playing field.

The Patriots mocked me by scoring again. I glanced at the TV then back at Camila.

She reached up and brushed her thumb across my cheek. "I love you." The focus in her eyes told me she meant it. Pushing two fingers deep inside her was my reply.

She inhaled deeply and settled into the carpet, closing her eyes as she let the breath out.

I moved slowly, like she had done to me, using more pressure than speed, brushing her clit with the heel of my hand, pressing up into her inner walls. I loved the way she felt, tight and hot, her slick muscles clenching around my fingers. Leaning forward, I brushed my lips over her dark nipple. She let out the sexiest sound, partway between a whimper and a desperate purr, so I did it again, adding my tongue to the mix, dragging it around and around the tiny ripples of skin and the hard tip. She began touching me back, dragging her fingers up and down my arm, then stroking lower to my ribs.

I added more pressure. And another finger.

Camila's short nails bit into the skin on my side. "Ginger..." she moaned.

"Does that feel good?" I asked, thrusting deeper.

"Yes."

"Seriously?" I couldn't hide my shock.

"Yes. Just like that. Fuck."

I latched my mouth back onto her nipple. I peered up at her as I suckled, mesmerized by the sound of her body. It was an addictive sound, an arousing sound. Her hips rose off the floor and I realized my hand had stopped moving.

"Oh. Sorry." I frowned and started my fingers working again. I did my best to ignore the way my body was reacting to her, the way my brain seemed to want to capture every detail of the moment and focused on giving her all the pleasure I could, with my hands and my mouth. It was like rubbing my stomach and patting myself at the same time. I knew I looked like an idiot doing it, and in this case, sounded like an idiot too, but if I focused hard enough, I always got the hang of it.

After a while, my fingers and my wrist started to get tired. The muscle in my forearm was starting to twitch. Camila liked it hard and deep, harder than I'd ever fucked myself, but I refused to give up. She had made me come so hard, with and without her bite, and I wanted to do the same for her.

Camila came without warning, growling and arching on the floor. She turned her head sharply, calling my name, and that's when I felt it.

I looked between her legs, making sure I kept up with the motions of my hand until she was completely finished. Come was leaking out of her bare pussy onto the rug. I swallowed thickly and fought the urge to replace my hand with mouth. It was the hottest thing I'd ever seen.

She sat up and gathered me in her arms, like I needed a few moments to recover. I stroked her back and her hair and softly kissed her cheeks and her forehead. She exhaled and held me tighter.

"It was pretty amazing, wasn't it," I said.

"Best orgasm I've ever had," she replied with a kiss to my neck.

"Yeah, right." My tone was bitchier than I intended, but I couldn't fight the tightness in my chest. I had decades of lovers to compete with. I shuffled off her lap and reached for my bra.

And I was flat on my back before I could get the strap around my arm. Camila ripped the bra from my hand and tore my sweats off my legs. When my lungs snapped back into action, she was on top of me, her hips pressing my body into the floor.

"I'm being honest with you," she grumbled fiercely. "It's very easy to fuck someone, but no one has ever made love to me before. Not before you."

"Really?" You are not going to cry. You are not going to cry.

Camila rolled her eyes then kissed me. "You drive me crazy, Red. I hope you know that."

"Good. I love you. And since you're already on top of me…"

Her fingers sliding into my pussy was her reply.

I swear Amy had set up a pup tent outside the elevator. I saw her out in the kitchen the moment the door slid open. The very second my big toe hit the landing in the pantry, she came bolting into the small space, screeching my name, ready to take me down for a thorough debriefing. She came up short the moment she saw Camila beside me.

"Oh. Hi." Her lips quivered as she tried to hold in a giggle of embarrassment.

"Hello, Amy. It's nice to see you too," Camila replied.

Her tone was suddenly formal. It made me happy to think that even though she was perfectly comfortable joking around with the girls, hanging out with them casually, she only seemed to relax with me. Amy wouldn't have known there was a difference, and I was okay letting that be the case.

Either way, Camila's tone and sudden appearance on the first floor of the house didn't stop Amy from flapping her gums. It just slowed her a little bit.

"Are you going to come bake with us?" Amy asked her. Camila took my hand and led me out of the elevator.

"As a matter of fact, I am. I've been neglecting you girls a little," she said.

"Oh, I fully blame Ginger for that." Amy grinned, the total suck up she was.

"I didn't miss you at all." I scowled back at her.

"Yes, you did. You love me," Amy replied, lacing her arm through mine on the other side as we walked into the kitchen.

Thanks to Camila and her amazing mouth and fingers and teeth, I had missed dinner, but at nine, my presence was required in the ABO kitchen. All of us new girls had several hundred cookies, brownies, and other miscellaneous treats to prepare for our Types of Hope bake sale. I barely finished my homework in time to slip back into some clothes and head upstairs. I'd every intention of sneaking a few baked goods.

When we stepped into the kitchen I saw that all of the new girls were there, except Anna-Jade, Benny, and Ruth. Cleo and Danni were missing too. I was surprised to see Paige and Samantha helping Florencia clean up the remains of an enormous meal. Apparently, we'd missed a formal Sunday dinner. They covered the last few dishes and slid them into the Sub-Zero while Gwen and Kyle helped Kate and Jordan set out enough sugar, flour, and eggs to make cookies and cupcakes for the whole university.

Amy followed Camila and me as we took up post near the fridge, trying to stay out of the way until Kate and Jordan had delegated baking duties. As our community outreach chairs, it was up to them to decide who got to do the fun work like decorating and who had to sit outside the cafeteria selling the goods.

Camila settled against the counter and pulled me between her legs. I let out a contented sigh, trying to ignore Amy. She was practically vibrating, just dying to get some dirt out of me. She knew better than to ask how good the sex was right in front of Camila. Or so I thought.

She leaned toward us and lowered her voice in a crappy attempt to be subtle, but the dramatics of talking out of the side of her mouth caught Laura's and Paige's attention. And Samantha's. I glared back at Samantha. She took the hint to mind her own business and looked away.

"I do have one question for you," Amy muttered to Camila.

"What would that be?" I could feel Camila's breath against my neck.

"Did you like her outfit?" Amy asked.

"Yes, Amy, I did." Camila laughed.

"Did you like what she had on underneath it?"

My head snapped in Amy's direction. "Amy. Jesus." Camila continued to take her prodding graciously, even though Amy deserved a good smack.

"I did, Amy. Thank you," Camila replied.

I had to get Amy to shut up. Asking where Cleo, Danni, and Benny were seemed like the perfect subject to use as a diversion.

"Hey—" I started. Just then Florencia appeared in front of me with a covered plate of food. My name was written on the cellophane.

"Oh. Thank you," I said, not bothering to hide my shock.

"It's still warm, but I would heat it up," she said. Florencia's voice, with its full accent, was so warm and inviting. It was hard to believe she was as unfriendly as Cleo had made her out to be. Camila took the plate from her with another gracious thank you, then stepped around me to slide the plate in the microwave. Her duties as occasional mother complete, Florencia slipped out of the room into the living room. Listening to Cleo hadn't exactly paid off in every department. As I watched her stocky form disappear through the swinging door, I made a mental note to try to have a conversation with Florencia sometime soon.

I retrieved my reheated food, and Camila and I plopped down at the table while Kate and Jordan divvied out tasks. Amy swore up and down she had the most amazing sugar cookie recipe so Jordan put her on the baking squad with Samantha, Laura, and Gwen, who all made similar claims. My baking skills were on par, but I was too busy wolfing down Florencia's cornbread and mashed potatoes to volunteer for the most urgent job.

Camila and Faeth, who appeared quite suddenly, volunteered to help Ebony, Kyle, and Maddie with icing and decorating. Their artistic vampire skills were far superior to those of us humans. Irene, Mel, and I were put on wrapping duty. Paige gave Mel a couple million baggies and red ribbons, playfully threatening our lives if we didn't make each little package of treats look professionally prepared. They told us then that Ruth and Benny were out with Cleo wallpapering campus with bake sale fliers. Amy threw in that Danni had a group project to finish.

Anna-Jade was MIA. I checked the clock. She still had three minutes to call or make an appearance. I wouldn't have been surprised if Paige had whipped out a stopwatch, but at eight fifty-nine, the front door slammed.

"I'm here. I'm here. Don't bake without me," we heard Anna-Jade yell from the foyer. Seconds later she came sprinting into the kitchen, flushed and grinning ear to ear. The whole room looked at her as she narrowly avoided slamming right into Laura.

"Hey. Sorry. I'm not late, am I?" she panted, shrugging out of her ABO jacket.

"No," Paige said. She reached into the fridge and handed Anna-Jade a plate Florencia had set aside for her.

"Thank—" Anna-Jade was interrupted by Amy's shriek.

"OMG!" Amy wiped her hands on a towel, then power-walked around the counter. Anna-Jade turned an interesting shade of white and shuffled back a step. Amy took her arm, then playfully grabbed Anna-Jade's head and craned her neck in our direction. "A.J. has a hickey."

"I do?" Anna-Jade broke free and whipped her body to the side. The front of the fridge was just shiny enough for her to get a look at the mouth-shaped bruise on her neck. "Oh gosh. It's huge."

"The girl comes in here with a hickey the size of a doughnut and says 'Oh gosh,'" Ebony said, shaking her head.

"Who the hell gets hickeys these days?" Amy said.

"A.J. does, apparently," I said. It was a huge hickey.

"At least we know Micah knows how to use those juicy lips," Paige said, and for the first time ever I saw her smile. I stared at her for a second. It was a little creepy.

Kate walked over to Anna-Jade and got a closer look at her neck. She snickered. "I'll show you how to cover that up. Go eat. You can be on wrapping duty for now."

"Okay. Oh, um, Micah said the guys will donate a hundred bucks if we make a cake just for their freshman." Anna-Jade blushed.

"Fine, but you have to ice it. Now eat," Kate said, swatting at her playfully.

After Anna-jade was thoroughly embarrassed, some of the girls scattered until their skills were actually needed. Kate plugged in her iPod and blasted the room with girlie pop. Anna-Jade skipped heating up her food and sat with me and Camila. I should have thanked her for taking Amy's attention off me. Mel, Irene, and Faeth joined us at the table with a deck of cards. I opted out of the games, deciding it would be more fun to feel Camila up under the table while she and Irene took on Faeth and Mel in a game of spades.

It all started as innocent caressing with one hand on her knee as I finished my dinner. She was mine now and I didn't see any reason not to adore her amazing body at every possible moment. Plus, I owed her for interrupting my productive afternoon of learning. I drew lazy circles across her thigh with my fingertips. I was making myself hot all over again just touching her, but soon I realized that part of her vampire strengths, particularly her nerves of steel, were not on my side. My super sexy efforts were getting no reaction out of her at all. That annoyed the hell out of me. I was powerless against her smallest attempts at seduction. I inched my fingers a little closer to her crotch, determined to prove that a certain redhead was her true weakness.

Mel's gaze shot to me when I dropped my fork.

Camila had caught my wandering hand and rubbed it against her crotch. I could feel the heat of her body through her jeans and that made my pussy instantly wet. She leaned over and kissed me just below my ear, holding my hand in place. I stopped breathing.

She whispered to me, swiveling her hips, "I love you, Red, but don't start something you can't finish right now." She quickly let go of my hand and turned right back to her cards.

Faeth let out a booming belly laugh that made her brown curls shake. "Keep distracting her, Ginger. She's cheating."

I picked up my fork and my pride and finished the last bit of my dinner. Camila was sweet to me still, giving me little kisses on my cheek and my neck between hands of cards. After a while, I didn't feel like such an idiot for blowing my attempt at turning her on.

Faeth kept taking little digs at Camila's shady approach to the game, and I noticed for the first time that Faeth had a little bit of accent. It may have been Australian, but I couldn't tell. It went nicely with her firm, husky tone.

"Faeth, where are you from, um originally? I love your accent."

"Don't tease her with compliments, baby. She doesn't respect me enough to keep her hands to herself," Camila joked. I think. And then I remembered what she'd said the night before about Tokyo and Faeth and their argument over me. I didn't think asking her, or even complimenting her about something as little as her voice, could be viewed as an invitation or a come on, but then again, I didn't know this sister-queen at all. I looked from Camila back to Faeth just as she gazed across the table at me. Her normally dark eyes were now glowing amber beneath her thick lashes. I swallowed, unable to look away.

"Faeth, cut that shit out," Camila muttered dryly. She grabbed my chair and pulled it closer, marking her territory. That snapped me out of Faeth's trance.

"I was born in New Zealand. It's your go, Irene," Faeth replied. I didn't miss the way her eyes started to dim.

"Oh. Well. It's nice," I muttered, cuddling closer to Camila.

Faeth just smirked and played her next card.

❖

Operation Bake Sale dissolved into a full on dance party the moment Ruth, Cleo, and Benny got back to the house. They came into the kitchen somewhere around the first few notes of "She Wolf" and Cleo couldn't stop herself from doing her best Shakira impression, which included seductively dancing up on Paige. Once my duties as packing elf were complete, Camila and I snuck away to bed. It had only been a few hours, but I wanted her to myself again. I needed her to touch me.

Around seven the next morning, Cleo came and grabbed me for breakfast. I saw then that early mornings were Cleo's down time. She seemed to be fine, but she was quiet and subdued as we walked to campus. I wanted to ask her what was on her mind, but I was also a big fan of moments where I could be alone in my head, even with other people around. By lunchtime, when I met up with her at our bake sale table outside the cafeteria, she was back to full Cleo crazy, calling Anna-Jade out on her hickey in front of Micah and Greg.

The bake sale was a complete success. Everything was gone before one o'clock, and the OBA boys were bragging all over campus about the cake we'd baked for them. We got some nasty looks from the Xi O girls and their rushes, but they didn't do a good job of portraying superiority over raging jealousy.

All day, I got texts from Camila. Not exactly notes in my locker, but still perfect reminders of why I fell so hard for her and why every free moment was filled with wanting her. I couldn't wait to get back to the house.

The sister-queens were having their weekly meeting, apparently to talk about us and any other vampire related matters that needed to be covered. My refusal to go through the switch and the fact that I was useless as a feeder, left me in this weird gray zone. Whatever happened between Camila and me in the future was our business, but I was still part vampire-demon, sort of. I would always be welcomed in their world no matter what role I took. Camila wanted me to see what went into being a responsible member of vampire society. Once the formal part of the gathering was out of the way, we would talk about my blood.

Camila and I dragged ourselves out of bed after a not-so-quickie and headed to Omi's quarters. I was glad Camila had thought to include me, but I had no idea how the other sister-queens felt about it.

"They don't mind that I'm coming?"

"Not at all. I spoke with them and Dalhem about you. No matter what you decide to do, you're part of the family now."

"I feel bad that I'm sort of worthless."

"You are very far from worthless. It's up to you where you want to fit in, and they want to help you figure that out. Even if a few of them also want to fuck you." I scowled at the playful wink she gave me and then she knocked on the door. I wondered where that wink was last night when Faeth was staring me down. My thoughts were interrupted by the door clicking open.

I had seen Omi four times, and I hadn't said a single word to her. All the sister-queens were beautiful in their own way, and Omi was no different. She opened the door to her lounge and greeted us with a warm hello. She looked completely at home and comfortable, but still elegant, even though she was only wearing a white bikini top and flowing white linen pants. Her long dreadlocks were braided in a crown around her head.

We stepped inside and I realized her wardrobe matched her design scheme. I don't know how she managed it, but walking into Omi's underground apartment was like stepping into some tropical beach resort. Blue, yellow, and green accents added splashes of color to the white and bleached wood furniture. Camila's room felt like a Gothic cave. I may have picked the right sister-queen to be with, but if I ever needed a tropical change of scenery, I knew exactly where to go.

Omi caught me looking at the bright track lighting. I felt like I was outside.

"Camila won't tell you, but some of us do miss the sun." Surprisingly, her voice had a hint of a British accent to it.

"Omi's from Barbados," Camila said.

"Oh. I've never been farther south than Disney World," I said.

"I'd tell you you must go, but it's far too sunny for your lady-queen," she replied with a grin. I couldn't help but smile back.

"Tokyo's running a bit late." I spun around at the voice behind us. Natasha suddenly appeared. Then Faeth right beside her. I'd seen Camila vanish and reappear, but only on camera. It was a little jarring to see it two feet in front of you. I blinked as they greeted us casually and made themselves at home. Camila and I followed, taking a seat on Omi's white couch. A few moments later, Kina arrived. She used the door.

"Where is Tokyo?" Camila asked.

"I'm here. Calm down," Tokyo replied before she took form. Her outfit shocked me more than her sudden appearance. The tight leather pants she had on flared over her thick-soled boots. Her leather zip front halter top was open, revealing the curves of her breasts and her belly button. Her black hair was messy, down around her shoulders. I was pretty sure she'd just finished having sex, or having sex had to her. She pulled a hair clip out of her pocket and arranged her straight-do on top of her head. I looked away when her nipples peaked out.

"Okay." She plopped down in the last available chair. "Where were we?"

"Close your shirt and we'll tell you." Camila frowned.

"Sorry. Ginger was enjoying the view." I looked up then over at Camila about to stutter a denial. "I'm kidding, Ginge. Take it easy." She zipped up her halter. "Better? Great."

"Were you downtown?" Camila asked.

"I was, and before you say anything, yes, I was with Moreland. Moving on." I did my best not to cringe at the thought of that particular vampire.

"That's fine, but just so you know, she seemed to have the wrong impression of how to address me. I had to remind her the other day," Camila said, putting her arm around my waist.

"I know. She told me. She is sorry," Tokyo said.

"Good. Natasha?"

"I'm happy to report Whitney-Pearl is adjusting very well..." Natasha paused for a moment while Camila explained to me what the heck she was talking about.

"Anna-Jade's mom is in prison. Some white-collar shit she got wrapped up in at work. Her dad has been drinking and taking his anger out on A.J. and her little sister. She's only thirteen. He's in jail now and we got Whitney-Pearl into a foster home with two very kind feeders."

I nodded, keeping my opinion and my shock to myself as Natasha went on. It went without saying that the truth about her family was not my business to share.

Natasha had spoken to the chancellor and secured Whitney-Pearl a spot at MU once she graduated high school. I liked Anna-Jade a lot. It broke my heart she'd been abused, her and her sister, but I was so glad to hear our sister-queens had done something about it, that Camila had helped to do something about it.

Camila filled everyone in on the redistribution of some feeders in Houston. Omi reported that everyone was on track with their grades, but Julia had requested a tutor for her advanced French class.

"How are the boys across the street?" Omi asked.

"It's good that Ginger is here," Natasha said.

I frowned at her sudden solemn look. "Why?"

"The boys are all doing very well," she said. "Except your laboratory partner, Gregory."

My huff of frustration gave me away. Obviously, we had no real secrets when it came to the sister-queens, and now the brother-kings, but Greg had tried to confide in me. I promised him I wouldn't mention the issues he was having with joining OBA. I knew they all had his best interests in mind, especially Rodrick, but my word meant something to me.

"What's the problem exactly?" I asked.

"Rodrick is concerned he's hiding something. He throws himself too enthusiastically into the feedings. Rodrick has probed his mind, but the young man is so truly conflicted, it's no indicator of where those feelings will take him."

"Mind reading isn't exactly our specialty," Kina chimed in. "It's thought altering. Humans don't think linear, clear thoughts unless they're in the act of forming a sentence or in the middle of making a decision. If Rodrick asks Greg, 'Does it make you uncomfortable when I feed from you?' Rodrick could get a sense of a feeling from him, no matter what his answer was, but Rodrick can't make informed decisions based on impressions. On the other hand, Rodrick could convince Greg that he enjoys every part of the feedings, but that's not what we're trying to do. We just want to know if you've noticed anything or if he's said anything to you that's more concrete. Everyone has intense emotions, even homicidal thoughts, but that doesn't mean we'll act on them. Greg could be thinking all sorts of things, but they aren't facts."

"You guys haven't talked to Samantha about this? She's going out with him. She spends way more time with him than I do."

"We've thought of that, but Rodrick says Greg trusts you more," Natasha said.

Why? Greg and I were barely friends. We weren't friends, actually. We were lab partners with mutual friends. Why did he have to trust me at all, let alone more than his girlfriend? I regretted giving my word in the first place.

Camila kissed my temple. "Look, Red. Greg seems like a nice boy, but he's aggressive during feedings. You don't have to tell us anything, just if you notice anything or if he says anything that suggests he could be a danger to Samantha or himself—"

"Wait, is he getting violent with her?" I asked.

"No. It's just Rodrick has had a few like him before, ones who were confused about their sexuality. He was able to head the problem off before anything happened, and we'd like to do the same with Greg."

I felt backed into a corner, but they had a point. All the guys seemed to understand that their relationships with the brother-kings were not a deciding factor in their sexual orientation. Rodrick preferred women, and even though Micah served Rodrick with no problem, he loved Anna-Jade like crazy. Something told me Greg would never be okay with the feedings. But if I could help, I wanted to. I nodded and mumbled my okay before resting my head on Camila's shoulder.

## CHAPTER TWELVE

After their meeting, Omi let us stay in her lounge while Camila and I met with Rodrick in private. When we were done discussing my genetic abnormalities, the sister-queens planned on coming back to test my powers, the ones I was positive I didn't have.

Rodrick appeared suddenly by the coffee table, with the results of my blood tests and his comforting smile that dulled the intensity of his electric blue eyes and his large fangs. He handed me the folder. I opened it and realized pretty quickly I didn't understand any of the results inside.

"Though you are not showing any outward signs of vampirism, the blood in you is very potent. Most pressing, Camila cannot feed you. Neither can I. If you are sick or injured, you need to feed from someone further removed from a bourne-demon. I am almost certain a small amount of our blood would jump-start your metamorphosis," Rodrick said.

"Oh. Okay." I hadn't even considered the effect Camila's blood would have on me. And then I was curious about Rodrick. "Um, how far removed are you, if you don't mind me asking?"

His grin made his bright white fangs seem even bigger. "I do not mind in the least. I am three times removed from a bourne-demon. All of my makers were very powerful."

"Okay. So I don't drink from you two. What else?"

"Hmm," Camila mused, reading over the papers in my lap. "We can track him. The levels aren't that high, but there is enough of our blood in you to track whoever saved you and your mother."

"If he's still alive," Rodrick said.

A twinge of hope flickered in my chest. "He?" I asked. "You can tell it was a man, for sure?"

Rodrick glanced at Camila before he answered me. "Yes. We may be able to locate him. We do not know him, or we would have recognized your scent, but the world is big. Still you must consider, Ginger—"

"That he might be dead," I said. That hope quickly burned out. I looked up as Camila took my hand.

"We could also track your birth father, if you'd like," she said cautiously. She must have seen the pain spread across my face as I started to understand what she meant. For a moment, I'd been thinking my birth dad and my blood donor were the same person, but they weren't. My birth dad could have gone through the change after I was conceived, like Samantha's father. It was possible, but it wasn't the case.

My adoptive dad had more than made up for the years of my life I'd spent without a father. Still, it hurt so badly to know there were two men in the world who had given me life and walked away just as easily.

I let Camila's arm slip back around my waist as she leaned against me. I leaned back.

"Can I think about that?" I asked.

"Of course you can," Rodrick replied. "I understand that the true concept of what we are seems dangerous and frightening, but we do love you, all of you. Any request you have of us, we will grant you."

"Track my maker. Not my father," I said. I had a father, an amazing dad who'd taught me all I could know about sports and still high-fived me when I'd finally picked out a prom dress. He was all the father I would ever need.

"Rodrick, please." Camila asked him politely to give us a moment. I didn't hear or see him vanish, but I sensed the moment he'd left the room.

"I don't want to know him. I can't not blame him. No matter what. Even if he didn't know she was pregnant. I'm not ready. I'll blame him," I said.

Her hand slid up the back of my neck and she gently massaged the base of my scalp. My eyes closed. I felt the tears threatening to spill over.

"Baby, it's your choice."

"I know. I just, I don't know what happened between my birth parents. And I don't think I want him to explain. I just—" I let out a huge breath. I couldn't deal with this, not now, not in Omi's apartment. I sniffled and wiped my eyes, shaking my head on another deep breath. "Rodrick can come back. Let's finish this and then I'll have a meltdown. I'm sure Omi wants her living room back."

"Omi is fine. If you change your mind, just let me know. We can find them both." I said okay and let it go.

Rodrick returned once I'd pulled it together and we talked some more about the precautions I should take. Camila told him about the incident that had followed her feeding with Amy. They both agreed that human blood shouldn't have any negative effects on me, but Camila still promised to be careful with me after her feedings.

When there were no more warnings, the sister-queens came back and they grilled me about my powers. And I told them again I didn't have any. Camila had explained that I had seen through her cloak for humans, and unlike the other girls, I could sense her mental influence, but wasn't capable of stopping it. They already knew about the Amy incident. There were a few cracks about the kind of mind control fun they could have with me, but those went silent when Camila growled.

"Nothing bizarre happened to you as a kid, nothing recently?" Faeth asked.

"Recently?" I mocked her.

"Other than all this joining our little club. Crikey, you are a smart ass." I chuckled at the way the words sounded with her accent.

"I have a pretty sensitive sense of taste and smell, but that's it," I said.

"Well, maybe we can teach her," Kina said. "Walk her through some things and then we'll know if there's anything lying dormant."

Camila looked at me, gently stroking my hair. "Is that okay?"

"Sure. I guess, but don't get your hopes up."

"Before we start, there's one more thing you should understand. Our powers reflect the functional needs of our master. A pure, powerful demon needs to be able to deceive, to appear in different forms, and to disappear on a whim. Some demons, not any of us, have the power of possession. All of these tricks are meant to do evil, I won't lie to you, but we use them for our own survival and for the good of our feeders. The downside to being born human is that the powers we don't use begin to fade over time. I'm excellent at shifting. Tokyo is better with the mind tricks. My mental skills are still sharp, but they would be better if I was mind tampering for the Feds every day. We can also communicate with each other through telepathy. You've seen Camila vanish and reappear?"

"Yeah." After Kina's explanation, the ability seemed even creepier.

"And she was able to read your mind?"

"Yeah. I sort of forced her into my thoughts involuntarily."

"Well, we can start there."

For two hours, they worked with me, and by the end, I was exhausted. Camila was afraid to overpower me and she didn't trust Faeth and Tokyo in my head, so Omi, Natasha, and Kina patiently walked me through several trials. Rodrick was in a similar situation as Camila. His influence would have been too strong. He sat back and did his best not to openly mock the ridiculousness that followed.

First, Omi opened her mind to me. I tried over and over to get in there and snoop around, hoping I could find some silly juicy bit to tease her with. But no. Nothing. We just ended up staring at each other until my eyes watered.

Natasha suggested that I try to vanish and reappear across the room. She gave up when I gave up and just walked over to the TV. I couldn't do it.

Other than Camila and Rodrick, Kina was the most skilled in changing form. I watched her become a German shepherd, a fluffy white cat, a bear (she knocked over Omi's coffee table with that one), a raven, and then as a final showpiece, she turned into Faeth. One moment I was looking at this Native American beauty, with her high cheekbones, full lips, and her long, ink-black hair, and the next moment I was staring at an exact copy of the vampire sitting on the floor beside me. Now that was a useful power to have. Just as quickly, she was back in her own body.

"The best shifters can alter parts of their body separately." Kina put her hands on her hips and looked around. "Let's try Camila's rack, Omi's arms, and Rodrick's package." She winked at Natasha. "And your hair." I blinked twice and Kina's arms were identical to Omi's—finely toned and a chocolate brown. The perfect breasts I'd come to love on Camila's body were too big above Kina's smaller waist, but they were Camila's breasts all the same. It was strange to see Kina with my red hair and just short of traumatizing to see how well hung Rodrick was.

"My tits look better than that," Camila said.

"And I think you're missing an inch, maybe," Rodrick added.

"Oh whatever," Kina said, but this time her voice sounded like Natasha's. I blinked once more, trying to pick my jaw up, and she had taken Faeth's full form.

"Do werewolves even exist or are you guys just messing with humans during full moons?" I asked, suddenly short of breath.

"Guilty," Tokyo said with a devious laugh.

"You want to give it a go, mate?" Kina said, copying Faeth's accent exactly. I stared at her standing there naked then over to the real Faeth who was playfully flipping Kina off.

"I know I can't do that," I said in defeat.

"Why don't we start small then?" Kina turned back into herself and slipped back into her jeans and T-shirt. I agreed and let her walk me through the small steps of shifting. We got as far as making my eyes appear brown and my hair look black. That's where it stopped. It was a neat parlor trick, but not really that useful to me. Camila hated it and threw a mini fit, insisting I always belonged a redhead.

After that, we gave up. The sister-queens had lives to get back to. I was tired and hungry and horny. Camila wanted to order

Chinese for us, and she had no problem thinking of ways to put me to sleep. I thanked the ladies and Rodrick for their help and their patience, then followed Camila back to her room.

"What's your strongest power?" I asked her.

"Dalhem taught me balance. None of my powers are stronger than the other."

"Oh. Is Kina the only one who can switch to someone else like that?" I asked as we walked down the hall.

"No. There are others."

"Oh," I said, feeling foolish for what I was going to say next. "What if someone turns into you?"

"They won't have my scent, baby. No one but me smells the way I do. You'd be able to tell."

"That makes sense." I hadn't set about sniffing the other sister-queens, but no one on earth smelled as mouthwatering, as delicious and sweet as Camila.

She smiled and pulled me closer. "And no one will want you more than I do," she said. That, I was willing to believe.

❖

I'd spent the following afternoon lying against a mountain of pillows on Camila's bed in my letterman's sweater and my underwear, reviewing my notes for a quiz I had in my dance and culture class. Just some dates and names to memorize, but I wanted to get it done before our chapter meeting at nine. Camila was busy having a conversation with Tokyo. I thought it had something to do with Moreland, but there was so much to their world I was clueless about, I couldn't be sure.

She was only gone for an hour or so. Still, I beamed like an idiot when she came through the bedroom door.

"Hi." I shuffled to the edge of the bed on my knees. My arms went around her shoulders and her hands slid down the back of my underwear. I swallowed when she palmed my ass, then I exhaled a tight breath as I pressed myself harder against her belly. Now was a great time for her to join me on the bed, naked. Instead of mauling me, she stood there. I tried to smooth the creases of concentration on her forehead, but she just blinked then focused on my ruby necklace.

"So, Red," she said slowly.

"What is it, my Mila?"

"I need to feed tonight."

"Oh." My mood and my posture deflated.

"What would you like to do about that?" she asked, squeezing my butt.

"I would like you to feed from me, but that'll get you nowhere. I don't know. Whose turn is it?"

"Danni. I can go out down the hall to Tokyo's room. She's out for the night. Or I can feed in here and you can watch?"

If it had been Benny or Paige, it would have been an easy decision. Hell. No. Paige was too much sex-crazed fembot and not enough compassionate human being. I'd watched her with Danni and then Barb and even with Amy. I was bothered by her limited range of facial expressions and intimidated by her overt desire to have sex with the closest attractive female. I'd rather not stare into her cold, emotionless eyes while she was coming in my girlfriend's lap.

And Benny, well, even with her acne gone, she had a hard time changing clothes in front of us. Feedings were probably the only time she allowed herself to come. I had a feeling she wouldn't want an audience for that. Danni, though, I could handle. She was so obviously into Amy. The two of them were a giggly, chatty pair, but their approach to the sister-queens had been all business. Chatty, giggly business.

"I'll watch, but can Amy be here too?"

"Red." Camila gasped.

"Oh, shut up. I'm not going to get it on with Amy while you feed. It's just, I'd feel a little left out if she was in the room while you were feeding from Danni and I wasn't invited. You can feed and Amy can take care of Danni."

"And what will you be doing while we're all being taken care of?" she asked before she gave me a soft kiss on the lips.

"What do you want me to do?"

Camila pulled out her cell phone. I heard it ring a few times and then she said, "Can you and Amy come down now?…Thanks." She ended the call and tossed the phone beside me on the bed. "I want you to stay where I can see you."

"I can do that."

Amy and Danni were probably busy hooking up when Camila called. It would take them a few minutes to rearrange their underwear and get to the kitchen. I hadn't logged the paces from the elevator to Camila's apartment, but I figured if we got started right away, we'd have a good five minutes of making out before they knocked on the door. But again, instead of attacking me, Camila stood there at the foot of the bed, gently pinching and rubbing my ass. It was just making me ache even more.

"A proper feeding lasts about three minutes, but it seems longer. We don't need as much blood as it sounds, but it's better for the feeder if we go slow. Better if we take what we need slowly," she said. Then she went right for my neck. I tilted my head back, bracing myself for her fangs. All I felt was her tongue tracing the curves of my skin. "When they get here, will you let me in?"

"Yes," I whimpered back.

"God, Red." Her voice dissolved into a growl. "I want you."

"Feed and then you can have me."

She drew the torture out for the both of us, licking at my throat, drawing her fangs up and down until Danni knocked on the door. When they stepped into the room, I realized I was panting, all flushed and wet. Under normal circumstances, I was in no condition to deal with company.

"Where do you want me, boss?" Danni asked.

Camila calmly walked across the room and sank into the big chair that faced the bed. She patted the ottoman between her legs. "Come sit here." Danni followed instructions and took a seat in front of Camila.

"Um, what should I do?" Amy asked.

"That is completely up to you and Danni," Camila said.

Danni pounced right on that suggestion, flapping her hands for Amy to come across the room. I had a second or two to wonder what exactly they were going to do. Amy dove between Danni's thick legs, ripping her shorts off. She didn't have any underwear on underneath, so it felt like a safe bet they were picking up where they left off upstairs.

Camila waited a few moments, letting the two of them find their groove. I couldn't drown out the sound of Danni's pants and commands as Amy went to work licking and sucking her clit, but all I could see was Camila. She gazed back at me with her glowing eyes. I watched her parted lips, her tongue gliding over the corner of her mouth and the tips of her fangs.

Gently, she swept Danni's honey colored hair off her shoulders. There was a moment of jealously when she stroked Danni's neck. She knew exactly where the vein was, but the way she was looking at me and the soft sound of her purring made me think she was playing my lust against me, trying to get me even more fired up. It worked. My neck started to tingle in the same spot and I wanted her more.

She tilted Danni's head to the side. "Let me in, baby."

I still wasn't sure how it worked, but I tried to relax, and suddenly, I felt Camila in my head. And then, like a cobra, she struck, biting into Danni's throat, hard and fast.

Danni and I gasped at the same time. She came immediately, gripping the back of Amy's head while she rode her mouth. My hand went to my crotch, cupping my pussy through my underwear. The cotton was soaked all the way through. The slightest brush made my clit jump and tingle, but I couldn't move my hand away.

"Will you talk to me? I want to hear your voice," Camila said. Her voice inside me was just as smooth and seductive as always, but now I felt it embracing my thoughts and my heart.

I'd never done anything like this before, touching myself in front of other people, but I felt like she needed me. She needed Danni's blood, but she needed me to get through the feeding. So she could fully enjoy it.

I nodded and then said yes.

"Lie back, baby, and take off your clothes."

I did what she said, trying to keep my eyes on hers as I pulled off my sweater, my underwear, and my bra. Once I was naked, I settled back on her satin pillows. Her glowing gaze followed the path of my hands as I stroked my body, over my nipples, under my breasts and back. My hips rolled to the side and I squeezed my legs together, pinched my clit between my swollen lips. My eyes fluttered closed then opened again. I wanted to look at Camila. Her perfect mouth locked in place. I shivered, knowing exactly what it felt like when her fangs bit through my skin.

"Do you still want to touch yourself when you think of me?" her voice echoed in my mind.

"Yes."

"Show me. Show me how you touch yourself."

"Okay," I breathed. I opened my legs and started teasing the tip of my clit with light flicks of my middle finger.

"Tell me what you're thinking about." She knew. She was in my head. She saw what I saw. Her gorgeous caramel slit spread before me, soft and wet. My tongue teasing her clit the way my finger was teasing my own. She felt my jealousy and my envy. I wanted to be in Amy's position, on all fours between my girlfriend's legs. Thoughts of pleasuring her swirled through my mind, and she was seeing every single detail. But she wanted to hear it.

My finger slid up the side of my clit, then I pinched it. "I want to taste you."

"Where, baby? Tell me."

"Your pussy. I want to taste your pussy again." I whimpered. My fingers moved down further, soaking my hand. I teased my opening, wishing it were some part, any part, of Camila touching me.

Danni's breath hitched. Her moan echoed off the high ceiling as she came again.

I slid a finger inside and then another. "I want to fuck you with my tongue. God, Mila." I'd been thinking of her that way for the past few days and just now realized it. She was mine, my Mila, and my body needed her.

I pumped myself slowly. My other hand went to my nipple, pinching and pulling on the already tight bud. My hips came off the bed. I panted through the clenching of my pussy around my fingers.

"Harder," she demanded.

I eased up instead. The burn was killing me. My body was on the edge, aching to explode, but not without Camila. She must have seen the thought flickering through my mind.

"Come."

I continued with the slow pumping glide, but eased up on the pressure even more. "No. I want to wait for you."

"Please, baby. Come. I want to see you."

I sat up quickly, tearing my hands away from my slit. "No." I frowned stubbornly. "I want you."

Her lip curled back in a snarl and she growled, her teeth still deep in Danni's vein. She was drawing her blood harder and faster, making Danni squirm. She wasn't in pain. The opposite. She was close again, pressing herself further onto Amy's tongue, but I could see the thumping of her pulse. Camila was rushing to get to me. I wondered how much of her was demon and how much was sensible as she fed. How much of her need was because of me. She gripped tighter, sucking deeper.

I crawled back to the edge of the bed, fixing my eyes on hers. "Slow down," I said. I swallowed the nerves her grimace spiked in me, but I didn't back down. Anyone would have thought I was crazy saying no to her. When someone that strong and deadly gives you instructions, you follow them. I should have stayed rolling in the sheets, with my fingers inside me, until she told me to stop. I didn't care how close I was to coming. I wouldn't without her hands on my body and not without my lips on hers. I dropped back on my heels, making myself comfortable with a smooth, deep breath.

"Slow down," I repeated. Her eyes narrowed, but her jaw relaxed. Danni whimpered, a high sound of longing, but that was her problem. Her orgasm wasn't worth Camila hurting her. I waited patiently, occupying my hands by twisting the blanket around my index finger. I could still feel her in my head. No words now, but emotions. Her desire for me was red hot, bordering on anger. She wasn't going to hurt me. She wasn't capable of it, but as soon as she was done feeding, she was going to fuck the hell out of me.

Gently, she pulled away from Danni's neck. She licked the bite marks closed, the strokes of her tongue healing the red and tender skin. She moved just as slowly, laying Danni on the chair. Amy was right there, crawling up Danni's body.

Camila's movement across the room was a blur. She was on top of me, her clothes tossed aside, her knee pressed between my thighs before the breath rushed out of my lungs. My blood boiled under my cheeks. She stared at me, then moved her legs, pressing herself, hot and slick against my hip. My clit throbbed against her skin. My chest rose and fell under her perfect weight, her nipples lightly brushing against my breasts, hard and full. Now would have been a perfect time for her to release all that passion and fury. But she held still, her tongue brushing over her fangs and lips the only part of her that was moving.

Until I twisted my hips. I was willing to wait for the sake Camila's health and sanity and Danni's jugular, but now was our time. I lifted my head and licked her neck and twisted my hips some more.

"I thought you wanted me too," I said and then whimpered as she shifted against me, bringing our slits in perfect line with each other.

She didn't reply right away. Instead, she rode me hard, but it wasn't the rough brushes of our pussies against each other that pushed me over the edge. It was the moment when she finally kissed me, when her tongue slid past my lips. I tasted her...and I tasted Danni. Her blood was sweet, traces still fresh in Camila's mouth. The small voice in my mind, the full human, was back and telling me I shouldn't have wanted more of the flavor, but I couldn't turn my head away. I moaned into her mouth, letting the electricity tackle me from my clit to my toes to the tips of my breasts. I arched against her body. I needed the grind and the push on the outside to match the burn on the inside. She pulled away, putting all her weight behind her hips.

"I do, Red," she said against my lips. There was something more she wasn't telling me, but as much as I could let her in, I didn't have the power to wander around through her thoughts. And I never would. She dropped a gentle kiss to my ear. "I love you."

It wasn't what was on her mind. Well, maybe it was, but it wasn't all of it. But it was more than enough. I leaned in close, and this time, I pressed my teeth into her neck, pinching her smooth skin.

❖

Something in the middle of my back popped when I stretched. It felt great. I was sore as hell, but the whole room didn't want or need to hear the sounds of me rearranging my spine. I snorted softly as I muttered my apology. Then I looked at my phone again. The library was closing in three hours and I knew I would spend every second of those three hours with Greg and our newly formed study group. Our first big test of the semester was on Friday, and we'd been studying since dinner with three other kids from our class—Vince, Jamal, and Alison, and this forty-year-old guy named Judd, who'd decided to take another crack at his degree.

"I need a smoke. Let's take five," Judd suggested.

"Let's take ten," Greg said.

We all agreed and I stretched again, watching Judd stride down the aisle. I would have been fine studying by myself or just with Greg. I was hesitant when Judd asked us if could study with us. He was a little too grizzled for my liking, but it turned out the guy took meticulous notes and he recalled everything our professor had said with an accuracy that redefined anal retention. I took good notes, but I had been a little distracted lately.

Camila liked to text me, a lot. She would have stopped if I asked her to, but my heart took off, sparking brainless, lip-biting grins every time the name Mila flashed across my screen. I was doing well in all my classes, but after seeing Judd's notes, it was obvious I could do better. I was willing to overlook the second hand smoke if it meant I was getting a supplement to my education.

I'd asked Camila to spare me at least while I was in the library. It was easier to sneak texts in a crowded lecture hall than it was at a small table, but it wouldn't hurt if I took the ten minutes to call her. I stood to make a break for the door, but Greg was on his feet at the same time, an expectant look on his face.

"You want to go for a walk?" he asked.

Damn it. "Yeah, sure."

He nodded toward the stacks and I followed.

"Marshall gave me a skeleton key to the whole campus," he whispered, pulling a golden key from his pocket. My mind went right to the gutter. I bit my tongue because the only thing I wanted to ask him was what he had to do to get that key. Greg was cool and all, but he was not up for that kind of making fun. I just nodded back.

I imagined there were plenty of neat nooks and forbidden places all over campus. I found the most important space under a certain sorority house. I didn't feel the need to go searching for more. Greg was probably still looking.

He led me to a door in a spooky, quiet corner in the back of the building. The corner was a perfect make-out spot. It was dark and lined with stacks filled with books that looked like they hadn't been checked out since the late seventies. He checked behind us before opening the heavy door. Then he ushered me onto the dark landing. I looked around as he closed us in. I'd seen the stairwell from the outside every day, and every day, I'd ignored it.

"Okay," I said quietly, trying to avoid an echo. "This is cool." The fourth floor of the library was just like every other building on campus, beige and blue with white walls and wood trim. The brick encased stairwell was made of a dusty concrete that ran the height of the building against its rear. Every landing had a large window that looked out over the campus. The lights were out, and the ventilation was crappy, but the air was cool. I peeked over the railing and looked down the white, rectangular spiral to the first floor. I had to high five Greg. This was the perfect study break spot to hide in.

"Come on. The stadium looks awesome from there." He pointed up. We ran to the top floor, taking the steps two at a time. When I reached the top, I was laughing breathlessly.

Greg was right. You could see the whole campus, including the football stadium that was lit up for a night practice. I couldn't stop myself from thinking of Camila and the night we'd spent in her penthouse only a few short weeks before. I was over the mishaps of that morning after. She was caught up on her sleep. I didn't see why we couldn't spend another night downtown with our toys and an alarm clock, just in case.

"So how's it going?"

I turned around. Greg was leaning against the brick wall.

"Pretty good, I guess. I want to get this test over with, but everything else is good. How are things with you?" I asked, raising an eyebrow to him.

"Better. I mean, same shit, but better."

"How's everything with the guys and stuff?"

His throat contracted as he swallowed and straightened up against the wall. "It's cool. I—I'm not gay."

"Greg, I know. You're with Samantha, remember? How are things with her?" Great job, Ginger. Bring up the girlfriend, not all the anal sex you know he's having and maybe loving. I figured he would appreciate that, but he just grunted and shrugged.

"She's all right."

"I thought things were going pretty well with you guys. She missed curfew twice because of you." I tried to tease him.

"Yeah, well, I heard you got promoted to like Most Important Freshman or some shit."

I snorted, instantly annoyed. Here I was trying to talk to Greg, trying to see if he was the type to go mental and snap Samantha's neck in a fit of sexually confused rage. I was looking out for her, and her nosy, big-mouthed ass was talking about me and Camila behind my back.

"Is that what Samantha told you?"

"She said you're dating the head bi—" He caught himself right before I punched him in the nuts. "Sam said things had actually gotten serious with you and the sister-queen Camila. You guys are actually dating."

"We are. And I wouldn't refer to her as a bitch, Greg. Rodrick answers to her. And she is my girlfriend."

"I know. My bad. I just..." he said. "I'm sorry. For real." He took my silence as a cue to keep his mouth shut while I cooled down. I knew he was confused and going through a rough time, but manners were manners and casual name-calling, especially in this case, was not okay. He didn't know Camila, and he obviously didn't know what she meant to me.

"So you can do that, like, date them?"

"Yeah." I sighed. His question reminded me how clueless he was to my situation. "I mean we just clicked, I guess. Dating them isn't off-limits; it's just not the norm."

"What happens when you graduate or if you want to break up with her? Not afraid she won't suck you dry in a fit of vampire madness?"

"No. I'm not," I replied, shaking my head. "It's been ten minutes. Let's go back."

"Okay. So you're a lesbian now or what? You're done screwing dudes?" he asked as we started back down.

I didn't know how to explain things to him so he would understand, because he wouldn't. I had no desire to be with a guy, but then I had no desire to be with anyone but Camila.

My throat ran dry at the thought. I didn't want to be with anyone but her, ever. And here was Greg, casually playing off his relationship with Samantha who did walk around campus, hanging off his arm like she was the head bitch. All the while he's taking to his secret sex life with an aggression that was making vampires nervous. He wouldn't get a simple explanation of love that saw past whatever was between Camila's legs and right to her amazing heart and her immortal soul. Greg didn't deserve an explanation.

He accepted the silent treatment I gave him, keeping any other questions he had to himself. I pushed open the door, grateful it didn't make a sound, and marched back toward our group.

Samantha was standing next to our table talking to Alison.

"Hey," she whisper-shouted when she saw Greg. She scowled when she saw me. I rolled my eyes right back at her. As if I would mack on her pig of a boyfriend. "Hey," she muttered at me.

"Hi, Sam," I said, taking my seat next to Judd. Greg leaned down and let Samantha kiss him. Her face lit up all over again.

"How'd you find me?" Greg asked.

"Your hat." His Cubs hat was sitting on the table. I wanted to burn that hat. "Is there room for me?"

"Yeah," I said. I ignored Judd's frozen shock and started packing up my books. "I'm going to go."

"We haven't started chapter four yet," Alison whined. Her eyes were begging me to stay, but I couldn't. Judd offered to cram with me the night before the test if I was still up for it. I told him I'd let him know. For now, I had to get the hell away from Samantha before I slapped her or Greg. Or stabbed one of them with a pencil.

I grumbled my good-byes and headed for the stairs.

"I don't know what the fuck her problem is," I heard Samantha mutter as I went. I almost reconsidered the pencil. And the slap.

I stepped out of the library and got a few feet closer to the engineering building before I realized I hadn't called for an escort. It was dark and windy and there was no one around. Perfect setting for me to get mugged by some transient passing through campus. I was so pissed, I didn't know who to call. I didn't want to bother the OBA boys. Micah was busy with Anna-Jade, and I wasn't in the right frame of mind to deal with Cleo's comedy hour.

I pulled out my phone and stared at my list of recent contacts.

I called Camila.

"Miss me already, baby?" she said as she answered. I felt terrible for not being in a playful mood, but a sudden sob bubbled from my chest.

"Red, what's wrong?"

"I'm at the library. Can you come get me?" I walked back toward the entrance and hid behind one of the marble pillars.

"I'll be right there." She hung up, and not four seconds later she was there, gently holding my cheeks in her hands. She still spent most of her time in her apartment in her underwear, but she'd thrown on some jeans and she was wearing my black ABO hoodie with my name stitched into the arm. She looked like another college student, minus the fangs.

"*Querida*, what's the matter?" she said. She still only whipped out her Spanish when she was really upset. I looked into her eyes and just burst out crying. She took my hand and led me over to a small bench on the side of the building. Two guys came walking from the direction of the cafeteria. They didn't notice us, which was good. I felt like enough of a complete fool for crying in the middle of campus. I didn't need people pointing and laughing.

I took a few deep breaths, trying to flush out the irrational tears. I couldn't believe I'd let something Greg said and then Samantha, make me cry. I swallowed and wiped my face with the back of my hand.

"Greg—he. God, he's such an asshole."

Her gentle expression fell. "What did he do?"

"Nothing, he was just asking me about you and then he called you a bitch." I sniffed and huffed some more before I kept going. "Well, he started to, but he stopped himself. And then Sam showed up and the two of them were acting like I'm the one who had the problem."

She laughed gently, pulling me toward her. "Aw, baby. Don't let them bother you."

"You're not mad?"

"No," she said, stroking my cheek gently. "Between myself and Greg, I'm pretty sure I know who would win in a fight. And Samantha is just Samantha. Ignore them."

"I—the way he was talking about you. I love you," I said. "I don't want anyone talking shit about you."

"I love you, too. And I'm not worried about anything Greg has to say. You should have heard Tokyo when I banned her from bringing her feeders down to Moreland's. She called me a lot worse."

"She did?" I gasped. "What did you do?"

"I punched her across the room. But we've gotten along great ever since," she said with a fangy grin.

"Greg said Sam told him that I got 'promoted' to most important freshman or some crap just because I'm dating you. You know I don't even give a crap about all this Greek stuff or being popular. I just—I just want to be with you. And pass chem."

"Come on." She stood and took my hand. "I'm taking you home. I'll help you study for your test and then we can have sex, okay?" she said, playfully pouting her way through the last bit. I laughed, sniffling one last time, and stood beside her.

"Are you just going to vanish us back to the house?"

"No," she said as we started walking.

"Why not?"

"Because we can only travel with inanimate objects. If I poofed you back to the house with me, your heart would stop, and that's if the stroke didn't kill you first."

"Nice night for a walk isn't it." I smiled cheerfully.

Camila's middle finger tickled my palm. "It's just what I had in mind."

## CHAPTER THIRTEEN

We walked slowly back to her place, hand in hand. I was happy just to be with her, and by the time we got back to her apartment beneath the ABO house, I had almost completely forgotten about my stupid lab partner and his stupid girlfriend. Camila and I crawled into her bed and she helped me review my chem notes. And then as she promised, she sexed me perfectly to sleep.

She was dozing peacefully beside me the next morning, and as I looked at her beautiful face I couldn't believe I had let Greg and Samantha get under my skin. The two of them were so screwed up and in a way, so perfect for each other. If Greg's refusal to deal with what was going on in his head got Samantha hurt, well, that would be awful, but that didn't mean I had to care what they thought about things that were so clearly not their business.

I kissed my sleeping beauty on her soft lips and smiled as she shifted closer to me under the sheets. I had the most amazing girlfriend in the world. She was intelligent, sweet, funny, not to mention drop-dead gorgeous, immortal, and mutant strong. And she loved me. I had made some great friends in Alpha Beta Omega, plus I had my ever-perky roommate, but Camila was the most important person in the world to me. Her happiness mattered, not the stupid things the likes of Greg and Samantha had to say.

Camila's eyes fluttered open when I kissed her again. And as she greeted me with her own hello and special brand of good morning, I made up my mind I wasn't going to care anymore about people who meant so little to me.

The first thing Greg did the next time I saw him was apologize. He pulled me aside a couple days later on our way out of class and said a bunch of crap about being out of line and understanding just how important Camila was to all of us, how much she cared about all of us. I wanted to tell him to go fuck himself, but it wasn't worth it. I accepted his apology and made a point to keep a cordial distance from him for a few weeks.

Things eased, because I'm just that nice of a person, and Greg wasn't so bad when he watched his mouth. I had no idea what was going on over at the OBA house in terms of his "feeding aggression," but Rodrick and Camila never brought it up again, so I figured he'd finally mellowed out.

I followed Camila's advice and flat out ignored Samantha. I wasn't mean to her or anything, but I stayed away from unnecessary small talk, and I never mentioned Camila in front of her. Camila was that special to me. If someone couldn't respect what we had, then they had no right to hear any of the amazing things I had to say about her. Unfortunately, Sam wasn't the real problem.

As the weeks passed, more people started to openly—in that sneaky gossipy sort of way—speculate about what exactly was going on between Camila and me. I'd been in such a love-induced sex haze when we first started dating I hadn't noticed the shifty looks I was getting from some other members of Alpha Beta Omega. Girls gossip. I know. I get it. It didn't make the shit talking any less annoying, and it didn't make their logic any less backward.

Anna-Jade had heard from Mel, who heard from Julia that the general opinion among some of Omi's and Faeth's feeders was that I was using Camila. Supposedly, I played the cool brainiac who was trying to sleep her way to the top and could care less about the sorority, which wasn't true at all. I never backed out on any of our activities and responsibilities, no matter how much I wanted to spend that time with her.

If I was so obviously using her, how would that help me win the popularity of the group and convince them to one day vote me in as chapter president? I didn't even want to be chapter president, but I had made a commitment to the sisterhood, and I had every intention of sticking by that pledge and every extracurricular activity that came along with it.

I would have spent every moment of my life with Camila, but I never sulked about having to be away from her because she always made up for our separation the moment we were back together. Still, according to Amy, a few of the girls actually believed that I was with the queen for the sex and the status and the bragging rights. I never had a serious conversation with anyone about my relationship with anyone but Amy. That may have been the problem. You don't give up the dirt and people make up their own.

And soon the rumors started to include Amy and Danni. Our foursomes during Camila's feedings became standard. We never brought it up to the other girls, but we couldn't keep it a secret. All the sister-queens had their own feeding schedules, schedules they stuck to. It didn't take long for a few people to notice that Amy and Danni were heading to the pantry twice a week, at the same time.

I'll admit that it was a little scandalous that the four of us had our arrangement, but what the hell. Every other sister-queen was screwing all of their feeders. Camila was the only one who was sleeping with just one person—me. I never touched Amy or Danni. Other than the biting, Camila never touched them either, but that didn't matter. The lie was way juicier than the truth, and trying to defend ourselves would only make things worse.

The overall mood on campus was that Thanksgiving vacation couldn't come soon enough. We had a couple long weekends between August and November, but none of them long enough to justify a trip back home or time away from Camila.

I had to go home at least for the carving of the turkey, but I did book a flight back a day early. Finals were going to be brutal and I wanted just one day with Camila, uninterrupted.

I left for the airport early Tuesday morning. We were only going to be apart for four days, but I cried when Camila kissed me good-bye. It was pathetic. I knew it was. We hadn't spent a full night away from each other in months. She reminded me that I was finally going to see my family. That perked me up a little, but didn't stop me from pouting as I rode the elevator away from her. It wasn't until I actually saw Dad waiting for me at baggage claim in Logan that I smiled again. He'd come back from South America just a few days before.

Dad looked older and tired, but a familiar smile lit up his face as I walked over to him. I'd settled comfortably into being Camila's girlfriend, but it felt good to be his daughter again. It felt great to hear his voice. He told me about Brazil, some of the people he'd met, a few of the patients he'd helped. Like always, he edited out the most grisly parts of his work, but the proof of the heartbreaking things he'd seen was clear in the weight he'd lost and the exhaustion that had settled on his shoulders. I thought of what Camila would have done in my shoes and told him that I loved him and I was glad he was home. That seemed to help.

Of course, then he asked me about school and Camila or Mila, the name Todd had passed on to my parents. I told him more about my classes, and our upcoming elections for ABO and Types for Hope. Camila's name worked its way into the mix, but I was afraid to say something that would even hint at the fact that she wasn't exactly human. He didn't seem to mind, or press me for details, so I just went on and on about school. We were still sitting in the garage when I looked up to see the patient smile on my dad's face. I blushed, feeling a little silly for rambling on.

"Sorry," I muttered. "Let's go see Linda."

He unbuckled his seat belt and went to open his door. "Don't apologize, Ginge. I missed you. That's all."

When we stepped into the mudroom, Mom descended on me with a shrieking frenzy that put Amy's enthusiasm for lingerie and Danni to shame. She kissed my face until I thought I would bruise and asked me a million questions and told me a trillion different things. I understood "Are you hungry?" and "I bought you new sheets."

"Go put your stuff away and I'll make you some lunch. And I just baked cookies."

I dropped my bags in my room and crawled into my New England winter pj's: fleece sweats and a hoodie, an ABO one of course. I was fully prepared to spend the day doing absolutely nothing. I split my time between the kitchen and the couch, listening to Mom as she stuffed me with grilled cheese and hot cider and cookies. A new family had moved in down the street. They had two kids, but they were four and five years old. She guessed right when she assumed I wasn't exactly dying to meet them. I told her about which finals I was dreading and she thoroughly examined my ruby necklace.

Then she sat down beside me, her mouth half full of sugar cookie. "So. How's Mila?"

"She's good." And hunkered down safely underground.

"You miss her already, don't you?"

"A little, but I missed you and Dad too. And Todd sort of."

"Oh, you love your brother."

"I guess. He's okay." I smiled.

"So tell me about her. If it's safe. I don't want to jinx anything."

"We're pretty serious now. I think it's safe to talk about her. I don't know. She's cool. And smart."

"And pretty. Todd showed me her picture. You two are so cute together."

I grimaced at Mom's ridiculous cooing. "Thanks."

She took a sip of her cider "Which one of you is the boy?"

"Mom!"

"Isn't that how it works? One of you gets to be the girl and the other gets to be the boy and then on off days you switch," she said with a faint twitch to her lip.

"You're hilarious. And neither of us is the boy. We're both ladies."

"Well, I want to meet her. I want to make sure she's good enough for my baby."

"She is, Mom. I promise. She's great."

"Good. Come here, honey." I walked around the table and let Mom pull me into a big hug. "I'm so proud of you. Even if you're not the boy."

"Thanks, Mom."

"Why don't you go keep your dad company while I get dinner started." She kissed my cheeks and kicked me out of the kitchen.

I lay out on the couch and kept Dad company while he watched football. He'd kept up with the scores online, but still felt slightly cheated by missing almost the entire NFL season. Todd had set up the DVR to record every single Pats game. I texted Camila pretty much non-stop during the season's recap. The semester and lunch caught up with me, and some time before dinner, I passed out. I woke up with Todd sitting on the floor beside me, his face disturbingly close.

"Hey Ginger," he huffed quietly, blowing his cider breath in my face.

"Todd, eww. Get away from me."

"Hug me first. I missed you, punk."

"Fine," I groaned, but when I went to sit up, I got caught up in the blanket. "What the hell?" I looked down to see that Todd had been nice enough to braid my hair into the tassels on Mom's afghan.

I sprang up like a jackal and punched my darling brother right in the arm.

"Ow!"

"It's not funny, you jerk."

"Todd!" Mom yelled from the kitchen. "Stop brothering your sister and come set the table."

"I'll be back for you." He pointed in my face then jumped out of the way just in time to dodge another punch.

"You really think he should be a doctor?" I asked Dad while I separated myself from the blanket.

Dad shrugged. "He'll make an excellent pediatrician."

Dinner hit the spot. Even though our chapter was small, I still spent most of my meals in a large group. It was nice to eat some real home cooked food and actually get a chance to hear everything that everyone at the table had to say. The four of us ended up back in front of the TV, vegging out. It was nice to be home, but by nine

I was going through Camila withdrawal. There was no use in hiding it, knowing that Todd would make fun of me anyway. I excused myself to go call her up in my room.

Camila picked up on the first ring and I found myself grinning like an idiot the second she said my name.

"Hi," I said, sounding chipper and twelve. "What are you doing?"

"We're remodeling the dining room at the Fontler. I'm adjusting the plans."

"Oh, cool. Show me when I get back."

"I have a few other things in mind to do when you first get back. And then I'll show you the plans. Where are you, baby?"

"My room."

"Do you have your laptop? I want to send you something."

I dug into my bag and pulled out my computer. Just to be on the safe side, I locked my door before I plopped on my bed.

"What are you wearing?" I teased as my laptop fired up.

"I'll tell you in a second, Red. Check your e-mail first."

"You're so pushy. I love you," I said with a wide smile, as if she could see me.

"I love you too." She laughed.

I pulled up my e-mail and opened a RAR file from Camila. A RAR file filled with a collection of clips from various security cameras. I opened the first one and saw us making out on her bed. I remembered the afternoon perfectly. My stats class had been canceled and Camila had the day free. We screwed for hours.

"Aw, baby," I cooed. "Did you make me a porno?"

"I did. I miss you. Which one are you watching?"

I looked at the file name at the top of the box. "Ten-oh-six."

"I watched that one twice this morning," she told me.

"You did?" I suddenly lost interest in the clip. "What else did you do this morning?"

"I touched myself, baby," she said. My pussy throbbed as the words left her mouth. On my computer screen the two of us were dry humping at the foot of the bed. I knew in a few minutes she'd pick me up and take me to the ottoman, but I wanted to hear more about the touching.

"How was it?" I asked.

"It was good, but not the same without you."

I leaned back and slid my fingers under the waistband of my sweats and into my underwear, feeling just how wet any thoughts of her made me. "Well, you have me on the phone now. And I'm alone in my room…"

"Gingey! Come look at the snow," my mom yelled up the stairs.

I pulled my hand out of my underwear. "Ugh, I have to go. My mom wants to bond over the weather."

"Gingey!"

"Mom. I'm coming!…I'll call you back in a little while. She's going to keep yelling until I go down. This better be the most majestic snowfall of the year."

"Okay, Red," Camila said. She was sweet enough to let me go without a fight. I closed my laptop and ran downstairs. My family was already out on the porch. Mom had left the front door wide open. I stomped into my boots and followed them outside. It was gorgeous out. Freezing, but gorgeous. Mom had told me it had already snowed a few times while I was still at school, but most of it had turned brown and gray or washed down the gutters. This snow was sticking and it was beautiful.

But not as beautiful as phone sex with my girlfriend.

"Oh, wow. It is snowing. Good night." I turned to make a break for the door.

"Get over here." Dad grabbed my arm and pinned me, shoulder to shoulder, between him and Todd.

"Just humor the woman for five minutes and then you can go back upstairs and talk to Mila," Dad muttered.

"Thanks. You're the best. Mom, this really is lovely."

"And you are a liar, young lady. I think monopoly and hot chocolate are in order," she announced.

My head whipped toward Dad and I stared at him in horror. "Please, no," I said through my gritted teeth.

"Come on, Ginger. You can be the thimble," Todd said, slapping me on the shoulder. I glared at him, ready to tell him just where he could shove the little piece of metal, when a sudden movement on the lawn caught my attention. My neighbor, the one I'd kissed, was walking up our snow-dusted pathway.

"Hi, Kristen. How are you, sweetie?" Mom said cheerfully. It was getting late to be dropping in on neighbors, but Linda was never rude.

"Hi, Mrs. Carmichael. I'm good." Kristen stood there for a moment. And that moment turned into an awkward moment as she looked nervously at me. Dad tried to save the day.

"Linda, why don't we get that hot chocolate started? Todd, you want to dig up the Monopoly?"

"Sure thing," Todd said, before he whispered to me. "Look at you, all two for two." I elbowed him in the side as he tried to slip into the house. My parents were right behind him and Kristen took that as her cue to join me on the porch.

I didn't know what to say. The last time I'd seen her, her tongue was in my mouth. I hadn't exchanged even an e-mail or a Facebook wall post with her all semester. So I asked her about how her soccer season went. She asked me about school. I told her I'd joined a sorority and she'd told me she'd thought about rushing, but soccer took up too much time. We avoided the subject of dating and the kiss we'd shared.

"I know we're only home for a few days, but maybe, do you want to go to the movies or something tomorrow night?"

"Oh, I—" Everyone I actually talked to knew I had a girlfriend, but how did I tell her without it sounding, well, bitchy?

"My parents are gone all afternoon too, if you wanted to come over and hang out," she blurted out.

"I'm going shopping with my mom tomorrow," I lied.

"Oh. Well." She started backing toward to stairs. "Come by if you change your mind."

"I will," I lied again.

I watched Kristen walk back to her house and silently, I prayed her mom and my mom didn't talk while I was home.

"Red, are you cheating on me?"

I spun around, my heart beating out of my chest. Camila was standing on my porch in nothing but her underwear and my favorite green v-neck. It was twenty-five degrees out and she couldn't have looked more comfortable. I assumed she had her cloak up. All Kristen, or my parents for that matter, had to do was look out the window to see a half-naked woman standing on our porch in the snow.

"Can anyone see you?" I asked anxiously.

"No, baby. The porch looks empty."

"Good."

And then I jumped on her, my legs wrapping around her waist, my big boots digging into the back of her thighs. She took my weight easily, carrying me to the corner of the porch, pushing me up against the side of my house. My lips latched on to hers, and instantly her tongue slid against mine.

I pulled away, just to make sure I wasn't hallucinating. "What are you doing here?" I panted before diving in for another kiss.

"Trying to keep you from giving your neighbor another crack at that beautiful mouth of yours." Her fangs trailed across my jaw.

"I'm sorry you heard that, but she doesn't have a chance. How long have you been lurking in my yard?" I asked.

"Long enough to know she still wants you."

"Doesn't matter. You're here. Kiss me." She smiled against my skin then sunk her teeth into my neck. My orgasm hit me like a Mack truck, sending my head spinning. Her cloak had to be soundproof, because I was moaning pretty loudly. She fed deeply, letting me come once more and again as I pressed myself against her stomach. I shuddered a final time when she pulled away and sealed the bites.

"Okay. I have to go now," she whispered softly between warm strokes of her tongue.

"What? No. Stay. Please," I said. "I have a double bed and new pink sheets. You'll love it. Just poof yourself to my room. I'll tell my mom I'm not feeling well."

"Really, Red. I have to go. Kina just came back to the house. The kindergarten teacher dumped her. She's a mess." She put me down, smoothing my hair behind my ear. "I told her I'd be right back."

"Fine. Will you call me later, if you can?"

"Yes. If it's not too late. You have to go shopping tomorrow," she said with a mocking smile.

"Har, har. I love you."

"I love you too, baby." And then she disappeared.

I kicked off my boots by the door and stumbled into the living room, dazed and soaking.

"What did Kristen need, honey?" Mom asked.

"Huh? Oh, uh she's fine. I mean, nothing. She was just saying hey. I'll be right back." I ignored Dad and Todd's bizarre looks and ran up to my room to change my underwear. I glanced at my neck in the mirror to make sure it wasn't too blotchy. It was, but that I could blame on the cold if anyone asked. I was back in the living room in record time, doing my best to play it cool as I took the thimble from Dad.

"If I have to spend time with you people I want to be the bank," I insisted.

"You okay there, champ?" Todd scoffed, nodding toward my arm. Unknowingly, I'd been running my fingers across my bottom lip. It was puffy and swollen. I dropped my hand.

"Yeah. Why?"

He just shook his head, smirking at the Chance cards he was sorting.

Monopoly was as fun as the Carmichaels could make it. I slid Dad money behind my back. Todd sold Mom some properties at a discounted price. We quit when Dad kept nodding off against the couch.

❖

I climbed into bed and texted Camila, telling her how much I loved her. I passed out before she texted me back. I dreamt about her, though, her kisses on my cheeks and my neck, the gentle caresses of her hands between my legs. We talked less than we made love, but I remembered her telling me that my bed was way too small. I'd laughed in my sleep, almost waking myself up, but not quite. I wanted to hold on to Camila and my dreams.

In the morning I found a piece of my mom's pink stationary folded on my pillow. But the swirly handwriting didn't belong to Linda.

*Enjoy the day, Red. Next time we're doing it on the floor. Luv, your M.*

I cursed out loud, careful not to crush the paper in my fist. I couldn't believe I'd missed her.

## CHAPTER FOURTEEN

It turns out Camila could hold her cloak in place while she fed, but she couldn't do it while I was busy twirling my tongue around her clit. She only came back once while I was home. Kina was devastated over her breakup with the kindergarten teacher. Camila and Faeth were on best friend duty on and off for the next day, but the afternoon of Thanksgiving, the kindergarten teacher had a change of heart and wanted Kina back. Camila texted me right before we started dinner, telling me to let her know the second I'd gone up to my room for the night. Needless to say, I was in an abnormally good mood while we ate.

I wanted to give Camila the same level of romance she'd shown me during our dates back in Baltimore. I made my bed and actually threw my clothes in the hamper. Then I downloaded a few movies for us to watch on my laptop. We had till dawn, and the nights were longer now. A few hours of romantic comedies would ensure that my parents were asleep before we tore each other's clothes off. She texted me right before she appeared standing across my room. I wanted to invite her to make herself comfortable on my bed, tell her the choice of movie was hers, but the words were trapped in the back of my throat.

Camila was already naked, her eyes glowing green and gold, lips parted, fangs exposed. I had no clue what had set her off, but she was hungry—for me. I walked toward her, my hand extended out. Her purr grew to a low panting growl the closer I got. I pressed my body against hers.

"What happened to your clothes?" I asked.

"Do I need them?" Her heated gaze focused on my mouth.

"No, babe, you don't. Did you just feed?" Her reply was more hiss than an actual yes as I ran my fingers down her side. Her soft skin was on fire. There was no need to bait her any further, but it was impossible to resist her heat. My palms found her breasts and my lips found her throat. I drew lazy circles with both as her head fell back. "Let me take care of you."

I sank to my knees, separating her slit with my tongue. She was so wet, pulsing hot. I needed more of her honey sweet taste. I swept my tongue deeper, closing my lips around her clit, my underwear soaking at the loving sounds rumbling from her chest.

She let me please her for a few moments, but I felt her body tensing, growing impatient. She never had a problem with me making her come, but she also didn't like sitting by and letting me do all the work. She pushed me away from her body, sliding to the floor beside me. In the next second she was underneath my hips, tearing my underwear off, pressing her face between my legs. I looked down, trying to get my bearings, pleasantly surprised to find her wetness still at my disposal.

I got lost in her, using my fingers and my tongue, tracing every inch of her pussy. Even though I thought her cloak was up, I tried to keep my voice down. It was difficult. She knew how to work me so good. Her tongue driving in and out of me with strong thrusts, her finger gently prodding my asshole. I was so close, dripping on the edge when she replaced her tongue with her other fingers. I shuddered against the dragging sweep of her fangs as they searched the inside of my thigh.

"Do it. Please," I begged, panting loudly. "God, Mila. Please."

And then there was a light knock on my door. Only my dad knocked like that. Camila and I froze.

"Ginge, honey. Can you keep it down? Your mom's trying to sleep." My eyes slammed shut, my teeth clenching together.

"Sorry, Dad," I called back, mortified.

"It's okay, kiddo. Night."

"Night."

We waited, listening until my parents' bedroom door shut. I crawled off Camila as quietly as possible, and shuffled to lean against my bed. She was right there beside me, nuzzling my neck and slipping her hand back between my legs.

"You distract me too much, Red. My cloak dropped."

"Yeah, I kinda forgot where we were too."

"Well, we'll just have to finish each other...one at a time," she said. Her fingers pushed back inside me and her fangs sliced into my throat. I bit the inside of my cheek, drawing blood, swallowing my cries while I worked myself against her hand. When I was done, she let me back between her thighs. I could still taste a hint of my blood in my mouth as it mixed with her delicious juices, but as she came silently, dripping on my lips, I couldn't help but wonder what her blood would taste like.

❖

The line to the ticket counter wasn't too bad, but the line through security was ridiculous. Dad was back from the short-term parking before I'd moved an inch.

"So I'm guessing Mila's going back early too."

"Uh, yeah." I'd told my parents I was heading back early to get a jump on my finals. Maybe texting Camila non-stop and leading them to believe that we were having phone sex gave away my true motivation for going back early.

"She's it for you, isn't she?" Dad asked.

I turned and peered at him. He was looking at his shoes, blushing a little. "What makes you say that?" I asked.

"That look you've had on your face all week. That's how I used to look at your mother," he said.

"What happened?"

"Nothing," he said, dismissing my worries of a divorce with a confident shake of the head. "I'm just old. My eyes don't get all wide and googly anymore."

"You're not old, Dad. Just seasoned and mature. And your eyes still get plenty googly when you're with Mom." The line moved forward a little. Dad followed the slow pace, sticking to my side.

"I guess that's true. She's a great gal," he said. "But I can tell with you two. The way you talk about her. The way you are now. She's the one for you."

"You don't think I'm too young to be so sure?" I asked. I think we both thought it would be a few years before we had this talk.

"No. Not at all. I was your age when I met your Mom. Plus, she can't get you pregnant."

"Ew, Dad." I scowled.

He chuckled before he got serious again. "If it's okay with her parents, we'll fly her up here for New Year's."

"Okay," I agreed uselessly. That wasn't going to happen. Ever. I knew she wanted to meet my family, but still after all these months we hadn't figured out how. I couldn't fly her up for an evening and then what, explain that she left before dawn to get us all coffee and wouldn't be back until dinner? But I would talk to her. I couldn't cut off my family, and I couldn't imagine not having her in my life. We would work something out. I just didn't know when.

When I was next in line Dad turned to me.

"Tell her I'm sorry I silenced your fun. Us old people still need sleep."

"Dad!"

"Come here, Ginge." He hugged me, chuckling his deep laugh against my hair. "Call me when you land."

"I will." I walked forward and threw my backpack on the belt and pulled off my boots. I glanced back when I got through the detectors and Dad was still standing there, still tired, but smiling.

❖

I felt bad that I didn't have more than three bucks to tip the driver Camila had sent for me. He turned down my measly wad of cash, explaining that Ms. Sanchez had already tipped him generously. He carried my bag to the porch and waited by the limo until I was safely inside.

The front door was locked, so I tried the doorbell. A minute later Florencia opened the door. She let me in and was on my heels as I walked toward the pantry.

I was so anxious to see Camila, a little bit nervous actually, but that anxiety disappeared the moment I stepped off the elevator and into her arms.

"Hi," I breathed against her neck. She held me close, wrapping her arms around me, but something was off. I took a small step back, shocked at the pained look on her face. "What's wrong?"

"Nothing, baby." She relaxed a little, but the look she gave me was way left of reassuring. "Well, Cleo's coming in an hour. She's trying to study for her anthropology final and her house is full of cousins. She won't bother us though."

"Okay. What else? Where Cleo studies never makes you this upset."

"I'm not upset. Come sit with me, *querida*." And then I knew things weren't good. I trailed behind her toward her apartment, trying to ease the death grip I had on her hand. My heart was thudding against my ribs and my stomach was clenched beyond tight. The worst things were running through my head. Maybe she wanted to end things. Or maybe she wanted to take a step back. What if I was smothering her? Maybe she saw me at home with my family and realized we didn't belong together.

"Are you breaking up with me?" I blurted out nervously.

"No, Red." She laughed for real this time. "I don't want to talk about this in the hallway."

She opened her bright red door for me and I followed her inside. Then I dropped my bags on the floor and sat beside her on the couch. I'd missed the smell of her apartment. The air was always so fresh and clean, but her cinnamon musk lingered everywhere. Still, her perfect scent wasn't enough to calm me down.

I took a deep, ineffective breath. "Okay, tell me."

Camila stared at the floor for a moment then looked me in the eye. "I've given this a great deal of thought and I didn't want to bring it up because I truly don't think it's fair to you, but it's just as much your decision as it is mine. I have to speak more with Dalhem, but if you would, after you gave it some real, serious consideration…if you'd like, I'd ask you to be my na'suul."

"Sounds pretty," I said with light hesitation. "What does it mean?"

"It means that you would be more than my mate. Our minds and hearts would be connected. If you wanted me, I would be yours forever. In your world and in mine."

I didn't think. I just answered.

"Yes."

"Red, wait. Let me explain first."

"No. You don't have to. My answer is yes." Even though part of me was just so overwhelmed that she wasn't kicking me to the curb, I loved Camila more than I ever imagined I could. There was no other response worth considering.

"Just listen, please. This is a serious bond, but that is why I want to speak to Dalhem. I want you to have an out clause."

"What do you mean?" I frowned.

"If you change your mind, three years from now, ten years from now, I want him to break our bond so you can go on with your life—"

"Don't say that," I pleaded, my voice sounding pathetically sad.

"Ginger, you're just so young."

"I know, but I'm not going to change my mind. I want to be with you. Till I'm old and gray and you have to spoon-feed me peas." I nudged her leg.

"Oh, I'm putting you in a home, but I'd love to keep fucking you until then, knowing you're mine," she said before the stern look came back to her beautiful face. "I am serious, though, Red. I do not want anyone else but you. But I have had years and years to know what I've been missing. You might find that you want someone else one day or that you just don't want me. And if that happens, I'm not going to stand in your way."

"You understand you've planned our marriage and our divorce before I even took my chem final," I said playfully. "My answer is still yes. We'll figure out the other stuff later."

"And you still have to understand, your family can't know what I am. It's fine now because we're both supposedly in school.

But if we're still together when you graduate, they'll want to see me in the daytime."

"When I graduate and when we're still together, we'll figure something out. We'll say you have some weird disease and you can't handle UV exposure. They'll think it's weird, but they won't turn away someone I love." I leaned forward and kissed her, trying to soothe her stress away. "And what about Dalhem? He's married to a human. Maybe he can help us think of something. I mean we still have, what, three years and half years till I graduate? And then I'm supposed to go off on my own anyway. You said yourself, let's just handle things as they come." I took a deep breath, looking at my hands. "My dad thinks you're the one for me."

"He does?" Her hopeful expression broke my heart. I wanted my family to meet her now more than ever, just to see the love she was capable of.

"Yeah. And I agree with him." I felt the waterworks bubbling over. I sniffled, holding them back. "So, yes. I want to demon-marry you."

"Okay, Red," she said finally. "I still have to talk to Dalhem. There's a certain amount of formality to it. Technically, you'll be considered a demon, but nothing else has to change. You finish school, if that's what you want, and then afterward you remain with me."

"I like that."

"I was going to wait until I talked to him, before we made things more official, but I did want to give you this." I looked to see a small box in her hand. The perfect wooden cube was stained a deep brown and there were roses and vines carved into every surface. Whoever made it could teach Tiffany a thing or two about presentation.

"You don't have to wear it. Or we can get you a different one, but I saw it—"

"On Amazon?"

"Yeah, on Amazon. I saw it and it made me think of you."

Camila didn't exactly know how to do it small. There was probably a hundred thousand dollars worth of lighting in her apartment alone. When she placed the box in my hand, I opened it expecting to find the Hope Diamond. Not my style at all, but a diamond that suited Camila's flare for the unique and the expensive. It took a little elbow grease to work against the small hinges. The ring inside was perfect. A large round-cut emerald sat nestled in a slanted arrangement of marquis diamonds fixed to a thick platinum band. The emerald was big, don't get me wrong, but the ring was elegant and something I never knew I would want so badly.

"I want to wait. I don't have to invite the whole chapter to the ceremony, do I?" I thought of all the rumors the ring would start.

"No. We can have witnesses if you like, but it's just between me and you. Natasha and Rodrick didn't have anyone at their na'suulaem—their wedding."

"Then I'd rather wait till it's done. I want to whip this bad boy out when everything is nice and demon-legal."

"Okay, baby." Her soft laugh was cut short by another kiss, a long and slow kiss. I found myself back in her arms, gently but passionately showing her that my answer was definitely and always yes. She pulled away eventually, laying a few more sweet pecks on my lips before she said to me. "Would you like me to hang on to it?"

"Yes. I'll lose it somewhere." I handed her the box back and she placed it on the coffee table. "I feel like we should celebrate or something."

"We can, Red. Would you like to go out or would yo—"

I tried to catch Camila before she doubled forward onto the floor, but I wasn't fast enough. I slid to the carpet beside her, leaning to see her eyes squeezed shut. And then pain came. It wasn't Camila's pain, but someone else's. Someone connected to Camila and to me. I couldn't feel it, but I could hear it. In my head, someone screaming, someone was in horrible pain.

❖

I looked through the thick glass of the hospital room. The person lying there was not recognizable as my friend. Cleo's body was covered head to foot in thick, gauzy bandages. The tan bottoms of her small toes peeked out through the dressings. Her right arm was elevated, supported by a brace. The intricate web of pins and supports was keeping her arm attached to her body. Tubes and wires ran from her face and chest to various pumps and monitors around her bed. Cleo's pain was muted now, but it was still there, a tight, constant scream. I felt like if she could have, she would have called out to Camila or me, but she couldn't. I wanted to help her, but I couldn't.

There had been two cars involved in the accident and a truck. Cleo had been pinned behind her steering wheel. Debris from the initial crash had severed her right arm almost completely above the elbow. Cleo's doctor had no idea whether she was conscious when the other car burst in flames, igniting the driver's side of her Civic. One driver had died at the scene and the driver of the truck when he reached the hospital. Cleo was barely holding on.

Camila wrapped her arm around my waist as she, Kina, Faeth, Omi, and Natasha got more details from Dr. Ronald Fountain, a feeder who belonged to the brother-king Pax. We stood in the center of the busy burn unit, shrouded by Faeth's cloak. I tried to pay attention, but all I could see were Cleo's toes. Suddenly, I wanted my dad.

"The burns cover ninety percent of her body, most of the damage being on the left side, and it remains to be seen whether she'll regain full use of her arm—if she lives through the night," Dr Fountain said. "But the tissue lost on her face and upper body will be a problem. She's heavily sedated now. She can't feel—"

"She's screaming," I interrupted.

Faeth whipped around in my direction. "You can sense her?" Immediately, I felt Camila's eyes on me.

"I didn't want to scare you," I said before I explained to the others. "I can't...feel her. It's more like I can hear her. I know I get no vote in this situation, but do something quickly. She's in pain."

I could tell the others had questions, but before they could ask them Tokyo appeared within the confines of the cloak with Moreland and her feeder Andrew, the brown-haired boy who had been with her that night at the restaurant.

"Why is she here?" Camila asked, her fangs flashing brightly.

"My Queen. I apologize," Tokyo said. "But I thought Moreland may be of some use to us. She was close by and she has feeders to spare." Camila looked at Moreland and then Andrew. He was taking measured, deep breaths, his gaze focused on the floor.

"Andrew, look at me," Camila said. He obeyed, his brown eyes peering at her respectfully. "Are you prepared to sever your bond with your Mistress?" she asked him.

"Yes, ma'am," he answered quietly. I hadn't noticed before, but his voice was deep and rough and carried much more confidence than the first time I'd seen him. "I want to help in any way I can." Camila seemed satisfied with that answer, although not particularly pleased with it. She turned her focus back to Moreland.

"Even though you do not deserve him, I know Andrew is precious to you. I thank you for your offering of sacrifice."

"Thank you, my Queen. If he is no longer needed, I will wipe him completely. He will have no recollection of this night."

Camila grunted decisively, turning things back over to Dr. Fountain.

"What are our choices?" Natasha asked.

Camila nodded to the doctor, urging him to give it to them straight. He glanced at Cleo through the glass.

"You can say it. No one will judge," Camila said.

"No. No," he stuttered, realizing she'd read his mind. "My assistance will be limited in the big picture, and her journey to recovery will be long and painful. I will do everything in my power to keep this young lady breathing, but I—if I were her lying in that bed, if she is feeling right now, I'd want you to end my suffering any way you can. As quickly as you can. If you can heal her completely? Tonight? I would do it, my Queen."

The sister-queens let out a collective mix of groans and swears.

Camila looked from the glass to Dr. Fountain. "I'll have to look at her, but I think the amount of blood she'll need for us to heal her will change her."

"Did you talk to her about the change?" Omi asked.

Camila shook her head. "I don't think she wants it, but we didn't talk about it at length."

"She…" I hesitated. I already felt like an intruder, but this was Cleo's life and it had been my suggestion that they do something quickly. Someone had to speak up for her if that something meant Cleo would no longer be human.

"What did she say, Red?" Camila said.

"A few months ago, we were talking and she said she didn't want to cut off ties with her family. She said she couldn't live with the idea of her mom thinking she was dead if she really wasn't. And she mentioned that she had some…religious reservations about becoming a demon."

"So do we just let her die?" Faeth said.

"No. We let her decide," Camila said. "Ginger is right. She is in pain. I can feel it. We can't leave her like this."

Dr. Fountain nodded in understanding. "When you're finished, I'll have the morgue prepare a body and the paperwork. I won't be far. Just call me if there's anything I can do."

"I will. Thank you," Camila replied. With that, Dr. Fountain walked down the hall. He hadn't turned the corner before Kina unsealed the door to Cleo's room and ushered us in. I ignored the beeps of the monitors and the buzzing of the bright lights overhead. We stood at the foot of the bed.

"Moreland, please. Cloak the room," Camila ordered.

"Yes, my Queen."

"What about Dalhem?" Kina asked. "He didn't exactly sign off on this."

"I'll deal with him," Camila replied.

"We're really going to do this?" Faeth asked.

Camila nodded. "She's mine and I won't let her die."

"She's going to be so pissed," Tokyo said.

"I know," Camila said. "But I want this to be her choice. If death is what she wants, she can have it. Just not tonight." She let out a deep breath, then let go of my hand. "Red, I don't want you to see this, but I'm not going to make you leave." She kissed me softly but quickly on my mouth.

I grabbed Camila's hand. "Wait. Please don't do this. Don't change her."

"Red, I—"

"I know you don't want her to die, but she doesn't want this. What about her family?"

Camila closed her eyes and let out a deep breath. When her gaze met mine again, I knew she'd made up her mind. "I wish I could explain it to you. She's mine. I can't let her suffer in pain any longer. She'll be upset for a while, but in the end she will have wanted me to help her." She kissed me once more, letting me know her decision was final. "You and Andrew go stand in the corner."

Andrew gently grabbed my other hand and pulled me out of the way. Silently, I prayed Camila was right.

Camila quickly started giving orders and the sister-queens followed them without hesitation. I watched as Omi and Tokyo rummaged up a scalpel and some surgical scissors and began cutting away Cleo's bandages. Faeth silenced the monitors and started unhooking Cleo from the wires and tubes. I wanted to look away as every inch and section of Cleo's destroyed body was revealed. My stomach flipped, twisted at the medicated smell of her burns. The bile rose in the back of my throat, but I couldn't look anywhere else but the bed.

The sister-queens kept cutting, splaying the bandages open around her. I swallowed a whimpering shriek when they reached her head. The left side of her upper lip and her cheek were completely gone. And so was her beautiful hair. Andrew's arm wrapped around my shoulder, and a moment later, I realized we were supporting each other.

Camila pulled off her jacket and threw it in the chair. "Natasha and Faeth, take her neck." As she spoke she held out her hand. Tokyo handed her a scalpel. "Omi, her right arm. Tokyo, Kina, take her legs." The sister-queens took their positions around the hospital bed. There was a brief moment of silent communication between the six of them and then at once, the five in their assigned positions struck, their fangs piercing Cleo's ravaged skin.

Not even a minute passed. They drank deeply, draining Cleo from arteries in her throat, her arm, and her thighs. Cleo's charred skin seemed to be pulsing as they sucked the life out of her. Out of the corner of my eye, I saw what Camila was getting ready to do. The point of a blade was pressed against her wrist.

Faeth lifted her head, making no move to be discreet as she wiped bits of loose, burnt flesh from her lips. "Now. She's empty."

"Just hold on for me," Camila said, not to Cleo, but to me.

The moment she slit her wrist, I threw up. Moreland must have sensed that I was about to heave because she appeared in front of me with a wastebasket the second the remains of my airline snacks came back up. Andrew took the trashcan from her and held me up as I continued to vomit. And then Camila had me.

"I'm fine, *querida*. Look." Her healed wrist appeared in front of my watering eyes. "I'm okay."

I nodded and stopped shaking long enough to take a bottle of water and a tissue from Moreland's hand. Even if the woman was a total creeper, she was handy in a clutch.

Camila gave me some space to do a little clean up while holding on to a tiny shred of dignity. When I was presentable, she handed the water back to Moreland, then Camila tucked me tightly to her chest. I looked over her shoulder, shocked at the change that had taken place in the few short moments where I'd been falling apart.

Cleo's healed lips were latched on to Kina's slashed wrist. Her eyes were still closed, but her throat was working, rhythmically swallowing every drop Kina gave her. When Kina stepped back from the bed, Natasha's wrist took her place.

And Cleo was healing, changing right before my eyes. It all happened so quickly. The puckered and drawn skin regenerated and smoothed itself out over Cleo's arms and legs and breasts. Hair sprouted from her head, longer and thicker than before, but just as rich and curly. Omi was last at the head of the bed, and as Cleo swallowed the final gulps, her now light brown eyes opened.

Omi took her wrist back and licked her wound closed. Foolishly, I'd been expecting Cleo to awake a screaming zombie. I expected her to come tearing across the room, mad with bloodlust, lunging for Andrew. But she simply sat up, as if she'd woken from a long, satisfying night's sleep, and looked around the room.

Her eyes fixated on Camila. She frowned for a moment, then bowed her head.

"My Queen," she said respectfully.

"How are you feeling?" Camila asked.

I almost smiled as Cleo's expression snapped back to normal. She scratched her head and tested the tips of her fangs with her tongue. "Fine. It's bright as hell in here." We all laughed nervously with relief. Cleo ignored us. "Did someone puke?"

"Yeah. Sorry about that," I muttered my guilt.

"It's all good." The sister-queens made room for her as she slid off the edge of the bed and stretched. "I'm hungry."

Camila nodded to Moreland. Andrew quickly pulled off his jacket and slipped it into the chair with Camila's. He was bare-chested under the leather except for the silver barbells that ran through his nipples and his collar. Moreland removed the thick black strap and handed it to Tokyo, then brought Andrew across the room to Cleo's side. As she approached, Moreland kept her eyes lowered respectfully, the way she'd done with Camila. She didn't look up as she spoke and Cleo didn't ask her to.

"The sister-queen Miyoko suggested that you may prefer a female, but all of my female pets are still away for the holiday. Andrew is very sweet and loyal and he will—"

"Yeah. I don't care. I'm fucking starving," Cleo said dismissively, taking the scalpel from Omi.

"As you wish." Moreland turned and gently lifted Andrew's chin with her finger. "I release you Andrew Edmond Franklin, Jr. Serve this sister-queen as you would serve the master himself. As you would serve me."

"I will," he murmured quietly. Moreland stood on the tips of her neon green stilettos and kissed him on the lips. Then with a sense of finality, she stepped back and Cleo took Andrew's hand.

The words Camila had spoken to me months before echoed in my ears in the overcrowded room.

"I thank you deeply for your sacrifice. Will you allow me to bind you to myself and to my sister-queens?" Cleo asked.

"I will," Andrew said.

"Thank you," she replied. Swiftly, Cleo sliced a deep gash across Andrew's palm. He shuddered, his head tossing back. It was hard to ignore how aroused he was. His erection was straining through the fabric of his jeans. He shuddered again as she licked the wound closed. Cleo raised her head with a low growl and tossed the blade on the bed, then her hands went to the fly of his jeans. Andrew was pretty muscular and a good six inches taller than Cleo, but she was in charge.

"I don't care about an audience, but I'm going to fuck the shit out of him. I'm not sure if you ladies want to watch. Of course, my Queen, you're welcome to," she said with a dip of her chin in Camila's direction.

"Thank you, but take your privacy."

None of us wasted a second following Camila out of the room. Cleo was safe, but back in the hallway, it was clear that this night, this life for her, had only begun. Camila thanked Moreland again, this time with more kind sincerity, then dismissed her. Before Moreland vanished, I caught a glimpse of the blue tears rimming her silver eyes.

Then, as if she'd called a huddle, the other sister-queens gathered around Camila.

"I'll get her some clothes," Faeth said.

"I will go tell Dr. Fountain it's done, and then I will go to Rodrick and inform our Brothers," Natasha said.

"And I'll call Sarah at the precinct and tell her when to release the details of the accident," Kina added.

"Thank you, my sisters. She's going to be very angry once she's fed. I'll let them stay in my quarters until we sort things out with Andrew."

"No," Tokyo said. "I brought him and Moreland into this. Cleo can stay in my place as long as she wants. I'm downtown half the time anyway."

"Fine. I'll agree to that, but only because I'm still pissed at you for bringing Moreland into this. Good thing I like you so much."

"My Queen." Tokyo flashed her fangy grin before she disappeared. The others were right behind her, going off to their assigned tasks.

Camila and I waited still under the protection of someone's cloak. The nurses passed us, completely unaware. We both ignored the sounds coming from Cleo's hospital room.

Camila pulled me into her arms. "Do you trust me when I say she'll be okay?" she asked.

"She seems like herself. That's better than months and years of surgeries and rehab, but her family…"

"We'll take care of her family. Baby, if they knew what we could do for her, they would want me to save her too. I swear it." I nodded, not knowing what else to say. Cleo was alive and safe and whole—physically. She sounded pleased with Andrew, but I was worried about her mind and her heart. "Thank you for speaking for her, though. She'll appreciate that." Fat lot of good it did, but at least I tried. Camila pulled me closer and rubbed her lips against my neck. "I love you," she whispered.

"I love you, too." But for the first time since we'd started dating, I wanted some time to be alone.

## CHAPTER FIFTEEN

I woke up to breakfast in bed complete with a bouquet of pink short-stemmed roses. On the way home from the hospital I'd considered spending the night at the dorm, but so much had happened, I didn't want to add to the drama by pushing Camila away without giving myself a little while to cool down. By the time Cleo and Andrew were settled and it seemed like Cleo wasn't going to flip out, I decided to stay the night. I looked at the tray on Camila's bed beside me, a little more than confused.

"What's all this for?" I asked as I rubbed my eyes.

"I'm sorry for last night. I hoped we'd be celebrating our engagement."

"We still can, just not now. And there's nothing to be sorry for," I said before I let her kiss me. The apology was sweet, but unnecessary. The pancakes, juice, and flowers were overkill. The night had been rough on all of us, but Camila didn't need to make anything up to me. "Have you seen Cleo yet this morning?"

"No. She and Andrew were busy screwing all night. I'll go check on them in a little while. Eat."

"This smells great. Thank you." My stomach growled as I picked up the fork. I hadn't eaten anything since I'd left the airport in Boston, and that hadn't stayed with me for very long. "So what now?"

"Now the complications." My mouth was full, but she continued when my eyebrow shot up. "Kina was in line after me. She's very powerful, but with my pure blood, Cleo is now third to Dalhem."

"Does that cause any problems for Kina?"

"No, and she doesn't mind the shift, but Cleo is very strong. A young, stubborn vampire with that much strength and power could be very dangerous. I love Cleo and I trust her, I just hope she can handle the responsibility."

Then why did you change her?

"But I wanted to talk to you about Benny."

I thought back to all of the times I'd watched them together. "She's in love with Cleo, isn't she?"

"Yes, she is. She will be back on campus in an hour and I think it would be better if she talked to you first. Her world is full of vampires and she lives with a full demon. I think having another human she trusts on her side through this will help"

"How did she find out?" I asked.

"Dalhem told her, but he said there was no reaction. That's why he's worried."

"He didn't read her mind for any 'general feelings'?"

"No. When he married her mother, he vowed never to read Benny's mind except in the case of a life-or-death situation. Benny is fairly honest with him so there's never been a need to."

"I guess details about your daughter's crush aren't a risk to vampire national security."

"You'd be surprised."

"Well, at least now Benny can feed Cleo."

Camila frowned. I rolled my eyes in frustration, trying to remind myself that sharing this information with Camila was important.

"Benny wanted Cleo to change so she could feed her. I don't know if Cleo feels the same way about her, but I'm guessing feeding Cleo is something Benny will suggest. How do you not know any of this? Some powerful vampire you are." I nudged her shoulder playfully. I had to offset the annoyance that was building inside.

"I don't have to tell you to keep this to yourself, but Benny knows how to block me."

"She does?"

"She's not invincible by any means, but Dalhem has taught her a lot of tricks to protect herself. I can breach her mind, but she would be able to tell."

"Like I can?"

"Exactly. And that's why I'm worried. Cleo is the only one she opens up to, and now that she's not human anymore…"

"I get it. So what now? What happens with Cleo and Andrew?"

"He's hers. She can do whatever she wants with him. She can give him back to Moreland if she wants to. She can keep him. If she does, I may have to move them out of the house. I don't know." Camila sat back on the bed. "I have to talk to her. I'll have to assign her two more feeders as well. At this rate, she'll drain him by tonight. I'll give her Benny if that's what they want."

"And what about her family?"

"The hospital contacted them last night. Florencia will let me know as soon as her family decides to come pick up her things. And her remains. We have a cadaver prepared."

"This is so weird. Because she's…"

"Not dead."

"Exactly. I mean, she's different, but even in the car last night it was obvious she was still Cleo, just more potent. I guess. If that makes sense."

"She is superior to everyone but me and Dalhem, and she knows it. Even Rodrick will have to bow to her."

"All because of your blood?" I asked still amazed at the power it carried.

"Yes. Because of me. I've never changed anyone for this exact reason. Dalhem and I and even Rodrick are very careful about that. I should have let her drink from Moreland instead. I couldn't."

"I think if she'd had a choice she would have picked your blood over Moreland's. I would have. I know it might throw off the power structure around here, but no one can blame you for making that call. What did Dalhem have to say about it?"

She made a slightly annoyed, dismissive noise. "Nothing. I think part of him is glad I saved her, for the sake of her friendship with Benny. He had some jokes about having to raise a teenager and then reminded me it was my responsibility to keep her in line."

"Are you worried she'll go on vampire pantie raids with Moreland?" I asked.

"I'm worried that she'll do something stupid. If she breaks the law, I have to put her down," she said bluntly. I could see where that would be a problem.

❖

The cold air helped me clear my head as I walked back to campus. I respected Benny's private nature, but I needed to leave polite at the door and get her to be honest with me. I had to share Camila before I even knew what she truly was. Even though our relationship had been full of surprises, she had always been a vampire to me. If Benny felt for Cleo a shred of what I felt for Camila, there was no way she was handling the news of Cleo's accident very well, even if it meant she could finally feed her. And if it was simply a matter of deep friendship, I knew Benny would still need some time to mourn what they had just lost together.

I texted her on my way over. She texted back telling me she'd wait for me in the lobby of her dorm. We didn't bother with any small talk as we made our way to her room. It gave me a few minutes to think of what exactly I was going to say and time to wish she hadn't been wearing one of Cleo's ABO hoodies, one with her name stitched into the arm.

She opened her still decorated door and I realized I'd never set foot in Benny's room. I looked around at her bed, twice the size of mine over in Cramer, and her bright purple decorations. There were pictures of her and her mom lining her dresser and pictures of us girls on her desk. There was a picture of her and Cleo next to her bed. I didn't see any evidence of Dalhem.

My dorm room would probably look the same way if I'd spent more than three minutes there a week. I glanced around once more. There was only one bed.

"You don't have a roommate?" I thought all the freshmen living in the dorms did.

"My parents sprang for a single." She held her hand out, motioning for me to sit at her desk. I took a seat and she flopped on her bed, pulling her stuffed panther into her lap. "How is she?" Benny asked.

"Fine. I think. I haven't seen her since last night. When did you find out?"

"Last night. My step-dad told me, but I knew before that. There's a database I have access to and her name popped up while I was getting ready for bed," she said, putting on a casual front. I winced, feeling my chest ache for her. Benny pretended she didn't notice my grimace. "I'm assuming she already has a feeder."

"His name is Andrew. He seems very nice," I said and then I blurted, "Benny, I know how you feel about her, but is there something more going on between you and Cleo?"

She looked up at me, a smirk touching the corner of her lips. "There's nothing going on between us anymore. She took Camila's blood?" I nodded.

Benny stood and placed the large stuffed animal back on her pillows. "Let's go."

"He's at the house right now, Benny. With Cleo."

"Where else would he be?" she said. I had no clue. If Andrew was anything like Benny, he'd never want to leave Cleo's side.

❖

As we walked back to the house, Benny shut down completely. I wanted to be there for her, help her bear the brunt of whatever was running through her head, but that just wasn't Benny's style. She was preparing herself to handle Cleo's pain, or maybe just dealing with her own.

Florencia let us in and told us Barb and Paige were back. They knew about Cleo and were both in their rooms getting their heads together. Florencia offered to make Benny breakfast, but she said no. We walked into the pantry and as we waited for the elevator, Benny finally spoke to me.

"I heard congratulations are in order for you."

"Oh, ah, yeah. Camila asked me last night, before all this happened." The elevator door opened and we stepped inside. Benny looked at the floor as I entered the code. Camila must have talked to Dalhem about her intentions with me while I was sleeping. Of course Benny would know about our engagement. At the moment I didn't want to think about it.

"Well, congratulations. My mother is patiently waiting for the day she can call herself my step-father's na'suul."

"I thought she and Dalh—your step-dad were married."

"They are married in the human world and she is his mate. A demon can only take another demon as their na'suul. They'll have their proper ceremony after she changes."

"Oh." I didn't know what else to say. Benny seemed to understand.

Camila had been trying to get me to stop knocking all semester, but I could hear voices on the other side of her door. I knocked twice and the door opened on its own. Camila was pacing in front of the TV and Cleo was sitting comfortably in one of Camila's chairs. Andrew was on the floor between her legs. They were both wearing the same clothes from the night before. He had on a shirt, but his shaggy brown hair had been shaved off. He looked a lot better.

Camila must have caught me staring at him as I walked over to the couch with Benny. "Did you cut his hair?"

"No. Moreland made him wear it long. He said he didn't like it. I said he could cut it. So he did. Hey, Ginger," Cleo said. Nobody missed the fact that she didn't acknowledge Benny.

"Hey," I replied, frowning slightly.

"Andrew, you know Ginger, and this is Benny," Camila said. He greeted us both with a nod and a polite hello.

Cleo took a breath and closed her eyes. "What do I do about my stuff?"

"I'd be happy to get your things for you," Andrew murmured, gazing up at her. Sometime in the night she'd broken him of his habit of looking at the floor.

"No, honey," Cleo hushed him sweetly.

"Andrew, it's very kind of you," Camila said. She was trying so hard to be patient with him and Cleo. "But I can't let you roam around the upper floors. It's a female-only residence."

"Can I have Barb bring my stuff then?" Cleo asked.

"No."

"Why?"

"Cleo, your family is going to want your things." Camila suddenly stopped pacing and her brows knitted together as she stared at Cleo. "Just say it. Get it out now."

"Thank you for saving my life. But…" Cleo tilted her head back, staring blankly at the ceiling. She tried to keep it together, but she couldn't. Several ragged, deep breaths puffed out her cheeks and then the blue tears bubbled over, sliding down the side of her face. Quickly, she looked back down and started wiping them away. She took another breath and more tears came. "Can I even say good-bye?"

My throat ran dry and somehow I managed to hold my own tears back. So did Benny, but I could feel her shaking, her leg trembling against mine.

"There are ways, but, Cleo, I need you to wait. I am sorry. You're too emotional and you're too strong," Camila said.

"When then?" Cleo wiped her nose and fixed a steady expression on her face. "When can I tell my mama I'm sorry for leaving her? When can I tell my daddy that I love him?"

"When I know you're under control. When I know I can trust you to deal with humans carefully so you won't accidentally reveal yourself."

"How much more under control do I need to be? I didn't hurt Andrew at all. And my powers are all in fine working order."

"You shifted?" Camila frowned.

"Yeah, last night. He likes to bottom sometimes." Andrew blushed and suddenly became very interested in the glasses lining the bar. That didn't hide the fact that his blush ran all the way down his neck. I glanced back and forth between Cleo and Camila. They were sharing something, something that Cleo accepted reluctantly as she rolled her eyes and leaned back further into the chair. Camila went on.

"You have access to the account. You can have whatever you want, but let your family clear out your room."

"Fine. Can he borrow the car? I'd like to let him grab his stuff. Faeth just brought him this shirt."

"Sure. Here." Camila tossed the keys to the Range Rover across the room. "You can have the car."

"Sweet. Thank you. What else?"

"You need two more feeders. If you're going to stay here, and you're more than welcome to, I'd prefer if they were female."

"So would I. Do I go out and find them or—"

"No. The sister-queens are letting you choose among the girls."

Cleo's gaze flashed to Benny's face, her eyes narrowing. She looked away just as quickly, but even Andrew had caught the tense glance between them. I swallowed nervously and reached for Benny's hand. She yanked it away.

"Okay," Cleo said to Camila. "Well, I don't want to step on anyone's toes. I'll let them decide who."

"Excuse me." Benny stood and marched out the door. I was surprised when it gently clicked shut instead of slamming.

I turned to Cleo "What did you just say to her?"

"I told her to go fuck herself."

"That was unnecessary," Camila said.

"Then she shouldn't have let me in!" Cleo shouted back. "Did you hear her?" she asked Camila.

"No."

"She was blocking me till the fucking second you said I could choose. This bitch said, 'she's ready to feed me whenever I'm ready to take her.' She is happy about this shit." Cleo waved her hands up and down her stomach. "She's fucking happy I died just so she could have me the way she wanted me. Listen, I'm grateful to you. I'm glad my face isn't extra crispy anymore. And Andrew told me I'd be missing an arm, but I didn't want this. She did."

"And this is what I'm talking about. I need to know you won't do that with someone in your family or someone in your mother's congregation you don't get along with. The human mind is fragile, Cleo. You can't just mess with it whenever the mood strikes."

"Okay, whatever. My bad," she said. She started stroking Andrew's bald head. He and I both exhaled once our vampires started to relax.

"So I'm on ice for a while. Fine. Is there anything you need me to do?" Cleo asked.

"Just lie low, please. Don't go where people will recognize you until I know you can hold a different form. And I would like for you to stay away from the girls until your feeders are chosen. They will sense your power and your need and they won't know how to deal with it. And please, feed the boy and let him get some sleep. Andrew, we'll talk more about work for you later."

"Yes, ma'am."

Cleo moved to stand and Andrew followed, immediately moving out of her way. Then Cleo walked across the room and hugged Camila.

"You should apologize to her," she said quietly as they embraced

"I will when I'm better under control." Cleo stepped back. "So we're like sisters now?"

"Yes. But I'm older and more mature and better looking. I'm going to let all this back talking slide for now."

"Yes, ma'am. Here. I won't be needing this anymore." Cleo reached behind her neck and unlatched her ruby necklace she'd reclaimed from Dr. Fountain before she left the hospital. She pooled the platinum links gently in Camila's hand. "I'll be back later." She turned to me with a casual nod. "Peace out, Ginge."

My good-bye came out hoarse, but Cleo pretended she didn't notice.

After they were gone, Camila closed the door. She leaned back against it, the necklace in her hand gripped in her tight fist. She let out a deep breath that I could almost feel from across the room. She looked at me and forced a grin, more apologies written all over her face.

"Come on, Red," she said, nodding toward her office. "You can pick out our new car."

It was none of my business, but I wanted to go after Cleo. I wanted to ask her how she really felt, without Camila's influence or without Andrew around. I wanted to tell her that I tried to say something on her behalf before the ball on this mess had started rolling, but I let her go. I met Camila halfway across the room and slid my hand into her warm palm. There was nothing I could say to make the situation better for anyone and there was nothing I could do.

❖

Camila made a few calls, and it was confirmed that her new silver Mercedes G55 AMG would be delivered on Tuesday. It was kind of weird and boxy looking, but I liked it because it was big like the Range Rover. All I could think about was Cleo's crushed and burned Civic. The last thing I wanted to do was hop in a little car. Camila liked it because it was expensive.

After our online shopping trip, she gave me some space to start studying for my chem final. We had three days of class left, then two reading days, which I think were for our professors to actually write the tests. The Monday after was my comprehensive chemistry exam. I had plenty of material to cover in a little over seven days, but it was useless. I couldn't focus.

Instead, Camila and I talked about Andrew. She wasn't bothered by having him in the house, but adjustments would be made. For one, he had no job. He was twenty-three and had been living with Moreland as her full time slave basically since he was eighteen. He'd dropped out of college after a month. Moreland had found him bed-hopping his way from meal to meal around Houston and asked for special permission to take him as a feeder.

The term slave weirded me out a bit. I didn't try to deny that, but Camila explained that in Moreland's situation, it simply meant that Andrew, and the other guy Luke, were at Moreland's disposal twenty-four seven. Her other feeders had jobs and lives of their own, but Andrew spent all of his time with her. Cleo didn't have the patience to deal with that kind of a pet, so Camila planned on asking Andrew if there was anything he wanted to do—go back to school, any skills he wanted to learn—and she would help him do it. Otherwise, they'd give him some sort of job working for the sister-queens. Idle hands and all.

We sat in her office chair, me in her lap, and for a long time she was quiet. When I started to get restless under the weight of my own thoughts, she offered to have lunch brought down. I wasn't hungry, but I did want to talk to Paige and Barb. I left Camila to make some more phone calls and went upstairs. I found them in Cleo's room clearing out her sex toys and porn. We searched the place for anything else her mother, the Reverend Cynthia Jones, might find unbecoming of a good Christian woman. We didn't find much, but under her bed we found a few Polaroids of her and Benny kissing the night of the Iota Halloween Party. I didn't even know people still used those old cameras, but it was obvious from the angle that Cleo had taken them herself. Barb suggested I hold on to them for Benny. I didn't argue and brought them back to Camila's apartment, hoping that at some point Cleo or Benny would want them.

After everyone was back on campus, the sister-queens gathered their feeders and told them exactly what had happened, about Andrew and Cleo's new role as a sister-queen in our bizarre family. Danni and Amy broke down and sobbed when they heard the news even though they understood that Cleo was okay. It was the accident that bothered them, that bothered all of us. As Camila told them about how we spent our Saturday night in the burn unit across town, I knew they were picturing every horrible moment that had put Cleo in that hospital bed and the horrible pain she had suffered until the sister-queens were able to reach her.

I wondered where in the world Benny was. No one had heard from her all afternoon, but she was back at the house in time for our emergency chapter meeting at eight. Camila wanted us to meet as a group, without the sister-queens, to decide who would feed Cleo. They didn't want anyone to feel pressured into it and they wanted to give us a chance to say whatever we wanted to say without them looking over our shoulders.

Camila didn't try to cover up the fact I was there during Cleo's change, but I almost wished she had. When all the details were out, I became the tragedy ambassador. The details of my relationship with Camila were mine to keep, but something that involved the chapter was fair game. I took my seat between Amy and Benny, avoiding eye contact with everyone else. Barb started the meeting before anyone had a chance to ask me what other details I knew.

"I'm going to cut right to it. We need volunteers. I'm looking for freshmen and sophomores. I'm not trying to say it has to be, but I know us seniors and juniors have a deeper connection—"

"I'll do it," Laura spoke up immediately. "Cleo is the coolest big sister I've ever had. No offense." She nodded in Kate and Jordan's direction, her nose stud gleaming. "But if she'll have me, I'll do it."

"Thank you, Laura. Okay, I just need one more person."

Things got awkward then. I expected at least ten clear volunteers from the start, but no one else spoke up. As the seconds turned to minutes, eyes started looking toward the floor. No one wanted to part from their sister-queen prematurely, and I couldn't blame them. Official demon proposal and pretty emerald ring aside, it would take a quarter horse to pull me away from Camila.

Finally, of fucking course, Samantha spoke up. "Benny. Ginger. What the hell? You're not going to volunteer?"

"Ginger can't," Barb replied before I did.

"Why?" Samantha asked.

"Because Camila said so, and if you have a problem with that, the elevator is through the kitchen, hook a left into the pantry. If you can figure out the code, I'm sure Camila would love to talk to you about whatever is on your mind." I could have kissed Barb, but that would have required Samantha keeping her mouth shut.

"Well, what about Benny? You two were attached at the ass. Daddy Dearest only want you feeding the best?" We all froze, waiting for Benny to walk across the room and finally punch Samantha in the face. But Benny stayed put. She gripped my hand, using me as an anchor as she spoke in a tone that was eerily calm.

"Because, Samantha, Cleo doesn't want me. She told me this morning, in front of the queen and Ginger and her new feeder, Andrew, who is quite polite. You'll all enjoy him very much. She told me that she didn't love me anymore and she doesn't want me to be her feeder. Now, Barb has asked very nicely for someone to volunteer."

I looked over as Mel started mumbling in Spanish. I'm pretty sure she was cursing. My Puerto Rican slang was as good as my Japanese.

She switched to English. "I'll do it. Tokyo loves Cleo. She won't mind."

The entire room exhaled.

Barb went on with the meeting, giving us all preliminary instructions on what we all had to do next. As far as the university and the rest of the human world was concerned, Cleo was dead. She now fell under the same jurisdiction as the rest of the sister-queens. We couldn't talk about her. Barb stressed this fact to Mel and Laura. Slipping up and mentioning her in front of other students might raise a few eyebrows. They would let us know when someone from her family was supposed to come for her stuff, and if asked, we were all expected to attend her funeral.

After the meeting, Laura and Mel were immediately ushered downstairs to be bound to their new sister-queen. I wanted to talk to Benny alone, but in the moment I turned my head to ask Amy a question Benny disappeared.

## CHAPTER SIXTEEN

Cleopatra Joy Jones is survived by her mother Cynthia, her father Barry, her three brothers Maxwell, 26, Stephen, 24, and Nathaniel, 19, and her Sisters in Alpha Beta Omega Sorority. The Chapter at 1444 Milson Avenue will be accepting condolences on her family's behalf. Donations to Types of Hope will also be accepted in her memory at the aforementioned address and at TypesofHope.org. Cleo was loved dearly by all who knew her, and it is an immense understatement to say that, although she is no longer with us, love will never diminish and she will never be forgotten." Ebony folded the university newspaper and let it flop onto the cafeteria table. "Well, at least Sam knows how to write something nice," she scoffed. Everyone around the table agreed. We were all a little surprised at the care she'd put into the piece.

I took another bite of my pizza and glanced around the cafeteria. At every table someone was reading or talking over Cleo's obituary. News about her fatal accident had spread through the whole university Greek association by Monday afternoon. By Monday night, the bottom floor of Alpha Beta Omega was filled with flowers. The *MU-Times* came out early Tuesday morning, complete with Samantha's eloquent tribute. It was a beautifully written article highlighting her recent life on and off campus, but it just added to the stress of pretending she no longer existed. Cleo's funeral was scheduled for Sunday. It would be a private family affair. In January, a larger service would be held at her mother's Baptist church in Richmond, Virginia. We were all invited.

Benny was trying her best to deal with their messy breakup, but that didn't stop Cleo from feeding from Mel. On our way to dinner, Mel had been stupid enough to admit that Cleo was amazing in bed, right in front of Benny. Mentioning how Andrew was an interesting addition to the feeding didn't help much either. Mel apologized the second she realized her screw-up. Benny didn't react, but I knew the words coming from Mel burned her inside. Benny turned as we neared the cafeteria and headed off in the direction of her dorm. She refused to talk to me about Cleo, but even though I didn't want her to be alone, I was glad she wasn't around to hear what people were saying.

"It sucks she died, but I don't even know who that chick is," some girl muttered to her friend at the next table. They passed the paper between them.

"This is going to get old," I said.

"I know something that'll take our minds off all this," Amy announced a little too cheerfully.

"What?" I asked. I knew exactly what she was going to say. My birthday was on Saturday. We had parties for everyone, and I had been looking forward to mine, but now it just felt all wrong. I just pictured Benny sitting across the room, watching Cleo with Andrew and Camila and me stuck in the middle. Not my idea of a good time.

"We need to pick a theme for Ginger's birthday party."

"Let's push the party till after break." I stood and grabbed my tray.

"Where are you going?" Amy asked.

"The house. I need a nap."

"I'll walk with you." We left Ebony and Gwen to finish their food. I listened as Amy suggested themes and plans for my rescheduled birthday party. She threw in her opinions on how Benny was doing and what she and Danni had planned for New Year's Eve. I listened, mm-hmming and nodding as we walked through the cold afternoon. There was no need to interrupt the perfectly good conversation Amy was having with herself.

We split once we reached the house. She booked it up the stairs to Danni's room and I headed to the elevator. When I got downstairs

I almost wished I'd followed Amy upstairs. I could hear Cleo shouting from the hall.

"Why are you being so stupid about this?" Cleo yelled.

"If by stupid you mean safe, then yes, I'm being stupid about this because I know you're asking for trouble," Camila said as I slithered through the door. She caught me and kissed me on the mouth before I got to a seat. "Hi, baby."

"Hey. I didn't mean to interrupt."

"You're not." I melted into her when she kissed me again.

I took Cleo's aggravated sigh as a sign I was interrupting enough for her tastes and slipped out of Camila's grasp. I joined Andrew on the couch where he'd been watching them argue it out. "How long have they been fighting?" I asked him. He glanced at the clock.

"Ten minutes."

"If they're going to be here, I can do it then. Just get it out of the way," Cleo said. Great. They were talking about her parents.

"I can't have them here after nightfall," Camila said.

"Why? You think I'm going to feed on them?"

"No. I think you want to see them. And I don't blame you, but I can't have you even thinking about going upstairs while they're here."

"Next week then. After my funeral. Let me go then."

"That was the plan!" I'd never seen Camila pissed like this before. "I told you. After the funeral I will go with you to your parents' house. I will show you how to enter your mother's dream and you can say good-bye. If Andrew is okay with it, we can practice on him in the meantime, but I have to be able to trust that you won't actually wake your mother up and start a conversation with her, but the more you keep arguing with me and suggesting that you appear to them in the middle of the sorority house, the less I trust you."

"I wasn't going to stand on the stairs and rattle chains. I just thought I could be in the room while they're packing. Drop some hints that I'm still with them."

"No." Camila was done.

"Fine. The day after the funeral. You fucking swear on it."

"The day after your funeral, Cleo. Do not make me regret this. You want to argue with me? Fine, I'll be okay with that for a few more months. If you mess this up, Dalhem will force me to come down on you. No exceptions. And stop fucking cursing at me."

"Sorry," Cleo said. "I'm just—this isn't cool."

"I know. Just give it some time."

"Come on, Andrew." He followed her faithfully out the door leaving Camila and me alone. I think Camila was at her breaking point. We all were.

❖

The next day after chem lab, I'd dragged myself back to the house to meet Cleo's parents. I'd been preparing myself for the absolute worst. I should have known we'd get much better from Cleo's family. Before they'd even set foot in Cleo's room, the Reverend Cynthia Jones had all of us unloading the fixings for an enormous Southern BBQ buffet. When Cleo's dad was stressed, he cooked, and man, did he cook. Her mother ordered us to eat while they packed her things, and almost to assure we wouldn't get caught under their feet, her brother Maxwell put a DVD on for us in the living room. The afternoon after Cleo's passing, he'd set about compiling a montage to show at her memorial service.

I curled up with Amy and Benny on the couch. The rest of the girls trickled in and gathered around. We watched footage of videos and scrolling photos of Cleo's short life: Cleo singing in her mother's church choir, receiving an award from her third grade teacher for citizenship. We all cracked up at several shots of Cleo scoring eight different goals throughout her soccer career in high school. The last clip had been shot just days before. Cleo was in her kitchen, helping her father make Thanksgiving dinner.

"What's the word, Mr. Maxwell Jones?" she teased her brother.

"You the word, Miss Cleo Jones." His laughter boomed from behind the camera.

"And don't you forget." I laughed even harder when she suddenly deadpanned. "Okay, put the camera down and help Daddy with the stuffing." Her brother had almost five years on her and even he couldn't resist her bossy charm.

We watched it three times before her family was done loading her things. Once Cleo's things were loaded up, her mother asked us all to join them out by their van before they said good-bye.

Cynthia Jones took Benny's hand and pulled her close to her side. Cleo had mentioned their friendship, but not the details. "Now I want you girls to pray with me." She glanced around the circle at our shocked faces, but didn't wait for a response. She bowed her head as I closed my eyes.

"Father God, our heavenly Lord. We gather before you to give thanks. We thank you for the life of our Cleopatra and the gift you gave when you sent her to us. We thank you for the power of friendship. We thank you for these girls and the sorority that brought them together. We thank you for the joy they brought to our daughter's life, and we thank you for the joy their faces bring to our hearts today."

I peeked up as she spoke, wondering who else felt like a complete asshole. Though everyone's eyes were closed, there was a range of rigid postures and wary expressions and not a few tears already running down some faces. Here her family was, doing everything they could to hold it together. Bringing us food, sharing more of Cleo's life with us, praying for us, and we all know that their daughter was alive and well somewhere beneath our feet. I wondered if anyone other than me wanted to tell Cynthia Jones the truth. Tears stung my eyes. I tried to blink them away, making a strange noise with my effort. Beside me, Amy held my hand a little tighter.

"We ask you, Father God, to please watch over these girls as we know you are watching over Cleo. Wrap them in your love, Father, and help them through this time. We praise you, always in Jesus' name. Amen."

"Amen," we all replied. I wanted to throw up.

"Now, I'm going to call up here in a few days, and I better get a full report that you are all studying for your tests," Mrs. Jones said.

"Yes, ma'am," we all giggled through our tears. I knew the others were seeing just what I was. Even though Cleo was alive, looking at Cleo's mother was like looking at the Cleo that would never be.

"Cleo will always be our baby, but you girls were her sisters, and now you're our daughters. You are welcome in our home any time," her father said.

"And you better show up," Maxwell said. Then her parents and her brothers hugged and kissed us, and just before they hopped in their vehicles, Barb gave Cynthia Jones Cleo's ruby necklace. Once they were out of sight, in the shuffle to get out of the cold Benny slipped away again.

I made it to the hall of Camila's quarters before I leaned against the wall and sobbed. Cleo's poor family. And I thought of my parents, what Dad and Mom would do if they lost me too soon and what Todd would have to say to the girls if he was in Maxwell's shoes. I knew Cleo would be okay eventually, but I wished there had been another way to save her parents from all this pain.

Camila walked out of her office as I came into the lounge.

"Are you okay?" she asked as her lips brushed my cheek.

"Yeah." I pulled away, annoyed for some reason that she wasn't more worried about the rest of the girls. I walked past her to sit on the couch and dug my chem book out of my bag. "I have to study."

❖

My behavior over the next few days was a little immature. I was angry with Camila and she knew it. I didn't know how to broach the subject with her without hurting her feelings, which wasn't my intention. I was happy that Cleo was still with us, but things were weird around the house. Benny had basically vanished from the sorority. I only saw her on campus, and she only offered up small talk if we were alone. She avoided everyone else, especially Laura and Mel. It made me so upset to see how hurt she was. Cleo too, was still wound tight. She didn't pick any more fights with Camila, but she wasn't happy, and that made me angry.

Camila kept saying things like, "Give it time," or "Don't worry. Cleo and Benny will make up soon." I wasn't so sure about that.

Despite my mood, every afternoon I studied at Camila's place, and even though we didn't have sex for those few days, every night

I ended up back in her bed. I needed some space, but I couldn't turn my back on her. That's where the real immaturity came into play. Not only was I keeping my feelings to myself, but I kept hanging around avoiding the subject when I should have dealt with the situation.

It wasn't like I didn't love her anymore, and I didn't want to end our engagement, but I needed something more from her to make the anger go away. This petty part of me wanted more proof she was actually sorry for something, but there was no black and white solution. Cleo was gone to her family now, Benny was broken, and Camila seemed confident it would all be okay. So confident she only talked about it if someone, usually me, brought it up.

The girls had no issue pushing back my birthday party. It was pretty obvious that throwing a rager for one of Cleo's closest friends would be a little messed up in the eyes of the student body. Instead, we all had breakfast together at the house. That more than made up for any sort of party. Presents from my parents were waiting at the university post office. I was too lazy to walk to campus to pick them up.

That afternoon I worked on my final English paper, an informative essay based on the many uses of sugar, a topic my chem lab TA gave me after he heard me bitching about not having a topic. I had almost finished it when Camila forced me to close my laptop.

"I know things have been a little tense between us lately, but I love you. So much. And I wanted to say happy birthday." Without me even noticing, she'd placed three boxes and a plate of cupcakes on the table. "Go ahead and open them."

The first two gifts were perfect: some pricey makeup I'd been coveting and my own leather strap-on that I would definitely use on Camila when I was thinking sexy thoughts about her again. I unwrapped the largest box, and when I pulled back the tissue paper, I gasped in amazement. The carved wood of the antique frame reminded me of the small piece of elegant woodwork that held my engagement ring. And even though I had yet to wear the ring, I knew what this frame held I would treasure just as much.

I looked at Camila then back at the painting.

Kina had used her unique graffiti style to capture a moment of my Mila and me together. It wasn't a particular moment I'd remembered, but a moment we'd shared so many times. On the canvas, I sat in Camila's lap, my legs wrapped around her waist, and she held me, her palms gently spread on my back. The two of us wore nothing but a black sheet covering our lower bodies. You could only see the slight profile of my cheek and chin, but that's not what I loved about it. Camila's beautiful face was completely visible, her full red lips pressed against the side of my neck. It captured my feelings for her in the most amazing way, highlighted the place and the person in this world I felt most whole with. I felt my anger and frustration from the last few days slipping away.

"It's beautiful," I whispered, softly kissing her lips. "We should hang it in the bedroom."

A knock on the door stopped Camila's answer. "Come in," she called out. I could see Andrew in the hallway, but Cleo poked her head inside. She was calm, but she looked like she'd just been crying.

"The sun is down. Can I go down to Moreland's with Andrew? He misses Luke."

"Yeah. That's fine," Camila said. "But during the holiday break you need to get him back on a normal human sleep schedule. Moreland likes to forget."

"I got it," Cleo replied. The fight in her was gone. I could see it in her face and hear it in her voice. When she closed the door quietly without even looking at me, I slid back on the couch, away from Camila.

"What's the matter?"

I paused for a second and stared at the door, literally biting the tip of my tongue. It was useless though. The words were already coming. "Is this what you mean by okay?"

"What do you mean? Are you talking about Cleo?"

"Yes. I'm talking about Cleo. Can't you just give her a break? She knows there are rules. She knows all the things she can't do. You don't have to keep reminding her." Camila's lips parted as she frowned. I'd shocked us both. Still, I wouldn't take it back.

"Are you angry because I'm being tough on her or is it something else?"

"You know what, it's everything. You don't seem to care that she lost her family. All you seem to care about is keeping her in line. And you don't even seem to find it a little odd that she won't separate herself from Andrew for a minute. I told you she didn't want this and it would have killed us all to lose her, but can't you see that for her that may have been the better option?" I didn't entirely believe that, but at the moment my temper was in control.

Camila exhaled, but tensed even more. "I have to tell you something. And I will tell you even though you won't understand. Our bond with our feeders—"

I smiled at her, huffing indignantly. This wasn't about vampires and magical connections. "Right, your bond is strong and it makes you feel like—"

"No, Ginger. Listen to me. I know you feel the feeder bond, but for us demons it's different. Our love for you girls is beyond unconditional. You have no idea the lengths we will go to protect you. It's the oath we've sworn to Dalhem, but you can't understand that because you're not completely one of us. You don't understand what it's like to have this precious thing linked to your very existence. Cleo has been with me for three years, and in that time I have grown to love her more than any feeder I have ever known with the exception of you. I could not let her suffer."

I knew what she was saying, but all I could hear was blood, blood, blood. We need you for your blood. We were the prize calves who must be protected from the wolves.

"I think that's crap," I said plainly. "You made a decision and you think you know how it's going to work out, because it worked out for you. Well, what if it doesn't work out for Cleo? What if Benny doesn't get over her?"

"Because I know Cleo. She will bounce back from this. I know what she told you, but people feel much differently talking with their friends than they do when they are staring death in the face."

"Right, but you didn't have to face Cleo's mom. You and your sister-queens risked a lot to save her. I get it, but you didn't have to eat all the food her father made us to keep himself busy. You didn't see her brothers forcing themselves to smile. You—" My voice cracked. "You didn't hear Cleo's mom praying for her soul, praying for us. You hide down here, and the rest of us—us humans—are dealing with the fallout. And what about Benny?" I asked again. "Have you even talked to Benny?"

"I tried, but she shut me out."

"I can't force Benny to open up, but maybe someone a little bit more powerful than me, someone with a connection may force her to talk. Maybe that's what she needs." I stood and shoved my laptop into my bag. "And you're right about one thing. I'm not a demon like you, but I know what Danni's and Amy's blood does to me and I'm not completely one of them either. I'm stuck in the fucking middle."

After stomping into my boots, I grabbed my stuff and rushed out the door. I didn't care if it was dark out, I didn't want a freaking escort.

❖

Hot tears ran down my cheeks as I power-walked through the snow. I needed someone to talk to, but someone who would understand my side and someone who wasn't involved in ABO. I texted Mom.

*Mila and I had a fight.*

We'd had our birthday chat that morning, but she called me right back. "What happened, sweetie?"

"Nothing. I-I just…I can't really talk about it. I'm just so mad."

"Can you tell me what she did? Did she hurt you?"

"No, no. Not like that. She did something that she thought was right and I didn't agree with her, but now we're just not seeing eye to eye."

"Hmm, not a fun way to spend your birthday. Is it something that makes you want to break up with her?"

"No…" I closed my eyes as the thought made my stomach ache. I loved Camila so much. What little part of me was a vampire needed her in my life, but why couldn't she see how much Cleo and Benny were hurting, how much she'd hurt me?

"Well, step away for a couple days. Take some time to deal with your feelings. Study for your exams, but if you love her, sooner or later, you'll have to forgive her. That's just how love works, honey. You can't hold on to the anger or it kills everything around you. I want to kill your dad sometimes, but in the end I still love him so." Of course she would get me to smile. I knew she was right, and maybe Camila was too. There were things about being a demon that I didn't understand. Time did heal some wounds, and maybe if we were all patient things would be okay. But Mom was right about one other thing. I needed some space.

"No, you're right. I think I'll take a break." I sighed heavily and wiped my face. "Thanks, Mom. I'm going to go." I climbed steps to my dorm.

"Okay. Did you pick up your gifts?"

"Oh. No, I forgot. I'll grab them on Monday."

"Okay, sweetie. You call me back if you need to talk some more. You wake me up if you have to. Your dad and I are here." I sniffled, nodding as if she could see me. We said our good-byes and our I love yous. Talking to her helped some, though not completely. As soon as I slid my phone into my pocket, I felt something behind me.

I slowly turned to see Faeth standing at the bottom of the stairs. "She made me follow you."

"Tell her I made it back in one piece. She doesn't need to worry."

"She'll worry until you come back," Faeth said. "Trust me."

I did.

I finished my paper and screened a few calls from Amy. I was not in the mood for an impromptu kegger at the Iota house. After a shower, I considered going to bed without another word to Camila, but that small, petty part of me needed that bit of contact before I went to sleep, that little jerk in me that would let her response determine how much longer we needed to be apart.

*Going to bed. I love you.*

I wasn't so mad that I wanted her to think I didn't love her.

She texted back right away. *I love you too, Red. I'm sorry.*

I realized then, time was exactly what I needed.

❖

The next morning I dragged myself to the library. I sat there all day reviewing my stats notes and polishing my paper until my chem study group showed up, four hours and seven chapters ago. The whole time I was in a fog, more sad than angry, and frustrated with myself that I couldn't just forgive Camila right away. I'd been ignoring her texts, but eventually we had to talk. After I aced this stupid chem final.

"I'm cheating on this test," Alison said. "No, I'm serious. Greg, sit in front of me. I'm tattooing the periodic table on the back of your neck."

"Fine, but who am I going to cheat off of?" Greg asked with a grim expression.

We were all going to do fine on our exam, but we were stressed and exhausted. Some of us for reasons that had nothing to do with preparing for this test.

"No one's cheating. Let's take a break. Then we'll cover sublimation," Judd said.

"See. I'm so screwed. I don't even know what that is," Alison said.

Over the course of the semester, Judd had recruited Vince as a smoking buddy. The two of them grabbed their jackets and headed for the door. Alison trotted off to the bathroom.

I stared at my notes. I never got headaches, but I was on the verge of giving myself one.

"Ginger." I glanced up. Greg tipped his head toward the stairs.

"Jamal, we'll be right back," I told him. He nodded, giving us a two-figured salute off his temple before he went back to his two-handed texting.

The stairwell was freezing, but it was nice compared to the stuffy heat of the library. It was weird to be in there at night, in the dead of winter. Only the lights from outside illuminated the echoing space, but the darkness didn't bother me enough to drive me back inside to the maze of books and stressed out students. We walked to the top and I stretched, gripping on to the railing. Still bent at the waist, I looked over the edge, down the rectangular spiral.

If only jumping would get me out of my finals and not break my neck.

Sighing, I looked up and gazed out the narrow window. The map of lampposts lit a misty golden trail across campus. It was a beautiful night, a night I should have been sharing with Camila. She could have helped me study and then we could have taken a break to do something silly like play in the snow together or make love.

Greg came forward and peered over the railing next to me.

"You okay?" he asked quietly. For the first time in days, I didn't feel someone was asking about Cleo.

"Yeah. I'm just tired. I'm so ready for this semester to be over."

"Just four more days," he said.

"And then we get to look forward to chem two."

"True. At least we get a break." Greg turned and leaned his back against the whitewashed banister. "Then three weeks of fucking, eating, and sleeping."

"Yeah…" If Camila and I made up in those four days.

Greg was quiet for a moment. It was time for us to head back. I stayed put as he moved toward the stairs. But then he stopped.

"We have some time right now," Greg said with an odd hint of suggestion in his voice.

"What?" I didn't connect what he meant until his hands came down on my hips and he ground his sudden erection against my ass.

I spun around and pushed him away. "What the fuck are you doing?" His green eyes glinted there in the dark, lustful and a little bit crazed. I didn't know Greg all that well, but I had no clue who this guy was.

"I said, we have some time right now." He stepped forward and his clammy palms gripped the sides of my neck. I tried to jerk my head away, but his thumbs dug into my jaw. "I thought the sister-queens liked to share," he whispered, tilting my head back so he could kiss me.

"Camila doesn't. Stop!" I gave him another hard, useless shove. Greg was tall, sure, but a lot more solid then he looked. He didn't budge. Just stepped closer, trapping my arms between us, and turned my head to lick my ear. He was hurting me now, gripping my neck too hard, holding my head at an awkward angle. I thought of the best way to hit his groin, the best way that wouldn't get me hurt even more in the process. I jerked my knee, but the railing caught my ankle.

"What's the big deal? Cleo didn't mind sharing Andrew the other night," he said, kissing the corner of my mouth, grinding his hard-on into my stomach. I gulped down the bile fighting to get out.

"Well, that's between Cleo and Andrew. Greg! Get the fuck off me!" I shoved him again, this time putting everything I had into the weight behind my forearms, and this time he let go. But it was way too little, way too late. There were so many fucked up things about this situation, the least of which was him ignoring my no. I was furious.

I made a move to punch him right in the nuts, but he jumped out of the way and grabbed my wrist. I jerked my arm back, out of his grasp, a bad move as I stepped backward toward the stairs. I should have been paying attention to my surroundings, but I was more concerned about getting away from my insane lab partner. My foot slipped and I let out a panicked gasp in the process.

I didn't fall, though. I caught a fistful of Greg's shirt and yanked myself back onto the landing. He gripped my elbows and held me steady. We stared at each other for a second, both shocked and relieved. It was that brief moment before Greg would have apologized for getting too familiar, realizing I wasn't playing hard to get, and I would have vowed never to end up alone with him again, right after I socked him in the balls.

And in the next moment, his expression shifted. A calm passed over his brow, his dark green eyes soft and pleading just before his jaw clenched with a flash of anger. His eyes narrowed. He smiled. And then Greg pushed me, shoved me with every ounce of strength he had, right off the top step.

# CHAPTER SEVENTEEN

The concrete and brick flipped past me in a quick blur. I was blinded momentarily as I hit the middle step, my wrist twisting under my back. My eyes snapped shut again when I hit the next step. There was a thick crack somewhere in my arm. I bit my tongue when I bounced to the landing, my head concussing off the floor. I lay there, completely in shock, staring at the dark bricks above me. I tried to sit up. It didn't happen. I tried to move my head to the side, but it didn't budge. Only my eyes were working, blinking open and closed, and I could hear.

Greg was gasping. "Oh, shit. Oh, shit. Oh, shit." The muffled sound of his voice mixed with the ringing in my brain.

I wanted Camila.

"What did you do?" Camila's terrifying growl echoed through the space.

A guttural whimper sounded somewhere above me and a flapping sound and another muffled snap. Then Camila was beside me. Her fingers brushed my forehead as she leaned over me.

"Talk to me, *querida*. Where does it hurt?" Her voice was harsh and strained and her eyes were blazing. Her fangs blocked her mouth from closing all the way. I tried to answer her, but nothing came out. My tongue was too thick. Panic forced my mind open.

*I can't feel anything, but my head hurts*, I told her. *Help me.*

She moved to cradle my head in her lap. My eyes closed as she shifted me. I felt the dull pressure of her thigh on the back of my head, but I couldn't feel the warmth of her body, the warmth I always felt when she held me. She grumbled out a curse then bit into her arm.

Her blood was flowing into my mouth before I even thought to stop her. The cooling zing hit my lips, and as I swallowed, her blood started working, doing exactly what it was supposed to do, healing me, changing me. My vision cleared, bringing things into sharp color and focus in the dimly lit space. I felt the stickiness of my human tears, tears I didn't remember crying, drying in the corners of my eyes and on the side of my face.

And then my fangs came. My canine teeth widened and grew longer. A sharp shot of pain lingered as my upper teeth inched back to make room. The gum and the bone shifted, new nerves grew and connected. They came in full and large and I didn't hesitate to use them to get a firmer grip on Camila's wrist. My tongue worked against her skin, massaging the vein, driving more of her blood down my throat.

Suddenly, we weren't alone. I felt Rodrick's inferior presence before he appeared in the stairwell.

"What has happened?" he cried.

Camila whipped around in his direction and let out a feral snarl, but she didn't pull her wrist away. I didn't stop drinking even though my nose was suddenly burning. I smelled human urine. Greg's and mine.

"Oh, Gregory," Rodrick moaned. I lifted my head and stared up at the pain written across Rodrick's face. He held Greg, dead, in his arms above us on the landing. Rodrick rocked him slowly, stroking his face affectionately even though Greg's head was twisted at an awkward angle.

My eyes slid back to Camila's face. She could feel the conflict inside me, the relief and the rage. I wanted to hit her, to scream in her face, but it was too late. We were bound now in a different way as more of her blood gushed down my throat. With the break in my arm healed, I reached up and touched her soft golden cheek.

"I'm sorry," she told me, gripping my hand and kissing my fingers.

I didn't answer. I couldn't trust my own response.

Her lips pressed against my forehead, and the warm, always gentle stroke of her fingers caressed my neck. "Just a little more."

I swallowed another mouthful and I was finished. Healed. Changed from human to demon-vampire, to sister-queen, completely.

I felt my connection to my other queens, each one of them individually and as a whole, a bond only Dalhem could break. I felt another level, another piece that made up what Camila and I were to each other. Now she was my maker, and no matter what happened between us, if I ever decided to turn my back on our relationship, something the human side of me was now all in favor of, this piece would remain. She would always be the one who created me, and I would always be hers.

I gazed up at her, watching Camila as she sealed her wrist, staring into her scorching eyes as she kissed me on my mouth, opening another chamber inside me. There was now a clear line between the part of me that was human, the love and the reasoning, and the animal with base, carnal needs. The full demon in me called to Camila, called to its mate. I tried to fight the emotions, but that draw was undeniable. The vampire in me knew no reason. It ignored the past pain. I rubbed my cheek against her face and licked the corner of her mouth.

"I'm hungry," I said, a growl lightly affecting my voice. My body was more than ready to hunt. I sensed the hundreds of humans on the floors below. Some closer than others, but I knew I had to wait.

"I know, baby. Fuck. Let me—"

"I'll feed her." I turned toward the rattled sound of Samantha's voice. She stood on the stairs just below us, shaking, but determined. The sleeves of her ABO sweatshirt were balled in her fists. She moved up one more step and relaxed her hands. I could smell her fear, but it wasn't directed at me. "I'll do it." Samantha tugged her hoodie over her head. My fangs ached as she exposed the ripe vein in her neck.

"Is that okay?" Camila asked me. She had to. She was powerful enough to force me to feed, but the choice was mine. I glanced at

Samantha again and my stomach rolled and clenched. My fangs throbbed, shooting pain through my sinuses, across my forehead. I didn't have much time before I took her.

My eyes squeezed shut. "Please," I begged.

Silently, Rodrick reached out to his wife.

In the next breath, Natasha appeared beside us. She bowed to me, calling me her queen. She pulled a short silver blade from a strap in her high-heeled boot and beckoned Samantha forward. Camila slid out of the way, letting me support myself. I shifted my weight and tucked my now powerful legs underneath my body, ignoring the wet patch in my jeans. Natasha and Samantha crouched in front of me.

I could have stopped her. I had the control over Natasha to keep her from initiating the ritual. We looked at each other for a fraction of a moment. There was distress in her bright blue eyes, but it was coupled with pleading and forgiveness. I nodded quickly, hating myself for my weakness and need. Natasha turned to Samantha and the words flew from her lips.

"I release you, Samantha Grace Phillips. Serve this sister-queen as you would serve the master himself. As you would serve me." The shift happened so quickly. Natasha had given Samantha to me. It would have been an insult for me to turn the offering down. I needed to feed so badly, but I didn't want to take Samantha away from Natasha. Not like this. But my thirst was too strong.

Sam and I looked at each other for a moment that seemed to stretch on forever. Her boyfriend was dead, and maybe at some point she might blame me, but there was no blame written on her face. And then there was the tiny issue of how much we completely loathed each other, but I was too hungry to be picky about where my first meal would come from. I frowned at her, asking the question one more time.

She grabbed my wrist and pressed the edge of the blade into her own palm.

I blurted my vow, reborn sister-queen to devoted feeder, and Samantha accepted. Our bond was made. I felt it to my core, but I found myself fighting it because it was not complete just yet, not until I sliced the upturned palm that was offered to me. I leaned forward and sealed the seeping gash. A sensual growl tore from my throat as I heard Sam's breathless sob.

There was nothing that compared to the taste of human blood, the rich mix of crushed berries, flavored with an unparalleled sweetness. I'd tasted its electricity on Camila's lips, wanted more of it because it made me want her. Now my demon body craved it, in essential ways that were impossible to explain. The connection between us made her flavor unique to me. It was spiked with her arousal and her desire to please me.

My heart was tackled by sudden, incessant need to protect Samantha and to make her feel loved and treasured. The lingering rationale in my brain recognized how ridiculous the urge was. I hated Samantha. Or at least, I used to. As the small trickle of her blood coated my throat, any negative thoughts I had about her were completely erased. She could do no wrong. I wouldn't let her. And anyone who even thought of harming her, would have to answer to me. If anything happened to her, I would be the one to protect her. She was mine.

My hand flashed to Samantha's neck and I yanked her forward, shifting her body so she was nearly pinned between me and the wall. Her whimper was far from a protest, but her body's plea for me to feed and then take her. It didn't take much pressure for my razor sharp fangs, their nerves pulsing with my own rabid heartbeat, to pierce Samantha's thin, soft skin. They punctured deep then retracted just enough for me to keep a hold on her, leave plenty of room for the blood to run free. God, she tasted so good.

She came in my arms, muffling her cries behind clenched teeth. My body soaked in response, my pussy wet and wanting. The tips of my breasts puckered hard and tingling, but I wouldn't satisfy my desire with Sam.

My gaze slid over to Camila and I told her, showed her, how I needed her to make this feeding complete. Samantha was satisfying one desperate craving. Only my maker, my mate, would quench the other. She reached out and stroked my cheek, projecting her feelings to me, making me purr. She would have me.

My eyes slid closed and I fed, slowly but deeply. I opened my eyes once more when the brother-king Pax appeared. He nodded to Camila, then I held his slate-gray gaze for a brief moment. He blinked in shock, then bowed deeply as his show of acceptance and respect. He would serve me now, if I allowed it, but beyond recognizing my sudden ascension, he was my brother and I accepted the bond, too. I wouldn't ask for anything from him, but I nodded slightly, my fangs still clamped onto Samantha's tender throat. I stroked the length of her spine gently, soothing her through another shuddering release.

Pax began speaking with Natasha and Rodrick. I listened to their low mutters as they mixed with the weak, panting sounds of my precious feeder in my lap. Rodrick and Natasha would take care of the body. Rodrick's suffering was tangible, but he was handling it well. He knew what Greg had done and only wished he'd done something more to prevent it. The remains of my human soul felt bad in a way, but my demon knew the aftermath of Greg's demise was Rodrick and the brother-kings' problem to deal with.

I probed Samantha's mind and quickly found the reasons why she'd been so close at the moment of my fall. She'd followed Greg and me into the dark stairs, partly out of jealousy, partly because she was worried about me. Despite that fact she was already his girlfriend and was sleeping with him willingly, Greg had raped Sam, more than once. Each time, he'd been careful not to leave any marks that couldn't be explained away. I thought about telling Rodrick and Pax to toss Greg's body off the top of the library, but it would have made a mess in the pristine snow.

A sudden jolt to my system pulled me from my daydreaming.

I felt Camila, her whole presence, slipping away from me.

My gaze shot to her, terror surging through my body. She grimaced, that tale-tell look of apology flashing across her face. I pulled my mouth away from Samantha's sweet vein, but before I could call to Camila, before I could beg her to stay, she was gone.

## CHAPTER EIGHTEEN

Where is she?"

"Where has she gone"? Rodrick and Pax gasped at the same time.

Instinct told me to bite the front of my tongue. My fangs pierced my own flesh and I used the small amount of blood that rushed to the surface to seal Samantha's neck. I wasn't done feeding, but I'd had enough to hold me over.

I shut out everything around me and focused on finding Camila. I found a piece of her, a shadow of herself. She was safe, but emotionally, she was falling apart. I just couldn't get a clear read on why she'd disappeared and I couldn't get a hold on where she was. I opened my eyes. Natasha, Rodrick, and Pax stood there, waiting on directions from me. My new demon instincts prepared me to delegate, but I had no plan.

"My study group is waiting for us," I told them. "I—" I flinched when Rodrick suddenly took Greg's full form. He even turned his dark jacket and slacks into Greg's jeans and long sleeved shirt. He grabbed Greg's Cubs hat off his lifeless head.

"Uh, I'll go with him," Samantha said, blinking at Rodrick. Her fear and her confusion grew stronger, but I was filled with pride. She might fall apart later, but she was going to keep a level head until we were out of the woods. "We'll tell them you threw up or something and we'll grab your stuff."

Rodrick nodded and started down the stairs. Samantha turned to follow him but stopped without a second thought when I gently gripped her arm.

"Thank you," I whispered. I learned forward and kissed her lips. There was no heat or desire behind the kiss, but another silent vow from me to her. I released her and she sprinted after Rodrick.

"I'll handle the body," Pax said. He slung Greg's body over his shoulder and vanished from the stairwell, leaving me alone with Natasha.

I felt her devotion as Natasha peered at me, her white-blond hair swaying.

"Sometimes the only way to protect your true love is to hide from it," she said, a sad bit of hopefulness on her face.

"Do you know where she is?" I asked.

"No. I do not have that power. She is blocking us all. We'll get you cleaned up and then we'll try to find her." I looked down. I was covered in dust. She took my hand and then winked. Her smile calmed me a bit. "You'll see, my Queen. It's like flying."

A soft rush of air went through my body. Natasha was right; it was like flying through a wind-blasted waterfall. When I opened my eyes, she and I were back in the lounge of Camila's apartment.

Tokyo appeared a moment later. She took two steps closer to Natasha and me, then stopped.

"What the hell happened? I mean—my Queen." The bowing and respectful nodding was getting on my nerves, but I had a feeling there was much more to come.

"Greg threw me down some stairs and then I pissed myself." I stormed off to the bathroom, turned on the shower, and shed my soiled jeans. Looking in the mirror, I saw the blood on my shirt. It was Camila's.

I reached out to her again and kept trying to sense her, over and over, as I bathed quickly, the frustration building. I didn't skimp on the soap between my legs or the liberal amount of shampoo I used to scrub out my dried human blood matted to the back of my head. I would have scrubbed myself raw if it weren't for my new resilient skin, still pale and covered with freckles, but tougher. I kept scrubbing though.

Where in the hell did Camila go? I could still feel her. She was miserable and she was crying, but I couldn't sense why. There was no pain, but something that reeked of guilt and shame. Still, not even the smallest hint about where she might be.

The past week with Cleo had been an absolute mess, and now we'd have to deal with the same issues with me. I had to die now, in the eyes of the human world, in the eyes of my family. There would be some elaborate plan to erase my life, some elaborate lie to make my parents think they had lost me forever.

I fought back the tears as the last of the soap washed down the drain. Crying now was useless.

I shut off the water and wrapped myself in a towel, grateful I'd gotten in the habit of leaving clothes with Camila months ago. Out in the lounge, all the sister-queens had assembled. I held my hand up to Cleo, Omi, Faeth, and Kina, asking them to save the bowing and the pledges until after I was back in fresh underwear.

I opened the drawers Camila had cleared out for me, and as I bent to grab my bra, I saw the small wooden box sitting among her things on top of the dresser. Ignoring the only proof of our engagement, I yanked on my clothes and went back to face the sister-queens.

I walked back into the lounge and stopped next to Kina's chair.

"I get it. I'm high on the totem pole, but I'm going to smack the next person who calls me queen. I'd like to find Camila, and we don't have time for all the bowing and praising," I said. They all nodded, taking my subtle hint. "Good." I walked over and squeezed between Cleo and Faeth on the couch.

"Well..."Omi said hesitantly, "You're in charge until she returns."

"I don't care about being in charge. I want to find her." I could still sense her, still upset, but nowhere around. "None of you can sense her?"

They all shook their heads.

I let out a breath in frustration and then I felt my feeder coming closer. I called out for Samantha to come in before she knocked on the door. Rodrick had seen her safely back to the house, but she was still shaken. She stepped inside and set our backpacks by the TV.

"They bought the puking story. Alison said she'd call you later," she said.

I couldn't stop my eyes from rolling. "Great. Come here." I held my hand out for her, comforted momentarily by the heat of her shoulders as she settled on the floor between my legs. There were the last traces of snow still melting in her hair. I rubbed her shoulders trying to ease the tension out of her body. She had nothing to worry about anymore, but it would take time before the worrying went away.

A voice in my head stilled my hands. A warm, soothing voice that I couldn't ignore.

It was Dalhem and he was calling to me.

*My Ginger*, he whispered behind my eyes. His voice was a low stroke to my temples.

"Ginger, what is it?" Faeth asked. I frowned, trying to concentrate, then moved Samantha gently out of the way. Natasha called for her and Samantha scampered across the room into her lap.

*My Ginger come to me now*, he whispered again in a gentle command.

"I have to go," I told my sister-queens. "It's Dalhem."

"Is Camila with him?" Kina asked.

"I don't know. I have to go." I didn't wait for them to ask me more questions. I closed my eyes and followed the sound of my master's voice.

I felt Dalhem's influence before I appeared in his living room. He was in my mind fully as I vanished through space. I knew before I even thought to block him or before I even considered his influence as intrusive, that I was in the presence of kindness and love. That love and kindness came with a sort of power I'd never imagined.

I came face-to-face with Dalhem in his half-human, half-demon form. I hadn't realized that a small part of me had been doubting the true nature of my sister-queens and Camila. Yes, they were vampires, animalistic, sure, but the demon part didn't truly make sense. The truth of the creature didn't all seem real until I looked into Dalhem's golden eyes and saw the crown of black horns that protruded quite naturally from his forehead. He was not of this world, not of heaven or earth.

His pure white hair fell gently behind his ears, almost to his shoulders. His wings were hidden. I imagine they would have ruined his crisp black suit. Even under the fabric of his clothes I could see how muscular his arms were. He grinned as I gazed back at him, showing off his enormous fangs rooted in the top and bottom of his jaws. Had he been human, I wouldn't have taken him for much older than thirty. Had he been human, he would have been very handsome, but it was hard to see past the horns and the teeth and the power in his eyes. His smile was warm and paternal, but I found it hard to smile back. Camila's suffering was ripping at my heart.

She was beside him on a large golden couch. The whole room was decorated in dark wood and creams and gold, but I couldn't take my eyes off Camila. She wouldn't look at me. She was too ashamed. Clear blue tears ran down her face in a steady stream. Dalhem's arm was around her shoulders. As she sobbed, he tightened his grip to comfort her, but she only sobbed harder.

"You are already a quick study. Using your powers with such precision and not even an hour old." My eyes fluttered back to his face.

"Master." I dipped my head to him deeply.

"My Rodrick. I thank you. You may go."

My head whipped to the side. Rodrick was standing in the corner looking back at Dalhem. I was too overwhelmed by Dalhem's power and Camila's tears to sense another vampire in the room.

"I thank you, Master, for your grace and forgiveness and your acceptance of my word," he said. Dalhem dipped his head with subtle appreciation in reply.

Then Rodrick took three long strides in my direction and hugged me. He was trying to tell me something, give me some sort of warning, but he couldn't. There was no way to keep any sort of communication from Dalhem and we both knew it. Instead, my arms went around Rodrick's waist and I squeezed back, my only way to thank him for at least trying to be on my side. Whatever side that was. And then he vanished.

I took a deep breath and turned back to face Dalhem.

"I'm afraid I have some unfortunate news. I'm going to have to punish our darling Camila, and I believe you know what that punishment will be."

"Please don't hurt her," I begged him as a sharp pain shot through my chest. I could hear Natasha's words pounding in my ears. Remove the head or the heart. The sun will do the rest.

"Oh, my Ginger." Dalhem frowned at me sternly. "I may be pure demon, hell-spawned, but I think you misunderstand my love for your mate. She is the only piece that remains of my twin. Though her execution is called for and just, I would no sooner harm her than I would harm my own daughter. But that does not erase the mistakes she has made. I overlooked the taste she gave you for human blood all those months ago. I should have corrected her then. But now she has changed you against your wishes and she has taken the life of a feeder that did not belong to her. If our Rodrick had not forgiven her immediately, she would have to answer to more than just me."

"But I begged her to change me. And Greg—"

"You begged her to help you. Let us not be confused. And yes, my Gregory harmed you and a feeder belonging to our Natasha. I would not have allowed him to live, but our Natasha and our Rodrick and even your precious Samantha, deserved their vengeance, and our Camila took that away from them because her only thought was of you."

"And she saved me. I don't understand. What's the difference between her changing me and her changing Cleo? We were both dying. She saved us both." I waited for his anger to rise as I kept up my arguing, but all I felt was his compassion.

"My Ginger, she saved our Cleo with the aid of her sister-queens. She trusted them, as she vowed that she would, to bring our Cleo across safely. Your sister-queens could have healed you and left you human, but our Camila let her emotions for you get in the way. She let her emotions overrule what she truly knew to be just."

He went on, speaking firmly but softly, all for my sake. I wasn't going to change his mind, but he was willing to explain.

"Though you have yet to commit the ritual, I only allowed our Camila to bind herself to you as her na'suul under the terms that she would be willing to let you go if you ever wished to leave her. Humans may be a very treasured gift to us, but they don't view time and bonds as we do. They don't treasure their own lives as we do. You may still love her very much, I sense that you do, but there is a large difference between fabricating stories to your family about your mysterious girlfriend and them believing you are dead."

Camila tensed, but stayed quiet as the tears dripped off her chin. I wanted to go to her. Trying to move was useless, though. Dalhem would not allow it, not until he was done. My feet were frozen to the floor.

"You will never see the sun again, my Ginger. And I hope you had no desire to have children of your own, because now that choice is gone. And there is also the small matter of your family. You may be content with our Camila now, but you have seen the behavior of your sister-queen, Cleo. If in a day or in a week or twenty years, when you see that your family is forever removed from you, you may hold our Camila responsible for taking your life.

"Our Cleo comes from an extremely loving flock, but they never would have accepted her as a demon. Her only choice was death." He stopped then, and looked over at Camila. Gently, he tucked a longer, spiky lock of her hair behind her ear. He was testing me, not my love for her, but my patience with him. I swallowed twice, waiting.

"You never tried to share the truth with your family, did you, my Ginger?"

What the fu—

"No. Of course I didn't. I thought it was against the law. And so did she."

He sighed wistfully. "If only she thought to ask. Again, her only thought was of her Ginger, and sometimes those sorts of thoughts work against you."

He had to be kidding, but I knew he wasn't.

"You're saying I could have told them?"

"I am saying, my Ginger, now I am afraid it is too late, and one day you may feel the sting of that regret. And when you ask that I cast Camila from your sight, the pain of losing you as a result of her own selfishness will be far greater than any punishment I could hand down. Our Camila will wish for death, and I will not grant it."

"Please. I love her and I still want her, with or without my family," I said.

"And what will we do about them now, my Ginger? Linda and her Fredo and Todd. You are probably wondering."

"I am," I replied. He was talking in circles. I had no idea what he was getting at.

"I will handle them."

"How?" I gulped.

"That is not your concern, my Ginger. Our Camila has forced my hand. But you will know the outcome. In the meantime, you will not contact them. When it is done, they will reach out to you or they will bury your memory. Either way, I will not allow our Camila to make those sorts of decisions anymore."

"Her punishment," I breathed. "What would her punishment involve? Or is this all?"

"Many things and one only. She may no longer act as the Queen of my Alpha nest. She has made some grievous mistakes. She may be old to you, but she is still very young, and now I have seen, too weak and too immature to handle such a responsibility."

Then I felt my jaw clench. I had a deep respect for our master, literally running through my veins, but Camila was my maker. No one had the right to insult her. Still, I kept my mouth shut. A slight smile returned to Dalhem's lips as he moved through my mind.

"A perfect example. You love her, but you know not to speak hastily. You are very young, but you know when to exercise restraint. Yet you know she was wrong. I can feel it, my Ginger. She went against your wishes." He took a deep breath, completely for show, and squared his shoulders. He still held Camila close. "You will be queen."

"But I'm younger than she is."

He grew very serious. I'd challenged him just enough for one night.

"The decision is mine."

"I—Sorry. If I become queen, what happens to Camila?"

"That is entirely up to you," he replied.

"So if I become queen, she can come home with me?"

"Yes, if that is what you wish. Her rank remains among the demon class. I would not have her weakened against others, but she will have no authority over the sister-queens within the confines of the house."

"What about her feeders?"

"Again, that is your decision, but I am trusting you with my daughter."

"I have to feed from Benny?" For some reason I didn't like this idea.

"No. I am trusting you to care for her. If you prefer that she continue on with our Camila, then so be it."

"If I don't want to be queen, then who will do it? What happens to Camila and me?" I asked. I didn't want to leave any nook unchecked. I didn't want Dalhem to catch me in some loophole when it came to my future with her.

"I don't believe you will refuse me, but if you do, Natasha will reclaim Samantha. I will then set you up in another nest. You are independent, but you do not truly desire to be alone. You may remain near our Camila if you chose, but she needs to remain near me. Here. I will only permit her to live amongst my young feeders in the Alpha nest if you are with her. Her mate seems to be the only one to control her.

"Cleo is strong, but her recent behavior displeases me. I would pass the throne to Kina. She has exhibited excellent control of her power and she respects me well. I treasure her as I treasure all of my queens, but my Benita trusts you. Her mother and I are never far. Though, in an interesting twist, I find that I feel as all human fathers do. This is her first time away from home. I worry for her and I would like her to have you near. The other sister-queens cannot provide her mother and me with that sort of comfort."

"I'll do it. And I'll take Camila with me," I blurted.

"Excellent." He smiled wider than before, flashing his tiger-sized fangs.

At that very instant, he took my breath, ripped it right from my lungs. He held Camila in the same motionless space, the two of us frozen as he took a piece of her mind and her soul and switched it with a piece of mine.

I exhaled sharply, feeling a new sense of power, different connections to not only all the girls and the sister-queens, but to Dalhem himself. The lives of forty-two humans and vampires were now my responsibility; Camila was my responsibility. If I failed them in any way, I had to answer to our master. The burden was immense, and it was mine to deal with. I was Queen.

"You grow accustomed to it," he said. "We are done here. In thirty-six hours, you will receive a call and you will know the fate of your former life. Do not reach out to them, my Ginger. Mistakes can, at times, be mended. Certain harms can be healed, but nothing can be undone."

"Yes, Master." I didn't know what else I could say.

"She asked for a life-bond with you, my Ginger. Did you know what that means?"

"No, Master."

"Our Camila asked me for your hand-na'suul, but she asked to die once your human form passed on. I would not allow it. Now you must excuse me. I'm going to have a few more words with our Camila." Gently, he stroked her soft black spikes away from her forehead. "Maybe you'd like to get better acquainted with your true maker."

At that moment, an enormous man, taller than Rodrick, appeared behind the couch. He nodded once to Dalhem before he nodded to me, skipping the bowing and the praising. He was dressed rather plainly in a white T-shirt, a black leather jacket, and jeans. His long red hair was pulled back in a tight ponytail. His thick red and blond beard was trimmed close to his face. I swallowed, gazing at him and reminding myself that this man was not my father.

"Seamus serves my sister, Caana. It was hard to locate him, but we did," Dalhem said, then he nodded toward the door behind me. "There's another sitting room right out there. Please take your time."

We stepped out of the room, but instead of making himself comfortable in a chair, Seamus stood across the small space, looking at me with his arms folded across his chest.

"Your name's Ginger?" His Scottish accent was so thick I could barely understand him, but the deep, rhythmic tempo of his voice was oddly soothing. I could have listened to him talk for hours. He seemed to be in a little bit of hurry, though. The night was moving so fast, especially now, the moment when I wanted him to stay.

"Yes. Ginger Carmichael," I answered.

He walked over to me and gazed at my face. He served another master, not Dalhem, and I sensed I was still important, but my power and rank meant nothing to him. I was just another young demon. I looked up, craning my neck to return his studying stare.

"Let me get a look atcha?" He gently grabbed my chin and tilted my head this way and that. "You've got the look of your mother."

Yes, I did, in a way. I had my mother's nose and the delicate shape of her face, but I had this man's lips and emerald eyes, even his cheeks. And, of course, his thick red hair and his freckles.

"Are we related?" I asked outright.

"Yes. I'm your uncle. Your father, Ian, was my brother," he explained, dropping his hand from my face. "Met your mother on a trip. I went home to tell my da I was going to marry an American girl. I would have made it back to her, but I was stabbed on my way to the pub the night before I meant to come back to Boston. My queen found me and changed me."

He went on, not skipping a beat. "My worthless brother waited a year after my headstone was in the ground, then he came to America and found your mother. He won her and you were made. I tracked them down. Janet was pregnant with you and he was trying to beat the life out of you both."

It was strange to hear my mother's name spoken out loud. It had been so long. But for some reason, I wasn't shocked by my birth dad's behavior. The few men my mother had brought home had been abusive creeps. It was no surprise my father had been one too. Maybe the violent streak ran on that side of the family.

"So you killed him?" I frowned.

Just then Camila came through the door. I'd waited eleven years to hear what Seamus had to say, to even find out that he existed, but at that moment, Camila was all I could see. We were in each other's arms before I could even blink, hugging each other tight, trying to breathe each other in as if our desperate embrace would keep the other from vanishing ever again.

I kissed her hard, and when I pulled away, I wiped her tears. She was back to herself, but still on edge.

"Are you okay?" I asked.

"Yes, baby. I'm fine." She glanced over at Seamus. "I'm sorry. I didn't mean to interrupt."

Seamus looked at us both for a second before he answered me, acting as if my tearful reunion with my girlfriend had never taken place.

"No matter. I was just telling Ginger what became of her father. Yeah, I killed him. Right in front of your mother. She didn't know what I was at first, but after I healed her, she made me promise I would never come near her again. I kept my word. I know I may sound a bit callous, but I loved her. Ian had no right to put his hands on her." A muscle twitched in his cheek and I knew then he was telling the truth about his feeling for her. He still loved her.

Camila's arm came around my waist. I gripped her hand against my stomach, more than willing to take her support. Whichever one of us was queen, I still needed her. She knew what I was about to say.

"She killed herself," I told him.

"I've heard." He turned his back for a second and stroked his beard. When he turned back around, all emotion was wiped from his face. "I'm glad I got to see you. You're a beautiful girl, Ginger. Probably the only good thing to come out of Ian, that piece of shit. I had best be going. My queen-mistress needs me."

"I don't—is there a way I can get in touch with you?" Seamus wasn't exactly warm and fuzzy, but if I never got to see my parents again, he was the only family I had. Him and Camila.

"You've your cell phone on you?"

"Actually, no."

"Here." Camila held out her phone to Seamus.

He took it and quickly entered his phone number. "Your Rodrick's been looking for me for a while, I hear. I meant to come see you before your next school term, but here we are. My queen-mistress has her demands, but you're my niece. You just call if you need me."

"Thanks. I—I will. Unc—Seamus, wait." The word uncle felt weird to say, but there was one more thing I had to know.

"Yes?"

"You exposed yourself to my mother as a vampire, but you never wiped her memory right? And she never became a feeder?"

"That's right."

"And your queen-mistress let you live, but was there some other punishment?"

"Na, there wasn't," he said. "She knew I was saving the life of my love and my rightful wife. And the baby that should have been mine."

He nodded once more, tight-lipped, and then he was gone.

I squeezed my eyes shut and let out a deep breath. Then I turned to Camila.

"Let's just—I have a lot I want to say, but not here."

"Okay," she whispered hoarsely.

I pulled her to me, wrapping my arms around her and we vanished through the night.

## CHAPTER NINETEEN

Camila was drained physically and emotionally. I wanted her fed and rested, but the moment we saw Samantha trembling in Natasha's lap, my focus changed. A new sort of trauma had just begun for Sam. Camila and I hadn't been gone that long, but it was long enough for Sam to start thinking about what had happened in the library stairwell.

She was across the room, throwing her arms around me before I got out a single word of explanation to my sister-queens. I picked her up effortlessly and just as quickly, her legs went around my waist. Her emotions were all over the place, such a mess that it was almost impossible for me not to enter her mind. She was thinking of Greg, dead on the stairs. I had come to terms with his death the moment the asshole had shoved me. The most he'd ever been to me was a lab partner, and at the least, he was an insecure jerk who didn't know how to watch his mouth. To Samantha, he'd been lover, tormentor, and her only human friend.

I sank to the floor beside the couch and held Samantha's trembling frame to me, cradling her head against my shoulder. It was slightly awkward because we were nearly the same height and build, but with my sudden strength, she didn't weigh a thing. And even if she'd been heavy to me, I wouldn't have set her down. Greg had hurt Sam, but somehow I felt responsible. We had all shut Samantha out at the beginning of the semester, simply because of her brutal, rude honesty. Maybe if I had just given her a chance, if we'd tried to get to know her, she would have relied on us instead of Greg for support and comfort. I couldn't take any of it back, but I could take care of her now.

Still holding Sam, I had a brief meeting with my sister-queens, my first official act as head she-demon in charge. They understood immediately that the shift had taken place. There was some confusion, but they all accepted me as queen, no questions asked, knowing they'd get the details when things were a little less crazy.

I made the decision to keep the girls in the dark about everything that had happened until the following morning, all but Barb. I'd need her to feed Camila tonight. I told them to let the girls know I was fine, but I didn't plan on going anywhere until I heard from Dalhem. If anyone on campus asked, I'd gone home on a family emergency. It was up to Rodrick what he planned to tell the boys about Greg.

My sister-queens offered, like they had with Cleo, to let me choose which of the girls I wanted to act as my feeders. I had been less than comfortable watching Natasha unbind herself from Sam. It didn't feel right picking and choosing. For a moment, I considered who'd I be most comfortable with, but then I remembered the moment I tasted Sam's blood. Previous comfort levels had absolutely nothing to do with the bond between demon and feeder. Even Andrew, who had seemed to be pretty devoted to Moreland. He'd latched on to Cleo so quickly and completely, it was as if they'd been bound together their whole lives. I cared for all the girls and would happily take the first two willing volunteers.

Sam had no interest whatsoever in leaving my side. I needed her to at least try to get through the week. Greg was gone, and I was clearly going to be a no-show for my exams the next day. I hated the idea of forcing her to do anything, so we compromised, agreeing she would get some sleep if Camila and I let her stay in our apartment.

After my sister-queens left, Camila and I got Samantha in the shower, and in my first real lesson in mind control, Camila showed me how to clear Sam's mind. I was horrified at all the things I saw as I sorted through the memories that kept her heart racing. Her emotionally dismissive mother, images of her father, who, in spite of his kindness, was a clear spokesman for Too Distant Dads. And then the parts of her that were clinging to Greg. She couldn't believe he was gone, and I couldn't believe after seeing the things he'd put her through, that she still loved him.

For the time being, I erased his face from her mind, soothing all the pain, pinpricks, and deep gouges, with calm and peace. Camila and I watched her for a moment as she drifted off between our satin sheets, both of us a little lost on what we would do with her when the morning came. And I wondered what Sam would have done if she hadn't followed us up the stairs, if Greg hadn't pushed me. How long would she have gone on letting him hurt her? How long had Greg been hurting others?

As if I'd asked the questions out loud, Camila took my hand. She showed me all the things Samantha hadn't seen. The girlfriend Greg had beaten all through high school, the unwanted advances he'd made on Micah, the rough way he'd handled Andrew just the night before, and countless other instances where Greg had lost his cool and crossed some lines. And then there were things I hadn't come close to expecting, like Greg's deep self-loathing and his obsessive feelings for me.

Greg hated himself and instead of turning it inward, he let his rage out on anyone unfortunate enough to get close to him in any way. He'd pushed me off the stairs because I was secure in who I was. He pushed me because I was happy with my love and my life and he knew no amount of seduction, intimidation, or force would make me give in to him. He had wanted me all along, knowing he'd missed his chance or that he'd never had one.

But no matter the reason for my death, Greg was a psychopath and all of us, in one way or another, had fed into his behavior. Whether it had been Rodrick's refusal to see anything but the best in his feeders, Camila's willingness to let Rodrick run his house the way he saw fit, or even my refusal to get involved simply because I didn't like Greg and his attitude toward my relationship with Camila, the human in all of us had let the monster in Greg get away with near murder.

"That's why I killed him," Camila's voiced floated quietly in the dark. "I grabbed him, and his mind opened and I saw everything he'd ever done, things Rodrick wouldn't have known unless he'd done a complete mental strip. I know he wasn't mine, but he was a monster. Like he said, Dalhem wanted justice for everyone. He wanted Greg to own up to what he did to Samantha in front of Rodrick and his father. I couldn't let him get away with anything more."

Then something else occurred to me. "How come Natasha didn't know what was going on with Sam?"

"You saw the other things, with her family, you've seen how she is with you girls. Sam has always been hurting. She's always been angry. The tone of her emotions was the same before Greg. Don't ask Natasha about it, Red. She and Rodrick already feel like they've failed us all."

"I won't," I murmured into the darkness. "I'm still not sorry you killed him. Who shoves someone down a flight of stairs?" I chuckled harshly. Camila huffed back as I squeezed her hand tighter.

It took a few breaths, a few moments in the dark silence, but a sense of calm settled around and in that calm, I was split in two. The demon in me felt strong and whole. I knew my place and what I must do. It longed only for Sam's blood and her safety and Camila's touch. My human side, the part that was still alive, was crying out. I would never see my family again.

I pulled my hand out of Camila's grasp and took a step away. I could see the pain in her eyes.

"I love—I need some time." I did love her, but I needed more than five minutes in a dark room to process what my life had become now that she was safe. I figured it would take a few years of mourning and searching for closure to find peace with my new life. I hoped it wouldn't take as long to come to terms with Camila.

She swallowed anxiously. "I'll just be in the office."

"Okay." I couldn't ask her to stay. Still, it sucked to watch her go.

I stood near the bed long after I heard the office door close, but eventually I climbed under the covers with Sam. She was warm and her body was an instant comfort, but she was a wild sleeper. I had to stop her from kicking me in the shins half a dozen times as she tossed and flopped around. When I spooned her body against mine and took a few passes at stroking her hair, she finally settled down. If only I could say the same for my over burdened mind.

Figure it out. Figure out what you're going to do, then go talk to her.

There was nowhere for me to run. I couldn't hide in my dorm room. I couldn't go home. The ABO house was my home now. Even if I escaped to another sister-queen's room, Camila was a part of me now. I knew exactly what Mom would say. Forgive her. She would tell me to embrace the change and to forgive Camila or I would poison everything we'd shared together. I would taint any chance of happiness in my new existence. Making things right with Camila was something I had to do, though at the moment I wanted something different.

I wanted to call Todd and my parents, even though it was the middle of the night. I wanted to call my brother and thank him for finding me and thank my parents for loving me. I saw Cleo's point even more now. I knew things would never be the same no matter what my master had to report, but I did want to say good-bye.

Dalhem struck me as a punctual man, so I knew when he said thirty-six hours, thirty-six hours was what he meant. We'd returned from his house a little before eleven p.m. I expected to hear from him no later than eleven a.m. Tuesday morning. And between now and then I would get on with my immortal life and let the rest—let my family—go. I had no other choice.

❖

Just before two a.m., Benny showed up at the door. I left Sam sleeping and let her in.

"I didn't walk over here alone," she said as we walked to the couch. "Faeth picked me up."

"I'll have to thank her. Your step-dad is pretty…interesting."

"Did you see his wings or his talons?" She chuckled quietly.

"No. But the horns and the teeth. I definitely saw those."

Benny frowned and leaned a little closer. "He is good, Ginger. I know he's intense, but he is good. He's just…not human."

I sighed sadly. I had no ill will toward Dalhem, and there was no need for her to think I did.

"I know. It wasn't him, Benny. It was the situation. I understand he was just doing his job."

"Where's Camila?"

I pointed over my shoulder to the office. "We're…taking a break."

"Faeth told me a few things in the car. That night in the hospital you couldn't have saved Cleo."

"I see that now. The bond is much stronger from this end. I should have listened to Camila." I stopped myself before my mind started with an impossible game of what if.

"It's not just that. Cleo had a year or two tops before her relationship with her mother fell apart. She was going to come out after graduation and her mother would have disowned her. And believe me, her church loves to make examples of homosexuals. My parents were already planning to support her. I figured if she became a demon it would soften the blow of her family's rejection. She just wanted to hold on to this charade she had going with them a little longer." Cleo has almost said as much that day in the mall, but part of me thought she was just afraid to tell her mom she was gay. I never thought her family would actually kick her out.

"But my family, my mom, they knew about me. They wanted to meet Camila. I need them, Benny. I need my family."

"You still have a family. You don't have to go through this alone. You have me and Amy. You have Sam. You have the sister-queens, a house full of sorority girls. Rodrick and the brother-kings are always around, and you have Camila."

Finally, I let myself cry. I couldn't hold it in any longer. Everything Benny was saying made sense, but I wasn't ready to accept the truth. Benny walked over to the bar and came back with some napkins. They were black, but I knew as I wiped my face they were now stained blue.

"Dalhem told me all humans get three chances at life, but most of the time we don't see them as opportunities, just obstacles. The time isn't right for me and Cleo. Her problem is with me, not the life of a demon. Don't let this stand between you and Camila. She loves you more than I think you know."

"I know. This just—" I laughed humorlessly. "This sucks."

"What's it really like?" I figured Dalhem could tell her everything she'd ever want to know about being a vampire, but Dalhem had never been human.

I sat back and wiped my face again. "I like the teeth. A lot." Benny smiled when I opened my mouth, letting my fangs grow to their full length. I hissed at her playfully, giggling myself before I sheathed them. "I don't know. I haven't thought about food in a while. I should be tired, but I'm not. Blood tastes really good."

"Cool."

"It's just weird. I don't feel like I'll ever be myself again."

"You won't, but that's the point of college. To grow up and change," Benny said.

"Literally. Listen. Sam's here, but do you want to stay?"

"Yeah. I think Samantha's in need of a second chance too."

I waited for Benny to kick off her boots and her jeans. She climbed into bed with Sam without a moment's hesitation. Minutes after they cuddled together, Benny was out like a light. I watched them for a few minutes more, gathering up the courage to take Benny's advice.

❖

"If I asked you to take me somewhere, would you?" I said quietly. Camila stood from her office chair.

"Of course. Where—" I didn't blink as I shared my thoughts with her, showing Camila my mind's image of where exactly I wanted to go. Sadness clouded her face, but she held out her hand for me. In the next breath, I was in Camila's arms. I shuddered as our cheeks touched. I could feel it in my bones, across every inch of my skin. This was home.

"Close your eyes," she said. I did as she asked, feeling the warmth of her lips against my neck and then I felt the heat of the Mexican night wind blowing through my hair.

I opened my eyes and glanced across the shallow river, lit blue and silver by spots of moonlight pushing through the trees. It was the very spot Camila had been that day, here on the fertile riverbank. I glanced around, seeing that Dalhem had kept his promise. The land remained untouched, and I knew as Camila exhaled a deep, somber breath, that almost nothing had changed in those sixty-five years.

We held perfectly still, letting the night creatures grow accustomed to our presence, and after a few moments, the small chirps of tropical insects and midnight birds rose again. Then I walked down to the water, letting my fingertips break the cool surface. Camila kept her eyes on me the whole time, not saying a word as I let the last few days roll around in my head.

It wasn't long before she'd had enough. She was having a hard time just standing on the bank with her back to what was once her home, but I had to know the truth. I had to hear the words from her willingly, without our connection or our relationship working against her in a moment of weakness. I turned to face her, keeping the physical distance between us.

"We were screwed from the beginning, weren't we?" I said, my voice sounding overly loud in the dark wilderness. "You would have saved me yourself no matter what. If I'd gotten hit by a car or choked on some broccoli, you would have saved me, no matter what I said." Her eyes darkened a bit in the moonlight. I could feel her fighting the urge to lie to me, but it wasn't going to work.

Camila swallowed then shook her head. "I'm sorry."

"Don't be. I would have done the same thing." I walked to her and gently tucked a short spike of hair behind her ear. "If I'd been in your shoes, I would have saved you too. A thousand times."

"Dalhem was right. Natasha or Faeth could have made you whole again, but I wasn't thinking, and I ruined your life."

"No. Greg is the one who pushed me. You just followed your heart. I feel it now, with Sam, even with you. You were right. This body and its connections—it's different. It's more. I'll miss my family. I already do, but you have to see I will never take that out on you. Ever."

"You will."

"No, I won't," I said, taking a step closer to her. Her breasts touched mine. "Here's what I realized. If I can't heal us, I'll never move on, and losing you will just add to the pain. Earlier…" I failed as the emotion caught up with me. My throat ached to close. I glanced back up again, and when our eyes locked, I knew I also owed her the whole truth. Uncontrollably, cool tears started streaming down my face. "Earlier tonight, I couldn't find you for twenty minutes, and those were the longest twenty minutes of my life. Do you understand how much I love you?"

She started to nod and speak, but I interrupted her. My point wasn't sinking in.

"I know you see it and I know you feel it, but you have to believe it. You have to believe me." I huffed painfully, swallowing as many tears as I could manage before I went on.

"Ginger, I know…I'm afraid," she finally said.

"So am I. I'm scared shitless about all of this. Everything but us."

"What if you can't forgive me?"

"Can't you see that's what I'm doing? I forgive you."

I closed the distance between us and crushed her to me. That's what broke her. Just a few tears at first, but soon we were both sobbing amongst the moonlit trees, probably scaring the crap out of the wildlife.

"There will be days where I'm sad and there will be days where I'm angry. There may even be days where I'm angry at you. All couples fight, but I will always, always love you." Wiping her cheeks seemed to affirm that fact. She was too precious to me, meant more to me than anyone ever would again. "I'll need you to help me through it. I'm going to need you to make me laugh. And I'll do the same for you. When you want to kill Cleo or Tokyo. Although, I guess they're my problem now. I just, right now, I need you. Why didn't you tell me about the life-bond?" I kissed her gently, tasting her sweet tears.

"I didn't want to scare you."

"Well, I wouldn't have let you do it. I wanted to grow old, but I didn't want you to die with me. We'll just have to live forever together." She pulled me closer this time, burying my wet cheek against her neck.

"What do we have to do for me to be your na'suul?" She leaned back as I fished the engagement ring out of my pocket. I took a bit of sick pleasure as her eyes popped wide when she saw what was in my hand.

"Um, it's quite simple actually. I just want you to be sure. Our divorce would be slightly more involved than lawyers and paperwork."

"I want to do it. Now."

"Red…"

"Don't you dare tell me no."

"Okay, baby," she said, trembling slightly. "Just remember, this is more than a marriage. It's an oath that surpasses the feeder bond and even the bond we have with our sisters. You'll be able to sense me always. Our minds will be connected."

"Perfect. Mila, will you marry me?"

"Yes." She nodded as the tears started again down her cheeks. She took the ring from me and slid it on my finger. It was a perfect fit. "Give me your other hand. And you take mine."

With her right hand over my heart and mine over hers, she cupped the back of my head with her left. I did same. When our foreheads touched, she whispered several words into the night air. Na'suul was the only one I understood, but that didn't stop me from feeling the weight of their meaning. Once she finished, she gently slid her ring finger between my lips. I guided mine toward her plump mouth.

"Bite," she said. I tasted her cool, sweet blood as her fangs pierced my skin. A drop was all we needed to seal our love, but we took more. And then she kissed me. I cried out against her lips, feeling whole, so completely loved without having to utter a single vow, and then like a movie playing in my mind, Camila showed me her life.

I saw her entire existence, human and demon. I knew the smells of her Mexican valley as it had been when it was filled with human life and joy. I knew the feeling of the rocky ledges and the cool riverbed under her feet. I knew the survival lessons her mother, father, and brothers had taught her. I saw the smiles of her children and heard the sound of their laughter as they called her mama. I felt the warmth and respect in the firm embrace of her husband's arms. I saw the devotion in Abrah's eyes, and I felt the unconditional love that dwelt in Dalhem's heart.

I knew, even more, exactly why she'd saved Cleo and why she'd changed me. I felt her love for me, how it swallowed up all her rational sense, how it made her feel alive and whole again. All her stresses, her hesitations and fears, I knew them and felt their sting, and then I saw how her love for me helped her push them away.

I whimpered desperately into our kiss, taking what she was giving me. Her life. And I gave her mine. Every moment. Every tear. Every smile. Things from my past I didn't want to remember and memories I didn't want to forget. They were all hers now. In every possible way, I was hers now.

And I am yours, Red, she silently whispered into my heart. I understood now that our na'suulaem had nothing to do with our need for blood and everything do with our devotion to each other. We were no longer two demon-vampires connected by our sister-queen bond, or demon and maker. We were one, partners of the soul. We'd be together for the rest of my life, and for the eternity of hers, she would be mine.

The kiss went on for what seemed like forever, but soon we pulled apart. I gazed at her, now my wife, overwhelmed and stunned into silence.

"Red," she whispered. "I want to consummate this, but there's something I want to show you first. Shift with me."

"What do I have to do?" I asked as we shed our clothes.

"I'll shift first and then you come into my mind. It's very simple," she said, wiping my cheeks with the backs of her fingers. I nodded then kissed her again. A moment later Camila was beside me, this time on all fours as a sleek panther.

"Got sick of the house cat costume?" I asked.

*No. There are condors out here that could swallow a housecat whole. They like to hunt at night. No need to tempt them.*

"Oh." I kept the rest of my commentary to myself and followed the cues my demon needed to shift. It felt the same as vanishing, almost like flying, only faster.

It took a second to get used to being so close to the ground, having whiskers and thickly padded paws in place of feet and hands, but I adjusted the moment Camila's large feline head nuzzled against the thick fur on my neck. I purred back deep in my throat, licking at her face and ears. In the next moment, she took off into the trees, bounding over rocks and ferns. I stayed close behind, letting her take me deeper into the night. I was still the queen, but when she knew where to lead, I would always follow.

# CHAPTER TWENTY

Camila and I took a quick shower, and while she was getting dressed, I called Barb. She was a little confused to hear from me at the crack of dawn, but much more confused when I opened the door for her a few minutes later. Shock flashed across her face when she sensed my power, and her eyes grew even wider as she fixated on my teeth. I explained to her quickly what had happened, skimming over the dramatics, leaving out details about Samantha that were hers and hers only to share.

Barb handled the news well, her own sense of duty as chapter president overtaking her shock and her confusion.

"So, uh, you'll need two more feeders, right?" Barb asked nervously. She couldn't stop staring at my teeth.

"Yes. We'll let you guys choose again," I said.

"I'd like to stay with Camila," she replied honestly. I told her that was fine, patting her arm as I sensed her relief. Titles may have changed, but I had no aspirations of grandeur, no bright ideas that said I had to mess with a good thing.

Camila came out of the bedroom dressed for bed in her tank and a pair of my shorts. I gave them a minute alone and went to check on Sam and Benny. In the darkness of the bedroom, through the closed door, I could sense Camila as she fed from Barb, deeply but slowly and safely. Barb did an excellent job of keeping her moaning and whimpering to herself. My body still flushed with heat, feeding off the lust rising in Camila. Knowing once the feeding was done, that Camila would be mine helped me keep my impatience in check.

I watched Benny and Sam sleeping soundly. How in the world had I gone from college student to married, crowned, demon foster mother in a matter of days? I thought of Seamus, wondered how much he and my birth father had in common, how often he thought of my mother. I wondered what exactly he did for Caana.

My thoughts drifted back to my Mila. Her feeding was almost complete, and with every swallow she took, my body bloomed for her, my skin flushing hotter, moisture rushing between my legs. I closed the bedroom door and walked quietly past her, into her office. Her gaze tracked my every step.

I left my clothes in a pile by the sideboard and leaned against her desk, leaving the lights off. I slipped my fingers over my tingling clit and let my head fall back on my shoulders, my purr vibrating the mouse on its pad.

Out in the living room, Camila growled.

I waited, listening as Barb slipped out the door. A second later, Camila appeared in front of me, panting and ready.

My body reacted differently to hers now. It invited her strength, ached for her physical power as a sign of her love. The animal in me would never be satisfied with the care she took with my former human self. I wanted all of her.

I watched her curves as she walked toward me, gazed over every inch of her as she came between my legs, licking my mouth, swirling her tongue around the tips of my fangs, sharing her feeder's flavor with me. The force of my lust rumbled deep in my throat as I took what she offered, sucking her tongue deep into my mouth. Barb's blood was sweet, but not as sweet as my Mila.

I ripped her tank top over her head and tossed it on the floor. My shorts followed as I yanked them down her smooth legs. I smiled at how wet the crotch was. Drawn forward, I cupped her breasts, massaging one and suckling on the other. I nipped her delicious brown nipple, teasing it with my teeth and my tongue, sucking it between my lips. Her fingers weaved their way into my hair, holding me closer, her body arching toward me.

"Ginger," her voice echoed in the darkness. My pussy clenched, my throat tightened as she called to me. I lifted my head, searching up her neck, and finding her mouth. My tongue slid inside with slow, dragging strokes, past the tips of her pulsing fangs. And then her fingers found my slit, digging inside, pumping me, filling each inch, making me want more as her thumb rotated over my clit.

Suddenly, part of me snapped. This wasn't how this was supposed to go. I knew it had to be Dalhem's doing, but I could feel it, clearer than a simple title change. I was in charge now. Camila's demon belonged to me.

Pulling away from our kiss, I looked up in her eyes. Her gaze softened, the caramel and green oddly muted for how turned on I knew she was. Slowly, she withdrew fingers and lowered her head. Normally, that would have made me beyond uncomfortable. This was Camila. She didn't bow to me. Ever. But the demon in me was pleased, aroused even more at the sight of her submission.

I cupped her face and guided her lips back to mine. I swallowed the whimpers that came from her mouth as I sucked her tongue past my teeth and licked her fangs and her lips and chin.

"Do you want it hard?" I said against her skin.

"Yes."

I plunged my tongue back into her mouth and walked us across the room, the drive of my desire to get inside her carrying more than enough momentum. More momentum than I realized. My body slammed into Camila's as her back slammed into the sideboard. The Colonial Williamsburg ashtray smashed to the floor, but neither of us made any move to stop it.

I gripped my Mila's hips and spun her around. Reading my mind, she bent over the wood surface, presenting her perfect ass to me. My knees met the hardwood floor with a loud thud. I wasted no time spreading her open and spearing her pussy with my tongue, coating my mouth with her cinnamon musk. I moaned, taking in her flavor, driving her with more force as my nails scraped her clit.

"Ah, fuck!" Camila cried while she scrambled up the sideboard. I helped her, gripping her thigh and shoving it up beside her elbow. One of the antique teacups and its saucer crashed and broke into pieces next to the ashtray.

The animalistic sounds we couldn't contain grew louder and louder together, and more and more, I felt my control slipping, the human in me getting lost to our fierce lovemaking, but I liked it. Camila did too. Silently, she told me so.

I stood, swapping my mouth with my fingers, grinding my clit against her hip.

"Come," I demanded, drilling my fingers harder and harder into her slit. When she didn't, I told her again, "Come." I clamped down on her shoulder with my fangs and her pussy spasmed around my fingers, soaking my palm.

"Ginger," she sobbed, rolling her head against her forearm. "Ginger, God."

"I'm not done with you yet," I said, licking at the small dimples I made in her skin. "On the floor, my Mila."

Camila vanished through my fingers. I spun around to find her stretched out on the floor, smirking in the darkness at the shock on my face.

"You think you're funny, don't you." I fell back to my knees and pulled her pussy flush to mine, throwing her leg over my shoulder.

"Just doing what my queen told me to do," she moaned as I rolled my thumb over her clit. I ground my hips in a punishing motion, rewarding myself with a violent shudder. Camila's fingers pinched at my nipples, pulling me closer. I leaned over her, riding her as hard as I could into the floor, shocked at how suddenly my orgasm tackled me.

I couldn't keep in the loud, roaring growl that tore from my chest. The sound pushed Camila over. She trembled beneath me, gripping my sides to anchor herself to the floor. I knew she was ready for more, but I rolled off her, my sensible self wanting to check in with her lover before things went any further.

Her eyes fluttered open as I licked her shoulder. I just had to kiss her now that I was thinking somewhat straight. "You okay?" I murmured into her mouth.

"Of course, baby. I'm fine." She wrapped an arm around my waist and gently trailed her fingertips up and down my back. I snuggled closer to her body, kissing and licking the scent of her sweetness off her chest. "We should have done this in Tokyo's room."

"Why?" I asked.

"Would have been nice to break some of her shit."

"Oh, sorry." I laughed, feeling more myself.

"Don't be. The ashtray cost me five bucks, and when was the last time you saw me drinking tea?"

"I don't know what came over me." I sat up and looked into her eyes. "Will it always be like that, now that I'm queen or whatever?"

"Only if you want it to be, baby." I thought about it for a little while as I listened to Camila's gentle breathing. Taking control was fun, a major turn-on, letting the demon in me be the animal it needed to be from time to time, but I didn't need more change. Sexual assault, temporary paralysis, and a shift to a different physical species was enough for one night.

I kissed her one more time, guiding her hand between my legs. "Let's take turns."

Camila agreed, pushing her fingers inside me.

❖

A while later, Camila put on a continuous loop of the slow tempo techno jams we'd made love to and I'd fallen asleep to so many times since we'd met. We climbed in bed, cuddling close on either side of Samantha and Benny.

I slipped my arm around Sam's waist and Camila gently stroked Benny's hair. I thought of the times she'd done that to me and wondered how many more times she'd touched me that way as I slept. It was such a sweet gesture, cute even to watch. Sam kicked my shin, taking unconscious advantage of my distraction. I pinned her legs between mine, just hoping she'd clobbered Greg a good one during the nights she'd spent with him. I glanced back up as Camila snickered, picking up on my thought.

She never yawned, but she blinked heavily for a moment and confessed she hadn't slept much since Cleo's accident. She didn't argue when I asked her ever so affectionately to take a nap. I lay beside them for a long time, watching the three of them sleep, wondering how I would pass the hours now, what I would do until I heard from Dalhem.

❖

Monday was the longest day of my entire life. I had to see it as a first day. My first full day with my true na'suul. My first day as queen of this weird but perfect family. The first day I could actually boss Cleo around, but as exciting as all of those things sounded, the hours dragged.

We sent Benny and Samantha off for breakfast and some last minute cramming, then we went into the office. Camila hacked into the Maryland DMV and had them send me a new driver's license. She changed my age to twenty-five. Then she ordered herself a new ID. It had been almost ten years since her last name change. I didn't complain. Camila Carmichael had a certain ring to it.

Then Camila gave me a guided tour to my new queendom. She had access to part of this mysterious database of vampire-demons Benny had mentioned to me. Dalhem had the names of every vampire and feeder in North America. I had access to all the vampires who fed on former members of ABO as well as a general list of all the vampires and feeders that resided in Maryland and the states that bordered, anyone who would accidentally stumble upon one of my girls. I had the names of every sister-queen and brother-king in every chapter and could call upon them whenever I needed to.

She went through the inner workings of the house. Florencia's kids—children I had no clue she had—owned every service we used, from catering to cleaning. They had their own schedule that worked so smoothly I never noticed their coming and going in all the hours I'd spent below ground. If I had any requests, which of course I didn't, I could go to Florencia herself. Two of her sons were Faeth's backup feeders. Her daughter fed Moreland. I decided to leave that one alone.

There were other tidbits like the fact there was a house the Alpha chapter owned in St. Martin that operated as a safe place for the girls to stay during spring break. It was supposed to be a surprise for us new girls next semester. I playfully pouted, whining to Camila that I wanted to go. She scowled back, reminding me that after dark we could go wherever the hell we wanted.

She lifted my hand, gently twisting my wedding ring, and generously offered to let me take part in all her personally owned business ventures. I told her I'd have to get back to her. I had no idea what I wanted to do now, and I figured it was best to get a hang of the whole queen thing before I started taking on part ownership in tattoo shops and hotels. Plus, I had some Japanese to learn.

She gave me Dalhem's phone number and Benny's mother's, just in case. That brought our joking and teasing up short. I just wanted to know what was going on with my parents. Tuesday morning couldn't come soon enough.

With exactly twenty-four hours left till I heard from Dalhem, I opened the door to Amy. She was a mess, tap dancing, sobbing like a fool in the hallway. After I got her to stop crying and yelling, "Oh, Ginger," she agreed to grab a few things from our room that my parents would never notice missing, my letterman's sweater and pair of flip-flops I'd spent all summer breaking in.

It eventually sunk in that I wasn't actually dead, and she asked me what my official story of death was going to be. I'd admitted I didn't know, but assured her I'd work Greg in there somehow as the villain. Danni came by to get Amy for her econ final. She just hugged me, thank God. She dragged Amy with her dramatic good-byes out the door, skipping all the crying and theatrics.

I went back to the office with Camila. Just as I sank back in her lap, I got a text message from Mom. She wanted to know if Camila and I had made up and if I was okay. She also wanted to know if I'd picked up my birthday presents from the university post office. I kissed away the pained look on Camila's face as she read the text over my shoulder, then I deleted it. I texted Amy and asked her to go to the P.O. to find out how long they kept packages before they returned them to sender.

After a few deep breaths, Camila explained to me the importance of subtle behavior around humans.

"People only remember a passing pretty face for a few minutes, a day at best, but they remember if you do something, say something, that stays in their mind. Always be forgettable, Red," she said. "Although that won't be easy."

"Don't worry. I'll just shift into Cleo if I ever feel like making a scene."

A few hours later, Natasha showed up with my two additional feeders. Paige and Anna-Jade. They'd volunteered as soon as they'd heard the news. Barb hadn't called a chapter meeting. I felt terrible for taking two feeders from Natasha, but she didn't seem bothered by it at all. She and Rodrick shared several feeders outside the house, and she could still see the girls every day. She hushed my buts and what-ifs and released Anna-Jade to me before I could argue anymore. I thanked her before she disappeared, promising her I would take care of Anna-Jade and Sam just as well as she had. She winked at me and told me she knew I'd do much better.

Before I accepted Paige, she turned to Camila.

"You're not angry, are you—that I'm leaving you?"

"No. Ginger's my wife. I'm willing to share."

"Oh," Paige said, shocked. "So I still can't sleep with her?"

Camila barked out in laughter, tossing her head back. "I release you, Paige Charlotte Plummer. Serve this sister-queen as you would serve the master himself. As you would serve me."

I accepted the little horndog's vow, shaking my head as I grabbed her hand and sliced a cut, nice and deep. She didn't even flinch. I sealed the bonding wound, licking the blood away, and somehow I should have known that out of all my feeders, Paige's blood would be the most potent aphrodisiac. I was very happy with Anna-Jade and Paige. I kissed and held them both, a little embarrassed at how sad the thought of them leaving for the three weeks after finals made me.

They headed off to class just as Rodrick appeared at the door. He had a letter from Greg's father, apologizing for Greg's "unfortunate" behavior. I told him I'd read it later, but thanked him sincerely for everything he had done. He and Pax had already returned the body to Greg's family, who had planned to officially report Greg's death as a suicide early next semester. They'd work me in however I decided—as soon as I heard from Dalhem.

Samantha was still a little out of it when she came back from the newspaper office that night. I had Cleo bring Andrew by and we ordered some pizza for them. Andrew was just so calm and gentle, it was impossible not to like him. He didn't hesitate to tell Sam how Greg had acted with him. Knowing Greg had been that cruel with more than just her helped Samantha relax a lot, but the comfort wasn't enough to keep her from spending the night in our bed.

❖

I thought it would be best to take the quick bullet from Dalhem and get on with my day. I invited Cleo to bring Andrew over for a nice breakfast with Samantha in our apartment. Florencia felt a little bad about all the dying and families breaking up, so she whipped up some pancakes for us. I had no desire to eat at all until we lifted the lid off the five short stacks and the mountain of bacon she sent down. I was good to go after one pancake, but I still groaned pathetically as I ate it. Butter and syrup had never tasted so good.

After Samantha left to take her algebra exam, Camila turned to Cleo.

"I have to apologize," she said.

"Why?" Cleo asked as she reclined against Andrew's chest.

"I should have asked you before it became a matter of your life hanging in the balance." Camila glanced at me and I took her hand. "I should have asked all the girls. And we will, from now on. We should know what you all want the very first night of initiation. It would have killed me to let you go, but it was your choice and I'm sorry."

"I'm sorry, too. I have been a complete shit head, but I understand why you did it," Cleo said. I didn't miss the gentle way her hand moved up Andrew's thigh. "I still want to see my mama, but I'm sorry for being an asshole to you." Then she turned to me. "I'm sorry I dragged you though any part of it too, my Queen."

"It's okay. I think I put myself in it. Tomorrow, with Camila's help let's go say good-bye to your mom." Camila nodded in agreement. We'd all been so caught up in my accident and my transition that the trip Cleo had been promised was nearly skipped over.

"No," Cleo replied. "They know I love them. I have to move on."

"You're sure?" I asked.

"Yeah." Apologies accepted, Cleo and Andrew said they wanted to hang around until I got the call. Faeth showed up to join in the wait. And then Tokyo dropped in. And Omi. We fought the awkward moments, filling silences with stupid stories, hatching ridiculous plans for the rest of my life. I liked Cleo's idea that we start a rumor I'd run off to join the circus. Camila played along for a while, joking that I would love a career in hotel management, but slowly she grew more and more quiet the closer it got to eleven a.m. Still, when I looked at her, she was sure to smile. I kissed her gently, every time reminding her it was the two of us, no matter what, forever.

Eleven o'clock, eleven oh five, eleven thirty came and went. By eleven forty-five, I'd considered whether Dalhem himself would come and break the news to me.

At noon, I took a moment and silently said good-bye to Todd, my mom, and my dad, knowing they would do much more than survive without me.

I glanced over at Camila once my prayer was over. I'd managed to keep it together, but her eyes were gleaming.

"Just let it go, okay?" I said hoarsely.

"Okay, Red," she murmured back, swallowing her tears.

I took one more kiss from my Mila, then let out a hopeful sigh. "Do you know what Seamus does for Caana?" I asked.

"He's her bounty hunter."

"Seriously?" Tokyo asked, her eyes lighting up a little too much.

"Yes. That's why he's so hard to find. He goes off the grid when he's working and Caana doesn't give him much time off. Dalhem had him summoned the moment you were changed," Camila said.

"Well, maybe I'll text him or something. I want to talk to him some more."

"About this Seamus…Is he fit?" Faeth asked with all the subtlety of a bull.

"Did you just ask me if my uncle was hot?" I scowled back at her.

"No, she asked if he was fit," Cleo mocked.

"He looks like Red, just a foot and a half taller with a beard," Camila replied.

"I can work with that," Tokyo said, flashing her fangs.

"You are not fucking my uncle."

"Why?"

Suddenly, my cell phone jumped on the coffee table. Cleo grabbed it and tossed it to me. I snatched it out of the air, snarling when I saw the name on the display.

"Yes, Amy."

"Omigod, Ginger. What happened? Did they call?"

"No, they didn't. They—"

The call waiting beeped. I pulled my phone away from my ear. Incoming Call: Alfredo Carmichael. Home

"Amy. I have to go."

"Ginger, wait."

"It's my mom! I have to go."

I hung up on her and switched to the other line, trying to hold down my small breakfast.

"Mom?"

"No, Ginge. It's me," Dad said. "…Linda, I will. Sorry, your mother is trying to talk through my head…Linda, I'll ask her… Sorry. How you doing, sport?"

I looked over at Camila, completely confused about what to say. She just shrugged, the same shocked look on her face. "I-I'm fine. Um, are you and Mom…"

"We're fine. Linda…Okay. Hold on. Your mom has to speak with you immediately." There was a space filled with some affectionate arguing, before my mom came on the line.

"Gingey?"

"Hi, Mom," I said, my voice shaking.

"Hi. Sorry we're late calling. We were supposed to meet that Dalhem man last night, but I got the time mixed up. Anyway, everything's all straightened out. Did you go by the post office yet?"

"No. Wait. Mom, what do you mean you were supposed to meet Dalhem last night? Are you okay?"

"Yeah, I'm fine. We were going to call you earlier, but we went into the city to meet the people we're supposed to feed. We had to pick up Todd on the way, and then your father got lost on the way back and then there was traffic. It was a big mess. Anyway"—she sighed dramatically—"I don't know when you're coming home, but I'll call the chancellor's office this afternoon and we'll withdraw you from your classes...Ginger, honey, what's wrong?"

I seriously had to stop crying. "Nothing, Mom. I—"

Camila was nice enough to take the phone. She pulled me closer, wrapping her arm around my waist. I buried my face in her shoulder, sobbing like a baby.

"Hi, Mrs. Carmichael...Hi, Linda...No, she's just a little overwhelmed at the moment." Camila paused. She held the phone away from her ear as she playfully rolled her eyes. Then she said to me, "Your parents want to know what we're doing for New Year's."

"Tell them we'll be there," I nearly shouted. And we would. I wanted my amazing, demon-wife to meet her new family.

# About the Author

After years of meddling in her friends' love lives, Rebekah turned to writing romance as a means to surviving a stressful professional life. She has worked in various positions from library assistant, meter maid, middle school teacher, B-movie production assistant, reality show crew chauffeur, D-movie producer, and her most fulfilling job to date, lube and harness specialist at an erotic boutique in West Hollywood.

Her interests include Wonder Woman collectibles, cookies, James Taylor, quality hip-hop, football, American muscle cars, large breed dogs, and the ocean. When she's not writing, reading, or sleeping, she is watching Ken Burns documentaries and cartoons or taking dance classes. If given the chance, she will cheat at UNO. She was raised in Southern New Hampshire and now lives in Southern California with an individual who is much more tech savvy than she will ever be. *Better Off Red* is her first novel.

# Books Available From Bold Strokes Books

**Sheltering Dunes** by Radclyffe. The seventh in the award winning Provincetown Tales. The pasts, presents, and futures of three women collide in a single moment that will alter all their lives forever. (978-1-60282-573-4)

**Better Off Red: Vampire Sorority Sisters Book 1** by Rebekah Weatherspoon. Every sorority has its secrets…and college freshman Ginger Carmichael soon discovers that her pledge is more than a bond of sisterhood, it's a lifelong pact to serve six bloodthirsty demons with a lot more than nutritional needs. (978-1-60282-574-1)

**Lucky Loser** by Yolanda Wallace. Top tennis pros Sinjin Smythe and Laure Fortescue reach Wimbledon desperate to claim tennis's crown jewel, but will their feelings for each other get in the way? (978-1-60282-575-8)

**History's Passion: Stories of Sex Before Stonewall** edited by Richard Labonté. Four acclaimed erotic authors re-imagine the past…welcome to the hidden queer history of men loving men not so very long—and centuries—ago. (978-1-60282-576-5)

**Detours** by Jeffrey Ricker. Joel Patterson is heading to Maine for his mother's funeral, and his high school friend Lincoln has invited himself along on the ride—and into Joel's bed—but when the ghost of Joel's mother joins the trip, the route is likely to be anything but straight. (978-1-60282-577-2)

**Holy Rollers** by Rob Byrnes. Partners in life and crime Grant Lambert and Chase LaMarca assemble a team of gay and lesbian criminals to steal millions from a rightwing mega-church, but the gang's plans are complicated by an "ex-gay" conference, the FBI, and a corrupt reverend with his own plans for the cash. (978-1-60282-578-9)

**Mystery of the Tempest: A Fisher Key Adventure** by Sam Cameron. Twin brothers Denny and Steven Anderson love helping people and fighting crime alongside their sheriff dad on sun-drenched Fisher Key, Florida, but Denny doesn't dare tell anyone he's gay, and Steven has secrets of his own to keep. (978-1-60282-579-6)

**Three Days** by L.T. Marie. In a town like Vegas where anything can happen, Shawn and Dakota find that the stakes are love at all costs, and it's a gamble neither can afford to lose. (978-1-60282-569-7)

**Swimming to Chicago** by David-Matthew Barnes. As the lives of the adults around them unravel, high school students Alex and Robby form an unbreakable bond, vowing to do anything to stay together—even if it means leaving everything behind.(978-1-60282-572-7)

**Hostage Moon** by AJ Quinn. Hunter Roswell thought she had left her past behind, until a serial killer begins stalking her. Can FBI profiler Sara Wilder help her find her connection to the killer before he strikes on blood moon? (978-1-60282-568-0)

**Erotica Exotica: Tales of Magic, Sex, and the Supernatural**, edited by Richard Labonté. Today's top gay erotica authors offer sexual thrills and perverse arousal, spooky chills, and magical orgasms in these stories exploring arcane mystery, supernatural seduction, and sex that haunts in a manner both weird and wondrous. (978-1-60282-570-3)

**Blue** by Russ Gregory. Matt and Thatcher find themselves in the crosshairs of a psychotic killer stalking gay men in the streets of Austin, and only a 103-year-old nursing home resident holds the key to solving the murders—but can she give up her secrets in time to save them? (978-1-60282-571-0)

**Balance of Forces: Toujours Ici** by Ali Vali. Immortal Kendal Richoux's life began during the reign of Egypt's only female pharaoh, and history has taught her the dangers of getting too close to anyone who hasn't harnessed the power of time, but as she prepares for the most important battle of her long life, can she resist her attraction to Piper Marmande? (978-1-60282-567-3)

**Contemporary Gay Romances** by Felice Picano. This collection of short fiction from legendary novelist and memoirist Felice Picano are as different from any standard "romances" as you can get, but they will linger in the mind and memory. (978-1-60282-639-7)

**Nightrise** by Nell Stark and Trinity Tam. In the third book in the everafter series, when Valentine Darrow loses her soul, Alexa must cross continents to find a way to save her. (978-1-60282-238-2)

**Men of the Mean Streets**, edited by Greg Herren and J.M. Redmann. Dark tales of amorality and criminality by some of the top authors of gay mysteries. (978-1-60282-240-5)

**Women of the Mean Streets**, edited by J.M. Redmann and Greg Herren. Murder, mayhem, sex, and danger—these are the stories of the women who dare to tackle the mean streets. (978-1-60282-241-2)

**Firestorm** by Radclyffe. Firefighter paramedic Mallory "Ice" James isn't happy when the undisciplined Jac Russo joins her command, but lust isn't something either can control—and they soon discover ice burns as fiercely as flame. (978-1-60282-232-0)

**The Best Defense** by Carsen Taite. When socialite Aimee Howard hires former homicide detective Skye Keaton to find her missing niece, she vows not to mix business with pleasure, but she soon finds Skye hard to resist. (978-1-60282-233-7)

**After the Fall** by Robin Summers. When the plague destroys most of humanity, Taylor Stone thinks there's nothing left to live for, until she meets Kate, a woman who makes her realize love is still alive and makes her dream of a future she thought was no longer possible. (978-1-60282-234-4)

**Accidents Never Happen** by David-Matthew Barnes. From the moment Albert and Joey meet by chance beneath a train track on a street in Chicago, a domino effect is triggered, setting off a chain reaction of murder and tragedy. (978-1-60282-235-1)

**In Plain View**, edited by Shane Allison. Best-selling gay erotica authors create the stories of sex and desire modern readers crave. (978-1-60282-236-8)